Also by Eric Almeida

Live from Moscow

Minsk Rises

Visit www.ericalmeida.com for details and updates.

Crimean Seas,
Kiev Skies

A Cove Rock Book

This is a work of fiction. The events and incidents described are products of the author's imagination. Any resemblance to actual persons is entirely coincidental.

Published by Cove Rock
A Division of Cove Rock Media
Clearwater, Florida

CRIMEAN SEAS, KIEV SKIES

CRIMEAN SEAS, KIEV SKIES

ERIC ALMEIDA

Published by Cove Rock

Cover photo by Anastasiya Gerasko
Cover design by Diane Whiddon

ISBN: 0692751688
ISBN 13: 9780692751688

www.ericalmeida.com

CHAPTER 1

Early in her final semester at Shevchenko University, Yulia Petrenko threw her options wide open. She entertained the whole gamut. Anything and everything. As long as the work offered decent fulfillment and a chance. Most important, she figured, was to find a solid starting point.

Along the way she got plenty of input. Much of it pointed her in contrary directions. Friends and relatives alike voiced their opinions. Her mother, as usual, did not abstain.

"You're obviously a talented writer, Yuliochka. You've had articles published. Plus your degree will be in journalism. Why not do it?"

"Mama. First of all, I don't really think I'm all that talented. Secondly, the pay is bad."

"Your editors think you're talented. Your father and I agree. So does everybody we know."

"And the pay?"

"You've got to start somewhere."

Yulia wished it was that simple. God knew Ukraine needed all the journalists it could get. Honesty in government had been in short supply since Yushenko's flare-out. Since then it had dwindled even further. Who else was going to probe the fouled recesses? Someone had to. The corruptions and misdeeds reached into every corner, from Kiev to the provinces.

She gave it serious thought. It would have been different if she could have hoped for a staff job at an established publication. But the odds of that were ridiculous. Which left what? Precarious and marginally paid stringer work—hardly enough to cover groceries and a half-share in a studio apartment...particularly in Kiev? In regional cities the situation was basically the same. Moreover she was young and female, which often meant closed doors and condescending attitudes.

Her main goal, just now, was self-sufficiency. Security as well. She knew Ukraine needed journalists. No...Ukraine *really* needed journalists. There was no doubt about it.

She just decided that she didn't have to be one of them.

Not that her overall view of her country was negative. In fact the opposite was true. Ukraine had lots of advantages. Dazzling coastlines, beautiful snow-blanketed mountains, and the most-fertile agricultural land on the planet, with a population—of which she was a bread-and-butter part—that was shedding old patterns through fits and starts: gamely embracing technology, democracy, Western-style business... the future. She'd been born in 1991, Ukraine's year of independence. Long term, she counted her citizenship a plus. Unlike her elder brother she had no desire to emigrate, to Canada or anywhere else.

She was just impatient with the pace of progress. How long would it take? Twenty years? Thirty...maybe more? She had only so many years available. Therefore pragmatism seemed sensible. Many of her friends thought likewise.

From there she'd excluded nothing, as long as it included a decent salary and wider horizons.

Airline stewardess seemed to fit the bill, at first glance. See and experience Europe and the Middle East on the fly, from a base in Kiev. The pay was all right. Her English was adequate. She even possessed passable French. It didn't have to be long term. However to her astonishment she discovered she was disqualified—simply by being too tall. Both of Ukraine's major airlines applied a height limit of 176 centimeters for female attendants. She was 178.

Other possibilities crossed her mind, including banks and corporate sales offices. However she'd investigated and found them wanting. Bank teller? Sales rep for a cosmetics company? Secretary to a resident Westerner? She had never cared for banks, and the rest appealed to her even less.

By contrast the hotel sector attracted her, the more she considered it. It called for communication skills and versatility. Human oriented, like journalism. So that's where she gravitated.

Of the various chains she evaluated, RadissonBlu seemed the most promising. It was part of a global conglomerate encompassing six additional chains, fifteen hundred hotels in eighty-three countries, and about eighty-five thousand employees. That meant chances for upward advancement and even postings elsewhere, if she ever wished. The company's managementtt-trackkk training program, described on its website, was open ended, promising the "widest possible exposure to the company's internal operations and guest services." Another phrase that had captured her fancy was the employee motto: "Yes, I can." She knew it was trite but liked it. It struck her as the kind of clear-minded approach that was too often missing from Ukrainian companies.

Best of all RadissonBlu had five locations in Ukraine. As graduation approached, two openings had appeared among them: events organization at the ski resort in Bukovel and receptionist in Alushta, on the Black Sea in Crimea. After interviews for both, she'd gotten the second, gaining selection over twenty-one other applicants, which boosted her confidence. She hadn't imagined Crimea in her schema but in fact it suited her fine. First, there was the fabulous climate and the beaches. Second, the low year-round living costs and proximity to her parents, who lived just a seven-hour bus ride away in Nikolaev. For a couple of years, at least, what could be better?

Only one thing troubled her somewhat. There was no sense evading it. Her diploma and experience mattered. But ultimately, she

suspected, she'd gotten the job because of her looks. One pronouncement in English by an Austrian businessman and would-be suitor in
Kiev during her previous semester—when she'd already become wary
of the male sex in general and soured on Western men in particular—
stuck in her memory:

"You make an impression on people, Yulia. How to put it? You seize
attention. Not just men's—women's too. When you enter a room, all
eyes go to you."

"Why?" she'd asked.

"There's no single reason. Call it overall effect."

It was true. Yulia knew it. And as far as she was concerned, it was
as much bane as blessing. First of all it was a little undeserved. Okay,
even she conceded that her facial features were eye-catching, when
combined with her figure. But she was hardly slender and certainly
fell short of the mass-media ideal in that regard. What bothered her
was the emphasis. Though from there, thankfully, her communications skills helped set things right. Reactions became more balanced.
If she did have a weakness, it was probably her tendency toward strong
emotions. Most of all in romance, she'd learned with unhappy result. In any case she'd gotten the job. Six weeks later she graduated
Shevchenko University, class of 2013. She'd now been employed for
more than two months.

During that time she'd found many things to like about her job.
One was that the reception desk put her front-and-center. Which
meant plenty of human contact, day in and day out, along with opportunity to prove herself.

Ninety-five percent of the guests came from Russia and Ukraine.
Affluent Muscovites made for a heavy contingent, thanks to the daily
direct Aeroflot connection from Moscow to Simferopol. Lots of couples in late middle-age. Also a surprising portion of single women,
traveling alone or in small groups.

Then there were the conference visitors—the ones who gathered for business, along with a little recreation on the side. They

were groupings unto themselves. Most of these were also Russian and Ukrainian. Westerners were rarer.

The conference now in progress was an exception: the last until September. Three days of closed sessions, under the English-language header *Investment Opportunities in Ukrainian Agricultural Reform*. The subject had piqued her interest straightaway. So had the participants: a noteworthy collection of Ukrainian government officials, English-speaking bankers, and at least ten big-shot Ukrainian and Russian businessmen who qualified as oligarchs—many of whom she recognized from media coverage. Half a dozen interpreters in full employ, along with numerous security personnel. Of the latter, each oligarch seemed to bring his own, and together they formed a small army in their own right, standing sentry at all the doors and windows of the conference room, beside the hotel's front entrance, and even in the interior garden facing the waterfront. Many of them, it was clear, were carrying concealed weapons.

The obsession with security had extended to materials as well. Each evening the organizers had removed all written documents, digital devices, and visual aids from the conference room, leaving nothing behind for the curious attentions of the cleaning staff and other hotel personnel.

A Wall Street bank had booked the event and footed the entire bill. Also on the tab: thirty rooms and suites for themselves, their support personnel, and about half of the Ukrainian officials. The rest of the officials and businessmen arrived in daily entourage by chauffeured car or motor launch from points further up the coast; vacation villas, she guessed—or in the case of five or six of the oligarchs—from garishly large yachts moored just offshore.

This evening Yulia was tending the desk alone. Her colleague Anna had been assigned to the cocktail party taking place in the lounge and terrace.

The party was still in progress. Through the open double doors behind her, Yulia heard a hubbub of voices and clinks of service trays, punctuated by laughs. There were other emanations as well. Most of all: corruption.

Her journalistic instincts, despite herself, were up and active.

Two men now descended toward her down the main stairwell, speaking English. One, judging by the stout fill of his suit and close-cropped hair, was a Ukrainian government official. The other was a lean-faced Westerner with glasses, in a trim-tailored blue blazer and light-gray slacks, expensive shoes flashing against the white marble. The banker mentioned another party later that evening, hosted by a Russian oligarch on his yacht offshore.

Both men swept their eyes over her at the desk. Yulia retained her polite expression until they disappeared, then exhaled. She could only guess at the schemes they were entertaining. Same went for the others in the lounge.

But she quelled the thought for tonight. She'd made her accommodation.

She turned her gaze toward her computer screen and pulled up the evening's anticipated arrivals. Because most rooms were already full, only two parties were due to check in. Both couples. One came with a pre-established customer profile through the hotel's loyalty program. Just as she clicked on it, a hired car from the hotel pulled up out front, visible through the smoked-glass doors. An athletic-looking young man in a suit emerged from the rear door on her side. Not Russian-looking, at first glance. Nordic, perhaps. She flashed her gaze back down to the profile onscreen.

Axel Thorsson
Residence: Geneva, Switzerland
Citizenship: US
Age: 33
Length of stay: 15 nights
Number of RadissonBlu stays over previous 24 months: 17
Loyalty program member since 2008

Total overnights: 57
Primary purpose of travel: business

The automatic sliders parted and he strode through toward her desk, followed by the porter. She took in details as he approached. Solid shoulders and longish hair, light brown. Well-cut suit, similar to those of the Anglophone bankers...perhaps a latecomer to the conference. Then she remembered his duration of stay. To her surprise he spoke precise, effortless Russian.

"Checking in, please. Axel Thorsson."

His voice was low-timbered and even. Stable, somehow. Grounding. She glanced again at his profile and then his passport to confirm that he was American.

"Welcome, Mr. Thorsson," she said. "I see you're staying for fifteen nights. Is that correct?"

"Correct. I've also requested a room with a covered balcony, on the second floor, with an unobstructed view of the water."

His tone was courteous, with no edge. She informed him that his request had been fulfilled, by way of room 212.

"I also see you've made a reservation for two guests. Will the other person be arriving later?"

A fissure of trouble showed itself, ever so briefly. But his Russian stayed modulated. "No. As it turns out, she won't be coming."

She offered a requisite, neutral smile. "That's fine."

As she stood to hand him his pamphleted keycard, he shifted his attention to the conference's sign stand several meters away. He appeared to take note. Just to be sure, she decided to ask him.

"Are you here for the Harcourt Bank conference, by chance?"

"No, I'm glad to say. Just here on vacation."

Somehow the response, like his voice, reassured her. One less participant in the corruption and scheming.

That could only be for the better.

CHAPTER 2

During the short elevator ride Axel Thorsson considered the girl at reception. She'd made an impression on him. Especially when she'd stood and he'd gotten a better look. Full lips, with their attendant associations. Large green-gray eyes on a roundish Slavic face. Medium-length dirty-blond hair. Plenty of lush contours further down. On first appraisal: a big, healthy, lusty girl, coursing with inborn appetites. Ordinarily a girl who would arouse his interest.

On this trip, however, he'd arrived here with a different purpose.

Upon entering his room he deposited his suitcase by the door, placed his laptop case by the desk, and surveyed the accommodations. Though the sleeping area adjoined the living section, the unit almost qualified as a suite and offered more than enough space for two people, let alone one. The bed was king sized, and the sitting area included two French-empire chairs and table, a flat-screen television, a sizeable minibar, and an ample desk area with easily accessible electrical outlets. Everything was high-grade, including the room's vertical dimensions. He'd read on the hotel's website that the building had been constructed for the holiday-going Russian elite in the early twentieth century, during the reign of Czar Nikolai II. And it still looked that way. He noted three tall windows and a glass door facing onto the balcony. Through the gauze of their curtains he discerned a direct sightline to the Black Sea. For confirmation he progressed outside.

At once he liked what he saw. The balcony, tiled and semi-enclosed, overlooked manicured interior gardens and afforded an unobstructed view of the water, between two stands of tall trees. Probably one of the best views in the house. Below and to his right, a cocktail party was underway on the large terrace, full of chatter. Several loud laughs burst upward.

He assumed the party related to the Harcourt Bank conference and paused to observe it in more detail.

The participants were mostly men, attended by interpreters and assistants, as well as well-attired hotel staff, employing both Russian and English. Mixed composition: Ukrainian, Russian, European, American. Based on appearances, a well-to-do and self-satisfied group.

The tableau was all too familiar. Self-enriching politicians, grasping officials, and voracious, high-rolling oligarchs. Minded as always by their Western moneymen, who stood ready with anonymous offshore trust funds and roundabout conduits through the City of London. Obscure transactions made outside public view. The same milieu he inhabited, more or less, in his own business activity.

He turned away and walked back into his room, then unpacked his suitcase and changed out of his suit. The hotel's dining area was on the other end of the terrace, adjacent to the party. Just now it didn't appeal to him. He decided instead to venture into the surrounding town and find a café.

He'd neglected to cancel the second reservation, though he'd already known for a week that he'd be coming alone. But by now that hardly mattered.

His intentions had changed.

* * *

Yulia raised her gaze when the American rounded the landing on the stairwell, maintaining her upward-angle longer than she wished.

He was now wearing an aquamarine shirt and white linen slacks. She forced her eyes back downward to her computer. Only when he reached floor level did she allow herself to look up again.

"Where would you suggest I go for the best selection of cafés?" he asked, holding to Russian.

"Turn right out the door, Mr. Thorsson," she said. "About one hundred and fifty meters down, you'll find yourself in the center of Alushta. There are numerous cafés there. Most are outdoors."

"Thank you." He held the smile on her before turning to go, more politely than the conference-goers. This particular foreigner had some tact.

Seconds later, several other men emerged in the corridor to her left, again speaking English. Yulia glanced left as they approached. One face was immediately recognizable, thanks to his media coverage: forty-nine-year-old Leonid Zherdev, owner of a large industrial group concentrated in iron and fertilizers and located in Donetsk— an associate of the president, and one of the richest men in Ukraine. Monotonous features: medium physical build, reddish-brown hair, and pale skin—overset by eyes of indeterminate color, which to Yulia suggested endless cravings and a barren soul. He was accompanied by two youthful bankers, whose faces also had become familiar over the previous several days. Several assistants and a security goon trailed behind at discreet paces. As the distance closed she could make out their smug expressions, as if they'd just concluded an agreement. Probably a crooked one, she guessed. All three had locked their eyes onto her, just like the others. As they neared the door to the lounge she sensed them slowing, and when she turned and looked again, she saw Zherdev give his cohorts a conniving glance before the group disappeared toward the party, followed by their entourage. Once again she was glad they'd gone.

Before she knew it Zherdev was standing hard by the U-shaped desk, just off her left shoulder. For some long seconds he took in her hindquarters from a back-angle. His thick-necked bodyguard stood several meters behind him in the doorway to the lounge, eyes forward and impassive.

"I've come back," Zherdev said, with the same entertained expression.

"I see that. Could you please walk around to the front of the desk? That way I can be of better assistance."

The two bankers also then reemerged, standing near the bodyguard. Zherdev shot a grin toward them and came round to face her. His eyes traveled to her name tag.

"Yulia Petrenko," he said, speaking Russian. "May I call you Yulia?"

"You may. It's hotel policy."

"Do you know who I am?"

"Yes, I do." Yulia showed him no deference, which seemed to amuse him even further. Standard courtesies: no more or no less. She grew more wary as he leaned toward her and adopted a mocking, confidential tone.

"Do you speak English, Yulia?"

"Yes, of course."

"What time do you get off work?"

Yulia tried to stay even, and held eye contact. "That's not information the hotel ordinarily shares with guests," she answered. "Is there a reason you wish to know?"

"Did you see the two men from Harcourt Bank over there?"

She flicked a glance toward the two men and nodded.

"The one with the combed-back hair?"

She nodded again.

"He's one of my bankers in London. Turns out he's taken a fancy to you."

This time Yulia refused to glance back at the pair. "So what of it?"

His eyes flicked toward her name tag again. "I'll get straight to the point, Yulia. He'd like to spend the night with you, and given that you're obviously..." he assessed her with a merchant's eye "...not the kind of girl who ordinarily does things like this, I'm willing to pay you generously." He paused again for effect. "Two thousand dollars. Cash."

Dismayed, she shot him a controlled glower. Zherdev took her silence as an opening and continued, keeping his voice low. "Let's talk plainly here, Yulia...he's not even thirty years old, a good-looking guy, and extremely well off, like most of them. So happens he sits on the boards of two my companies. He even owns his own plane...a prize, I would say. You might even find him pleasant. And he's not leaving until Saturday. If it goes well, there could be a second night as well—same price. After that, who knows? His fancy might even turn into something long term. Then you win both ways...a dream come true."

"Forget it. I'm not interested."

"Two thousand dollars...what's that? Five or six weeks' salary for you?"

Again she held her glower. She was determined to stay in control.

"Okay. Let's make it three thousand then."

"I'm not interested at any price. In fact..." she amped up her glower and raised her voice slightly, feeling her face flush, "your proposal is revolting and offensive."

Zherdev stood back from the reception counter, startled. He quickly recovered his amused confidence. "You know I could probably get you fired, if I wished," he said.

"For what? Having some decency?"

He laughed. "I didn't think there were many girls left in Ukraine with that attitude. But I'll let this go. I've got business to attend to." Without any further remark or courtesy he rejoined the two bankers and reverted to English. On their way back to the terrace she heard them laugh. The bodyguard followed, still unthinking and impassive.

When he was gone Yulia took several deep breaths. Most men showed her at least some civility and respect. These oligarchs and their international bankers were different. They comprised a class unto themselves. They made up their own rules, endlessly leveraging their crooked advantages and obscene, ill-gotten gains.

They thought they owned Ukraine and everyone in it, including her. At some point, it had to stop.

CHAPTER 3

If there was one facet of business travel for which Axel Thorsson had retained his enthusiasm, it was an abundant, well-prepared breakfast buffet. Which for him meant, at minimum: fresh-scrambled eggs, several varieties of sausage, high-grade bacon, just-baked croissants and pains-au-chocolat, fried potatoes, and a variety of fresh fruit. All washed down by gourmet-style coffee.

The subterranean breakfast room at the hotel lacked windows and natural light. But he figured he'd soon have plenty of the latter. With a rush of hunger, he sprinkled salt and pepper on his scrambled eggs, picked up his fork and knife, and got started. He'd eaten several forkfuls of egg and two sausages when a quartet of men walked into the room, looking self-important. Other breakfast-goers in the early crowd sported summer wear; these four wore blazers and trousers. All four sized him up as they passed near his table. Probably wondering if he was one of their own. Two Ukrainians and two banker types—Anglophone by the looks of them. Unable to identify him, they proceeded along the buffet and selected a table at the other end of the room.

One of the bankers pulled out an electronic tablet and began a discussion at low volume, while the other leaned to the side with a cupped hand and talked on his cell phone. Fragments of both English and Russian were audible. For Thorsson the scene resembled those he saw on his travels—in Moscow, Almaty, Baku and everywhere else. Only the setting and timing made it unusual.

When he returned to the buffet for more pains-au-chocolate and fruit, the foursome interrupted their confab and gave him additional scrutiny, taking in his shorts and sandals. They didn't resume their discussion until he'd filled his plate and seated himself again.

He could make certain educated guesses as to what they were up to. But he didn't really care. In any case he'd been noticed. That tended to happen with him.

$*$ $*$ $*$

After returning to his room and changing into his beach gear, Thorsson made his way back to the elevator. Inside he noticed a small flash-memory stick on the carpet, and picked it up. The device was conventional—small, black, and plastic—and bore no identifying markings, tabs, or neck strap. The Harcourt breakfast group had been the only business contingent he'd seen thus far; he guessed it belonged to them.

The thought occurred to him of keeping the item and reading the contents later, back in his room. But he dismissed the idea in short order. The men at breakfast might occupy dubious moral ground, but they weren't villains. Indeed, probably not so different from him, at the baseline. He pressed the button for the ground floor and continued down.

At reception the same girl was present as the evening before, looking a little more on- guard. All the same she summoned an upbeat greeting. Her wide, green-gray eyes caught the morning light as he addressed her.

"I'd like to turn in an item that was apparently lost. I found it inside the elevator just now…a flash-memory stick." He handed it across the reception counter between his thumb and index finger. With care, she took possession of it in the same manner, grazing his fingers in the process. Her eyes concentrated.

"Perhaps it belongs to someone from the business conference that's going on here," he added, glancing again at the sign at the side of the lobby.

"Perhaps…" She colored slightly. "The conference finished yesterday evening. But many of the participants are still here. We'll try to identify the owner."

"Worth a try. Someone might be searching for it."

"Yes. Thank you for helping."

Her chromatic irises refixed on him as he slung up his beach bag and stepped away toward the lounge. Rounding the corner of the desk, he glimpsed her contemplating the item, holding it between the digits of both hands. He liked her attitude. Conscientiousness was an underrated quality, in his view. One he appreciated. From rear view, he also realized that she was even more voluptuous than he'd comprehended.

Colors and horizons of the Black Sea loomed up ahead through the windows of the lounge. He redirected his thoughts to the morning ahead.

*   *   *

Yulia examined the memory stick with the same kind of intense absorption that had once seized her during university exams and a handful of stringer reports she'd written under deadline. She sensed at once that the item was less innocuous than it appeared. The American was probably right; it belonged to someone from the conference. She recollected whom she'd seen pass through the lobby since she'd come on duty at seven and in particular who'd used the elevator. Several possibilities came to mind, all of them conference-goers.

She tried to clear her head and think calmly. Here was a chance to learn what the bankers and high rollers had been discussing over these past few days…and to know what, exactly, had drawn a figure like Leonid

Zherdev here, away from his yachts and penthouses and huge industrial complexes…The digital clock on her reception panel read 8:13 a.m., and Anna was scheduled to join her behind the desk at 8:30. If she were to do anything with this quirk of chance, her minutes were diminishing.

She took a deep breath. Shortly her options came into focus.

Her computer—one of two at the reception desk—had two USB ports and Internet access. She pulled the cap off the flash stick and prepared to stick it in the closest port. At the last instant she hesitated. She knew she was crossing a threshold.

Then she remembered Zherdev's crude proposition the previous evening.

She stuck the flash in the slot. When the contents came up on screen she drew a sharp breath.

There was a list of about fifteen file names: four in Russian and the rest in English. Mostly Word, a couple Excel. As far as she could tell none were encrypted. Her eyes widened as she scanned down them. The first two held a list of attendees and the conference agenda. Others bore more specific headers:

Grain Production in the Cherkassy and Poltava Regions: Capacity versus Potential

Grain Production in the Cherkassy and Poltava Regions: Prospects for Consolidation

Land Ownership in the Cherkassy and Poltava Regions: Fragmentation and the Obstacle of Small Land Holders

Harcourt Bank—Proposal for Offshore Restructuring of Zherdev Holdings

Her heart fluttered when the elevator doors opened. With a quick movement of her mouse she minimized the window. To her relief, a Ukrainian couple in their fifties walked out, bound for the beach. She managed a smile and greeting as they passed by into the lounge. When they'd gone she glanced again at the digital clock in her pane:

8:19. Only minutes remained before Anna showed up. Her pulse accelerating further, she thought fast.

Opening the files was out of the question. The action would be registered. That left just one option.

Copy them.

With a buzz she remembered a holdover from her student days—a flash stick of her own in her purse. She reached under the desk and fished it out—and after quick checks right and left and up the stairs—stuck it in the second slot. She remaximized the first window and pressed the control button on her keyboard.

Copy. Click. Click. Paste. The operation was over in seconds.

When it was complete she closed the open windows, removed her flash, and dropped it back in her purse. Finally, with trembling fingers, she pulled the original flash out of the port, reapplied the cap, and placed the item on the desk surface. She managed several short breaths and looked around the lobby. To her relief, there was still no one in view. Her body relaxed a bit…

Until she remembered the overhead security cameras. With a wave of dread she looked up.

Two black half-globes. One mounted over the reception desk. Another positioned near the elevator. Meant to be discreet and unnoticeable, to guests and staff alike.

But always active, always watching, always recording.

Before she had time to compose herself Anna walked through the sliding doors of the entrance, in a bright mood.

"Good morning Yulia. Anything interesting or unusual happen so far this morning?"

Yulia made an effort to steady her voice. "No, nothing really. Just a lost-and-found item. Pretty typical."

CHAPTER 4

Thorsson selected a lounge chair near the middle of the beach, spread his towel over the cushion, and stripped down to his swimming briefs. Once he'd settled in under the umbrella, he looked out over the water.

If he was honest with himself—and he almost always was, in the end—he didn't blame Theresa. This vacation had been just another holding pattern. For him, just one in a long series. Seven months had transpired. He'd sidestepped a summer sojourn with her in the States, which would have meant engagements with his parents, his brother's young family, and his American friends, along with the inevitable queries about the future.

He and Theresa were both better off that the reckoning had occurred abroad. And before this vacation rather than afterward.

He recalled their final conversation, the weekend before. Early evening, and they'd been sitting on a bench, on the shore of Lac Leman. The waters of the lake had lapped gently against the stone embankment nearby. Casual strollers had passed in backdrop.

"I'm willing to take responsibility for our current impasse," he'd said.

This time, when she spoke, her voice had become more adamant. "And do what next, Axel? We have to be moving toward something."

"Of course. But can't we put off these resolutions until a little later?"

"That's just another deferral. And you know it is."

"Does that mean this is your final decision?"

"I made mine months ago, Axel. You're the one who's failed to decide."

Before they'd concluded he'd characterized her decision as "a blow...one from which I will require weeks to recover." He'd also pledged to elaborate upon his emotions—and his interpretations of their relationship—in subsequent e-mails. To this she'd neither objected nor approved, but rather resigned herself.

Resigned herself because she could predict their contents. Thorsson could, too. As usual he'd already thought them through.

*   *   *

When Anna got settled Yulia informed her in more detail about the flash, treating the matter as ordinarily as she could. If no one claimed it by day's end, she suggested, they would place it in the lost-and-found collection in the back office. For the time being the item remained next to her computer terminal. Over the next fifteen minutes she could hardly keep her eyes off it. In the meantime she tried to muster some calmness.

Her peace quickly dissolved when two Ukrainians emerged in haste from the elevator and headed straight to the reception desk. Both were around thirty, with close-cropped hair. One bore tattoos on several fingers—the marks of a convict. Yulia recognized them as participants in the conference. She thought she'd seen them with Zherdev.

Their faces were grim-serious. The one with the tattoos addressed Anna first. "We think we lost a lost a flash-memory stick this morning. Probably in the elevator. Has anyone turned it in?"

"You're in luck," Anna responded. She gestured over to Yulia.

The pair imposed themselves in front of her. Despite her jangled nerves, Yulia didn't like their demeanors. She'd had her fill the previous evening. "Is this it?" she asked, holding it up between two fingers, determined to show no unease. She didn't immediately proffer it across the counter.

"Yes it is. Can we have it?"

With the courtesy required by her job, she handed it over. The one with the tattoos examined it up close and appeared to relax a little. All the same his frown persisted. His compatriot's as well.

"When was this turned in?" he asked.

"Oh, about twenty-five or thirty minutes ago."

"By whom?"

"A foreign guest. He said he found it in the elevator, just after breakfast."

"And he brought it to you immediately?"

"As far as I know, yes. He was on his way to the beach."

"What's his name?"

"With respect, I don't think that's relevant."

"You said this happened after breakfast...rather tall guy...sportive type, around thirty?" He made a pause, laced with acidity. "Walks around like he's got his own special category?"

Yulia looked back at them and said nothing. Still serious, the pair exchanged glances and without further word turned away and strode into the lounge, in the direction of the beach. With no pretense of civility, just like their boss.

Yulia, still standing, took a deep breath and turned to Anna. "Not so much as a thank you," she commented. She hoped the pair didn't try to interfere with Axel Thorsson. For a moment she wondered if she should call hotel security. She decided against it.

*   *   *

Thorsson reflected further, now that the relationship was over. Theresa had vested considerable hope and effort in him. In the end, though, he'd only brought her disappointment and pain.

Morever this was a repeat pattern.

Over the previous five years he'd visited grief upon one woman after another.

Money had yielded the temptations, been the enabler. Made women suddenly available, in a way they'd never been to him in college and graduate school. Allowed all the careless choices and attachments. And prompted him toward dissolution and indulgence, one slippery gradient after another. Along the way, he now realized, he'd acquired attributes he'd never had before. Materialistic. Selfish. Degenerate. Sex-obsessed. Measured, according to his own calculus, by the luxury of his apartment, the size of his financial balances, and the quality of his suits. And perhaps most of all, he had to admit, the number of his liaisons. Outwardly he enjoyed ease, status...endless choice. The very definition of twenty-first-century Western success. In reality he'd become irredeemable and corrupt. Squandered his advantages, rather than applying them toward proper ends. Become the author of his own torments.

There was however now a chance for rectification. An upside to this disrupted vacation. Namely: solitude and detachment. And for the next two weeks he'd have those in abundance.

In his revised plan, two templates would now predominate. The first was physical: forty-five minutes of vigorous swimming every morning, supplemented every other day by pre-breakfast calisthenics. At university he'd competed in water polo and swimming. But his fitness level had slipped a little lately. The exercise would revitalize him and clear his head of distractions. The second was intellectual. He'd already downloaded a selection of titles to his Kindle e-reader.

Time had come to bring philosophy to bear.

As he reached into his beach bag, he sensed attention from two figures to behind and to his left and glanced back over his shoulder.

They were standing six or seven meters from the semicircular terrace that protruded out from the pool area, flanked by stairwells. The two men were wearing suits. He also recognized them at once:

the Slavic types whom he'd seen at breakfast with the bankers from Harcourt. Both had fixed their gazes squarely upon him—with expressions that were altogether too blunt and aggressive. Despite the angle he stared back at them for a full fifteen seconds. At last they looked away, exchanging complicit glances. Thorsson redirected his gaze toward the water and wondered why. Their attentions had started at breakfast. Then the most likely cause quickly occurred to him.

The flash stick he'd found near the elevator.

After about twenty seconds he glanced again over his shoulder. The two men were still there, with eyes refixed. Displeased with the way this was developing, he stood up from his lounge chair to full height and turned to face them. The two men looked him over from head to toe with the same blunt stares. For the first time he noticed tattoos on the fingers of one of them. The other one glanced down the stairwell that led down to the beach, and made a remark to his tattooed cohort. They decided to keep their distance. Only after another ten seconds did they turn back toward the hotel, offering another display of aggressive looks before they went.

Thorsson watched their retreating heads and shoulders from his position on the beach. He knew he had plenty of defects. But he thought he'd performed a good deed with the flash.

Malevolence of that kind was the last thing he needed in return. Particularly when it was baseless.

CHAPTER 5

What struck Oleg Konstantinovich Mikhailov most of all, now that he was standing here in the flesh, was the immensity of the space. The countless television images he'd seen, ever since childhood, didn't quite convey the scale, grandeur, and might of the soaring ceilings, gigantic chandeliers, and glittering gold. This was Russian power, evoked on big, vivid canvas: massive and monolithic, a progression of authority running from czars through commissars to the modern Russian state.

Here in Grigorsky Hall, he was reminded what it meant to be Russian. To be a part of large and consequential nation, with achievements that stretched across all fields of human endeavor. Which over many centuries, through frequent upheavals, had forged a society that encompassed 150 million souls, bestrode nine time zones, and remained central to the world in the twenty-first century.

There was another subtext as well. Individuals in this grand schema were expected to subordinate their own interests to the greater whole. And submit to the state in the process.

That was the part that now gave him pause.

For the moment, though, his role had been assigned. He glanced down the line of twenty-one officers, all men, already arrayed along the red carpet. They were attired in uniforms of various hues and colors, from the light gray of the Interior Ministry to the olives of army intelligence to his own midnight blue-black.

There were no news cameras or reporters present here this afternoon, despite the familiar public setting. Just an official Kremlin videographer and two photographers. The officers were called to attention by the senior official present. After a protracted pause, two Kremlin guards swung open the massive arched doors that led to the companion hall of Alexsandrovsky.

Additional seconds punctuated the silence before the president of Russia entered, a lone figure against the backdrop.

Upon attaining the line, he stopped to shake the hand of the first officer and offer congratulations. He then did likewise for the remaining twenty men, including Mikhailov. Upon conclusion he walked briskly to a lectern in the middle of the hall, while Mikhailov and his fellow officers, in keeping with predefined choreography, reformed into a right angle around him. Some fifteen senior officials and ministers arrayed themselves opposite. The president opened his remarks:

"Comrade Officers!

"I am pleased to congratulate you on new success in your careers, with appointment to higher duties and assignment to next ranks. As leaders of your corresponding structures, you are vested with significant authority…"

After precisely eight minutes the president paused and stood aside while the director of Mikhailov's own branch moved to an adjoining lectern for a brief address of his own. The entire ceremony lasted seventeen minutes, almost down to the second. Before it was over, Mikhailov realized that he'd ascended near the pinnacle.

Most incongruous to him, in this grand setting, was that the higher he'd ascended the more his doubts had taken hold. Over recent months, indeed, they'd only multiplied—especially when combined with his personal upheavals.

His promotion today wasn't borne of aspiration. Having come this far, he didn't really even want it.

*   *   *

"What was the president like, up close?"

"Powerful presence, to be sure. Mainly by virtue of his position, I would say. But also very human."

"What do mean by that, exactly?"

"I mean he's not larger than life. He struck me as just as fallible as anyone else."

Vera, Mikhailov's wife, gave him a curious look. It was not a comment she'd expected at this particular time and place. But she chose not to explore it for now.

"You'll tell me more about it at home, right?"

"Of course."

The two of them took several additional steps toward the side of the ground-floor reception chamber of the Kremlin Palace, raised their cups and saucers to draw sips of tea, and surveyed the room over the tops of the porcelain. The president and most of the ministers had departed toward other business at the conclusion of the ceremony, leaving a collection of deputy ministers, directors of the security services, and the wives of the promoted officers. Waiters in military livery were in attendance, distributing hors d'oeuvres on platters.

In short order the director of the FSB made his way over, a subordinate in tow. He fastened his eyes on Mikhailov's and offered a firm handshake.

"Your husband has been a capable servant of the state," he said, turning to Vera. "His promotion today reflects his contributions."

"Thank you Director Stepanov. We're honored."

When Stepanov moved on, Mikhailov registered numerous, discreet glances in his direction from the assembled officers and deputy ministers. They'd observed the vignette. They always did. This was his first real taste of Kremlin politics. Everyone surveying the matrix, looking out for rivals, plotting trajectories to the top. Among them, Mikhailov had gained a reputation as something of a loner. Also someone unstained by corruption.

Nowadays, that set him apart from most of the rest.

Half an hour later, as the gathering wound down, he and Vera finally detached themselves, filtered out of the hall, and made their way out. Within minutes they emerged onto Cathedral Square, the gold domes and bell towers of the Kremlin's churches looming up on three sides, glistening in the late-afternoon sun. They drew to a stop in the center of the space, and at last Vera took a moment to observe him, also glancing at the new insignia on his epaulettes.

"My dear Colonel Mikhailov..." She let the pronunciation hang in the air for several seconds. "You realize you were the youngest officer in the group today, don't you?"

He nodded once.

"Also, if I may say so, the best looking in a uniform."

Mikhailov looked back at her with a restrained smile, showing little self-satisfaction. He said nothing.

"Putin himself was thirty-nine years old when he attained the rank of lieutenant colonel in the KGB. The same age as you are now." She gestured around the square and then over at the Kremlin Palace. "Do you realize how far you've come? What this means?"

Again Mikhailov held her gaze, showing no enthusiasm. By quick increments her expression transmuted to sympathy. "What happened last winter has been hard," she said. "But six months have passed. Maybe this presents a chance to put those events behind us...to look forward." She gestured around the square again. "After all, what more could we want?"

Mikhailov reflected for a moment. "You've cut to the crux," he answered. "It's the main question."

CHAPTER 6

Pedestrians were thick on the sidewalk, many still clad in bathing suits and beach gear. Yulia's heart pounded again as she turned right out of the automatic glass doors and melded into the flow. Under the dusk-light their carefree faces and conversations seemed surreal, given the information she was carrying in her handbag.

She reached across and pulled the straps higher on her shoulder. She had never committed such an audacious act in her life.

The subterfuge unsettled her most. She'd violated rules. Put her job at risk.

At the end of the hotel building she almost had to gasp for air. Fifty meters further she reached the pedestrian-only seaside promenade, with its outdoor cafés, amusement rides, and street-style entertainments. Half of the mechanical attractions remained unilluminated and inert for now, and music was not yet blaring from the clubs along the waterfront, which helped her steady herself. She maintained her stride and refrained from walking faster.

Glances swung toward her from all sides; she felt them, glimpsed the turned faces. Tonight, with extra effort, she ignored them. All the same she glanced back over her shoulder.

Sticking to her standard route, she cut left up Kvitnya Street, away from the beachfront, and ten minutes later attained the courtyard of her 70s-era, Soviet-constructed apartment building, where she found the usual gaggle of *babushki* on the benches near her entrance. She offered them her customary greetings before walking inside and taking the lift up to the seventh floor.

The apartment was a one-bedroom rental with furniture that had seen better days. Upon entering she spotted her roommate, Oksana, sitting on their balcony, staring at her tablet computer. Oksana was also a recent university graduate; she worked as a salesperson at an art gallery during the day and doubled up three or four nights per week as a waitress at a waterfront café. Yulia deposited her handbag on the couch and suggested iced tea. She then retraced to the kitchen, extracted a jug from the refrigerator, and poured out two glasses. Out on the balcony she handed one over and sat down.

Her next question was whether Oksana was working that evening.

"Yes, eight to one."

Oksana picked up her glass and took a sip.

"What about you? How's your weekend shaping up?"

"Looks like I'll have Monday off," Yulia answered.

"Me too. Maybe we can make it to the beach for a few hours."

"Sounds good."

Yulia already felt the urge to confide in someone, to seek advice. And Oksana was trustworthy, as good a candidate as any. Yulia's first task tonight, though, was to explore the flash in more detail.

Twenty minutes later, Oksana had changed into her waitressing clothes and was out the door.

The instant she was gone, Yulia rose from the balcony and reentered the living room. Her laptop was on the coffee table; she seated herself on the couch, opened the screen, and pressed the on switch. During boot-up she reached for her handbag, and for the first time since morning, pulled out the flash-stick and held it in her fingers.

She was about to take another step forward. She sensed this gambit was becoming irreversible.

*   *   *

She started with the conference agenda and worked out from there. What appalled her most as she read one file, and then another, was not the aims of the participants—she knew that Zherdev and other oligarchs were corrupt to the core—it was the brazenness of this latest scheme. And that this one happened to be agriculture, perhaps the biggest prize of all.

One of the Harcourt Bank presentations included a recent history of the sector, in English, which helped refresh her memory:

In the post-Soviet land reform of 1992, more than 97 percent of agricultural land then in cultivation or generalized usage was distributed to the existing, in-place worker-occupants of residual Soviet-era collective farms, who in turn became freeholders and titular owners. Most of these allotments were small, ranging from three to five hectares. These newly created freeholders, however, were prohibited from selling the land that they now owned. This was deemed to be for their own protection, based on the apprehension—which appeared very real in the chaotic conditions of the 1990s—that they would be preyed upon by speculators and opportunists.

The result was a fragmented system with inadequate levels of overall investment. Aggregate national agricultural production—encompassing fruit and vegetables, meat, and dairy products—plunged by 67 percent from 1991 to 2000, according to various international agricultural organizations.

In response to this state of affairs, the Ukrainian government implemented legislation in 2000 that allowed a small number of foreign firms to assemble leasing rights, particularly in the Vinnitsa, Cherkassy, and Poltava regions. These foreign leasing operations have had limited success in boosting production on the land under their management, but their development has been hindered by corrupt local officials, burdensome bureaucracy, and an aging rural workforce...

It was the usual dysfunction. She read on. Gradually the present picture came into clearer focus:

In early 2013 the Ukrainian Parliament undertook to draft legislation which will remove the twenty-one-year-old moratorium on the sale of agricultural land...However the obscurity and complexity of the rules that will govern this process and that have emerged thus far, as well as widespread corruption in the Ukrainian judicial system, have made foreign observers and opponents of the current government extremely critical of the legislation in its current form and skeptical about its prospects for success.

To date, the reform remains uncertain and in flux. In our view these circumstances present risk, but also enormous opportunity, if married to bold strategies and decisive action...

The overriding aim of the conference-goers became clearer and clearer. These oligarchs, with Zherdev at their head, were preparing to divide up Ukraine's agricultural sector like Mafia chieftains, assigning each boss his own territory. Much as they'd divided up Ukraine's industrial sector in the 90s.

And at every phase, their Western bankers would be ready with advice and practical assistance—creating obscure trusts and shell companies to facilitate the swindle, reaping monstrous fees along the way. Money and wealth would be flushed out of the pockets of poor Ukrainian farmers and cycled back through the City of London, and from there to be spent across the four corners of the world, on penthouse apartments, yachts, ski chalets, and God knew what else.

After forty minutes Yulia noticed that her head was spinning again and her face felt hot. She stood from the couch and walked back onto the balcony, then turned her eyes toward the darkening sky and drew several deep breaths.

She herself was descended from countless generations of peasant stock, as most Ukrainians were. The issue therefore cut deeply.

If this plan went forward, Ukraine's latter-day villagers would be exploited and repressed all over again, much as her own ancestors had been through the centuries, by Mongol and Russian overlords alike. Screwed over in this latest instance by the likes of Zherdev... who'd intended the same treatment for her with his insulting and outrageous proposition the previous evening.

The main question now was what to do next.

CHAPTER 7

In analyzing his serial breakups, Thorsson had identified the common threads. The starting point was always mutual attraction. Perhaps boosted by some shared intellectual bents—enough at least to make a long-term union plausible. Little in the way of premeditation. Then, in short course, the woman's go-ahead. Minus any real long-term decision on *his* part. Just the more immediate one. When the opportunity arose, he plunged ahead. And why not? Sex was for the taking. Especially when money was part of the mix.

The next phase was just as predicable. An ongoing *relationship*, and all that went with it: deeper ramifications, encroaching commitments, obligations…he soon found himself looking for the exit.

The only benign angle, thus far, was that he'd avoided any pregnancies. He'd taken some chances. He'd simply been lucky.

He cast an unfocused gaze out over the water. Theresa happened to be American, which had perhaps given them some extra affinities and a few additional months. But in the end that was beside the point. The careless choices and decadence had gone on long enough. Time had come to break free of them. He adjusted the backrest of his lounge chair to a more forward position, reached down into his beach bag, and pulled out his e-reader.

Prior to arrival he'd downloaded *Enchiridion* by Epictetus and *Meditations* by Marcus Aurelius. Then, in his room, Seneca's *Letters from a Stoic*. He'd started *Enchiridion* the previous morning on the beach. Thus far he'd covered ninety pages.

He checked his watch. According to his program, he would wait until ten o'clock for his swim. That now left about an hour and a half for reading.

At one time, in university and graduate school, he'd considered himself fairly cerebral...before, that was, the materialism, the easy indulgence, and the torments that had resulted. He'd wandered away from his foundations. Now he would employ the same instrument for course correction.

The Stoics' prescriptions, he'd decided, were just what he needed. Self-control. Detachment. Application of reason. All leading toward a more stable and forward-oriented way of life. He clicked open the ninth chapter of *Enchiridion* and resumed reading.

*   *   *

During the first two hours of her shift, Yulia resisted the urge to look straight up. But she knew it was there: an inconspicuous half-sphere of black glass, mounted on the ceiling above reception. Inside was a digital video camera with a view that encompassed the desk's interior work space, the raised U-shaped customer counter, and about half the lobby. Another was mounted by the elevator, and yet another inside it, more discreetly concealed. Other orbs were positioned over the landing on the stairwell, above the main entrance outside, and throughout the hotel complex, including the pool and enclosed grounds. All streamed live digital images to the security room down in the basement, where they were displayed on a battery of small screens, monitored round-the-clock by at least one of the hotel's security personnel. Yulia had seen the room just once, during her initiation training. She'd been told that the videos were retained in digital storage for ten days before being erased.

She also knew that members of the security detail tended to be athletic types in their twenties and thirties, disinclined to sit for long hours indoors. In nice weather they preferred to walk the premises rather than watch the screens. Her best guess—her hope—was that her quick and inconspicuous operation had gone unnoticed.

All the same she flicked a glance up at the orb as she returned after mid-morning break. Anna was checking out several Ukrainian government officials. As Yulia took her seat two younger figures emerged from the elevator, wheeling their suitcases.

They were Zherdev's lieutenants. The same two who'd lost the flash. She put on a neutral expression as they drew up in front of her. The one with the finger tattoos handed their keycards over, squinting with recognition from the previous morning.

"Both our rooms are to be charged to Harcourt Bank."

"Yes, I see that's indicated here. Would you like to review your charges?"

He reacted with dismissive smile. The other did likewise. "Should we?"

"That's up to you."

His smile faded. "What for? The hotel is trustworthy, yes?"

"Of course…in any case I'll print out your receipts."

Yulia felt a slight reddening on her face as she stood, coming eye to eye with both men at full height. She asked them if she should call a taxi.

"No need. A motor launch will be collecting us out at the landing."

"I'll have someone assist you with your luggage." She signaled the bellhop, who was standing near the entrance, then folded the men's account summaries, placed them in two envelopes, and handed them over. "Thank you for staying with us."

Neither man offered any return courtesy. For good measure they gave her one last, hard appraisal as they followed the bellhop into the lounge area and out toward the water. Probably headed out to Zherdev's yacht. In any event she was relieved they were gone. If it was up to her, she'd never see them again.

She'd also thought ahead to her plans for the evening. With the way now clearer, she felt ready to go forward.

*   *   *

Sexual decadence was not just an outgrowth of money. It also, Thorsson had determined, issued from surplus physical energy. How could he focus on philosophy without a clear head? And swimming, with its full-body exertion, provided the perfect means of release.

Raising his forehead, he glimpsed the breakwater about seventy meters away. He re-submerged his face, and blew a hard exhalation into the water. Amid an eruption of bubbles and frothing water, he launched into his final power-fifty.

As he accelerated he felt his ventricles slam hard in his chest. Each stroke delivered a new explosion of power and surge through the water. Thirty strokes in, he allowed himself one last glance forward before putting his head back down and ripping off his closing sprint.

Forty-eight...forty-nine...fifty.

With the last stroke, he drew up several meters short of the barrier, which was made of poured concrete. Gradually his pulse and breathing moderated. Three laps between the breakwaters the previous morning; today five. This was his second day back to the sport this summer, and he felt like he was already finding his groove.

The rumble of an inboard engine also reverberated through the water. He soon identified its source. A sleek, deluxe-looking motor launch was idling at the boat landing, halfway down the barrier. It was tended by two men, one standing. To steer clear, Thorsson kicked ten meters back, out of the boat's prospective path, and began an easy breaststroke back toward shore. As he drew closer he took a better look.

Everything about the vessel transmitted excess from the oversized forward hull, to the leather-and-mahogany cockpit, to the electronic equipment on the dashboard. No expense spared. Same for speed; judging from its contours and the engine-bay dimensions, capable of shooting up the coast to Yalta in twenty to thirty minutes. Thorsson was familiar with the type. He'd encountered such boats on previous visits to the Caspian and Russia's inland waterways, and been invited out by a few of his business interlocutors. They'd almost become standard accessory for the ex-Soviet elite.

Two men in suits caught his attention on the breakwater. They were walking from the direction of the hotel, assisted by a bellhop. Both sported sunglasses, but their features were unmistakable in the bright sunlight.

The same pair that had stared him down the day before. They noticed him at once in the water. Their attentions didn't waver as they made their way up to the boat.

The boat pilot helped stow their luggage, and the two men climbed aboard and took their places on the upholstered rear seating, just six or seven meters away again. The one with the tattooed fingers placed his hand on the gunwale.

They reestablished their stares as soon as they were seated.

From his lower position, Thorsson looked straight back. He was accustomed to drawing generalized attention; as a teenager he'd realized it was his lot in life. But he'd also recognized that there existed a certain class of males—for reasons that were never quite clear to him—who identified him, instinctively, as a threat. Someone to be challenged and opposed.

These two men fell into this latter category.

The pair held their glare while the launch maneuvered out the inlet and out to sea, until finally turning their gazes forward. Lesser types, he confirmed, consumed by their own petty vindictions. He was glad to see them go.

CHAPTER 8

She could still backtrack. It was not too late. This next step of hers, however, was a decisive plunge forward. Yulia tingled with nerves and adrenaline as she clicked the video-call button. Seconds later the audio connected and the image came onscreen via Skype, clear and unadulterated.

"Hello Pavel. Thanks for connecting. On a Saturday evening, I wasn't sure I'd reach you."

Yulia saw her cousin smile over the link. His hair was a little longer than the last time she'd seen him in May, and his face bore stubble. Otherwise, though, he looked vigorous. Not just because he was twenty-six. He was also a man animated by purpose. That was one reason she'd contacted him.

"Lately Saturday night is almost like any other for me, Yulia."

"You're not the only one. And I just graduated."

He laughed. "Anyway, an unexpected pleasure. With video, no less..."

"Actually there's a reason for Skype." Yulia stopped to take a breath. "As I wrote in my message, I'm calling about something serious..." She observed his reaction. "Don't worry, though...not illness or accident." She hesitated. "I'm calling you because you're my cousin, Pavel. I trust you...you're also one of the best reporters I know. I chose Skype because I didn't want this conversation to be monitored."

Now she really had his full attention.

"I'm listening."

"There was a conference at my hotel this week, called Investment Opportunities in Ukrainian Agricultural Reform. Some big players were there: Ukrainian oligarchs like Zherdev and Girenko, even a few from Russia...for example Mironov and Zaslavsky. Some government officials as well, mostly deputy ministers. The organizer was Harcourt Bank. Wall Street, I think. Have you heard of them?"

"Of course. But that's not what really grabs me. You know this has been one of the main stories I've been covering over the past couple of years...trying to, anyway. The stakes are big. You know that...were you able to get hold of an agenda?"

"I'll get to that."

On-screen she saw him edge his chair forward and lean forward on his elbows, closer to his computer. All the same she held off with the lead item, choosing to fill out the surrounding picture first: the strict security, the yachts offshore, the cocktail parties, and the business conducted after hours and on Friday. She omitted Zherdev's crude proposition for the time being.

At last she got to the critical event—Axel Thorsson and his discovery of the flash memory. In a news story, she would likely have kept Thorsson anonymous. She also withheld his name from her cousin, at least for now.

"After all the tight security, are you telling me this American businessman, with no connection to the conference, just found the flash in the elevator?"

"Yes, and I'm telling you first."

"Amazing. Don't tell me you copied the files..."

"That's exactly what I did. And just in time, too. Zherdev's lieutenants came around looking for it as soon as they realized it was missing. They were uptight and aggressive. And that's an understatement."

"Have you examined the contents?"

"Yes. Two of the files are password protected. But I read all the rest. They're everything you might imagine and probably more: agenda, participants, strategies, even a division of regions…of spoils, you could say. It doesn't surprise me. But it's still appalling. Which is another reason I'm calling you, Pavel, and no one else. This is dangerous stuff."

Her cousin absorbed this. She could see his mind working. He sensed this was big. "I'm glad you have, Yulia. Particularly since I'm still just a boot-strapping reporter at medium-sized online outfit… you also could run with this yourself. You're a trained journalist. This could be your chance to break out. Launch yourself."

"You give me too much credit, Pavel. First of all, I don't have any publication behind me. You do. You're also in Kiev…I'm in Crimea… with a job I'd prefer not to lose. Secondly, I doubt I could handle this. It would be too much for me…I simply don't have the talent. On the other hand you know what you're doing."

"Don't sell yourself short, Yulia."

She averted her eyes from the webcam and dismissed the notion with a shake of her head. "There's something else I don't have," she said. "That's the courage. For me this would be a leap into the un-known. This story needs someone who's capable of seeing it through. You've got that, Pavel. I also know that you'll look out for me. I wouldn't entrust this to anyone else."

"I appreciate that. I also take it seriously. So what do you propose? To send the files to me by e-mail?"

"That's what I have in mind."

"Then I'm glad you contacted me first. Also that you had the sense to use Skype. I'm fairly certain both my cell phones are moni-tored these days by the Interior Ministry, not to mention my messages through the newspaper's e-mail system. Same for my personal e-mail."

"I figured as much."

"Here…I'll give you a separate, nondescript web mail address that I use only for situations like this. I only access it from Internet cafés, libraries, and the like." He gave her the address, and she wrote it down. "Tomorrow's Sunday, and it so happens I'll be out of the city during most of the day, where secure Internet can be a problem. I also want to have time to read through all the materials and think this through carefully. Can we Skype in the evening?"

Yulia informed him that her shift at the hotel would run through evening.

"What about Monday morning?"

"I may be on the beach with my roommate. But I've got Skype on my mobile. We'll work it out. The first task is to send you these files."

"Ready and waiting..."

Yulia clicked the red end-call button to break off the connection. She'd already placed the flash next to her laptop. She reached down and inserted it in the serial port. The dynamic was now in motion. There really was no going back.

CHAPTER 9

One set of Soviet-made cross-country skis and poles still leaned against the wall of the storage shed, off to the side of the newer and more sophisticated European equipment. Through the various upheavals and transformations that had transpired since the late 80s, somehow, the arrangement had held. Mikhailov straightened several pairs and made sure everything was in order, then turned off the lights and locked the door. As he turned round and redonned his gloves, his cocker spaniel ran up to him from the edge of the forest and barked, ever loyal and enthusiastic. Mikhailov reached down with both hands and grabbed him by the ears. He'd given him an Anglo-Saxon name, a tribute to both the dog's British provenance and his own lifelong study of the English language.

"Good boy, Rufus," he said. "Time to head back."

The canine pivoted and sprinted back toward the house, kicking up snow with his hind paws. Mikhailov followed, smiling slightly. Halfway back he released a couple of sharp exhalations into the frigid air, generating bursts of frost in the dusklight.

Windows on the first floor of the dacha glowed with illumination. It, likewise, had seen change since his parents had acquired it in 1977: enlarged and upgraded in the early 2000s; foundation buttressed, new windows installed, and new roofing and siding applied. Trees had grown taller around the clearing, perhaps. But the setting remained as pristine as ever, surrounded by nature—relentless, enveloping, and undeniable—another quality that Mikhailov found reassuring.

Three cars were parked next to the house, outlined by floodlights. As Mikhailov drew closer he observed his father stowing skis in the trunk of his parents' vehicle, a Renault sedan. During the 80s and early 90s, he'd strapped the gear to roof rack of the family Lada. His father looked at Mikhailov's empty hands.

"During the week you and Dima are always welcome to come up around campus. We could get out before dawn."

"I know, Papa. Thanks. But I've stored our skis here again. I have to leave the country on Tuesday."

His father glanced at him sideways with his sharp, light-blue eyes. His attitude toward Mikhailov's career still fell short of full sanction. He was a professor of Russian literature, nearing retirement. Wariness toward the security organs came naturally. In his father's case the instinct was lifelong.

"Near abroad, as usual..." Mikhailov added, with his usual obliqueness.

Mikhailov's work was not the only thing left unspoken between them. There were many others, going back years.

His father looked down to reposition some items before standing up straight. He was five centimeters taller than Mikhailov, with a full head of silver hair. Despite his advancing age, he remained strong boned and vigorous, even handsome, with skiing endurance to match.

"Are you ready to start loading?" he asked.

"We should be."

On the shoveled walkway back to the house they encountered the husky figure of Sasha, Mikhailov's brother-in-law, hauling two duffel bags. Trailing behind him were his twin university-age daughters, each armed with a cell phone. During high school, both had blossomed into head turners.

"Just about ready?" his brother-in-law asked as they intersected.

"Think so," Mikhailov answered.

Rufus rejoined him on the front porch and accompanied him inside to the kitchen, where they found Vera organizing leftovers, along with Mikhailov's mother and his sister Ksenia. Dmitri, age sixteen, almost full-grown, on the crossover between adolescence and adulthood, sat at the kitchen table with his iPad.

"Bags all packed?" he asked Vera.

"In the hallway."

"We'll load those first; then you can bring the food out." He turned to Dmitri. "Let's go Dima."

His son touched a button on-screen and rose at once. Two soft leather bags with zippered compartments, Mikhailov's and Vera's, stood near the main door, along with Dmitri's sport bag. They carried them out front, Rufus leading the way. When Mikhailov had stowed the bags in his Audi, he turned back to Dmitri.

"Go see if your mother and grandmother need help with the food," he said.

Without a word, his son turned and walked back to the house, preceded again by Rufus. Observing the exchange from nearby, Mikhailov's father said nothing but his reaction was evident. Ratification on at least one score, Mikhailov figured.

His father then also retraced to the house to turn out the lights and lock up. Several minutes later, loading complete, their entourage exchanged hugs and farewells. Mikhailov reserved a special embrace for his mother. "Big thanks as always, Mama," he said. The women and Dmitri then took seats inside their respective cars, leaving Mikhailov, his father, and Sasha still standing outside next to the Renault. Mikhailov's father also reached down to grab Rufus' ears one last time.

"Shall we follow our usual route back to the Inner Ring?" Sasha suggested.

"Sounds good," Mikhailov answered. "You go first, Papa, then Sasha. I'll bring up the rear, even if we get split up."

They agreed and shook hands. Aware of what came next, Rufus raced over to the Audi and jumped into the backseat with Dimitri. The three men took places behind the wheels, illumined their headlights, and wound out of the clearing down the driveway.

CHAPTER 10

Traffic was thick on the two-lane artery, little to Mikhailov's surprise. Cars were moving along in dense single file at thirty to thirty-five kilometers per hour. They'd managed to merge in from the side road but became separated by multiple vehicles.

"The usual nightmare," he commented.

"We've seen worse," Vera responded.

Mikhailov glanced at the rearview mirror. In the backseat, Dmitri had donned earpieces and refixed on his iPad, while Rufus looked ahead through the windshield.

Two headlights moved up fast from behind. Mikhailov looked sideways as the passing vehicle zipped by only twenty centimeters away, swaying their Audi: a large black Range Rover. Inside he glimpsed a young couple in the front seats, smug expressions illumined in blue light—probably in their late twenties. The woman's face was angled down toward a smart phone. A short distance ahead they veered back hard into the procession to avoid an oncoming vehicle, also an SUV, provoking a cacophony of horns.

"Idiots," Mikhailov exclaimed in a low tone, suppressing his irritation. "They probably came close to Sasha."

"Didn't hear any collisions, thank God," Vera said.

"Easily could have been, with that stunt."

Mikhailov could surmise the type. Moscow's new golden youth, with their hallmark attitudes of entitlement and generalized immunity. Flush with cash and backstopped by well-connected parents—possibly government ministers or Gazprom officials. One facet of twenty-first-century Russia, along with a few others, that rubbed him the wrong way.

The thought was still fresh when the Range Rover shot back out again, accelerating rapidly. As soon as it did, headlights loomed up in the opposite lane along the bending snowbank, high off the asphalt—a trailer truck, also traveling fast. Neither vehicle reduced speed.

"This looks worse," Mikhailov said, with more alarm. Distance between the two vehicles closed rapidly, casting the Range Rover in stark relief. At the last possible instant, the driver attempted to veer back into line.

It was too late.

The truck clipped the front-left corner of the SUV with a crunching eruption of sparks and glass, disintegrating much of its left side on impact. The remainder catapulted two meters into the air in half rotation, and after slight, almost surreal delay, smashed upside down onto the roofs of two vehicles on the other side of the center line. Screeching tires and secondary collisions ensued immediately among the cars behind, provoking a chaotic multicar tangle and bringing traffic to a dead stop.

"Good God, Oleg," Vera said, wide-eyed. "That happened up around your parents."

Rufus stood up on his hind legs with his front paws on the seat back, also sensing something was wrong.

"Stay in the car, Vera. You too, Dima. I'll leave the key."

Mikhailov jumped out the driver's side door and ran up the center line. Sasha had already leaped out ahead of him and was tracing up the right shoulder. Car alarms and panicked shouts perforated the night air while fires rose up from the wreckage. Fifteen strides he spotted the black Range Rover, half-obliterated and resting upside down on top of another vehicle. The bottom of its engine compartment was smoldering with smoke and flames.

The car underneath was his parents' Renault.

"*No!*" he shouted.

The Renault's roof was compacted and its left side was bent inward. A bloody forearm extended out the narrowed, blown-out opening of what had been the driver's-side window, bent at a grotesque right angle with the sleeves half torn away. At once Mikhailov recognized the sleeve of his father. Slicing with horror, he hurtled forward and looked down inside.

Half his father's head had smashed in at impact, ripping open his thick, gray scalp. A morass of his blood and brain tissue covered the bent-down headrest and air bag. One lifeless eye looked back vacantly from what was left of his face.

His father was unmistakably dead.

From inside a woman's moans wailed out—his mother's. With new shots of dread, he scrambled around the front of the two sandwiched vehicles, where he found Sasha also bent over, tugging on remnants of window glass. His brother-in-law's face had reddened from desperation and the heat.

"She's still alive. Let's get her out!"

Sasha had created a twenty-centimeter opening. Through it Mikhailov could see his mother's face. The top of her head was pushed up against the compacted roof and her body remained strapped in place by her seatbelt. Her eyelids moved and her lungs expanded and contracted. Her face was lacerated by glass and plastic and coated bright red with blood. But she appeared still conscious. His words rose up out of instinct.

"Hold on Mama!"

He helped Sasha tear away the rest of window glass, then groped inside and released the power lock. They gripped the top of the mangled door and heaved back. Three attempts later it remained jammed. Wailing sirens became audible in the distance.

"Let's try to pull her out!" Mikhailov shouted. He reached down the side of seat for the fastener on her seatbelt then pressed the button and pulled the buckle back up and across her body.

Just as he did she convulsed. Thick, gelatinous blood gurgled from her mouth and she gagged, unable to breathe. His desperation growing, he reached two fingers into her mouth to clear her airway.

"Mama!" Mikhailov shouted again, willing her survive.

Her next paroxysm was accompanied by a wrenching, visceral moan. Mikhailov watched in horror as life drained out of her. His fingers soaked with viscous blood, he pressed them to her throat, hoping against earthly odds to find her pulse.

There was none. His mother's heart had stopped beating.

*   *   *

Russian cemeteries tended to be tranquil and immaculate places, and this one, six months after the accident, was no exception. In the summer sunshine discreet but impressive views opened in several directions: on the right, a short distance up the verdant hillside, to the towering main spire of Moscow State University; on the left, down the lower reaches of Sparrow Hills and over lush green treetops, to the sweeping horseshoe bend of the Moskva River and the oval ring of Luzhniki Stadium just beyond, on the opposite bank. Gravestones on either side of the winding walkway on which Mikhailov now progressed with Vera and Dima were elaborate and hewed from fine materials, often bearing carved or inlaid portraits of the deceased. Most were for lifelong academics and their spouses. Almost all were bedecked with combinations of seasonal plantings and cut flowers, testimony to the reverence Russians held for the departed.

Somewhere along the line, long ago, Mikhailov had realized that foreigners often misperceived the Russian attitude toward death. They assumed, based largely on twentieth-century history, that Russians took an unconcerned and even casual approach to human life, relative to other Western cultures.

And given his inclination toward detachment, and his staunch acknowledgment of sad realities, he had to admit there was an element of truth to it. And not just because of the Communist record, either. The recklessness of the driver and his unthinking companion in the Range Rover on the fateful evening in late January had provided gruesome, latter-day examples.

But the condition of the cemetery told the other side of the story. The dead, for many Russians, were really not so distant from the living. They were therefore never to be demoted or forgotten.

Mikhailov knew because he held this attitude himself. It was what brought him here with Vera and Dmitri each month, on or around the seventeenth, the date of the accident.

They drew up at the dual gravesite, with the two headstones placed side by side and ornamented by planted blossoms. Vera kneeled down and placed a bouquet of cut chrysanthemums against the slab for Mikhailov's mother, and Dima did likewise with a bundle of white lilies for his father. The three of them then stood back with heads bowed.

Mikhailov caught his wife's face in profile. Her eyes were closed. She crossed herself, and he looked down at the graves again.

His father had been a lifelong atheist, and his mother had discovered faith late in life. In deference to his father's views and his mother's late conversion, he and his sister had split the difference, placing Christian markings and inscriptions on their mother's stone only. On the day of the funeral, however, Ksenia had also added a bronze Orthodox cross, which remained anchored between the two.

Behind his sunglasses, Mikhailov closed his eyes with his usual inured fatalism, and performed a genuflection of his own. He'd never quite come naturally to the practice. After a moment he felt the warmth of the sun on the hair on top of his head and looked up.

"Thanks for helping Ksenia," he said to Vera. "The graves look flawless, as always."

"My help's been modest. Ksenia has done most of the work."

Mikhailov looked over at Dmitri, set off by the bright backdrop of the river and the city beyond. "I'll never forget them, Papa," his son said, meeting his gaze. "I'm glad we still come."

Vera withdrew her eyes from the graves to look at each of them in turn. Her husband's promotion had hardly set things right. "These upcoming weeks in Crimea will do us all good," she added. "Remembering is important. But we also need to unweight ourselves... to look forward. Correct?"

Vera had the essence right, as was her habit. Still, she hadn't framed the vacation quite the same way as Mikhailov had done, at least to himself.

He did agree however that it would present a chance for new directions.

"Correct," he answered.

CHAPTER 11

Through her employment at the art gallery Oksana had secured two discounted season passes to a semi-private beach just north of the Radisson. Today Yulia was glad they had them. Unlike the bathhouses at public beaches, the bathhouse here offered several quiet nooks to which she could retreat when the call came from Pavel.

Oksana rolled off her stomach and sat up on her beach towel. After a glance at her smartphone she looked out at the water.

"Can you watch my things, Yulia? I'm going in for a dip."

Yulia's ears were already wired to her own device. She checked the display. "Right now I'm still waiting for that call from my cousin…I'll tell you what. If I get it when you're in the water, I'll bring your bag with me."

"Okay, thanks."

Yulia watched her walk into the water, adjusting the edges of her bikini bottom. Almost on cue, her earpieces chortled with Skype-tones, and Pavel's profile flashed onscreen. She clicked the green video-connect button and squinted at his image through her sunglasses.

"Give me a minute Pavel. I'll try to get some privacy."

She scrambled up from her towel, scooping up her beach bag and Oksana's. The usual array of gazes swung her way as she navigated the maze of bathers and mounted the concrete stairs to the bathhouses. On the shaded terrace she scanned the three long rows of chaises, and spotting an unoccupied section in a far corner, strode down the back aisle and sat down on a chair against the bathhouse wall. She performed one last survey, removed her sunglasses, and held up her phone. Her cousin's face now came into view, framed by bookshelves in the background. Yulia tried to keep her voice steady.

"Sorry for the delay...I admit this whole thing is making me nervous. Maybe I'm paranoid."

"No problem. The video feed gave me a little taste of the sea, here in the city."

Yulia could tell he was trying to calm her.

"Anyway your carefulness is warranted, Yulia. These files you sent are extraordinary. Truly explosive stuff."

Even with all his experience, Yulia could also sense he was excited—almost as much as she was nervous.

"Thanks to a tech guy at the paper I managed to open the two encrypted files as well. They've got even more details. Taken together, they spell out not just the division of territory by these oligarchs and the payoffs to government officials but also specific blueprints by Zherdev to shunt thousands of small farmers around Vinnitsa and Zhitomir off their properties, in order to create massive, consolidated farming operations. Then turn them into profit machines, manned at low wages by the very villagers who'll be displaced."

"Incredible. I knew this stuff was going on. But nothing this outrageous."

"Me too...It's even worse than I thought. I'm still assimilating it all and coming up with a story plan. I've scheduled a meeting with my editor this afternoon. Then I'll probably need three or four days to perform additional reporting here in Kiev and write the initial articles. At this point I'm thinking about a big-play, three-part series, to get the essentials out quickly. These are scandalous revelations, Yulia. There are bound to be aftershocks."

Yulia took in the word "aftershocks." It only compounded her nervousness. "Where do I fit into this plan?" she asked. "I'm the source, after all."

"You're right to ask. It's also something I've thought over carefully. Let me ask you this. Have all the participants in the conference departed the hotel?"

"Yes. The last ones checked out on Saturday."

"Before they left, did you get the sense that you'd fallen under their suspicion?"

"I'll put it this way. They knew the flash had been in my sole possession for thirty minutes or so. That put them on edge. They sized me up...took note of my name."

"Did they say anything directly to you about it? Threaten you?"

"Not directly. No. The threats were implied."

"What about the American businessman? Is he still there?"

"Yes, for almost two more weeks, according to his reservation."

"Did he come to the attention of Zherdev's men?"

"Well, they were keen to identify him. I refused to provide his name. But they clearly figured out it was him."

Pavel paused; onscreen, Yulia could tell from his face that he was also concerned by this. It also occurred to her that she was folded into an uncomfortable position. She uncrossed her legs and leaned rearward against the backrest, propping the smartphone on her knees. Shouts of children and teenagers emanated from the water.

"Can you tell me about him?" Pavel resumed. "For example, is he there alone?"

"Yes. Apparently he was supposed to come with a girlfriend. But seems the plan fell through. Otherwise he's thirty-three, according to his profile. Resident in Geneva. Tall, athletic guy, rather good looking, I will admit...wearing a fancy suit on the evening he arrived. I don't know the nature of his work, but judging from his lodging record with RadissonBlu, his business takes him all over the former Soviet Union."

"Thanks. That helps fill out the picture. He's an innocent by-stander in all this. So he shouldn't experience any consequences. Or at least...let's hope not."

The word "consequences" unsettled Yulia almost as much as "af-tershocks." "Will you keep me informed? Don't forget I'm on the line here. Along with everything else, I'm risking my job at the hotel."

"Of course I will."

"What about Oksana, my apartment-mate? She already senses I'm up to something. She also knows I was going to talk to you today. Should I reveal anything?"

"Good question..." Yulia watched him over the connection as he pondered this angle. "How about this. Tell her you're working with me on a freelance piece. Perhaps imply that it has something to do with Crimea or the resort business. But don't go into any details. Later on, just before the stories are released, you can tell her the specifics."

Yulia knew she would trouble holding the information to herself for so long. Nonetheless, she agreed.

"One final note...the conference participants are all gone from Alushta. That should simplify our situation somewhat. I'll also hint in the pieces that I uncovered the information in Kiev or through con-fidential informants who were involved in the conference. With luck, you and this American will never get drawn into it."

"Please do, Pavel. The lower the risk, the better."

Their conversation had run to conclusion. When they'd finished, Yulia sat looking at the blank screen for a moment then turned her gaze out to sea. The small flotilla of yachts that had idled offshore several days earlier, during the conference, had all departed.

Yes, the matter was in Pavel's hands now. And its locus had shifted to Kiev and elsewhere.

But here in Alushta, she would have to keep her guard up.

Over the maze of blankets and beachgoers she spotted Oksana emerging from the water, reaching back and squeezing water from her hair. Rising to her feet, Yulia hoisted the two bags onto her shoulder and retraced to the beach.

CHAPTER 12

Thorsson was now into his fourth day of reading. As he'd supposed, the Stoics had a lot to offer. He revisited a passage he'd highlighted from Epictetus:

> When you imagine some pleasure, beware that it does not carry you away, like other imaginations. Wait a while, and give yourself pause. Next remember two things: how long you will enjoy the pleasure, and also how long you will afterwards repent and revile yourself. And set on the other side the joy and self-gratification you will feel if you refrain.

And another he'd underscored from Marcus Aurelius:

> When you have been compelled by circumstances to be agitated or excited in manner, quickly return to yourself and do not continue out of tune longer than the compulsion lasts.

Beneath the shade of his umbrella, Thorsson lowered his e-reader and looked out over the sparkling surfaces of the Black Sea, now dotted with Jet Skis and other watercraft. He'd studied some ancient history.

From it, he knew that Crimea had been inhabited by Greek-speaking settlers through most of the Roman Empire: farmers and maritime traders who had employed the same language in their daily lives as Epictetus and Marcus Aurelius had chosen for their writings.

The coincidence was apropos.

His knowledge of the period was also enough to form some impressions. One was that sex was approached openly in the Roman world. Erotic images were abundant. There were few practical restraints on carnal indulgence, particularly for men.

Women were accorded less leeway. But they were hardly repressed, either.

At the peak of the Empire during the first two centuries AD sexual morality was consequently a matter of personal ethics and self-restraint. Not prohibition. The Stoics had formulated their views accordingly.

Which in turn made them, he'd concluded, quite relevant to the early twenty-first century. To a society at the peak of influence and affluence. But also showing fissures, corruption, and precursors of decline. In a word, decadence.

He figured he should know. He was one of its out-front products. He recalled one of Theresa's penultimate pronouncements: "Maybe one of your problems is too many advantages."

"What do you mean?" he'd asked.

"I mean you got some lucky breaks starting off...looks, athleticism, education, and so on. Now, thanks to your work, money and travel besides. You're well received wherever you go. The good life. Endless choices."

"I think that's a bit overstated. But, okay. I'm lucky. Is that bad?"

"It can be. With so many choices, one risk is that you never have to make any."

"I assume you're talking about women."

She'd let the point stand, implicit and self-declaring.

"Would you be interested in lunch today, sir?"

Thorsson became aware of a waiter, leaning his head below the edge of his umbrella. The previous day the waiter had first addressed him in English; today, remembering him, he spoke Russian. Thorsson glanced at his watch. It was already time for lunch. He said he was and accepted a menu.

"Any drink to start?"

"Perrier please, with lemon."

Thorsson chose a chicken-and-Roquefort wrap off the list, then glanced around the beach. It had filled out further since his mid-morning swim, and was now a smorgasbord of bared bodies. Twenty or thirty people waded at water's edge or paddled lazily a short distance off. Over his shoulders, from the pool area, he heard splashing and the shouts of children.

Within seconds one woman seized his attention, about thirty meters down the beach. She was tilting her head back and wringing water from her hind-locks, from hair that was thick and dark and glistened in the sun, like the droplets covering her body. She was tall, but sensuous rather than angular, with a bikini that made proper emphases. Rather than towel off, she kept her eyes closed and her face angled toward the sun.

She was far and away the most beautiful woman he'd spotted since he'd arrived. Indeed, the most attractive woman he had seen in quite some time.

His first guess, upon closer scrutiny, was that she was his age, or possibly a year or two older. Somewhat further along the scale than his usual preference, but in her echelon that hardly seemed to matter. There also appeared to be no man in her vicinity, which only aroused his interest further. All the more when she sensed his gaze, opened her eyes, and turned to look straight back at him, locked-on and sizing him up.

Seconds later her expression showed no ambiguity. The interest was mutual.

Until a fair-headed boy of about five ran up to her carrying a beach toy, amending the tableau. Thorsson surmised at once she was a single mother. He'd already noticed several others around the pool area, who'd registered him as well, given that he appeared to be alone. All seemed nice enough, and he sympathized with their challenges. Indeed, they often struck him as female equivalents to himself. Possessed, at one time, by illusions of mastery over the world. Heedless in their couplings. Casualties of their own dubious choices.

The difference was that they bore ongoing consequences.

He gave the woman with the dark, glistening hair a polite smile, which she returned. He figured he might strike up a conversation a little later. But that was as far as it would go.

He wasn't here to save the world. He had to save himself first.

The waiter returned several minutes later with his Perrier and took his lunch order. When he was gone again, Thorsson regripped his e-reader. The commonalities between the early Roman Empire and latter-day West held. Then, as now, the male of the species had to engage his reason before acting.

CHAPTER 13

"I admit, Yulia. You've stirred my curiosity with this. You're sure you can't tell me more?"

"The story is in progress. So it's probably better if I don't. Moreover it's Pavel's story, not mine. I'm just helping out."

"But I'll eventually read it, right? You said by the end of the week?"

"That's the plan."

Oksana contemplated the prospect. Her intrigue persisted. "By then the story will be public," she said. "There'll be nothing to hide. So what's to worry about?"

"Nothing, I hope. I'm just a little nervous about it, that's all."

The two of them were walking back to their apartment building along Volodomirskomy Street, approaching the town center, both wearing flip-flops and sheer body wraps over their bikinis. Yulia had already deflected numerous inquiries on the beach. At the supermarket she grappled for a diversion.

"I need to pick up a few things," she said. "Do you want to stop by also?"

"Actually I intended to pick some fruit at that stand around the corner. Peaches, blueberries, and apricots. Can you buy me some bread and cheese, while you're at it? We'll settle the balance when we get home."

"No problem."

They agreed to meet at the same spot in ten minutes.

Veering into the store, Yulia locked her beach bag in a storage compartment and scooped up a plastic handbasket. In addition to Oksana's request, she gathered a few other items, including half a sausage and a bar of chocolate. Near a magazine rack at checkout, she stopped in her tracks.

The face of Leonid Zherdev stared back at her from a glossy magazine cover, photographed in portraiture with his wife. The backdrop was opulent. The publication was a monthly called *Elegant Ukraine*, and its headline read "The Good Life with Leonid and Victoria Zherdev in Kiev, London, Crimea and Courchevel." Separate, secondary headlines mentioned horse racing by an ex-government minister, an upcoming art auction in Zurich, and an exclusive resort in Bali.

Blood rising, Yulia grabbed a copy off the rack and flipped it open. Among full-page advertisements for Swiss watches and French and Italian luxury brands, the article and photospread on Zherdev and his wife comprised much of the middle section. Thumbing through its thick pages, she glimpsed lavish, over-the-top interiors, French landscaping, and a shot of Victoria Zherdev exiting a Rolls Royce, a chauffeur holding open the door. Another photograph, taken over water, showed their three-story seaside villa just up the coast near Yalta, complete with marble colonnades and private beach. The magazine had not even bothered to mention the Zherdevs' residence or businesses in Donetsk, his city of origin.

Yulia realized she didn't have time for further perusal. Despite its high price she dropped it her handbasket. After checkout she re-encountered Oksana at their appointed spot. Oksana looked at her closely.

"Everything okay, Yulia? Your face is all red."

"Oh, it's nothing…in the store I was just thinking about the way things are going in our country."

"Why? Something go wrong in the store?"

"No, it's nothing new. Just more of the same."

Now Oksana was eager to change subjects as well. She glimpsed the banner of *Elegant Ukraine*, which Yulia had stuck in the side pocket of her beachbag rather than stowing it with the food items.

"I didn't know you read that magazine, Yulia."

"I don't, usually."

"Can I look at it when you're done?"

"Sure."

As they covered the remaining distance, Yulia tried to remain companionable. But her mood was now spoiled.

She held such journalism in low regard. Tonight, though, she would suppress her distaste. She needed to know more about the types she and Pavel were up against.

*   *   *

One of the captions, transposed above a photograph of Victoria Zherdev cuddling her poodle aboard the Zherdevs' sumptuous private jet, read: "When asked which residence she prefers, Victoria says, 'That depends on the season and my mood. Lately, I find myself spending more and more time in London.'"

The poodle appeared to have just undergone a multi-hour grooming session—and judging by his contented expression, was quite comfortable with private air travel. Victoria, for her part, seemed to move among her various habitations with aplomb, returning to Kiev with her husband only when protocol demanded. During peak-summer she preferred their Crimean villa, or cruises on their yacht along the south of France.

The images grated on Yulia. Not because she was opposed to wealth, generally speaking. She respected hard-earned money as much as anyone.

What bothered her was the source of Zherdev's riches.

Over the years she'd gathered the gist. Around 1992 or 1993 he'd acquired an import license from Moscow to resell Russian gas to Ukrainian utilities—a quick source of wealth in the chaotic years just after independence. Soon thereafter, in 1995 and 1996, various media accounts mentioned a series of shadowy transactions with regional politicians in Donetsk, also involving state industrial boards in Kiev, in which Zherdev acquired several steel, cement, and fertilizer plants at fractions of their real value. Rumors of violence, intimidation, and multiple payoffs abounded. Similar divisions of spoils had unfolded all across Ukraine at the time—just as they had in Russia.

Around Yulia on the balcony dusk had turned to darkness. Disquieted, she rose from her chair, reentered the apartment, and made her way to the refrigerator. To improve her mood she poured out a glass of plum *kompot* from a jug supplied by her mother, broke off several squares from her chocolate bar, and transferred to the couch for better light.

When she'd settled herself she plopped the magazine on her lap and bit off a morsel. The pages fell open to a photograph of the Zherdevs in their chalet in Courchevel the previous March, wearing après-ski fashions and seated on an extravagant leather sofa. Their feet, donned with embroidered slippers, rested on a rug made from an animal pelt. A massive stone hearth with a roaring fire framed the backdrop. Victoria had her hand placed on her husband's knee. Her gaze was pointed at the camera, while his fell on her with an affectionate expression. Another quotation from Victoria was transposed overhead: "I make a special effort to lure Leonid with me to Courchevel. It's the only place of ours where he can forget about his business for a few days."

The opposite page showed the couple at one end of their colossal dining table and its parallel tall-backed chairs. The couple's pale complexions were set off by deep-brown wood paneling of the room's walls, as well as the snow outside, visible through tall windows. Several bottles of vintage wine were positioned on a nearby serving cabinet, in front of a shelf of crystal goblets. Zherdev stood behind his wife, who was seated, embracing her from both sides while she clasped his forearms. Another portrait of domestic idyll…suggesting, once again, that the Zherdevs were actually a rather conventional couple: altogether decent and devoted to each other.

Thanks to her encounter with Zherdev at reception, Yulia held a different view. She also had little doubt that he would have tried to purchase her for himself rather than the banker, if he'd had the time or the urge.

In the latter two photographs, to enhance the glow of domesticity, she noticed that the Zherdevs' dog was included, just as he'd been on the private jet.

She didn't begrudge him, though. The poodle was just along for the ride.

CHAPTER 14

Finally Yulia tossed the magazine onto the coffee table, exhaled through her nostrils, and leaned back on the couch. She'd had about as much as she could take.

Oksana could flip through when she returned home. In the meantime Yulia decided to check her e-mail and get ready for bed. Anything to take her mind off Zherdev—at least until morning. However the cover stared back at her. The oligarch's face as well.

She couldn't fight off the images, despite herself. Her mind still swirled with mahogany furniture, plush carpeting, and vintage wines. Other associations flushed up, too. The taste of chocolate on her tongue helped them along. Recollections from seventeen months earlier—ones she would have preferred to avoid.

"Parlate italiano?"

"Un poco," she'd answered.

One of the first things Yulia noticed about him was his tailored blazer. Next his white shirt and crisp collar, emphasizing his olive tan. The latter contrasted with her pale tones in February. Later she realized it was his natural hue.

"Inglese?"

"Yes, of course."

The opera was *La Traviata*, at the National Opera and Ballet Theater. First intermission, and Yulia was standing in a queue at the refreshment bar, while her friend Lesya visited the women's room. Other impressions: he was about her height, though she actually stood a little taller just now due to the heels on her winter boots. Longer hair than her ex-boyfriend's and more styled. Somewhat older, but to positive effect. His eyes were brown and looked straight into hers. His English, though rather basic, carried an accent that disarmed her.

"Have you ah…seen *La Traviata* before?"

"No, this is the first time."

He smiled. "What do you think about it?"

"I like it so far."

Another smile. He seemed to appreciate the response.

"Please tell me later…*piu tardi*. I would be happy to hear."

At second intermission he found her again and beguiled Lesya as well. Yulia had envisioned an early exit. But for reasons she couldn't spell out in the moment, she decided to stay, while Lesya stuck to plan. From there she hadn't objected when Massimo—by then he'd introduced himself—occupied Lesya's vacant seat, even though his was more expensive and closer to the stage.

A light snow was falling when she streamed out onto Teatralna Square with him afterward, along with other opera-goers. By then the segue seemed natural. On their walk back to Yulia's hall of residence, all his questions were directed at her, with an attentiveness she'd half-forgotten was possible in the human male. About all she managed to learn about him was that he'd just arrived on a three-month assignment, to supervise the opening of a new Prada boutique on the Passage downtown.

Nonetheless she felt a rush of misgivings as they approached her dormitory. She was still reeling from her breakup. Out of self-defense she raised her guard. However at her entrance—to her relief—he kept polite distance and behaved like a gentleman, asking for nothing except for her mobile number, which she provided. Climbing the stairs to her corridor a minute later she was overrun with a giddiness she hadn't experienced in a long while.

He called the very next morning, and the two weeks that followed were a whirl of charm and ease. The pleasant surprises only multiplied. Other European men Yulia had encountered Kreschatik since coming to Kiev—most of them older and full of self-importance—were intent on quick pickups and could be observed circulating on the boulevard's broad sidewalks in the company of fortune-seekers or glorified hookers. During spring and early autumn such men were thick on the ground.

Massimo was different. First of all he was thirty-two, looked younger, and was attractive besides. In addition, his evening and weekend program consisted not just of restaurant outings but also two museum excursions, the opening of an art gallery, and a reception at the Italian Embassy. And through each one his gestures were subtle and incremental: a hand on her waist on an icy sidewalk, a gentle brace and smile from behind as he helped her off with her coat before a mirror, a playful phrase as he leaned toward her in front of a painting. After one week, he gave her a gift of hand-crafted leather gloves from his store, ones she would never have purchased for herself even if she could have afforded them. They fit perfectly. That evening, as he saw her off again at her hall of residence, she gave him a kiss, rather than vice versa. Once again he didn't push matters further.

Still, the restaurants formed the primary delights. Over the course of two weeks, seeming to wear a different, perfectly-fitted Italian-made suit or blazer and elegant silk tie on each occasion, he conducted her to six or seven of the most exclusive restaurants in Kiev: Terracotta, Fiore, Citronelle...the list only grew. Places Yulia had never visited or even dreamed of entering: venues with rich upholstery and patterned fabrics, expensive silverware and customized moldings. Somehow, at every one, he managed to garner a secluded table and rapt service, disarming the waiters and waitresses with the same amiable mix of

Italian and English he'd used at the opera. Three or four courses always ensued in perfect progression, comprised of impeccable cuisine that she was too inexperienced to fully appreciate, always accompanied by a bottle of wine and completed by coffee and elaborate chocolate dessert which made her head spin with pleasure. On this last score he'd identified one of her core indulgences.

But that's where the indulgences stopped. Not due to lack of attraction—simply out of the way he organized things. From their very first walk home after *La Traviata*, through each of their succeeding encounters, the vibe of sex always pulsed in the background. Always looming but never realized, which she admitted to herself at that point was a welcome change.

Indeed the trauma of Vitali, for her, had scarcely subsided. She'd first met her now-ex-boyfriend at a party during first year at the journalism faculty; he'd attended with friends. An engineering student, two years older than she was, but on the same graduation graphic due to his military service. Tall, big-boned, and healthy, like she was, from respectable parents, and seemingly ambitious. Which she supposed gave them a foundation to build upon. After a five-month build-up their romance had expanded to a full-blown coupling that lasted three years. He was the first with whom she'd crossed the critical threshold. And she'd also hoped…believed, really…that he would also be her only. She never pressed the issue, but acted as though they were pointing toward marriage—if not by graduation then soon thereafter.

Instead, in their second year, he'd slipped toward indifference. The slide had been gradual, and to her alarm she could do nothing about it. Her turmoil grew in tandem. By their third year together he seemed to prefer weightlifting or watching Kiev Dynamo football games and drinking beer with his friends—to the point, as far as she could tell, that she'd become little more to him than an offhand accessory. Their relationship degraded into a repeat cycle of arguments, public scenes, and bouts of rough, groping lovemaking, interspersed by frantic attempts by her to revive what they'd lost. The final devastation came during the holidays, when she'd been visiting her parents in Nikolaev. He'd informed her by text message that he'd met another girl at a disco. He wanted a total break. Four short paragraphs, without even an accompanying phone call.

Three years in which she'd given herself over. Utterly and without restraint. And four paragraphs were all she'd gotten.

All of which made Massimo the perfect corrective.

It was now Saturday night, and she and Massimo were walking down the center of Kreschatik from Maidan, after yet another elegant dinner. The boulevard, as usual on weekends, was closed to traffic. Light snow was falling, creating a surreal hush and illuminating facades with a make-believe glow. Massimo had his hand around her waist. During dinner he'd lavished her with another bounty of adoration. She examined his profile in the softened light as he contemplated the tableau.

"*Bellissima*," he said. "It is…beautiful."

"Yes it is."

"*E così tranquilla.* So quiet."

Yulia looked ahead to his building on the left, the tallest on the street, where he'd taken a short-term rental. Soon they would pass it, en route to her dormitory. Her two roommates were gone for the weekend. She imagined her empty bed.

Two months had passed since Vitali's gruff sendoff. Many more before that—longer, barren ones—had passed since she'd experienced true male affection and closeness. She yearned for those again. To override past thresholds. Also to reclaim them. Even to hope, possibly, for love.

The time had come. She knew it would.

"I can imagine this moment with no one else, Yulia. *Solo con te.*"

"I was thinking the same about you, Massimo."

She looked toward his building and stopped directly in front of it. With both hands he drew her toward him into tight embrace and brought his mouth down onto hers. She kissed him back without hesitation.

That night, in the surprisingly large and sumptuous bed of Massimo's apartment, she tumbled into the most exhilarating sex of her life, ascending to pinnacles of euphoria and release she'd hardly imagined with Vitali or never even known existed. Massimo, previously so genial and gracious, played her up and down the scale with the dexterity of a virtuoso, sending her panting with new possibilities. Over the next seven weeks she seldom slept in her dormitory, and in the blink of an eye, she fell in love again.

So much so that she hardly thought about the impending endpoint of Massimo's work assignment and ninety-day visa allowance and his return to Milan—particularly when he professed his sincere desire to stay. He talked expansively of introductions to his parents and brother at his family's homestead on Lago Maggiore in July.

In late May, five days after his return to Italy, Massimo sent her an e-mail. This one was two pages, and despite its fervent emotion and ardent apologies, had an effect even more devastating than the shorter variant she'd received over the Christmas holidays.

In the third-to-last paragraph, with his usual admixture of English and Italian, Massimo admitted that he was engaged to be married. That, in fact, he had been for two-and-a-half years. His wedding was planned for the end of June.

Crying copiously in her dorm room that evening, as her two roommates consoled her, Yulia tried to find something redeeming about the affair—anything at all. About all she could identify, through her veil of tears, was that she picked up some Italian and even become conversant.

The thought provided little relief.

One particular recollection made her feel even worse. The opera that first evening had been *La Traviata*. In Russian: *Padshaya Zhenshina*. The Fallen Woman.

Seven days later, when she started to recover her senses, she came to another realization. And with it a resolution, one that she vowed to retain in all circumstances, and for all time.

Never again would she allow herself to be seduced by money, extravagance, and the trappings of wealth.

Never again would she allow herself to be bought.

CHAPTER 15

Twenty-eight, twenty-nine, thirty...Thorsson finished his last set of squat-leaps and checked his watch: 5:43 a.m. The sea was still calm with first light, and the poolside terrace remained empty. Next, from the collection of equipment around the lifeguard enclosure, he located a children's water toy of suitable size and shape, set up a lounge mattress on an open quadrant of tile, and covered it with a beach towel. Lying on top, he then performed a rotating series of scissor kicks, push-ups, bicycle crunches, planks, and improvised leg raises, employing the water toy for stability and extra load. Forty minutes later, he concluded with three minutes of upward-facing dog, a yoga pose to stretch and elongate his spine, breathing deeply and angling his face toward the rising sun in the southeast. Finally he rolled over onto his back and placed his hand towel over his face, relishing a new flush of endorphins.

He then got up, put away the accessories, and walked to the stone wall along the beach. He placed one foot on top to stretch his hamstring, looked out over the water, and remembered one declaration from Epictetus with which he did not agree: "It is the sign of a weak mind to spend too much time on things having to do with the body, such as exercising a lot, eating a lot, drinking a lot, excreting, and sex.

Such things should be done incidentally; let your attention be concentrated on your mind."

Thorsson could see the logic of the last bit. Not the first, though.

Thrusting one leg straight back to stretch his Achilles tendon, he spotted a school of dolphins several hundred meters offshore—seaborne mammals also well known to the ancient Greeks and Romans. The creatures leapt out of the water at intervals, arcing over the sparkling surface and cavorting among their own, exulting in their prowess and vitality.

His swim of about forty-five minutes would come later that morning, after breakfast and another spell of reading. Four days into his regime, he could feel improvements in his power and endurance. He was getting fit.

Logic and detachment were fine, he reckoned. But prowess and vitality did have their place.

CHAPTER 16

During dinner most of Vera's questions were directed at Dimitri. Conventional subjects: what Dima had done that day, his plans for the rest of the week, and his preparations for their vacation in Crimea. Throughout them, however, Mikhailov noted that his wife aimed her longest, most intent glances across the table toward him. Meanwhile Dmitri made quick work of his meal. When he was finished he looked over at his father.

"I think I'll pass on dessert," he said. "May I be excused, Papa?"

"Back by eleven, as usual?"

"Yes, of course."

He cleared away his plates and utensils and departed the kitchen, while Mikhailov and Vera resumed eating. They remained silent until they heard the door close. Mikhailov sensed that his wife had something to say and looked up from his plate.

For the moment she held off. She asked him instead if he wanted extra servings. Mikhailov declined.

"For dessert," she said, "I bought some fresh blueberries. I also have some cake with chocolate and banana filling, which I purchased at that new bakery in the next building."

Mikhailov agreed to the blueberries. He passed on the cake.

Vera loaded their used plates and utensils into the dishwasher and doled out their servings. Still preoccupied as she reseated herself, Mikhailov noticed that she'd cut a generous portion of the cake for herself. Over the previous four or five years she'd started to add weight. He never commented, though. In fact, the trend did not trouble him.

Recent discords issued from other sources.

Now he waited for the next stanza, which came after Vera consumed her first two forkfuls of the sweet. "I know what happened in January was hard," she said. "It was hard on Dima and me also. I've just figured you need time to recover…you and Ksenia have also had to organize things."

Mikhailov placed a spoonful of blueberries in his mouth and said nothing.

"But there are other questions, too," she continued. "And now seems like a good time to talk about them. For example, what am I supposed to do with my own time, now that Dima's almost grown?"

Mikhailov took another spoonful as he considered his response. She pressed on before he had one.

"I mention this because Sveta and I had a talk this morning over coffee. We're interested in starting a small business together…maybe a florist shop…we noticed that empty retail space next to the new bakery."

"Sounds like a decent idea to me."

Vera displayed a flicker of frustration, as if he'd missed her primary thread.

"That's not the real issue here, Oleg. Before I take a step like that, I have to make sure we're on the same page. I don't take anything for granted with your promotion. Still, the wives of high-ranking officers seem to face a lot of expectations and demands…dinners, concerts, and so on…"

"I'm not part of any inner sanctums yet."

"I know. But as far as I can make out, you're just one step away… am I right?"

"Maybe; maybe not. I'm different from most of the others. You know that. That may work against me."

For the first time that evening, Vera reacted with a compassionate smile. "That's one thing I've always admired about you," she said. "You've stayed yourself. And you don't take anything for granted."

"No, I don't. Even less than I did before."

Mikhailov had not intended to evoke sympathy but watched tears well up in her eyes. She reached her hand across the table and grasped his forearm. After a slight pause to wipe them away, she readdressed her cake and blueberries. A moment later, she continued in softer tone. "Is that the reason you've been spending so much time alone in the study lately? Extra work?"

"No. Not really."

"If not that, then what is it? Until now I've only been able to guess. Reading? Thinking? Praying…even? You do seem to spend a lot of time at the computer or looking out the window. Several times I've found you with an open book in your hands…I've just been glad you haven't turned to drink, like a lot of our men do. Therefore I haven't pried."

"I've appreciated that, Vera. You've disturbed me very little."

By now Mikhailov had finished his blueberries and couldn't resist a quick glance at his watch. The flick of his eyes was not lost on Vera.

"Are you planning another evening in there tonight?" she asked.

"Well, yes. First, though, I was going to walk Rufus." As if on cue, the dog appeared at the kitchen door. Mikhailov reached for his pack of cigarettes, lying nearby on the windowsill, which provoked the usual glance of rebuke.

Tonight, though, Vera seemed to have other preoccupations. She took a deep breath. "I'll tell you what," she said. "I won't object to you enjoying a cigarette or two tonight. But I would ask that we spend some time talking. Can you do that for me, Oleg…at least for one evening? That way, maybe we can go on our vacation in Crimea with a cleaner slate."

Mikhailov took a deep breath of his own. This was not the evening he'd envisioned.

"Yes, I guess we can do that."

"Good. I'll put on some green tea. It will be ready when you get back."

CHAPTER 17

When Mikhailov let him off the leash Rufus raced out to a cluster of bushes near the children's playground and performed his evening ministrations. He then retrieved a large stick he had concealed nearby that morning, clamped it in his jaw, and romped out to a parcel of mowed grass. Keeping the dog in view, Mikhailov paused along the walkway and pulled his cigarette pack and lighter from his shirt pocket. His daily intake had seldom been great, even during university and graduate studies. He'd now gotten back down to two or three.

Though the tobacco still brought clarity, which he reckoned he needed. He placed a cigarette in his mouth, lit up, and continued walking.

Three high-rise apartment buildings loomed over the semi-enclosed yard, anchored by underground parking garages and schematic landscaping—part of the building spree that had overrun the green fields west of the city during the 2001-2008 real estate frenzy. Thanks to accidental and opportune timing, he and Vera had purchased right after the crash, drawn by the fresh air, the straight-line commute, and a backdoor subsidy from the Service. But he'd always perceived it as more intermediate stop than destination.

That had been even truer since winter.

Ten days after the funeral there had been a second installment. Mikhailov dragged on his cigarette and gazed out over the manicured bushes and winding walkways, still awash in the long daylight of northern summer, and blew a plume up toward the sky. The nicotine rushed his brain and roused his memories from that particular February morning, a Saturday. The skies had still been dappled with darkness as he and Sasha had rendezvoused at the clearing. The outing ahead had promised affirmation. Maybe even renewal. He remembered their aspirations well.

*   *   *

After locking the door to the storage shed Mikhailov glanced back across the yard. This morning no lights or activity emanated from the main house, as they had on the evening two weeks before. Beside him, in the grays of first light, Sasha's expression was grim, pensive, sympathetic. Without a word they carried their skis and poles around the corner toward the start of the trail, frost pockets forming with their exhalations. Rufus cantered alongside over the fresh snow cover, affected by their mood.

"Looks like there's about twenty-five centimeters of fresh snow out here," Sasha observed.

"I hope we can find our old tracks," Mikhailov responded.

"Don't worry about it…I'll lead the way." His brother-in-law caught sight of the sauna cabin, then straightened and turned. It was the first time Mikhailov had seen him flash his customary bonhomie since the accident.

"We'll fire up the *banya* as soon as we get back, right? Have it ready for the wives and kids?"

"Of course."

They reached the trail opening and plopped their skis onto the unbroken snow. Rufus barked and began scampering around them in half circles, kicking up clumps of powder. Sasha placed his feet in the bindings and reached down to snap in, while Mikhailov followed suit. "I'm quitting cigarettes," he said, still bent over. "None for three days already." Mikhailov glanced at him from the side, somewhat surprised, given his brotherrr-in-law's heavy habit. "I'm doing it for Ksenia. She's been urging me to quit for years. Now I figure she needs me more than ever."

"Maybe I should follow your example."

"I suggest you decide that later," Sasha responded, displaying another flash of energy as he donned his gloves and slipped his hands into the pole straps. "Anyway this is a chance to breathe some fresh air and get our blood pumping. Right?"

"It is. I need it."

Sasha looked over at the trail opening, clapped one open hand over his fist, and released two sharp exhalations. "Ready?" he said, glancing back. Mikhailov thought ahead to the route they planned, covering seven kilometers and numerous inclines. He hoped he had the endurance. "Ready as I'll ever be," he answered.

"Let's not hold anything back, agreed?"

"Agreed. You lead the way."

"*Davai!*"

With a quick hop Sasha pivoted his robust frame toward the forest, blowing several hard exhalations as he took off. Intent not to fall too far behind, Mikhailov did likewise. Rufus barked and brought up the rear. They rounded a bend and met an incline, where Sasha refound their old tracks, easing the way. The pace was nonetheless demanding. His brother-in-law had been an accomplished hockey player in his youth and his baseline athleticism still showed. Mikhailov fixed on his heaving torso and pumping limbs and tried not to lose distance. He looked down at Rufus alongside the track. The canine was also panting as he churned through the snow. So far they were keeping up.

"Good boy, Rufus," he said. "We can do this."

Rufus glanced up at him, then forward again, determined as ever.

Minutes later they entered a gradual, five-hundred-meter down incline. Mikhailov picked up speed and let his skis run, welcoming the respite, while Rufus fell two or three meters behind. At bottom the trail leveled again, and Sasha glanced back over his shoulder. Mikhailov could see sweat stains showing through his brother-in-law's tunic and steam rising from his neck.

"Kak?"

"We're still here."

Sasha flashed a grin in profile, angled out a raised fist, and gripped his poles and for full combustion through several familiar agglomerations of boulders and jagged rock. A grove of birch trees followed. Mikhailov couldn't tell for sure whether his cocker spaniel recalled what they'd face next, but he did: the most punishing uphill incline on the course. Sasha soon opened up another twenty meters of separation. Then another ten. And yet another fifteen. His brother-in-law seemed to have found his glide-rhythm. Mikhailov struggled to get some words out between exhalations. The dog was also panting.

"Come on, Rufus!" he said, hardly looking down.

At the rise began Sasha glanced back again to make sure they were still within view. His face had gone even redder than before, with the sweat to match. Mikhailov had seen him in this frame of mind before on countless occasions, many involving vodka. Once he got going, he could become difficult to slow down.

"Davai!" his brother-in-law shouted again, waving out and sweeping a pole forward. "Leave it to God!" He then charged up the hill, heaving breaths and planting his poles hard.

The incline formed a long, gradual bend to the right, and Sasha disappeared from view around a cluster of spruce trees, by which point Mikhailov estimated that he and Rufus had fallen at least seventy meters behind. He was now ruing his smoking habit more than ever. His only salvation lay in the small plateau at the top. The biggest challenge would be over.

Halfway up Rufus riveted his snout and issued three loud barks, then burst ahead, agitated.

Fifteen kicks further, the peak came into view at last. Sasha was already across. Rufus continued surging ahead with even greater urgency. The final stretch grew even steeper, exacerbating the burn in Mikhailov's thighs. He lowered his head and performed a final ten-count, pushing hard off his pole-plants and grunting through his last several kicks, while Rufus accelerated faster still and disappeared over the apex, his barks even more frantic. When Mikhailov reached the crest himself and looked up, he understood why.

The tracks that Sasha had laid and had traced for three kilometers thus far veered suddenly right. At their culmination Sasha lay in a heap, with his face half-buried in the snow and his legs splayed back at wrenched angles, with one of his skis detached. He wasn't moving. Rufus drew up to him, let out a piercing yelp, and looked back at Mikhailov with desperate eyes.

"Sasha!"

Mikhailov bolted another kick and released himself from his bindings, threw aside his poles and hurled himself into the powder. He twisted Sasha's shoulders and brushed the snow from his face. His brother-in-law's eyes were half-closed and his respirations were shallow. Fluid oozed from his mouth. Mikhailov tried to restore consciousness with a slight shake to his shoulder. It was to no avail. His next exhortation was even louder than the first.

"Hold on Sasha!"

Rufus reacted with another yelp, churning back and forth a meter away. Mikhailov pushed himself back, released Sasha's remaining binding and freed his wrists of their pole straps, straightening his legs. He then rolled him at once onto his back and brushed away additional snow from his head and shoulders. He also raced his memory. His last refresher course in CPR had been five or six years earlier. He remembered that time was critical. So was the sequence.

Yanking off his gloves, he cleared the mucus from Sasha's lips and with two fingers felt his carotid artery. His pulse was faint but constant. Mikhailov tilted his head back, splayed his mouth open and inserted two fingers, extracting as much remaining fluid as he could.

He then injected two exhalations and straightened to execute thirty chest compressions.

There was no effect. With hardly a pause, he repeated. Still nothing happened. Mikhailov swore, unzipped the top of his jacket, and pulled out his cell phone. He had an emergency number on the speed dial. The call was answered at once. He kept his voice clear and concise.

"My brother-in-law has collapsed unconscious in the woods. Skiing...it looks like a heart attack." He conveyed the exact location with his GPS tracker. "I urge you to send a team by snowmobile...even helicopter if possible."

"We'll draw upon all available resources."

"Please hurry!"

As he clicked off Sasha emitted a guttural groan, and his body wrenched with a single, violent convulsion. All at once his skin went white. Feeling his carotid artery again, Mikhailov found that his heartbeat had stopped.

"Sasha!"

Mikhailov injected two more breaths, locked his hands together, and thumped Sasha's chest with thirty more quick compressions. Making one last-ditch attempt as Rufus looked on, he repeated the action.

The effect was null. Sasha was dead.

Mikhailov sat back in the snow, gazed skyward, and howled into the forest. Rufus did likewise.

CHAPTER 18

While Vera prepared tea in the kitchen, Mikhailov surveyed their flat-screen television, modernistic leather furniture, bookshelves, and glass-topped side tables. He'd hardly watched television of late; indeed he'd spent very little time in the living room at all. Even Rufus, now lounging on the patterned rug at his feet, seemed perplexed to be here. Whenever his master was home, the canine had grown accustomed to evenings in the study.

Perhaps Vera was right. This talk was overdue.

Wearing light slippers, his wife entered with the tea tray and placed it on the coffee table. She poured out two cups and set Mikhailov's down on the side table by his armchair. Taking her preferred position at the end of the couch and facing him at a diagonal, she removed her slippers, reached for her own cup and saucer, and curled up her legs to the side.

"Thanks Vera. What you said is true. It's been a while."

"It has been. You've always been gone a lot, Oleg. But when you were home, I usually had you to myself…here in the living room watching TV, reading, whatever. I miss that."

"I do too. However what I've been doing is necessary."

She took in the word "necessary" during a sip of tea, as well as his employment of the present tense. Neither seemed to allay her. "I know how hard it's been for you...with your parents and Sasha and so on," she said. "Therefore I've tried not to intrude. I've assumed you needed time for reflection...to grieve, in your own private way. As I said, I've just been glad you haven't turned to drink."

"No. That would solve nothing."

"But at a certain point you have to move on," she continued. "Or I should say *we* have to move on."

"We will, Vera. I'm with you to the end. You know that."

"I do, deep down. That's why I've been patient. But as your wife I still need to ask, Oleg...can you at least tell me what you're doing in there in the study, night after night?"

Mikhailov drew a large sip of tea, then a deep breath. Time had come.

"I'm working on a novel," he said.

Vera's eyes widened, and she stopped in mid-sip. Collecting herself, she lowered her saucer to her lap, now fully alert. From the floor Rufus glanced up, sensing import.

"A novel...you mean fiction?"

"Yes."

"What's it about?"

Mikhailov took a sip of tea before responding. His intelligence training, even in his marriage, was relevant. He'd anticipated such questions. Also that they'd come fast and furious, once the truth was out. "My storyline and characters are still in development," he answered. "If you don't mind, I'd rather not go into that kind of detail, just yet."

"Can you at least give me a general idea? A love story? Historical novel? Something that relates to your work?"

"A qualified yes to the first question. No to the second...that is, it's set in current times. And yes to the third, to certain limited extent."

"So it's a spy novel, then."

Vera's voice had already acquired tones of almost desperate urgency. The news, to her, struck like a thunderclap. He made another deliberate pause.

"That term would also be a misapplication. I do intend to use my work as a window onto modern-day Russia...onto larger moral questions that we're facing currently, the state of our politics, and so on. And the book will likely contain some intrigue, for narrative momentum."

She seemed to take particular notice of the word "plan." Also to take heart in it, as if it was still provisional.

"How many pages have you written?"

Mikhailov took another sip of tea and rationed a breath of his own. "That question is also premature. Until now, I've been working on character sketches, plot outline and so on...reflecting on themes I wish to advance. I've drafted a handful of opening pages, more as experimental exercises than bona fide writing. They're very rough and preliminary."

Again Vera took absorbed this. "That makes it sound as if you're aiming to write the next, great Russian novel...as if you want to be the next Tolstoy or Dostoevsky or Turgenev, or something like that."

Mikhailov couldn't help but smile. "Please don't put that kind of pressure on me, Vera. Don't forget this is my first novel. These are very early stages."

"But you're talking as if this book isn't just some hobby or a way to deal with grief." A ping of accusation entered her voice. "You sound quite serious."

"I am serious."

"What about your motives? I mean...what drove you to this?"

Here Mikhailov became more circumspect, opting for question rather than statement. "Remember what caused my parents' death?" he asked her.

"Of course. How can I forget?"

"That young couple, with their oversized vehicle and reckless driving? They're rife in Russia today. Over-the-top materialism, joined to an absence of social conscience. Especially here in Moscow. Part of it flows from Westernization, perhaps."

"So you blame the West?"

"No, not really. I'm more troubled by trends of our own making... not least political ones."

This was another comment Vera didn't expect to hear from a newly promoted officer of the FSB. It resembled the one he'd made at the Kremlin. She almost hesitated to inquire further.

"And you're seeking to change that, politics and all?"

Mikhailov released a slight laugh through his nostrils. "Politics and all? That's rather beyond the scope of a novelist, wouldn't you say?"

Vera didn't appreciate the riposte. Her features became troubled again. She raised her cup and saucer and took another sip. Again the herb appeared to provide little comfort. She promptly lowered her feet to the floor, transferred the saucer back onto the tray, and felt the teapot with her palm. "The tea's gone cold," she said. "I'm going to go to the kitchen to make more. Can we continue this discussion when I get back?"

"Of course. I'll be here waiting."

Along with Rufus, Mikhailov watched her exit the room, carrying the tray. She appeared to be formulating her next line of inquiry. Indeed the next big question appeared to have already occurred to her. One that she almost dared not to ask.

And the fact was Mikhailov had not disclosed the whole truth. These ambitions and motivations had been building for years, not months. They came down to purpose. His place on the planet, before his time expired. His relation to society, too. The deaths of his parents and Sasha had just brought the requisites into clearer, more urgent focus.

Most of all, he had some things to say.

CHAPTER 19

Vera was the first person to whom Mikhailov had made his admission. He supposed that was natural and even obligatory; she was his wife. All the same he'd already foreseen reactions from others as well: Ksenia, Dmitri, his small circle of long-term friends. Among them there would be some common strains, at first: surprise, curiosity, skepticism, joined, perhaps, with well-meaning concern. The reasons were understandable. The creation of a novel, for most people, entailed too many unknowns. It was tantamount to a gaping black hole.

From there, as the revelation took hold, he expected further reactions. Unease. Discouragement. Even outright opposition. From Vera most of all. That was also natural. She had the largest stake. Also, potentially, the most to lose.

These responses were already evident on her face when she reentered the living room with the tea service. She set the tray down, poured out two fresh cups, and resecured her position on the divan. From the rug, Rufus examined her expression for a moment and lowered his head. The canine sensed this would not lead to the usual sequestration in the study. This would take a while.

Vera now transmitted a compassionate gaze over the top of her teacup. "This really has caught me by surprise, Oleg dear. But as it sinks in I can understand what drove you to this. What you've been through would be enough to shake up anyone. Even I felt numb for about a month. It was a lot to handle."

"Yes. I suppose it was."

"I haven't pushed you this way until now, but might faith achieve the same thing? That's what Ksenia has done...and she's your own sister. I would say she's visited church at least three times per week since the funerals. Dima and I have gone with her sometimes. But you never have...except for Easter." She waited for a reaction from him. When there was none, traces of desperation reappeared in her face, and she cleared her throat. "You know, sometimes I'm not even sure you believe in God, Oleg. We never really talk about it. Yet you've worn that cross around your neck for the past three or four years...even before all these events. What does it mean to you?"

Instead of answering straightaway, Mikhailov returned his gaze to Rufus and took another sip of tea. At last he looked up at her. All the same he couldn't help but smile a little. His tone was neither severe nor sarcastic. "Call me an aspiring Christian," he said.

"I'm your wife, Oleg. Is that all you can say?"

"That's about the best I can offer."

Vera straightened her back, a little frustrated, and turned her face in the direction of their flat-screen television, staring into indeterminate middle distance. "Your response sounds a little offhand, if I may say so," she said, "like you haven't given religion much of a chance. This writing of yours, by comparison, is much more individualistic."

"Is that so bad?"

"It can be. For one thing, it causes you to be by yourself much of the time."

"Yes, that's true...although don't forget Rufus."

His wife glowered at him. She did not appreciate the joke. "Please be serious, Oleg."

Mikhailov drew a sip of tea and took his time answering. "If solitude is an offense, then I plead guilty."

She appreciated this remark even less. "Well! That's a peculiar attitude. Are you sure this isn't just a means of escape…a flight from reality?" This was about as close Vera came to straight-out indictment—especially since he'd been tagged for promotion.

Mikhailov took a deep breath to gird his patience. "It's actually quite the opposite," he answered. "It's a means of confronting reality head on."

"How? It's just fiction."

"Therefore there are no restraints. It affords total freedom."

"Freedom? The freedom to do what?"

"The freedom to grapple with hard questions. Uncomfortable, impolitic ones, that people often can't address in any other way."

"Is that what you intend to do?"

"I intend to try."

Vera stared back at him.

"Let me frame it another way," he said. "I had some things I always wanted to say to my father. Now, of course, it's too late. And for a while now—even before the events of January and February—I've also had some things to say of a general nature. Worthwhile things, I hope… to everyone, far and wide. And I want to say them before that also becomes too late. Don't forget I'm only two years younger than Sasha."

The elaboration hit like another thunderclap. Vera was now more off-balance than aggressive. Her eyes went wide again as she drew rest of her tea. "And your career?" she said. "You've always been on a successful track, Oleg…this promotion is everything we've dreamed about."

Mikhailov raised his eyebrows and shrugged. He showed neither thrill nor satisfaction. It wasn't an act.

"Where does your novel fit with your job?"

"The two spheres are bound to collide, at some point. It's inevitable."

Additional stillness engulfed her, as if she was too disturbed to return her cup and saucer to the table. Finally she had attained the question that she almost not dared to ask.

To save her the trouble Mikhailov held up his hand. "However rest assured that I have not lost sight of two other central considerations," he continued. "The first relates to my chances for success. These are absurdly improbable, to say the least. The second relates to my material responsibilities to you and Dima," he gestured around the living room and down at the dog "and Rufus too, for that matter. For the foreseeable future, therefore, this novel will remain a sideline."

Vera's next exhalation was born of relief. For the first time since he'd sprung his announcement, her tension ebbed. "Thank God," she said.

"All the same I should note that I plan to continue my work in Crimea," he added. "Starting as soon as we arrive. Early mornings, rather than evenings. Pre-dawn, before we head to the beach."

"You're sure you won't get tired? That doesn't sound like much of a vacation."

"I'll manage."

As long as there was movement toward the desired endpoint, Mikhailov figured. For now, that was what mattered most.

To make the full leap, he would probably need another catalyst.

CHAPTER 20

The melodic tones were familiar yet unassociated with anything in her dream. Preferring the gripping scenario now in progress, Yulia tried to ignore them. But the sounds persisted and only grew louder, until the voices and images in her head dispersed and she stirred awake. With reluctance she half opened her eyes. At first she couldn't identify the source.

"It's your phone, Yulia," Oksana said from the bed nearby.

"Huh? What?"

The tones identified the call as Skype.

Oksana emitted a slight moan. "Sounds like you left it in the kitchen," she added.

Yulia pulled off her single sheet, swung her feet to the floor, and blinked her head clear. The room was already flooded by early light, despite the closed curtain. The digital clock on her nightstand read 5:47 a.m.—almost half an hour before she was due to get up. Emitting a moan herself, she rose and exited to the kitchen wearing panties and a tank top. The melody was now at full volume. She realized the device was in her handbag, which she'd dropped by the kitchen counter. With another moan she squatted down, rummaged inside, and pulled it out. Rising and bringing her eyes into focus, she jolted to alertness when she observed the Skype caller profile.

"Pavel?"

"Sorry for calling so early, Yulia. Since we last spoke, everything's been unfolding fast."

Yulia doubled back and quietly closed the door to the bedroom. She also inserted her earbuds, muting the external speaker on the phone. "No problem," she said, making her way into the living room. "What's going on?"

"What's going on may be the biggest story of the year, thanks to you."

"That big? Good God."

"Since we last talked, I've been going flat out. I spent much of the week following up on several angles here in Kiev, filling out some of the surrounding elements...do you want to activate video?"

Glancing down at her tank top, Yulia saw her breasts splayed out and her nipples outlined. Elsewhere she was all lush flesh and skin. However this was too important for niceties. "I'm not really decent," she answered. "But I'll just keep the lens pointed at my face." She sat down on the couch and kept the phone at close range. Pavel's image came onscreen from his cramped but empty newsroom, in an aging building not far from Zolotoi Vorota. He looked like he was wired on coffee.

"You know lots of journalists have been sniffing around this story for the past couple of years, right?"

She nodded.

"Well, these files you provided from the conference in Alushta contain the first hard references...names, banking institutions, planned allotments in different regions, and so on. It's the very sort of information that's been lacking so far. Therefore I spent the first part of this week running these down...staying careful, of course, not to let on about the details in my possession."

"So the story's taking shape?"

"Taking shape? The story is already written. We're going online with it at noon, in our Ukrainian-language edition."

Yulia felt her throat tighten.

"That's why I'm calling you so early," he continued. "I wanted to catch you before you left for work...to give you a chance to read it, before it goes public. Can I send it to you by e-mail, encrypted under password access?"

"Of course."

"The password is the name of my cat."

She had no trouble recalling it. Due to her nervousness she dropped the angle too low on her phone for an instant, though Pavel seemed not to notice.

"The best thing you can do to start is to read the story. Then call me back if you find any inaccuracies, especially about the Alushta conference. That way there will still be time to insert corrections." He paused and looked at her over the connection. "I know this is moving fast, Yulia. But I told you I would keep you in the loop. I'm keeping my word."

She thanked him. This was moving really fast.

"Some other details," he continued. "This morning I'll finish up the English translation with our in-house translator. Also at noon, Ukrainian time, we'll send this out to wire services and major news outlets in Europe and North America, to get it into their Friday news cycle. On Saturday and Sunday, we'll release second and third installments of the story in Ukrainian and English, which fill out today's lead piece. Our Russian-language web pages will come out with the same three articles on Saturday, Sunday, and Monday, six hours after the initial cycle. The weekend rollout is deliberate. Half the country is on vacation now, and any government officials and other bigshots still in Kiev are likely to be leaving early on long weekends. We aim to catch them flat-footed. Not to give them time to react and cause any nastiness...blockages to our website, server shutdowns, sudden tax inspections, and the like."

Yulia's throat tightened even further and grew dry. "You're worried about that kind of retaliation?"

His expression became no-nonsense over the link. "It wouldn't surprise me at all," he answered. "These are powerful interests we're up against, Yulia, with huge wealth at stake. In fact, that's one reason I made a point again of calling you on Skype. We shouldn't take any unnecessary chances."

The past several days had offered a lull of sorts. Yulia's edge and apprehension now regrabbed her. "Should I be taking any precautions?" she asked.

"The best thing to do is to maintain your routines, especially at the hotel. I'd be particularly concerned if any of the participants in the conference show up again and make inquiries. Meanwhile, stay alert to sudden attentions from unknown people—especially as you come and go from your job."

Yulia gulped. It didn't assuage her dryness. "Do you think these people...I mean the ones we're exposing...will ever draw the connection between you and me?"

"Let's hope not. For my part, I've kept your identity completely confidential. I've told no one apart from my editor Alexander Brisiuck, whom you know. The fact that we have different last names should also help. Have you mentioned to anyone at the hotel that I'm your cousin or even that you have a cousin in Kiev who works as a journalist?"

Yulia thought for several seconds. "No. I don't think so."

"Good. Anyone else?"

Yulia looked over at the closed door to the bedroom. She lowered her voice even further. "Just my roommate, Oksana, as we discussed. To this point, all I've told her is that I'm assisting you with a story."

"Obviously she's a variable I can't control. I'll leave it to you to manage her properly."

"I'll do my best."

Yulia observed Pavel's face on the screen. She could tell he took these risks seriously. But she'd known him her whole life. His main objective now was getting the story out. She couldn't mask her nervousness when she spoke next.

"What if they *do* make the connection?"

"Then we'll have to come up with a Plan B."

They paused for several seconds as both of them considered the prospect.

"The first thing to do is to send you the article. We'll take it from there."

When they ended the call, Yulia sat and stared at the blank screen for ten seconds. She then sat up straight and placed the phone aside. Her laptop remained atop the coffee table. She carried it back to the kitchen, set it up there, opened the lid, and turned it on. There was little time before work. Everything really was speeding up.

*　　*　　*

During boot-up Yulia brewed a pot of coffee and threw together a quick breakfast. When she seated herself, her plate alongside, she opened a browser and checked her Google Mail account. Pavel's message was already waiting, together with the password-protected Word document. For an instant she visualized his cat, a black-coated female, then typed her name: *Octavia.* Her pulse quickened when the text opened in the Ukrainian language. The opening paragraph set the tone:

> Oligarchs and Government Officials Plot Takeover and Division of Agricultural Landholdings
>
> KIEV—On July 25 and 26, while many Ukrainians turned their attentions away from everyday business and politics and toward vacations on beaches or in the countryside, Harcourt Bank, a large international institution headquartered on Wall Street, pursued more acquisitive objectives, sponsoring a closed, secretive conference at an exclusive seaside hotel in Alushta under the nondescript moniker of "Investment

Opportunities in Ukrainian Agricultural Reform." The gathering included twenty-two Ukrainian government ministers and high-ranking officials and thirteen of Ukraine's wealthiest oligarchs, as well as representatives of Russian agricultural and business interests. Despite its innocuous heading, the conference carried a brazen and far-reaching purpose: specifically, development of strategies for the wholesale buyout and seizure of Ukraine's small landholdings and their consolidation into large agricultural concerns, to be owned and controlled by some of the country's wealthiest figures, most associated with President Viktor Yanukovich...

Yulia reached over to her plate, placed a sliver of cheese on a piece of bread, and took a large bite. Pavel tended to employ a hard-hitting style. This article also didn't pull any punches. She swallowed hard and read on:

Tight security prevailed at the conference, which took place at the RadissonBlu Alushta, an elegant resort complex dating from the time of Czar Nikolai II, with its own private beach and enclosed gardens. All journalists and other uninvited observers were excluded. Nonetheless, through a confidential source, *Ukraina Sevodnya* has obtained a complete agenda and full list of participants. Most prominent among them was Leonid Zherdev, one of the richest men in Ukraine, who reportedly stayed offshore on his private yacht for the duration, commuting daily to the hotel by motor launch...

Zherdev's name, so straight out and up-front, made Yulia's next swallow go down even harder. He hadn't intimidated her. Still, he was a powerful man to cross. To clear her head, she got up to pour herself a mug of coffee. When she was reseated she took a gulp and read on.

Pavel's initial article comprised five pages, and he'd been thorough and well organized, addressing all relevant angles, in a way she probably couldn't have done, had she tackled it herself. As she expected, he'd written the story for maximum impact.

Before she dressed for work she wanted to allow time to finish her banana and apricot. She sensed she would need her energy for the day ahead. And in the days that followed as well.

CHAPTER 21

For a plethora of reasons, and one in particular, Mikhailov knew this parting was going to be even more difficult than that of the previous summer. Rufus seemed to sense likewise. By time they reached Patriarchs' Ponds and parked outside Ksenia's apartment building, the dog was unsettled and on alert. He now understood what was coming. Mikhailov reached over and snapped the leash onto his collar, which he disliked doing.

"Neither one of us wants this," he said, opening the car door. "Come on boy."

The dog had become integral to his new routine. And the recognition was mutual. Now, down on the pavement and observing the pond and sniffing its familiar scents, he calmed down somewhat. Still, he gave Mikhailov a baleful look as Mikhailov pulled out his smartphone. "We're down near your entrance," he informed Ksenia. "Do you still want to take a short walk?"

"Of course. I'll be right down."

When his sister emerged from her building Mikhailov was pleased to see more color on her face. She was also minus her headscarf, which had almost been a fixture since the funerals. They kissed, and after Ksenia reached down to stroke Rufus, they walked the dog to the

corner and crossed into the waterside promenade. Trees along the perimeter provided a partial canopy overhead, and the afternoon skies
were cloudy and serene, the pond gray and glasslike. There were only
light dispersals of pedestrians and bench-sitters. Mikhailov decided to
remove the leash.

"My brother the colonel!" Ksenia exclaimed, as they watched the
dog run up alongside the cast-iron interior fence, pausing to sniff at
frequent intervals. "This is the first time I've seen you on a workday,
since your promotion. Does that qualify you for police escort now or
special traffic lanes?"

"Hardly," Mikhailov laughed. "One reason I was intent on quitting
early today. Avoid the rush-hour snarls."

"I don't blame you."

Mikhailov looked at her from the side. She also appeared more at
ease now than ten days earlier, the last time he'd seen her.

"You look good, Ksenia. Everything well?"

"It's been a good week," she said, smiling in a way Mikhailov was
gratified to see. He recalled recent timelines. "You mean the girls
passed their entrance exams?" he asked.

"With superb marks. The results came out just yesterday. They'll
both be entering Moscow State in September. Katya to the history faculty and Tanya to the law faculty."

"That's great. Dad and Mom would be proud of them. And I am
too, as their uncle."

"Thanks."

Rufus, picking up their positive tones, doubled back on the walkway and appraised their faces. Ksenia maintained her moderate smile
and reached down to pet him. So did Mikhailov, before the dog noticed a Scottish terrier thirty meters ahead and raced off again to perform a reconnoiter.

"At last, the future's coming into clearer focus," she added as they
resumed.

"As it should."

They remained wordless for a moment. Mikhailov supposed that Ksenia would now be more inclined to hold onto their parents' former apartment in Sparrow Hills, close to campus, in which case he'd get their dacha, which he preferred. But that decision could wait until September.

Rounding a corner, they came upon the most famous stretch of the promenade: the setting for Bulgakov's opening scene in *Master and Margarita*. Rufus bounded back and forth along diagonals, reacquainting himself with the area. Mikhailov suspected the dog would fare just fine during his absence.

"Shall we complete the loop?" he suggested to Ksenia. "After that I'll accompany you and Rufus up to your apartment."

"Agreed," Ksenia answered. "Before you go I'll fix you some tea."

During the drive over, Mikhailov had decided not to tell Ksenia about his novel, just yet. That was another open question. Also one better addressed in September.

*   *   *

While Ksenia busied herself at the kitchen counter, Mikhailov laid out Rufus's food and water bowls. As he did Katya and Tanya returned after an outing in the center. Mikhailov hugged and congratulated them. They'd adapted to the year's traumas more quickly than their mother and appeared more vibrant than ever, taking Rufus happily off into other rooms. "You're lucky with the twins," he told Ksenia after they'd seated themselves at the table. "Also that Sasha left the three of you in comfortable circumstances." He gestured toward the kitchen doorway to the rooms beyond. The apartment was pre-Revolution and possessed of high ceilings and big windows, grand by Moscow standards. "I've always liked this place."

"Yes, I'm grateful for that," she responded. "And for the twins most of all. But I admit that's not what's gotten me through these past months."

Mikhailov divined the allusion. On the way in he'd noted the growing complement of crosses and icons, including several in the kitchen. By way of acknowledgement he glanced up at the Christ portrait, with the gold inlays and bearded visage, mounted on the wall above the table. She caught the signal.

"In fact it's all come down to faith and prayer," she confirmed.

"I know, Ksenia. I've been glad you could draw on that."

She studied him over the top of her teacup. "What about you, Oleg? You never reveal much about yourself, as usual. Getting back on course?"

"For the most part. The process continues."

Her evaluation continued as she lowered her cup. "Is your promotion helping?"

"Somewhat," he responded. "I do welcome my new rank."

His intonations were not lost on his sister. With a thoughtful look, she paused. "It's not just a matter of pressing on, you know," she said. "Or moving up. One also has to find sources of hope…"

Mikhailov could see her line of progression resembled Vera's and was therefore glad when Rufus reentered the kitchen with an interruption, wagging his tail. He bent over and reached down with both hands to grab the dog around the ears and bring his snout to his face, where they made full, wet contact. When he straightened and looked again at Ksenia, he displayed a revived smile. "I'll miss Rufus when I'm in Crimea," he said. "You'll take good care of him, won't you?"

"Of course we will."

Mikhailov's thoughts traveled back to his book, and his smile widened further. Upon his return to Moscow, according to his plan, he and Rufus would recommence their regime in the study. His future was also looking up, just like his sister's.

CHAPTER 22

At the start of her forty-five-minute lunch break Yulia stole away down the first-floor corridor outside the conference rooms, now empty, and verified that there were no hotel personnel in the vicinity. Only then did she go online with her smart phone. *Ukraina Sevodnya* had given the story supersized lead play, just as Pavel had promised. Her pulse accelerated when she read the headline, in big, bold characters, just under Pavel's byline: *Oligarchs and Western Bankers Plot Strategies for Takeover of Ukrainian Agricultural Sector.*

Three photographs were arrayed below. The first showed the headquarters of Harcourt Bank in lower Manhattan, name on prominent display above the entrance. The second pictured Leonid Zherdev, emerging from the back of a limousine, attended by a bodyguard. And the third framed the RadissonBlu, in a shot taken from the water, emphasizing its private beach and whitewashed pre-revolutionary grandeur.

During lunch in the cafeteria and the ensuing afternoon she remained sensitive to signs of trouble: inquiries by the hotel manager at the reception desk, some new live current among the staff, or even worse, a sudden visit by representatives of Harcourt Bank, Zherdev's organization, or other oligarchs. None occurred. Meanwhile waves of new guests arrived for conventional Saturday check-in—fresh off planes from Moscow, Nizhny Novgorod, Kharkov and other points north. None of them mentioned the story either.

Her activations shot higher when she saw Thorsson return from the beach around five- thirty, en route to his room. He looked as steady as ever—also as if he also hadn't read the story.

Somehow she managed to hold herself together until her shift ended at six o'clock.

As soon as she was out the entrance she veered left, away from pedestrian traffic, and found a quiet nook under the hotel's front portico. She selected a position between two potted boxwoods, pulled out her phone, and found a new Skype text message from Pavel, his first since early afternoon:

Yulia—Things have accelerated since we released the story. Within two or three hours, my editor received angry calls from a government minister and lawyers from Zherdev. Similar salvos have followed from other oligarchs. Because of international coverage, it's probably too late for the government to shut down our servers. At least five major European news organizations have already picked up the story, including Le Monde and the Guardian, which gave it prominent play on their international page. Argumenti e Fakti has even published it in Russia, and just minutes ago I spoke with a reporter at the New York Times, who says they plan to go live with it on their website during the next hour or two…any signs of trouble at the hotel? If so, call me at once. Meanwhile stay vigilant! Also keep an eye on Axel Thorsson, if possible…

She'd barely looked up, seconds later, when Thorsson emerged from the sliding glass doors, giving her a jolt. He paused under the portico, no more than fifteen meters away. For an instant she dreaded that he would glance left and spot her. Instead the American donned his sunglasses against the early-evening sun and headed into town. She shoved her phone back in her handbag, donned her own sunglasses as well, and followed him, a short distance behind. All her senses were now fully engaged.

She'd already noted that he was eight or nine centimeters taller than she was. This evening he was wearing leather sandals and trim-cut khaki shorts that reached almost to the knee. His coral-colored silk shirt made him easy to keep in view. He was also carrying an electronic tablet. He seemed to pay no heed to passersby, many of whom noticed him straightaway. He drew attention—just like she did—whether he wanted it or not.

Tonight she would have preferred him to be less conspicuous.

Thorsson seemed to have a destination in mind. Sixty or seventy meters further, he cut left to Hotel Lidia, just off the promenade, and ascended onto its covered restaurant terrace. Keeping careful distance, Yulia walked another ten meters past a kiosk and half-empty bench and sought cover behind a cluster of pine trees. Pretending to check her smartphone, she watched him take a table by the concrete balustrade and receive a menu from the waitress. He placed an order at once, without consulting it. A moment later, the waitress returned with a tall glass of draft beer and a bowl of nuts. He looked up while she poured it out and thanked her, showing a polite smile. As soon as she was gone he turned on his tablet. The device was small and dark-gray, and appeared to be an e-reader.

The thought occurred to her that he might be calling up Pavel's article. She kept her eyes on his expression.

Thorsson reached out for a small handful of nuts, took a sip of beer, and focused on the screen. Her position gave him a three-quarter view of his face. Was he was reading something long-form, rather than the article? Literature? History? And in what language? In any case he appeared fully concentrated.

A separate sidewalk cut alongside the terrace on the other side of the pines, creating a foreground of moving pedestrians, while

Thorsson sat at elevated level on full display. A steady stream of pass-ersby flowed by just a meter or two from his table, separated by the balustrade.

Among them she detected the same phenomenon she'd registered on the promenade. Thorsson got noticed. By males and females both. Most of them just curious. People accorded him attention, for what-ever reason.

For his part, he remained focused on his reading. Alert to no danger, either. Though at least for now, there was none in view.

She noticed the time on her smartphone. The American appeared to have settled into place. She gave him one last appraisal and turned to go. For the rest of the evening he'd be on his own.

CHAPTER 23

The girl was polite but businesslike. There were five other families waiting in line, with multiple suitcases ranged nearby. When she found Mikhailov's record on her screen she paused for several seconds and looked up again with an extra measure of regard. "I see here that a lux-category suite has been booked on your behalf, Mr. Mikhailov. Three guests, for a period of three weeks. Is that correct?"

"The period is correct. However I booked an ordinary two-room unit. Are you sure there isn't some mistake?"

Her eyes returned to her terminal. She appeared to review some special notation before she addressed him again, with the same undertone. "It says here that your ministry in Moscow telephoned last week and requested the upgrade. The additional cost has already been paid."

Mikhailov presumed the perquisite had issued from his promotion. And that the girl had noted the originator, even if the FSB hadn't identified itself directly. More than twenty years after breakup of the USSR the aura still loomed large, even for the young. Ukraine was no exception. "I suppose I can't object, then," he said, keeping his voice low in order not to advertise his status. "Is the suite also located in this building?"

"Yes, on the twelfth floor. You have a direct view of the sea."

Upon collecting the keys Mikhailov then rejoined Vera and Dima, who were waiting alongside a column in the expansive, light-filled lobby. He told them about the upgrade, still keeping his voice low. Vera refrained from commenting until they'd gotten their luggage into the elevator and they were ascending behind closed doors. "I know you explained that the FSB has some kind of ongoing connection down here," she said. "Still, we're in Ukraine. I'm surprised that Russia maintains that kind of sway here."

"It's not what it was. But we never really went away."

Mikhailov saw no reason to gloat. They reached their floor and found their unit at the end of the hall. Upon entering Vera looked around, inspected the half-kitchen, then crossed the living room to the large glass door onto the balcony, where she opened the curtains. The panorama encompassed lush mountainsides to the left and sparkling sea to the center and right. "Quite something," she said. "If this is one perk of being Russian, then I'm not complaining."

Mikhailov responded with a sardonic look. It went a little further than that. "You know that statement has to be qualified," he responded.

"I know."

While Dima inspected his own room they stepped out onto the balcony, taking in the view more completely. Children's playful shouts and the gentle sounds of a fountain filtered up through the pines below and from the beach further down. Out on the water, two hundred meters from shore, a tourist ferry hummed past along the smooth surface, en route from Alushta to Yalta. They stood wordless for a moment. Mikhailov sensed that his wife was already considering the social dimension.

"You said five or six of your colleagues were already here," she commented. "With two others arriving this weekend, including Department Chief Rykov?"

"That's what I've gathered."

"Will that mean any special obligations? Socially, I mean?"

"Nothing's been formalized, but as I said, some might arise, given that we'll run into them down in the dining hall and on the beach. But they're all here to relax. No one is here to work."

Vera paused, examining him from the side.

"I just want to know what to anticipate," she said. With one hand she gestured back toward their suite. "That is…if all this status and privilege will come with new strings attached."

"I wouldn't worry about it. Don't forget we're in Ukraine. We try to keep a low profile here."

"All right. Just checking."

When his wife fell silent again, Mikhailov pulled a deep inhalation of the sweet Crimean air through his nostrils. For the moment at least, Vera seemed to have forgotten about his novel. He looked over at the small table and two chairs at the other end of the balcony. It offered the perfect location for his laptop, separate from the common areas inside. He visualized himself there at first light every morning, even earlier, with a mug of coffee close at hand. The only component lacking was Rufus. Everything else looked propitious.

CHAPTER 24

The amusement rides, as usual this early, were turned off. Workers had already cleaned up around them after nighttime merrymaking, and the first beachgoers were only starting to emerge. Yulia kept a watchful, uncluttered view as she neared Lenin Street and the hotel. At the bend out of the pedestrian zone she kept particular lookout for high-end Mercedes, BMWs, and Range Rovers—a response team from Zherdev or Harcourt Bank.

Instead the street also looked dormant. Fruit vendors on the opposite side, also as usual, were just opening for business. The only deviation came from a pair of men in their early thirties, idling under the portico and smoking, who eyed her as she crossed into the hotel entrance. Before the doors slid open and she crossed the threshold she glanced back at them. One of the men was holding a camera and had a large photographic case slung over his shoulder. The other appeared to be holding a notepad. She recognized them at once, in part because she was once one herself. *Reporters.* Pavel was just one of a breed. They were bound to appear. The good guys, in general. Still, her nerves tightened as she crossed the lobby to the reception desk. She observed the expression of Andrei, who was just coming off night duty.

"Did those men try to talk to you outside?" he asked, before she'd even reached the counter.

"I didn't give them a chance."

"Good; they're journalists. Are you aware of what's going on?"

She paused and collected herself. She decided, on the spot, to appear unknowing. "No...what?"

"The hotel's in the news, thanks to that conference a week ago. I read the story online, and it's scandalous. Vladimir Nosko has issued an instruction not to talk to anyone from the media. He's already scheduled several staff meetings to make sure everyone understands."

"Vladimir is here on a Sunday?"

"He got here at six."

Vladimir Nosko was the hotel manager. Since Yulia had started work, he'd never shown up on Sunday, let alone at this hour.

While she rounded the desk and prepared to take her station, Andrei consulted a printout in both hands. Rather than getting up to leave, he remained in place.

"In fact you're slated for the seven-thirty group," he said. "I've been told to stay here until you get back."

Yulia took a deep breath. The early-morning calm had been misleading.

*   *   *

Through her interview and her first two months on the job, Yulia had perceived that Vladimir Nosko fit the chain's corporate prototype. Well-groomed, Westernized, and responsible-looking, with a degree from Kiev Polytechnic. Hired as part of the company's long-term development, assigned to two junior-level stints in Western Europe, then elevated in his early thirties to the rank of hotel manager and redeployed to his homeland. Just now he stood before twenty-some staff members in the windowless basement meeting room for employees, wearing his characteristic suit and tie. Whatever plans he'd

made for the remainder of the weekend with his wife and two young
children had fallen away.

Copies of Pavel's article had been distributed in advance to all
those in attendance, now scattered among the four rows of chairs.
Continuing her play-act, Yulia perused it as if she was seeing it for the
first time.

"Those of you who didn't know about this news story have now had
a chance to skim through it," Nosko began. "Therefore I'll cut right to
the main issues involved, as far as the hotel is concerned.

"The first and most serious is the possibility that someone here on
the staff leaked the information." He scanned the faces in the room.
"There was obviously tight security during the conference. Did any of
you gain access to this information or know anyone who did?"

Yulia's heart pounded several hard beats. Like the majority of those
present, she glanced to her right and left. Otherwise she remained still.

"Good. Thus far I've assumed this wasn't the case. However if this
does happen to be true, it would represent a serious violation of our
employee regulations, with which you're all familiar."

Yulia swallowed hard and felt her face flush. She hoped against
hope that no one noticed—particularly Nosko. However he was already intent on his next point.

"Second is the image of this hotel—and more broadly—our worldwide brand. On this, I've already communicated at length with our
management in Brussels. They've determined this presents complexi-
ties. There are of course certain negative connotations…the big money
interests, politics, the secrecy, and so on. But we have to admit there are
also several positives…most of all the free publicity. This news story has
been disseminated all over the world. It's already all over social media.
Many thousands of potential visitors and guests in dozens of countries
are learning about us—maybe reading about Crimea for the first time.

"The key is to project the right message. That means keeping controversy out of the mix, especially rumors. Unfortunately that's exactly
the kind of information news reporters want. You may have seen several

of them milling around the hotel this morning. Some of you may even have been approached by them. And more are likely to appear here over the next day or two. But you are now under strict instructions not to speak to any of them. You are to refer all questions either to me or to Alyona Smirnova, our deputy manager. Is that clear?"

Nosko scanned the assembled faces. Yulia also glanced left and right. Most nodded.

"Same goes for incoming phone calls from the media, into reception or the administrative office." Nosko scanned again. Yulia was the only receptionist present. "Is that also clear, Yulia?"

Yulia gulped and tried to keep her voice even. "Yes, of course."

"Good. Correspondingly, hotel security has been instructed to exclude all unaccompanied reporters, photographers, and cameramen from hotel grounds. They are only permitted on site if they are accompanied by either Alyona or myself. If you see one or more of them wandering around on their own, you are to alert hotel security immediately. Is that also clear?"

Again Yulia glanced left and right. The nods replicated.

"In that way, we'll project the image we want. Who knows? This sudden, unexpected coverage may even boost our guest traffic and overall business, which is good for all of us." For the first time Nosko's sternness eased, and he smiled. "Are there any questions?"

Evgeni, one of the pool attendants and lifeguards, raised his hand.

"Yes, Evgeni."

"Those sound like mostly positives to me, Vladimir Anatolovich. What's the worst that could come from this?"

Nosko thought for several seconds. His face clouded again. "Mainly just one," he said. "That's if this leak occurred from within our hotel. If so, it would damage our reputation for customer confidentiality and professionalism...our brand." He paused, took a deep breath, and returned to more neutral aspect. "But I've already addressed that angle. Any more questions?"

There were none. Yulia was glad the meeting was over.

CHAPTER 25

The thought had flickered through the back of her mind, off and on, for more than a week. Now Yulia could think of little else. All the more because the source of her worry was located just three just meters away, over her right shoulder. Ever present, always watchful. Never relenting. Black and opaque—which disguised its serious purpose.

The small, semi-spherical video cam, mounted on the ceiling over the reception desk.

This one, like all the others, fed constant image streams to the security station in the basement, for both live viewing and digital recording. They'd become so pervasive in public buildings that Yulia gave them little consideration.

Until this past week, that was.

Since Nosko's meeting she'd fought the reflex to glance back. The arrival of her lunch break brought a respite. Rather than head down to the employee cafeteria, she scooped up her handbag and strode straight out the front entrance. Today she eschewed the portico proceeded to the end of the building, crossed Lenin Street, and sought refuge under the shade of a tree. To her relief Pavel answered her Skype call on her first attempt. She inserted her earpiece and kept an eye on the front of the hotel. He came onscreen instants later.

"I was just getting ready to contact you, Yulia. You sound a little strained. Is everything okay?"

"Not exactly. The hotel has gone into crisis mode. Reporters from other publications have now arrived. I've already attended a meeting about them. But that's not what worries me most."

She recounted Nosko's reaction. To this point, to Pavel, she had not mentioned the video monitor. Her voice cracked a little as she told him. As usual, he offered no reproach.

"So your worry is that the camera caught you sticking the flash stick in the computer?" he asked.

"Exactly. I'm not sure about the angle. But I think at least part of it was visible. One thing I am sure of, though. The visit later by Zherdev's two henchmen was in full view."

"Do you know how long the images are retained?"

"That was mentioned in my employee orientation. For ten days, I think. Then they're scrubbed and overwritten, to save disk space."

There was a slight pause on Pavel's end. "If I'm not mistaken that episode occurred eight days ago. Correct?"

"That's right. Believe me, I'm counting."

"Which now means that we have two days before we cross the safety threshold. In the interim, I think it's unlikely that you'll be singled out for particular scrutiny. Don't forget this episode transpired after the event was over. The participants were already checking out."

Yulia took a deep breath and felt her nervousness subside. Pavel had a way of calming her down.

"Thanks, Pavel. I feel better already."

"That's the girl. I know your lunch break is limited. Do you have time for a quick update?"

"Sure."

Her cousin had scarcely started when a black BMW 7-series with tinted windows entered Yulia's line of vision on the right and pulled up across the street. Two men emerged at once from the opposite side of the car, wearing suits and sunglasses. After brief survey of the area, they marched promptly into the front entrance of the hotel. Meanwhile a third man stood up from the driver's-side door and remained with the vehicle. Even from across the street she could see the bulge beneath his suit, under his left armpit.

Yulia recognized the first two at once. Zherdev's lieutenants. The same pair that had mislaid the flash stick.

"Tomorrow, as planned, we'll post the third and final article," Pavel continued. "By Monday, when Kiev opens for business, we'll be able to take fuller..."

Yulia cut him off. "Sorry, Pavel. We've got trouble. Zherdev's guys just showed up—the same two as before. I've got to go." She barely caught his closing words as she tugged out her earpieces.

She'd always feared the worst. It now appeared to be in full progress. She kept her eyes off the driver as she approached the hotel, in order not to draw his attention. Inside, she was already girding herself.

*   *   *

Deep down, Yulia had prepared for this moment. She knew was capable of presenting a composed front, when it mattered. As the doors slid open and she reentered the lobby, she anticipated seeing the pair at the reception desk in aggressive stance or already in dialogue with Nosko. Instead she only glimpsed their backs as they disappeared through the door into the lounge. She tried to stay professional as she drew up in front of Anna.

"I just saw those two guys walk in. I recognize them from the conference. Trouble?"

"I don't know," Anna answered. "They didn't ask me for anything. They just said they were looking for a guest, who was probably down on the beach. Because they weren't reporters, I didn't object and let them through."

Yulia paused. To chase straight after them would be too flagrant.

"Does Vladimir Nosko know about them yet?" she asked.

"Not yet, unless he's spotted them on his own."

"Hmmm. Maybe I should follow along and make sure it's nothing to worry about."

"Not a bad idea, I suppose."

Yulia wasted no more time.

CHAPTER 26

From the veranda Zherdev's men were not immediately visible. To relocate them Yulia halted at the banister and swept her eyes over the interior gardens and recreation area. Her survey didn't take long. They were already halfway across, at full stride toward the beach. Keeping them in her sightline, she descended the steps and followed.

About fifteen seconds later the two men pulled up at the seaside balustrade. Wary that they might glance back, she slowed.

Her caution was unnecessary. Their full attention was on the water.

At the corner of the pool terrace, she angled aside and stopped between two empty chaise lounges, holding her discreet view line over a row of sun-tanners. All at once the men's heads stopped moving. Their postures became taut and hostile.

Yulia could guess their quarry. She'd fretted over this scenario as well.

*   *   *

Thorsson had started with four. Then five and then six. Today, one week into his vacation, he'd attained his target. The session had required about forty minutes. Seven aggressive laps between the two breakwaters, with minimal breaks at the turns. At any level of conditioning, the pace and distance made for a tough workout.

But that had gone earlier. This was the more languid aftermath, to cool off before lunch. From the beach he turned over and performed an easy backstroke to the midpoint, where he stopped and floated, eyes half-closed and face turned up toward the sun. His arms and legs splayed out straight from his torso so that his body formed an X. The shouts and splashes of children and teenagers on the beach sounded a world apart.

His endorphins and endocannabids only amplified the effect. When he'd cooled off he rolled over onto his stomach and headed back to the beach on a relaxed crawl. The strokes came easily. At chest depth he put his feet down on the small polished stones at bottom, rubbed the saltwater from his eyes, and surveyed the beach. At noon-hour the resort was now in full activation. Waiters were circulating among the chaise lounges, dispensing drinks and taking orders. Same on the pool terrace above.

At water's edge, when he looked up, two figures up along the balustrade caught his attention. The pair was incongruous because of their dark suits. He recognized them at once.

The same duo who had twice stared him down the week before. Same dark sunglasses. Same unambiguous attention.

Only today their snideness and posturing had become something else. More than just sizing him up as an adversary. As if preparing for attack.

He walked back toward his chair and held their stares. When he reached it, he stopped again. His perplexity persisted and his irritation along with it. This had now gone beyond spontaneous dislike. While he watched, the one with the tattooed fingers pulled out a phone.

Thorsson thought he caught Russian but couldn't make out any phrases. When the call concluded, then men didn't linger. After levelling one last hostile stare, they abruptly turned heel back toward the hotel, their objective fulfilled.

There was little room for misinterpretation, this time round. These men had returned with malevolent intentions.

CHAPTER 27

Yulia's nerves jolted when she detected a presence outside the door. For an instant she froze, then jumped from the couch and scrambled across for closer listening. Her nerves calmed somewhat when she heard a jangle of keys and insertion into the lock.

"Oksana...is that you?"

There was a pause on the other side. Oksana now sounded on edge herself.

"Yes, Yulia. It's me."

Yulia let out an exhalation and slid back the deadbolt. Oksana watched with concern as she hastily shut the door and reapplied the lock before they traced to the living room.

"I know you were nervous about Pavel's story, Yulia. I also read it today. It's all over my Facebook feeds. But this is pretty extreme."

"We'd better sit down."

Oksana's face draped with new worry as she deposited her handbag on the table and perched herself on the couch. Yulia recounted the appearance of reporters and the staff meeting. Then the visit by Zherdev's two associates. Oksana listened with rapt attention throughout.

"So after they charged down to the beach, they just left?" she asked.

"That's right."

"Did they pay any attention to you?"

"No. Only the guest on the beach, as best I could tell."

"Who?"

"He's male. Other than that I'd rather not say."

Oksana absorbed this. "Sounds he's the one they're after," she observed. Her face became puzzled. "Do they think he passed on the information to your cousin Pavel? I don't get it. Does this guest know Pavel?"

Thus far Yulia had been sparing with details. But now the stops were off.

"I've got to come clean, Oksana. I copied some confidential files from a flash-memory stick. I'm the one who sent them to Pavel, not this guest. Sorry for not telling you this until now. I figured it was for your own good. Please don't reveal it to anyone. Not even my parents."

Oksana's eyes widened as more of the pieces came together. Yulia watched her, worried how she'd react. "Now I understand why you're on edge," she said. "If they ever find out your Pavel's cousin, they could show up here, too."

"Tell me about it. But that's not even my main worry. I much more worried about the guest. Zherdev's men seem to suspect him. But he's innocent."

"Shouldn't you tell him that he's in possible danger?"

"I've thought of that. One problem is that I don't really know him. Until now I've just tried to keep an eye on him. I followed him to a café after work yesterday evening, just before I met you at the art gallery. This evening I stuck around again, with the same idea. Turned out I didn't have to, though. Tonight he stayed in and ate dinner on the hotel veranda."

"Is he on vacation?"

"As far as I know. But he's here alone. Apparently his girlfriend didn't show up."

"A Ukrainian guy?"

"No, actually American. Seems to be a businessman of some kind… though that's about all I know."

"Interesting…Do you think that's why he's grabbed such attention from Zherdev's people?"

"I'm sure it doesn't help."

"What's your next move?"

"Right now I'm just taking it one day at a time…let me show you something." She swiveled to her laptop on the coffee table, grabbing her mouse. Oksana scooted closer, shifting her attention to the screen. "Pavel's story has spread far beyond Ukraine. Here's an article in the *Guardian,* from England." The headline read, "Ukrainian Oligarchs Conspire with Wall Street Bank for Takeover of Ukrainian Agricultural Sector." Yulia allowed Oksana to take in the opening paragraph before switching browser windows. "And here's another from Le Monde: '*Banque internationale orchestre acquisition massive de terres agricoles par des oligarques Ukrainiens,*' which as you can see has also gotten big play." Yulia switched windows yet again, showing her another from the *New York Times.* "Check it out." A file photograph of Zherdev was affixed, along with another of the Harcourt headquarters.

Oksana's eyes widened even further. "Wow," she said. "Can I take a look at these?"

"Of course. There are others here as well." Yulia slid the laptop over on the coffee table. "As for Zherdev, I think the international attention is a good thing. It might keep him in check. His power does have limits…right?"

Oksana looked skeptical…even a little fearful. "Don't forget this is Ukraine, Yulia," she said.

This was not the answer Yulia wanted to hear. Her nerves jolted again, just as they had when Oksana had arrived at the door.

"The last thing you want," her roommate added, "is for this guest to be martyred for an act he never committed."

* * *

The essence was the same in Partenit as it was in Moscow. Only the particulars differed. The hardest part was getting started.

This was the thought that occurred to Mikhailov as he waited for his computer to boot. Here in Partenit his revised routine was now in its second day. Step one: switching off his alarm clock at 4:00 a.m. with a quick hand before its high-pitched chirps roused Vera. Step two: sitting up and swinging his legs out of bed so that he didn't slide back into slumber. Step three: standing and making his way across the darkened bedroom, shutting the door quietly as he exited, and proceeding by direct path to the half-kitchen to brew a pot of coffee. Step four: carrying his closed laptop through the living area out onto the balcony—taking care, en route, not to awaken Dima in the other room; setting up there on the small circular table; and hitting the on button. Step five: positioning his chair at an angle that afforded both a diagonal toward the sea and easy access to the balcony door, in order to refill his mug. Then seating himself in comfortable, upright posture, entering his password, and activating the Russian edition of Microsoft Word. And lastly, opening several reference files he'd created, as well as the all-important story file.

All of which led to the point of the drill, which was also the most intimidating. His confrontation with the blank page. There was another one every day. And there would be for long while.

In Moscow he'd drafted a rough prologue. Sketched out his three protagonists. Outlined his story, though more as guideline than blueprint.

Numerous voids remained to be filled. He was still short on secondary characters and subplots. Those, he decided, would have to arise in process.

On his first morning he'd written three hundred words. Not many, perhaps. But a decent beginning.

While the coffee maker sputtered indoors, he reviewed what he'd written and made a few adjustments. Just five paragraphs, stark on the page. He already knew they would require reworking and redaction later.

By then, according to his outlook, Rufus would be back at his side.

When the brewing cycle concluded, he rose from his chair and retraced to the kitchen to fill his first mug. Back at his table he took his first sip, a big one, followed at once by a second. Verdant scents reached his nostrils from the trees and gardens below, and he pulled a deep inhalation. As the caffeine and oxygen entered his bloodstream, he swept his eyes out over the becalmed surfaces of the Black Sea, still illumined by moonlight, over Utos Point, then northeast up the coastline. Lights of Professorski Ugolok and Alushta were visible in the distance, and beyond them, on the horizon, he discerned the first light of morning.

He could sense the arcs of his story. But at this early stage they remained ephemeral, elusive. Their realization would require effort. He positioned his fingers over the keyboard and refocused on his screen. His outline and vision were provisional. There were many angles and elements still to discover.

The ending remained very much contingent.

CHAPTER 28

Yulia's heart thumped when Axel Thorsson emerged from the elevator at 8:15 a.m., clad in shorts and tee-shirt and carrying an aqua-blue beach bag. He diverged from standard path and stopped at the desk, smiling and offering his habitual morning greeting. He also appeared curious and ready with questions.

"Your hotel is very much in the news," he said. "Are you aware of that?"

She stiffened. She hoped the reflex wasn't evident. "Yes. The hotel management alerted the staff yesterday," she answered.

"I first read reports last night in the *New York Times,* of all places. Then similar articles elsewhere, in French and Russian media. And more this morning…there are a lot. It's also being re-posted extensively on Facebook. The story seems to have gone worldwide." He smiled again, also bending slightly to lower his beach bag to the floor. "I got here just as that Harcourt conference was concluding. I admit it caught my interest. If I may ask, was the hotel aware of any of the details of what was being discussed?"

Yulia paused to compose herself. "No…none. Everything was very confidential. Harcourt and the others came with their own security."

"That's what I thought." He turned his head to the side for an instant, as if he'd already decided upon his next query. "Remember when I turned in that flash stick on my first morning...the one I found in the elevator?"

She struggled to hold her voice steady. "Yes...of course."

"Did someone ever claim it?"

The thumping in her chest cavity was now continuous. "Actually it belonged to one of the attendees at the conference. Two men came to collect it about fifteen minutes afterward."

Thorsson's eyes narrowed. But he refrained from inquiring further. He smiled again. "Does the hotel have any additional information on this matter for guests?"

"Just one, really. You may have seen some reporters milling around outside the hotel. We're excluding them from the premises. We suggest that guests avoid them as well."

"Will do," he said. "Thanks for the advice."

Yulia did her best to project a calm facade as he bent down to collect his beach bag. When he disappeared into the lounge area, she exhaled. He'd appeared relaxed, despite his questions—as if the visit by Zherdev's henchmen the day before had not disturbed him, if he'd noticed them at all. She was unsure whether to be reassured by this or the opposite. Minutes later Anna arrived for work, providing some welcome reinforcement at the desk. For Thorsson's sake, Yulia determined to stay on guard. If Zherdev's henchmen made a repeat appearance, she and Anna would serve as first line of defense.

*   *   *

Thorsson angled his eyes to surface level for an instant to gauge his remaining distance to the breakwater, then lowered his head and unleashed a power-thirty. Around the ten-count, he heard the all-too-familiar and unwelcome reverberations through the water. Upon attaining the barrier, he put his feet down on its concrete ledge, and breathing hard, looked around to identify the offending vessel.

A Jet Ski came into view around the corner, in-board motor rumbling. This particular example was a two-seater, larger than most, bearing two men. The only positive was that they were keeping their speed down.

The pair examined him for extended seconds, with impassive faces behind their wraparound glasses. From his lower vantage Thorsson looked back. They were a different duo than those at the hotel. Both of these men sported shaved heads; they were also muscled-up, tanned, and wearing bathing trunks—perhaps locals. And unlike the suits these men didn't hold overlong gazes, passing by instead and continuing to the next breakwater. Thorsson watched them until they rounded into the next beach zone, which was semi-public. Ten seconds later the sound ceased altogether, indicating they'd tied up or coasted into shore.

He then refocused. Four laps down. Three left to go. He launched out into the water, firing his first exhalation. Forty meters across, he glanced up to confirm that his lane remained unobstructed and lowered his head. Closer to the breakwater he took one last quick glance ahead and unleashed his concluding power-thirty.

On his next down-stroke another human body closed in fast, as if out of nowhere. A split- second later a large forearm rose up from under the surface and made vicious impact with his forehead, snapping back his momentum and sending a flash of pain through his skull. His body came to a violent, sudden stop.

When his lids opened he came face-to-face with one of the shaved heads from the Jet Ski, minus the sunglasses. He was looking him straight in the eyes. The man's expression bore no surprise or apology.

On the contrary; this looked intentional. To Thorsson's dismay he raised a fist up out of the water.

"What the f—?"

His final consonant coincided with the crack of bone on bone as the man's knuckles made contact with his cheek.

CHAPTER 29

The force and abruptness of the blow drove Thorsson's head and shoulders underwater. When he resurfaced he heard a motor sound and jerked his vision left. The man's accomplice was rounding the breakwater on the Jet Ski—preparing to join in. There was no doubt now about their purpose. Thorsson's next reflexes were rage and a will toward survival. He heaved several fresh intakes of oxygen, growled, and put his arms up for combat. The first assailant lunged up and out toward him with both hands, aiming for his head and neck. Thorsson pushed off the man's chest and drove himself backward.

His counteraction came too late. The man lurched around behind him, encircling him in a headlock and forcing him underwater again, leveraging his weight from above. Seconds later Thorsson felt the man's bulky forearm tightening like iron around his larynx, constricting his windpipe.

With a bolt of clarity he knew he had little time left.

The realization activated a tactic from his water-polo days—one he'd very seldom used, even in the dirtiest of matches. He twisted his torso, made a fist, and swung it as hard as he could into the man's groin. The man's headlock came loose at once, together with a wail of pain. Seizing advantage, Thorsson then drove his elbow to the man's solar plexus, broke free, and with furious leg kicks and churning arms propelled his head to the surface.

Back above water he also caught sight of the second man, who'd now pulled up close. He leapt straight off the Jet Ski toward him, with the same malice in his eyes.

Round one now seemed moot. The second attacker had arrived to finish him off.

The first assailant, also resurfacing, grappled him again from behind. Aware his chances were dwindling, Thorsson lashed up and out with one of his free legs, employing the body weight of the first man as a backstop. His heel made crushing, savage contact with the second man's solar plexus.

The effect was immediate. The man torqued backward, grunting and gasping for air. As his head came forward again Thorsson employed another water-polo move, twisting sideways and leveraging his weight again off the first attacker. He then delivered another kick-blow with the sole of his foot, this time to the middle of the man's face. Bone and cartilage crunched as he made direct contact with the man's nose. The result was another wail of pain, together with a fountain of blood. The man sank back in the water, semiconscious.

Staying on the offensive, Thorsson heaved another lungful of oxygen and lashed back with his elbow.

Again his blow found its target, making blunt impact with the man's temple and outer eye socket. Thorsson felt his attacker's arm go slack for an instant and hit back with a second lashing move from his elbow. This one seemed to find the man's cheekbone. New blood sprayed into the water and onto Thorsson's arm and shoulder. At last, the man's arm went limp and Thorsson shook himself free, thrusting himself away with five hard strokes and scissor kicks.

Only then did he turn to look back, still panting, bracing his arms in case either of the attackers followed.

Neither did. His first attacker remained in the same section of water, one side of his face veiled in blood, reorienting himself. Three meters away, his cohort appeared barely conscious, choking on water and sinking below the surface. The Jet Ski was already drifting away. After brief hesitation and a howl of fury, the first abandoned the attack and swam over to assist.

Thorsson swung his view toward the breakwater, just twenty meters away. To his relief, twenty to twenty-five people were lined up along the poured concrete, largely teenagers. Other bathers, closer to shore, were shouting toward the beach. Still gasping and jacked with adrenaline, he launched back into a crawl and attained the ledge seconds later. Two middle-aged men and a teenage boy reached bent down to offer assistance, but he climbed out under his own power.

"Are you okay?" one of them asked.

Thorsson felt his cheekbone, which had sustained the first blow, finding it only moderately swollen, with a slight cut. He nodded and struggled to choke out a response.

"We saw the whole thing...they attacked you. Someone's already called the police." He nodded again, too winded to say more. Waving off further assistance, his legs still hanging over the top edge, he tried to recover. At last he looked back out onto the water.

His first attacker had now pulled his cohort back toward the Jet Ski, about ten meters away. The second man appeared almost lifeless, sputtering water from his mouth and breathing irregularly. His eyes were closed and his face remained covered in blood. The first struggled to haul him onto the gunwale, with no success. After two laborious attempts, he let go another howl of frustration and started making for shore. Thorsson could see that the first attacker was also depleted—scarcelyyy able to keep his head above water. By now the second appeared to be turning blue. "Help him!" the first shouted, barely getting the words out as he drew closer.

Only when the pair attained the barrier did several teenagers reach down, guardedly, and brace the second man against the concrete. At the same instant Thorsson heard whistles and commotion toward shore. Turning, he saw several lifeguards running out along the breakwater. A pair of blue-uniformed policemen trailed a short distance behind, grasping their weapon belts. The lifeguards scrambled straight down to the second attacker and with considerable effort, given the man's size, dragged him up on top. The two policemen also drew up, panting. The middle-aged man who had earlier addressed Thorsson moved immediately to intercept them, joined by another man holding a phone. After a few seconds one of the policemen raised a walkie-talkie. Thorsson had mostly regained his breath.

"Were you involved in this altercation?" the second policeman asked him in Russian.

"Yes. I was the one attacked."

"Are you in need of medical attention?"

"No, I don't think so."

"Stay there."

The policeman turned his attention to the first attacker, still down in the water. He spoke again, this time more forcefully. "You there, with blood on your face...get out." Chest still heaving, the man stared back through his good eye and scowled, making no move to climb out. Instead he glanced back out to his Jet Ski. A water-borne siren became audible further down the shoreline. Seconds later one or two other wailing signals erupted from and land side as well.

"Don't even think about trying to flee..." the policeman added.

The two policemen descended to water's edge to corral him. Blood still trickled down onto the man's collarbone and chest. When standing, he looked even bulkier and more muscle-bound than Thorsson had realized. The other attacker, now receiving CPR, was of similar build. Thorsson was half surprised he'd fought them off.

His conditioning, he figured, had probably saved him. That and his water-polo experience.

The Stoics, after all, had erred on some counts.

CHAPTER 30

The howl of sirens sliced through the mid-morning lull and made Yulia look up from her computer. A flashing squad car barreled past the entrance, followed several seconds later by an ambulance. They filled her at once with fright.

"Sounds like they're heading along Naberezhna Quay, toward the beach clubs," Anna observed.

"What do you think it is?"

"Maybe be a drowning or some kind of boating accident."

"At least they're not coming to the hotel, thank God."

Yulia's fright deepened when the sirens seemed to stop just a short distance south. The placement sounded like Demezhki Beach. Less than a minute later, even within thick-walled interior of the hotel, she detected another siren from the direction of the water. "Something's going on," she added, hearing her own voice quiver. Her remark hung in space for a moment until two blue-uniformed policemen ran up abruptly to the sliding glass doors. They had to pause while they opened and hardly slowed as they approached the desk. "Can we cut through here to the beach?" one asked. "There's been an incident."

Yulia's fright made her slow to respond. Anna filled the void. "On the hotel beach?"

"Out on the breakwater."

Anna gestured over her right shoulder and gave clipped directions. The policemen resumed their fast trot and disappeared through the double doors. As soon as they were gone Yulia turned back toward the entrance and glimpsed two reporters and a photographer peering inside. Surmising that the action was down on the waterfront, they quickly bore off to the left—toward Demezhki. She thought fast. "This might involve a guest," she told Anna in hurried syllables. "One of us should probably go out and check."

"Shouldn't we alert Vladimir Nosko?"

"Good idea. Can you call him? I'll head out."

As Anna picked up the phone Yulia was up and on her way. Near the pool she caught sight of a crowd around the end of the south break-water. She pulled up at the balustrade and looked across. Through the mill of people, she couldn't make out details. Her first impulse was to shed her heels and make her way out barefoot. Before she did Nosko drew up behind her with his tie loosened and in shirt sleeves.

"I just heard, Yulia. What's going on?"

"Some kind of incident. Maybe a drowning. There are rescue personnel and policemen out there."

"Is a guest involved?"

"That's what I came to find out."

"I'm going to head out there to know for certain."

"Should I come with you?"

"Better you stay here, in case additional emergency personnel show up. Please also keep guests from congregating in the area or interfering in any way." Before she had a chance to object, Nosko double-timed down the stairway onto the beach and out across toward the breakwater. When he was gone she braced one hand on the balustrade and shielded her eyes from the sunlight with the other. Squinting, she thought she could make out Thorsson in the throng of people but couldn't be certain. Otherwise the scene across the water only deepened her fear.

"Oh my God," she said.

* * *

During the next three to four minutes Thorsson watched as numerous additional policemen arrived, along with emergency medical technicians carrying a stretcher and portable resuscitation equipment. Two policemen were assigned to supervise him personally and ensure he didn't venture far from the scene. Nonetheless he rose to his feet to gain a better view. He made two quick assessments. First, his initial attacker wasn't talking, despite rough handling and aggressive questions by the police. Second, his second attacker was showing no indications of revival.

Onlookers continued to gather in the meantime along the breakwater and on the two adjacent beaches. A contingent of photographers and reporters appeared closer to shore, brandishing notepads and cameras. They proceeded at once to snap photographs and elicit witnesses. One reporter tried to venture out on the barrier before being intercepted by a policeman.

Thorsson also caught the approach of another figure: a man in his mid-thirties, wearing shirtsleeves and a loosened tie. Looking more closely, he spotted a badge from the hotel and signaled him over. The man took in his two police minders as he drew closer, as well as the more ominous scene nearby.

"Are you from the Radisson?" Thorsson asked him.

"Yes. I'm Vladimir Nosko, the hotel manager."

"My name is Axel Thorsson. I'm currently a guest."

Nosko looked him over again, noting his cheekbone. "Are you hurt?" he asked.

"Not seriously."

"What happened?"

Thorsson told him. The incident sounded even more surreal in summary.

"Just like that, for no reason?"

By now Thorsson had a decent idea. Still, he refrained from declarations. "Completely unprovoked," he answered. "Let's put it that way."

On the water, a police launch arrived and quelled its siren. Several loud thuds emanated from the resuscitation area. Thorsson and Nosko looked over again and saw one of the medical technicians holding twin defibrillation pads over the chest of the second assailant, while his collaborators performed another round of CPR. As the other rescuers leaned back, the man's body convulsed up off the rocks. There appeared to be no response. Faces around the circle appeared grim as he tried again, again with no result.

"Unbelievable," Thorsson said.

The hotel manager's face became even more somber. "Are you here alone?"

"Yes."

"Foreigner, I take it?"

"Yes. US citizen."

"Whatever happens next," he said, gesturing toward the rescue team, "I'm here to assist you."

"Thanks." Thorsson gestured over toward the resuscitation effort. "This could become complicated. I may need a lawyer or at the very least, consular assistance."

"Understood. Would you like me to call anyone on your behalf?"

"Yes, if you wouldn't mind. The top-ranking consular officer at the US Embassy in Kiev. You can find contact information on their website."

"Certainly."

All of a sudden the commotion and commands in the resuscitation area ceased. Thorsson and Nosko turned back to the scene and observed the rescue crew leaning back from the body. One of them stood and addressed a policeman who appeared to be the ranking officer. "All vital indicators have stopped," he said. "He's dead."

"Any point in transporting him to the hospital?"

"No."

The officer raised his radio transmitter. "I'll alert the medical examiner." Several additional policemen in the vicinity corralled the crowd as the crew loaded the body onto a stretcher and covered it with a white, water-resistant sheet. The policemen then cleared a path off the breakwater. As the stretcher passed, less than two meters away, Thorsson observed the man's profile and physiognomy, outlined under lightweight fabric, and shuddered. Less than fifteen minutes earlier he'd looked the man squarely in the face.

"You'll have to accompany us to the station," said the officer to his left. Thorsson nodded.

"I'll follow along to the station in my own car," Nosko said. "I'll also call your consulate en route."

Thorsson thanked him again. He was glad he had backup.

Before they departed, the second assailant also passed close by, also just two meters away. He was now handcuffed, with his arms pinioned behind his back. From tight range he leveled a noxious, lethal-looking stare, together with sneering, arrogant smile—an expression not just of malevolence but of confidence. As if he was unconcerned about the aftermath. This feature assured Thorsson rather less.

CHAPTER 31

Thorsson remained standing, pacing the windowless room in which the police had deposited him twenty minutes earlier. Apart from his bathing suit he wore only a towel—gray, department issue, redolent of cheap detergent—which he'd wrapped around his waist. A man of about forty entered, carrying a small bundle and dressed in a rumpled suit. His expression fell short of adversarial but was devoid of conventional courtesy. "My name is Yosyp Yezhov," he said, speaking Russian rather than Ukrainian. "I'm with the local prosecutor's office. I'll be conducting your questioning."

"Am I being charged with a crime?"

"Based on initial accounts by witnesses, at this point we consider you the victim of this assault rather than the perpetrator. Nonetheless a man has died. We therefore need to ascertain the facts." He handed Thorsson the bundle. "Here are some dry clothes. Please change into them before we start."

Looking at the items, Thorsson realized they were his own, collected from his hotel room, thanks to Nosko.

"Because you are a foreign citizen," Yezhov continued, "I've also agreed to let you speak to an official from your embassy in Kiev." He gestured to a desk and chair against one wall, which was empty except for a Soviet-era landline phone. "The call will ring there shortly. I'll give you five minutes."

Yezhov turned at once and exited, closing the door behind him. The room was awash in florescent light and under-ventilated. A large horizontal window with blackened one-way glass occupied the wall opposite the desk. Thorsson had also noticed a small black video sphere, mounted in the corner. Ignoring both, he slipped out of his swimsuit and into undershorts, trousers, and a silk shirt. He was still tying his shoes when the phone chortled. He crossed over, sat down at the desk, and picked up the handset.

"Hello?"

"Am I speaking to Mr. Axel Thorsson?"

"Yes."

"This is Heather Robinson, consul general at the US Embassy in Kiev. First, I need to establish some background. I also understand we just have five minutes, so please keep your answers concise. Are you a US citizen?"

The voice was female, American. Modulated and well educated. Probably mid-to-late thirties. Thorsson answered in the affirmative. He also checked his watch, to keep the time allotment in mind.

"Birth date?"

"May 13th, 1980."

"Are you traveling alone?"

"Yes. Currently on vacation."

"I've understood you're now in Alushta, in the central police station. And that you've been detained in connection with a death by drowning. Also correct?"

"Yes, that's correct. I was swimming off the beach in front of my hotel. The drowning victim was unknown to me. Also for reasons unknown, I was the target of a premeditated attack…"

Robinson cut him off. "I should note, Mr. Thorsson, that this line is almost certainly monitored and recorded by police and other officials.

I therefore advise you to refrain from revealing any more information than I request or is absolutely necessary."

"Understood."

"To your knowledge, are you being charged with a crime?"

"To my knowledge, no. I've been told I am being questioned only for purposes of investigation."

"Nevertheless I would also advise you to proceed with caution. The Ukrainian criminal justice system is known for being arbitrary, corrupt, and unpredictable."

"That was what I'd gathered, even before this happened. Will I have recourse to an attorney?"

"I'm afraid not. Not at this stage. Accordingly, I should underline that things operate differently here in Ukraine than they do in the United States. Rights of individuals in your circumstances are much more limited."

"Duly noted. How should I respond during the questioning?"

"Based on our previous experience in such matters, you are best served if you cooperate with the investigating magistrate but only to the minimal extent necessary. Provide facts but nothing more. Refrain from interpretation or speculation of any kind."

"Makes sense. Assuming I am released afterward, what should I expect next?"

"First, I would not necessarily assume you will be released upon the conclusion of questioning. For that reason, I will remain in ongoing contact with local police officials and the Alushta prosecutor's office until you are free from custody. After that, we should communicate as soon as possible over a private connection. We can then speak more openly."

"And if I am detained further—for example, overnight?"

"Then I or another US consular representative will travel to Alushta with all possible dispatch to intervene on your behalf."

Before Thorsson could formulate his next question the door opened and Yezhov reentered the room, accompanied by a uniformed police official Thorsson had not seen earlier. He checked his watch. Only three-and-a-half minutes had elapsed.

"My questioner has returned early," he told Robinson.

She did not sound surprised.

*   *   *

Apart from the desk ensemble, the only other piece of furniture was a straight-backed metal chair situated in the approximate center of the room, under a bank of harsh lights. Yezhov directed him to seat himself there instead. Thorsson did as instructed. Meanwhile the police official made cold, wordless eye contact, assuming a standing position near the desk, arms behind his back.

"As preface," Yezhov began, "Let me say that this is not an interrogation. At this stage I am engaged purely in fact-finding. To establish precisely what happened."

Thorsson just nodded, heeding Robinson's counsel.

"How did you happen to come to Alushta, Mr. Thorsson?"

"I came here on vacation."

"Alone?"

"Originally I planned the trip with a female friend. However she cancelled out just beforehand."

"Are you married?"

"No."

This response elicited a brief glimmer in Yezhov's eyes—as if the fact made him a readier suspect. "Why Alushta? American tourists aren't so common here."

"I do business in the region. I had appointments in Tbilisi and Kharkov earlier this week. I flew into Simferopol immediately afterward."

"What kind of business?"

"I work for an American company that sells equipment and services for natural-gas exploration. I'm the regional manager for Eastern Europe."

"And you travel all the way from the United States for this activity?"

"No. My office and residence are in Geneva, when I'm not on the road."

"What is the name of your company?"

"Allegheny Exploration, based in Pittsburgh."

"Can you spell that, please?"

Thorsson complied, pronouncing the characters in English. Neither Yezhov nor the police official took notes, which didn't surprise him. He'd already assumed that the exchange was being recorded on both audio and video. Yezhov paused again and examined him.

"You look rather sportive for a traveling businessman, Mr. Thorsson. Are you also an athlete of some kind?"

"I was. I swam and played water polo at university."

Yezhov looked at his passport and repeated his birth date. He then appeared to perform a calculation. "Same age as Jesus Christ..." he observed with undertones of mockery, which Thorsson found jarring and incongruous. The magistrate then swung a complicit glance at his colleague and changed tack.

"From what we gather, this encounter you experienced with the two men on the Jet Ski, including the drowning victim, occurred about fifty meters from the beach, in front of the RadissonBlu Hotel. Correct?"

The word "victim" discomfited Thorsson a little, but he showed no fluster. "Correct."

"Had you ever seen these two men before?"

"No."

"Or had any prior awareness of their identities?"

"No. None."

"How did you happen to be in this area when this encounter occurred, so far from the beach?"

"I was swimming laps between the two breakwaters."

"For exercise?"

"Mainly."

"Now, if you will, recount everything that happened from the time you entered the water—from your initial sighting of the men, through your physical contact and confrontation with them, right up until you climbed up onto the breakwater. Please leave out no details. I'll only interject if any elements appear missing. Otherwise, I'll withhold my questions until the end."

Through Thorsson's experience in sales and contract negotiations, he knew the downside to open-ended monologues. This was quite different but bore similar dynamics. He took a deep breath and began, proceeding by careful increments. Yezhov listened with a studious expression, evaluating every word and inflection. In keeping with his preface, he refrained from questions until the end.

"When you kicked the victim, Mr. Thorsson—the 'second attacker,' as you call him—you kicked him once in the chest and once in the face. Correct?"

"That's correct."

"With the second kick—the one to his face—did you intend to inflict lethal injury, or even to kill?"

Thorsson took another deep breath and weighed his words. On this question, some measure of interpretation was unavoidable. "I wasn't thinking in those terms," he answered. "Those two men were trying to kill me. I was just trying to survive."

Yezhov contemplated the statement. After a moment, he glanced at the police official.

"This interview is over, Mr. Thorsson," he said, somewhat to Thorsson's surprise. "You are free to go, although I may have to ask you back in for additional questions later, if that proves necessary. I believe that Vladimir Nosko, the manager at your hotel, is waiting for you at the front desk."

Thorsson rose, walked over the desk, bunched his swimsuit in his hand, and followed the police official toward the door. On the way out, Yezhov extracted a smartphone from his breast pocket, refraining from eye contact. Thorsson wondered if his first attacker would be questioned next. In profile, Yezhov's expression offered no clues. As if he was keeping all options open.

CHAPTER 32

The image, for Yulia, remained lurid and front-center, secured against the riptide of churning rumors and general agitation that came just afterward and had extended through her lunch break into mid-afternoon: Axel Thorsson, barefoot and clad only in swimming briefs, conducted off the breakwater by two somber-faced policemen—one of them grasping the American's arm as he would a criminal—forming the rear of a grim procession that included a shrouded body on a stretcher and a menacing, thug-like character bearing handcuffs and a bloodied face. In fragments and from elongating distance, she'd last observed him force-marched onto the adjoining beach and out through Demezhki Beach Club. A gaggle of reporters and photographers had followed close behind.

Dozens of hotel guests had already vacated their lounge chairs and umbrellas for a closer look. Less than a minute later Nosko emerged from among them, striding across the beach pebbles. He stopped to briefly address several of the most querulous, resumed progress, then quick-stepped up the stone stairwell, perspiring through the armpits on his dress shirt. She'd been so anxious she'd spoken first, even before he'd drawn up on the balustrade.

"What happened, Vladimir?"

"One of our guests was attacked by two men who arrived on a Jet Ski. His name is Axel Thorsson. According to witnesses, they tried to drown him."

Yulia's head felt dizzy for an instant. In her peripheral vision, she glimpsed numerous onlookers down on the beach. Other guests in the pool area had also trained their attention her way. Many looked frightened.

Nosko squinted at her in the sunlight. He took her elbow gently with one hand and gestured back toward the hotel. "I've got to head to the police station," he said. "Let's talk as we go." Yulia fell in a half-step beside him, struggling to keep up in her high heels. They'd passed two middle-aged women, gaping from behind sunglasses with half-open jaws.

"Yulia, some of the guests saw what happened on the water. And almost everyone saw the police and the dead body. People naturally have questions. They're going to want answers."

She'd drawn a deep breath. She also wondered when she'd have the chance to call Pavel. "What should I tell them?"

"The bare minimum, which is what we know so far."

* * *

Now, for perhaps the thirtieth time, Yulia carried out the instruction. She'd almost gone on auto-pilot to conserve her nerves. "At this point, our information is limited," she told an elderly couple from Perm who had just returned to the hotel building. "There was some sort of altercation out on the water. A man drowned, for reasons that still aren't clear. One of our guests was involved, but sustained only minor injury."

"We saw the whole thing," the man said, grim and a little shaken. "This young guy went in for a swim between the barriers...we've seen him do it before. He'd been out there awhile. Then, suddenly, two men came on a Jet Ski. Before we knew it, they attacked. Looked like they meant to do away with him...and that they'd planned the whole thing beforehand. All in plain view...as if they didn't care who saw."

Yulia took a deep breath. "That corresponds to other accounts we've heard," she answered. "But as I said, we're still trying to learn details. Vladimir Nosko, our hotel manager, has gone to the police station. He's there now."

"This guest...he's a foreigner, isn't he?" the woman asked. "Does that have something to do with it?"

"Please, ma'am. The police are now investigating. We hope to have more information from them later today or tomorrow."

Their attention was diverted by a chaotic chorus from the street. Glancing at the entrance, Yulia saw Nosko and Thorsson arrive through the sliding doors. Behind them, Vassily, a member of the hotel security staff, blocked out a posse of reporters and photographers. Once they were through Nosko glanced back and guided Thorsson to one side. Yulia cringed when she saw the swelling and redness on his cheekbone. At least he was now wearing the slacks and shirt that housekeeping had fetched from his room. He still looked a little taut with adrenaline. But given what had just happened to him several hours earlier, he appeared nonetheless composed and lucid.

"In view of today's events, Mr. Thorsson," Nosko said to him, "and this continued media presence" he gestured an open palm back toward the door "I might respectfully suggest that you remain within the hotel grounds for the rest of today and dine in our terrace restaurant this evening. The dinner will be compliments of the hotel."

"Thank you very much," Thorsson answered. "That's quite generous. Though I admit I have the urge to at least go out a walk beforehand. Blend with people a little...just now I could benefit from a little normalcy."

Nosko pondered this, too well trained in customer relations to object. "Quite understandable...what if you encounter more trouble or are accosted by the reporters?"

"I've considered that. But I figure this may be my last chance before this story gets out in earnest tomorrow. After that it may be impossible."

Nosko nodded. "You might be right."

"Could you possibly help me slip out a service entrance?"

Thorsson's attitude struck Yulia as reckless, in the immediate wake of a murder attempt. However Nosko again held to form. "We can do that," he said. "Perhaps we can take some extra measures, for safety's sake…at what time would you expect to head out?"

Thorsson glanced at his watch, which Yulia had also instructed housekeeping to collect from his room. "About seven, I suppose."

"And for how long?"

"Oh, probably twenty or thirty minutes. If any trouble occurs of I'll course come back straightaway."

"Would you object if Stanislav" Nosko gestured out the entrance, "and one of our other security guys accompanied you? They're both well trained. They'll remain a discreet distance behind you in the crowd, alert to possible threats or interference."

"Sensible idea. I suppose not."

"Good…consider it a precaution. Temporary, we hope. With luck, we'll gain more clarity from the police tomorrow. Shall I meet you here in the lobby at seven, then, as you prepare to head out?"

"That's fine. Thank you again for all your assistance today."

They shook hands. Before Thorsson turned toward the stairwell, Nosko spoke again. "I also have an idea on how to deal with the media. I'll offer some kind of general statement while you're out for your walk. Distract them for a while."

Thorsson was only halfway up the stairs when Yulia's thoughts turned to Pavel in Kiev. Her shift was over at six-thirty. That left her just enough time to call him before Thorsson exited. This walk of his, she figured, might be her best chance to make discreet contact with him outside the hotel.

She finally needed to come clean with Thorsson, too.

CHAPTER 33

From the backdrop, Yulia could see that Pavel was again sitting at his desk near a wall in the *Ukraina Sevodnya* newsroom. "Thank goodness you're safe," she said, staring at the Skype screen on her smartphone. "Did you get my text message earlier? I had to be brief."

"I did," he responded, keeping his voice down. "I also read the reports filed by the reporters from *Korrespondent*, the *Kyiv Post*, and a few others who are down there. This is even more extreme than we feared."

"I'm still in shock. I'm just thankful Thorsson survived."

"I am, too. These men were likely professionals, hired by Zherdev or someone else from the conference. It could easily have gone the other way."

"That's why I'm worried to death about you, Pavel. You wrote the pieces."

"The difference is that I entered into this with my eyes wide open, Yulia. I know the score. Consequently, I've looked over my shoulder these past few days as I've walked the streets…stayed alert on the metro and so on. By now I'd like to think this story has gained too much prominence for Zherdev or any of the other powers-that-be to go after me directly. Since Gongadze, they've been wary of killing journalists. There'd be too much international outcry. In fact I'm meeting two foreign reporters for dinner tonight, British and German. They've now also been assigned to this story, if you can believe it." Pavel paused. "Still, I'm taking nothing for granted."

"God, I hope not."

"Thorsson, by contrast, has until now been anonymous. That's made him more vulnerable. I hate to say it, but this attack may have been intended primarily as a message to me and a warning to other journalists." Pavel paused again to examine his feed more closely. "Where are you now, Yulia?"

"I'm across the street from the hotel again. I just got off my shift."

Pavel asked if Thorsson was back from the police station. Yulia confirmed that he was and provided a general update, including the conversation with Nosko in the lobby. Looking up, she also observed that the assortment of reporters and photographers lingering under the porticoes had now grown to seven or eight. "This is getting bigger and more complicated by the hour," she said, her voice cracking a little. "What should we do next?"

"By my reckoning, there's now no choice. This has become a moral obligation. We've got to inform him. Tell him what we did."

Yulia exhaled, partly from relief. "I agree one-hundred percent. This has already driven me crazy. After what happened this morning I can hardly bear it."

Pavel studied her again on screen. "You realize, of course, that the ramifications of this are more profound for you than for me. Depending on how he reacts, you could lose your job."

"I'm aware of that."

Her cousin absorbed this. "Will you be able to make contact with him without drawing attention to yourself?"

"It won't be easy. Hotel policies prevent me from meeting him one on one in his room, for all practical purposes. And talking with him anywhere else on hotel grounds is almost impossible to do discreetly. That leaves his time outside. Problem is, tonight he'll have a two-man security detail assigned by Nosko. And he's only going out for twenty minutes or so."

"I see what you mean. However I may have a solution. It's high time I traveled down there anyway. Perhaps even by tomorrow. Then I could talk to him."

Her head snapped back a little in surprise. "What?"

"I'm serious. The story warrants it. And given the importance it's acquired over these past few days, I may even be able to convince Alexander to spring for a night or two in the RadissonBlu."

"Are you sure that's a good idea, Pavel? Maybe we should think about this first…" Yulia caught sight of Nosko emerging from the front entrance and turning left under the porticoes. Several meters further, he stopped and addressed the gaggle of reporters. "Hold on," she said. "Nosko has just walked outside."

Thanks to Nosko's clear diction and authoritative tone, she could make out almost every word from across the street as he invited the group inside to a conference room. The reporters fired off several questions, but rather than respond Nosko asked them to present their credentials to security, and turned back inside.

"Sorry Pavel, got to go…Thorsson should be leaving shortly."

"Good luck, Yulia."

She pulled out her earpieces and put away her phone. When she passed the corner of the hotel she sighted the side-door, keeping her distance. About a minute later, right on script, Thorsson emerged in the company of Stanislav and Konstantin. She watched him cut up to Lenin Street, then curve toward the beachfront promenade, melding in with the crowd. The two security men, both in their late twenties and with athletic builds similar to Thorsson's own, fell back into double-flank formation, six or seven meters behind.

Yulia melded into the flow as well. From thirty meters behind, Thorsson appeared more observant and alert to her than the first time she'd followed him. Also still a little coiled with adrenaline, judging from his taut posture. In any case Stanislav and Konstantin appeared to be taking no chances. Her best hope, she reckoned, would be if Thorsson stopped somewhere. She watched the American closely as he approached a cluster of cafés around the central fountain.

Instead he kept walking straight along the Post Office plaza, as he'd done before. He hardly broke stride near Hotel Lidia, his dinner venue two evenings earlier. About one hundred meters further, he finally stopped to observe a pair of exotic show dogs with luxuriant white fur, mingling with a cluster of onlookers. Among them was a gaggle of teenage boys who noticed him, with looks of fascination—even awe—and exchanged some furtive comments. Nearby, two teenage girls did likewise. Yulia guessed they'd been on the breakwater during the attack, and also seen the death of Thorsson's assailant. Maybe because of the latter, they also kept their distance.

Stanislav and Konstantin remained on guard nonetheless. To appear less noticeable, Yulia pulled out her smartphone and stared at the screen. When she dared to look partway up again, Thorsson had resumed progress, with the two security men still in trailing position. She spotted the columned pavilion fifty meters ahead that marked the promenade's endpoint.

This evening, for understandable reasons, Thorsson would not be stopping for a beer.

Instead he found a vacant spot under the columns, rested his hands on the balustrade, and gazed out at the sea. Her throat tightened as Stanislav and Konstantin turned around for a ninety-degree scan of the crowd in the area. They didn't take long to pick her face out among the others. She saw that she was now committed. As she drew closer, she addressed Stanislav, who was nearest.

"I was on my way home and found myself walking behind you," she said. She nodded toward Thorsson, who continued looking out at the sea a short distance away. "Everything going okay?"

Stanislav didn't object to her presence. But he also seemed to find it a little unusual, so far from the hotel. He maintained his security face, while Konstantin's head turned sideways, also meeting her eyes with a curious glance.

"So far," Stanislav answered.

Thorsson pivoted his head and looked over. To flat-foot the two security men Yulia raised her voice and addressed the American in English across the short distance. "I heard about what happened to you," she said. "Just thought I'd ask how you were doing."

"Yulia, right?" Thorsson answered, also in English.

"Yes, from reception."

"Well...this walk helps. Thank you for asking."

Before moving closer, Yulia glanced at Stanislav, who in turn cast a cautious, skeptical look toward Thorsson, who nodded and raised his palm in approval. "*Normalno*," he said in Russian.

Yulia walked over, keeping her voice loud enough to be heard by the two security men and holding to English. "Excuse me for interrupting your walk," she added. "But I feel a kind of responsibility."

He took in her face. "That's very kind." Still, his voice bore a slight undertow of suspicion—the same kind he'd conveyed that morning at reception. The American seemed intelligent. He'd drawn connections. She angled her body more toward the water and lowered her voice.

"I wanted to talk to you privately," she continued in English. "To admit something..."

When she paused, his gaze bored straight into hers, absorbing every detail.

"I think I know why you were attacked. I'm also pretty sure I'm to blame."

"I'm listening."

"I don't have long," she said with a crack in her voice, flicking her head back toward Stanislav and Konstantin. "Remember when you found the flash stick in the elevator?"

He nodded.

"I saved the files that were on it. Then I transmitted them to a reporter I know...my cousin, in fact. That's how all these stories came out."

His expression stayed even. He scrutinized her for several seconds.

"Look, Mr. Thorsson, I know you have every right to tell hotel management, which will almost certainly get me fired...which I probably deserve." She thought of Zherdev and shuddered a little, though she kept that to herself. "But I would ask that you give me a chance to talk to you longer. At least explain myself a little. Is that possible?"

"Yes, I suppose so."

"Do you use Skype? It's the most secure."

"Yes."

"Can you remember my Skype name?" He nodded again. She gave it to him. "Please call me tonight, when you're able to talk," she added.

She was about to contrive an exit when Konstantin shouted suddenly. Both she and Thorsson pivoted their heads and shoulders across the plaza. *"You there, stop that!"* the security man shouted again, gesturing toward a painted plaster-cast bear about thirty meters away, a commemorative relic of the 1980 Olympics. He took several aggressive steps in the same direction as nearby pedestrians took notice. Looking more closely, Yulia spotted the offending figure lurking between the bear and an adjacent bush. Her heart pounded a few hard beats when she perceived the details.

The man was a photographer, training a telephoto lens on her and Thorsson. Another two or three seconds elapsed before he lowered the apparatus with a look of satisfaction. Nosko's ruse had not worked on every member of the media. And her situation had just gotten even more complicated. Her throat tightened again as she readdressed Thorsson. "We'd best part ways now," she said. "I'll wait for your Skype call later."

CHAPTER 34

Thanks, Thorsson presumed, to instructions from Nosko, no fewer than three waiters tended to his wishes and requirements during dinner, maintaining appropriate distance from his table, intervening whenever necessary without being intrusive, displaying courtesy at every stage. Under other circumstances he might have appreciated the extra attention. Tonight, though, he would have preferred to remain less conspicuous. Nosko had warned him of what was to come:

"Word about the attack seems to have spread all through the hotel," he'd said after Thorsson's walk. "Not just among the staff, but among the guests as well. There are two main strands. One is that you were attacked by two professional assassins. The other is that you killed one of them with your bare hands."

"The first may be true. But the second is a little skewed, to say the least."

"*I'm* aware of that. But you know these situations. People traffic in exaggerations."

Meanwhile first reports of the attack were appearing on the Internet.

For perhaps the fifteenth time during his dinner, a party crossed the patio, identifying his table. This one consisted of middle-aged parents and two children in their early teens. Once they'd descended to the gardens, the son and daughter turned around and gawked, just like the teenagers on the promenade. Thorsson barely managed a sip of wine when the lounge emitted another party: this one the single-mother-and-son duo from the beach. He'd already chatted with her before the attack. Now she was nicely turned out in a short skirt, heels, and jewelry. She waved, flashing an even more available gaze than she had earlier. Her son looked over with thrill in his eyes.

There were eleven or twelve other tables on the patio. Every one or two minutes, it seemed, at least one person from each would cast a prolonged glance. And that was not to mention his waiters, who despite their tact were treating him as though he was some sort of celebrity.

"More wine, sir?"

"Yes, please."

The waiter was well groomed and conscientious, in his early twenties. After topping off Thorsson's glass, he surveyed his place setting. "If you're finished, may I take this away?"

"Yes, thanks."

"Would you care for dessert?"

"I'll just finish my wine, thank you."

The waiter collected his plate and utensils, while one of his cohorts appeared to scrape crumbs off the tablecloth. Tonight Thorsson's e-reader lay idle on the table, also a casualty of the day's events.

And now Yulia Petrenko was part of the mix as well.

Dusk had settled when he rose to leave, thanking the staff. Under gazes from all quarters, he descended the stairs and made his way down through the gardens. At the pool patio, he turned left and crossed to almost the end of balustrade, to the most secluded corner available, next to a stone wall. He set down his e-reader and raised his smartphone. Yulia's Skype moniker—now in his address list—was green and active. He already had questions. He was starting with those. On screen, she looked even more nervous than she had face to face. Her voice cracked as she greeted him.

"First, Yulia, I should say first that I appreciate your approach on the promenade," he said. "And Skype is a good idea. There are obviously dangers involved here."

"Can you talk now?"

He looked around. "Seems so. I'm in the far end of the hotel grounds, away from everyone."

"You have every right to be angry with me, Mr. Thorsson. But I never imagined it would come to this."

Thorsson examined her face again onscreen. She looked not just distraught but sincere. "You can call me Axel."

She looked back at him.

"You said on the promenade that this issued from the flash-stick in the elevator. Correct?"

"That's right...that's where it all started."

"Can you begin there and tell me how all this developed?"

For the next ten minutes Thorsson listened carefully, interjecting occasional queries. He let Yulia do most of the talking, taking in her image on screen. Halfway through, he glanced down at his e-reader, still lying nearby.

He'd delved into the Stoics, at the start of this vacation, to quell rampant urges and indiscriminate unions. However he'd never imagined challenges of this kind.

He'd aimed for clear thinking and self-containment. They were now more essential than ever.

CHAPTER 35

Tonight Oksana had returned early from her shift at Zanzibar. Yulia was glad that she had. She needed the moral support. When her roommate entered from the bedroom, wearing the loose tee-shirttt she employed as a nightdress, Yulia signaled her over to the couch. Pavel's Skype icon remained inactive. At the beep, Yulia felt another hollow ring in her chest cavity and heard her voice crack as she recorded the message. It was her third. She tapped out yet another text message, more from desperation than real purpose: "Pavel please call! I'm worried out of my mind."

Oksana sat down at perpendicular angle on the couch and examined her with alarm. "What's happened Yulia?" she asked. "Has something gone wrong?"

"Something's gone very wrong..." Yulia choked on her own words. "Have you heard what happened at the hotel today, out on the water?"

"I heard there was a fight of some kind. Also that somebody died."

"Well, it was connected to me and Pavel. That foreigner was involved... the guest I mentioned...though he wasn't the one who got killed."

"Good God."

"Good God is right. Now I'm trying to reach Pavel to make sure he's okay. He said he was going to have dinner this evening with two reporters from Europe. But it's now ten minutes after midnight. And he still isn't answering."

"Aren't reporters known to drink a lot when they go out together?"

"Tonight Pavel should know better."

"Why don't you just call his mobile number?"

"That violates the system we agreed upon."

"I would say these are special circumstances."

Yulia thought a moment. "You're right," she said. "I'm nearing my wit's end." She opened her call list and tapped Pavel's name. The connection rang just twice before a tone series cut in, succeeded by a message in both Ukrainian and English: *The number you have called is either inaccessible or out of service. Please try again later.*

Yulia turned up the volume and held the phone out so that Oksana could also hear it. When she clicked off she sat frozen, staring out with a pleading, almost frantic expression.

"Isn't there someone else you could call?" Oksana asked her.

"Pavel is from Nikolaev, like me. He doesn't have any immediate family members in Kiev. There's his girlfriend, but wait…I forgot the obvious…I do have the number of his editor. His name is Alexander Brisiuck. He knows me. I've written some stringer articles for him in the past."

"That makes sense. This is an emergency."

Yulia thumbed through her list and found the entry. Before going further, she considered possible consequences. Until now she'd hewed to her role as an anonymous source. For better or worse she was crossing another boundary—one that Pavel himself had insisted upon.

She tapped Brisiuck's name. Pavel's welfare was first and foremost. And her hollow ring had turned to a jangle.

*   *   *

Somewhere between the hours of two o'clock and four, the night slipped into a blur. Fatigue mixed with fear and nerves to keep her awake, more or less functional, and able to answer her phone for Brisiuck's periodic updates, long after Oksana had retired to the bedroom. Through each one, Yulia fought off despair, as best she could. Around four thirty the first flickers of dawn showed through the windows. At five, with the flush of full sunlight, she remembered that she was due at work in three hours. Minutes later she reclined on her side and succumbed to sleep.

She was in the nascent stages of a perturbing, ominous dream involving Thorsson and Pavel when the ascending melody of her smartphone pulled her back awake. Sitting up and reaching for the device, she saw that the caller, once again, was Brisiuck. The time was 6:37 a.m.

"We found him, Yulia."

Suddenly Yulia couldn't breathe. She imagined Pavel's bloodied corpse body in a roadside ditch. She could also guess who was responsible.

"He's alive," Brisiuck continued. "But he was badly beaten. Earlier this morning, shortly after dawn, he staggered to the edge of a village about forty kilometers southwest of Kiev called Kodaku and collapsed. A villager was out working in his fields and called for an ambulance. He was transported to a regional hospital in Vasylkiv. He's apparently been in and out of consciousness, with multiple injuries, including broken ribs, a badly damaged leg, and a fractured cheekbone. Also internal bleeding. And that's just the short list."

Yulia still couldn't get enough air. She hesitated to ask the most obvious question and struggled to get the words out. "Is…is he going to survive?"

Brisiuck made a somber, considered pause. "Thus far I can't get a definitive answer from the medical staff. The hospital in Vasylkiv is relatively small. All the doctors have done for now is to stanch the bleeding and stabilize his vital functions. But he's going to require extensive surgeries. For that reason, within the next twenty minutes or so, he's going to be transferred to another hospital in Kiev."

"Which one?"

"The National Emergency and Trauma Hospital on Bratislavskaya Street. I'm heading over there right now."

"Please keep me informed, Alexander Vasillievich, either by phone or text. I'll be at work this morning. If I don't pick up I'll call right back."

"Of course. Meanwhile Yulia..." Brisiuck paused again. "Say a prayer for him."

Oksana had not yet stirred. For several minutes Yulia sat and stared into empty space in the living room. She visualized Pavel on a hospital gurney and drew another constricted breath. She then did as Brisiuck had advised.

CHAPTER 36

On Gorkovo Street the morning migration to the beaches was already in progress, with usual bared limbs and bright colors. Yulia felt in a daze, keeping her smartphone clutched in one hand. As she approached the waterfront it vibrated her palm and she jerked it up to eye level. The text was from Brisiuck: *Upon arrival here in Kiev Pavel was wheeled immediately to the emergency room. I saw him briefly on the stretcher. He remains unconscious. I am now awaiting further information from the doctors.*

Her nerves jangled again as she imagined the scene. At the Agora she cut a hard right onto Lenin Street and heard an unusual confluence of voices from the hotel's front face. When she finally caught sight of the building, she saw why. Three squad cars and another official-looking sedan were arrayed around the entrance. Nine or ten journalists and photographers jostled and maneuvered under the porticoes, including a female television reporter and her cameraman. Five or six policemen were trying to maintain clear passage amid the commotion.

There were no emergency vehicles. But everything else pointed to trouble. The commotion only intensified as she drew closer, craning her head. Five paces further she slowed and almost stopped.

The scene she observed hit her just as hard as Brisiuck's phone call.

Thorsson was being led out of the entrance, preceded by one policeman and flanked by two others. This time he was wearing handcuffs. Cameras trained and clicked, together with their video equivalent. Questions erupted—most in heavily accented English: "Why are you under arrest, Mr. Thorsson?" "Did you know the victim?" "Mr. Thorsson, what is your business activity?"

When a path had been cleared, the policemen loaded Thorsson into the backseat of one of the squad cars, pressing his neck forward under the doorframe. Once inside he leaned back and spotted her through the windshield. She sidestepped a knot of journalists and pulled within two meters of the side panels.

The rear window was smoked but she could discern his face. He looked on edge but balanced, just like the previous evening. With a combination of desperation and bewilderment she opened her palms toward him and shook her head. She still wasn't sure what was happening. But she thought she could read his expression.

As far as she could tell, he still appeared to be on her side.

*   *   *

Thorsson's head and shoulders were briefly visible through the rear window before the squad cars disappeared from view, and for a moment, Yulia continued staring after them. She realized that she was over-ventilating. She tried her best to moderate herself before going inside, where she found Nosko engaged in an exchange with a middle-aged man in a suit and tie, while yet another policeman stood by impassively two meters away against the staircase. She guessed the man was the investigating magistrate. Nosko's eyes registered her arrival as she walked past him toward the desk. But he did not interrupt his dialogue.

"I was on the scene myself, just afterward," he said. "I talked to a few of the witnesses. They all said Thorsson was attacked…that he acted in self-defense."

"Nonetheless a man died," the magistrate responded, bland faced and unaffected.

"So what are the charges?"

"Several are possible, beginning with manslaughter. Our investigation is continuing."

When Yulia reached her position behind the desk she stayed cued to every word. Nosko was not given to emotion. But she knew that he could be direct.

"At least thirty or forty people observed the attack," he said. "Maybe more. What's changed since yesterday?"

"Let's just say new information has come to light, Vladimir Denisovich. I'll leave it at that."

"And the other man who attacked Thorsson? Will he face any charges?"

To this question, the magistrate did not even deign to respond. Like most of her fellow citizens, Yulia made certain assumptions about the function—or malfunction—of Ukrainian criminal justice. She'd come across examples in her freelance work. "New information" meant often outside influence. The kind that flowed from money and politics. Nosko knew the score as well. He now regarded the official with a hard look.

"We are now gathering all possible information on Axel Thorsson which we deem relevant to the case," the magistrate resumed. "We know you employ a video-surveillance system here in the hotel and maintain an archive. Do these records encompass Thorsson's visit since he checked in on July 26?"

Bolts shot through Yulia's innards.

"Yes, they do," Nosko answered.

"Are they in disc format?"

"Yes."

"Could you please assemble them, in their entirety, from July 26 to the present?" The official checked his watch. "I'll send someone back here to collect them at eleven o'clock."

Nosko knew the civility was symbolic. In reality he had no choice. "As you wish," he said.

The magistrate did not shake Nosko's hand before departing. As he exited the front door with his police consort, Yulia realized her anonymous role in the background, now almost ten days running, would be starkly and unequivocally exposed—and very soon. The only question was how much time she had left.

CHAPTER 37

Through her cinematic acquaintance with American westerns, Yulia remembered that outlaws were often hung in the mornings. And that the practice stemmed from both mercy and efficiency. Condemned men did not have to suffer the ordeal of waiting. And the rest of the world could get on with its business.

She now appreciated the reasoning.

When the prosecutor departed Nosko had called the hotel's in-house technician, summoning him at once to the basement security room. Before heading down he'd also given her a meaningful glance. He'd heard, no doubt, about her conversation with Thorsson on the promenade the previous evening. Soon he would learn the rest. The magistrate would too.

Now she was just waiting, like a doomed outlaw. Her only diversion came from interactions with guests. She also told herself—again and again—that she had acted in good conscience. That she wasn't a criminal any more than Pavel was. That they'd done the right thing.

Just after ten o'clock her smartphone chirped in her handbag. It was another text message from Alexander Brisiuck: *Pavel regained consciousness briefly and his condition has now stabilized. However the surgeons are now repairing numerous broken bones and other serious injuries to ensure against any further internal bleeding. I will remain here at the hospital and provide updates as they come available...*

Yulia pulled a deep breath of relief. She also made a determination. The sooner her fate was decided, the better. Once she was fired she could board the first overnight train from Simferopol to Kiev and rush to Pavel's bedside. Eleven o'clock couldn't come soon enough.

Several minutes before the appointed time, Nosko emerged from the elevator, carrying two hard cases of DVDs. He gave her another loaded glance as he passed the desk. A deputy official from the prosecutor's office was already waiting. The handover transpired with minimal formalities. When it was over, Nosko's gaze resettled on her immediately. His voice was weighted.

"Could I see you in my office please, Yulia?"

Yulia rose from her chair, fatalistic. She was ready to face her sentence.

*   *   *

Nosko closed his office door behind her and invited her to sit down. Yulia examined his face as he rounded his desk and detected a vibe she hadn't expected. As best she could tell it seemed like sympathy. She supposed the rendering would be easier that way. Nosko would be a merciful executioner. He paused to examine her over the desk before speaking.

"I assume you observed what happened this morning, Yulia? Not just with Thorsson. But also the prosecutor's request for our video files?"

"Yes."

"Are you aware what's on those files? Specifically...the images that relate to you and Thorsson?"

Yulia inhaled and exhaled. It was now clear to her that he'd viewed the incriminating segment. She prepared to confess. The moment had been long in coming.

Instead Nosko interrupted, sparing her. "I saw you copy the files from the flash, Yulia," he said. She opened her mouth, but he stopped her with a raised hand. "In fact, I stayed late last night, and viewed the relevant images on my own, even before the request from the magistrate." He paused again, as if more intent on summarizing facts than presenting an indictment. "I assume you're the one who transferred the files to the reporter in Kiev?"

Yulia felt almost liberated as her answer tumbled out. "Yes, the reporter is my cousin. Pavel Krylov is his name." Tears layered her eyes, and she choked on her words. "In fact it's been a horrible, stressful night...just after dawn, I learned he was abducted last night. Severely beaten...he's now in the hospital, in serious condition. I assume reports will soon be all over the media."

Nosko took this in, with a flash of pain in his eyes. "I see..." He placed his elbows on the desktop and interlocked his fingers, studying her over his knuckles. "Does Axel Thorsson know any of this yet?"

"I doubt he knows yet about the beating. But he knows everything else. I told him yesterday evening."

Nosko nodded, and her next words came out in a blurting jumble. "I just want to say that I acted in good conscience, Vladimir...I didn't like that conference two weeks ago...the usual foul corruption. You know what I'm talking about."

"And you decided to do something about it?"

"Well, yes. I just didn't think it through...especially for Thorsson."

Nosko unlocked his fingers and leaned back in his high-backed executive chair, examining her again before speaking. Several framed family photographs were visible behind him. "Do you realize everything you've done—from your violation of guest privacy during the conference to your endangerment of Thorsson—was strictly against company policy?"

Yulia pulled another deep breath to steady herself. Her voice cracked anyway when she answered. "I do, Vladimir Denisovich. And I'm prepared for the consequences."

She prepared for the chop. Instead Nosko lingered, she assumed out of compassion. "Before getting to those," he said, "what do you intend to do next?"

"My first priority is to get to Kiev to be with my cousin in the hospital. To be honest it's the main thing on my mind right now, apart from Thorsson."

"I understand. If I was in your position I would go as well."

Yulia was confused. This seemed like a roundabout dismissal.

He filled the void further before she could react. "However not under the conditions you have in mind…I'm not going to fire you. I'm going to give you a three-week leave of absence."

"What? What about the video? Won't I be incriminated now?"

"I'll be frank, Yulia. Last night I saw what you'd done. I returned home thinking it over. Then this morning I received a call from the magistrate, asking if Thorsson was on the premises. Naturally I rushed right over. I also immediately understood what had happened. Since yesterday some powerful people intervened. Perhaps Zherdev or another oligarch…perhaps some corrupt officials in Kiev as well. We both know the way things work in our country." He paused and held eye contact. "This morning, therefore, before the magistrate arrived, I reached a decision. I erased the relevant images and reformatted the DVD, with the help of one of our technical guys. With luck, the magistrate won't notice anything amiss."

Yulia's head spun. She'd always had a decent rapport with Nosko. But nothing like this. She felt a swell of emotion. "I…I don't know what to say, Vladimir. You did this to protect me?"

Nosko now showed another facet that was new to her. "You've always been a conscientious employee, Yulia," he said. "And that was something I considered. But I took this action for many of the same reasons you did. I've seen plenty of corruption in my time, like most of our people. I decided I'd finally reached my limits. Call this my own way of making a stand."

Somehow she'd never perceived the manager as an idealist. His words levitated in the air for a moment. They were not ones that Yulia ever expected to hear in the administrative office of a hotel, least of all in Ukraine. "I'm grateful, Vladimir," she said, "almost beyond words. But won't that put you at risk as well?"

"I've made my choice."

Her thoughts ran back to Thorsson. She asked Nosko what he foresaw next.

"My ability to influence this situation is limited," he answered. "But I'll do everything I can. I'll keep you informed of ongoing developments by phone, if you wish." Yulia said that she did. She then asked him what he was going to do about the media. "At first I saw them as a problem, even an irritant," he continued, "albeit with a possible upside. But now I see them as a godsend. They were on the scene at the time of the attack. Now they'll throw a public spotlight on his arrest as well and its connection to the conference. All these travesties will be on full display."

Hearing this, Yulia felt a sudden new swell of emotion. She wiped away another coating of tears, first on one eye, then the other.

"This whole matter has gone far beyond Alushta, Yulia, and even Kiev. The wider world is already taking notice. My sense is that this is just getting started."

CHAPTER 38

Each session, Mikhailov was realizing now that the process was in live motion, required in many ways a new beginning. Whatever momentum he manufactured on a given morning—through the hours that commenced before first light and progressed through to breakfast—subsequently dissipated and dissolved during his lolls on the beach with Vera and Dima, light swims in the sea, lunches and dinners in the cavernous babble of the dining hall, and gentle evening strolls through the botanical grounds. On their third afternoon, eager for some solitary reflection, he'd slipped away by himself for a ninety-minute hike up the bluff, amid the scents of cypress. But the effect was more inductive than tangible. Throughout the off hours—delightful, distracting, and pleasant as they were—he kept a pen and several notecards in his beach bag or in his rear pocket to scribble down ideas that occurred to him during quiet interludes or spontaneous musings. All while his book remained in the back of his mind. Still, when his alarm sounded at 4:00 a.m. and the next installment rolled around, he essentially resumed from standing start, re-summoning his resolve with a potent infusion of caffeine. That was the daily reality.

Each session also bore another trait that he was now recognizing. Whatever the quality and quantity of his output on a given day, the resulting increment was small. Completion just of his first draft, at his current rate, was likely to require at least eighteen months. And then he faced yet other recommencements as he embarked on endless improvements and redrafts. This was going to be a protracted struggle. And that was the optimistic case. One that assumed he'd be able to keep pressing ahead when this vacation expired and he returned to his primary job.

Primary, at least, in Vera's eyes.

Through the crack in the door he heard his wife emerge from their bedroom, round past the kitchenette, and traverse to the bathroom. Thus far she'd kept her distance from his labors, largely by virtue of their time frame. She'd also avoided questions. He'd discerned the subtext. She'd be quietly, indeed deeply, grateful if this proved to be a passing phase, after which he'd return to the halls of power and discreet briefing rooms at the Kremlin. He glanced at the digital display at the lower corner of his laptop screen. He still had about fifteen minutes until they headed downstairs for breakfast. He refocused on this last paragraph, moving to wrap up and save his work.

Less than a minute later the room phone rang, jarring the silence. *Chortle-chortle. Chortle-chortle. Chortle-chortle.*

The olive-plastic apparatus was located on a side table by the sofa. This was the first time it had sounded since they'd arrived. After she closed the tap, Vera's footfalls sounded across the living room and she walked over to answer. Mikhailov thought he heard a deep, tobacco-cured voice on the other end. Seconds later Vera opened the door and leaned out, with her face toward his worktable on the right.

"Sorry for the interruption, Oleg. But Anatoli Rykov is on the phone."

Anatoli Rykov was head of the Near-Abroad Subdirectorate at the FSB and Mikhailov's immediate superior. Currently inhabiting, along with his family, a four-bedroom cottage in a pine forest just up the hillside.

"Rykov, this early? Did he say what it was about?"

"No." Vera leaned out further and kept her voice low. "But he sounded rather businesslike."

Mikhailov pushed back from his computer and went inside as Vera retreated. He remained standing as picked up the phone. "Hello Anatoli Sergeivich."

"Good morning, Oleg Konstantinovich. Excuse me for calling at this hour. You're aware of my attitude to vacations."

Mikhailov did. For all Rykov's cold professionalism back in Moscow, the senior man valued rest periods. Mikhailov glanced across the room at Vera. She'd paused on the threshold, worried. Not because his writing might be compromised but because of the ramifications for their vacation. She held his gaze for an instant before closing the door. Rykov resumed.

"However a certain matter of interest has arisen. In close proximity...just down the coast in Alushta. Did you read news reports over the weekend about the investment conference that took place there recently, organized by an American bank?"

Mikhailov said that he'd taken passing note of the coverage, during quick newspaper perusals on the beach.

"As usual, the Ukrainians have been inept in managing the situation. Consequently the scandal has now escalated."

Mikhailov remained silent. He could already see where this was pointing.

"Do you, Vera, and Dimitri have any excursions planned for today?"

"No, just the usual. Beach and relaxation mostly."

"Will you be at breakfast during the eight o'clock seating, in your usual place?"

"Yes."

"Good. I'll swing by with the dossier. A little later, after you've had a chance to absorb it, we can discuss the particulars." Rykov paused. "With luck, this matter will require minimal attention, and your rest and relaxation can resume in short order."

After the call was complete Mikhailov glanced again at his watch and walked over to knock on Dimitri's door. His son's voice replied at once from inside: "I'm up, Pop. I'll be right out."

Mikhailov retraced to his station on the balcony, sat down, and concluded his work. As his laptop powered down, he looked up the rugged bluffs and cypresses of the coastline, toward Alushta. Seawaters were calm and the sun had risen higher in the sky, to idyllic, shimmering effect. This vacation had gotten off to an encouraging start.

He also visualized his study at home, with his laptop open and Rufus at his feet. Then his father's old desk at his parents' dacha.

To this point, he'd imagined that this kind of collision, between his writing and his career, would come later, back in Moscow. In fact it was happening much sooner.

*　　*　　*

The preliminary, as Mikhailov had anticipated, was both understated and free of severity, in part because breakfast was in progress. Amid the hubbub of voices and clinking utensils, he'd spotted Rykov on the approach across the sprawling space, down an alley encompassing five or six rows of tables. The unsentimental career intelligence officer, thirteen years his senior and with close-cropped salt-and-pepper hair, was wearing shorts, a tee-shirt, and beach sandals. He'd circumnavigated two staff women with a serving cart as he closed the gap. Before he drew up Mikhailov swallowed a spoonful of cottage cheese, then pushed his chair back to stand and greet him. They'd shaken hands and made the exchange, and he'd extended brief verbal courtesies to Vera and Dima.

This was still vacation, after all.

Now stripped down to his swimming briefs, with his legs stretched out on the beach chaise, Mikhailov looked down at the folder that Rykov had given him. The cover of the file was stamped Secret: Grade

Four Clearance. The service, in keeping with its Soviet origins, had not lost its predilection for paper files. Mikhailov often saw the practice as cumbersome. Today, though, it presented distinct advantage. It meant he could absorb the contents ten meters from water's edge, while Vera and Dima took their first dip.

First he reviewed the original reports on the Harcourt conference by Pavel Krylov, a Kiev-based reporter for *Ukraina Sevodnya*, followed by further Ukrainian and international news coverage in English, French, and other languages. Next he reached the service's internal production on key personalities, which included Krylov, Zherdev, several executives from Harcourt, and other key participants. His concentration intensified when he reached the material on two foreigners who had appeared at the episode's epicenter.

Axel Thorsson
Born 13 May 1980, age 33
Birthplace: Pittsburgh, Pennsylvania, United States
Citizenship: US
Ethnicity: unknown, assumed northern European
Education: Upper Saint Clair, Pennsylvania public schools 1985–1998; University of Pennsylvania, Philadelphia, Pennsylvania 1998–2002, AB Russian language and literature 2002; Kellogg School of Business, Northwestern University, Chicago, Illinois, 2004–2006, MBA 2006
Employment: various 2002–2004, Pittsburgh area; 2007–present, regional director for Eastern Europe and the CIS, Allegheny Exploration
Employer: Allegheny Exploration, Masontown, Pennsylvania, natural-gas exploration technologies
Current residence: Geneva, Switzerland
Family background: father, insurance executive; mother, nurse; one younger brother
Marital status: unmarried

Children: no known children

Religion: unknown

Miscellaneous: varsity water-polo player and swimmer at the University of Pennsylvania

Profile: intelligence derived from Thorsson's business dealings in CIS countries indicates he is an effective, well-respected manager, adept at interacting with both governments and private enterprises at a high level, typically in the Russian language. Since beginning work in 2007, he has concluded at least fifteen major sales and consulting contracts in the region for his company's shale exploration technologies.

Attitude toward the Russian Republic: assumed to be neutral, though his activities are often at odds with Russian state energy interests.

Thorsson's passport portrait accompanied the text, along with nine or ten recent news photographs. In the portrait he was clad in suit and tie. Full hair, somewhere between blond and brown. Detached expression. The various other shots were mostly full length, captured by Ukrainian photojournalists in Alushta over preceding days. The first showed him being escorted off a breakwater by police in bright sunshine, clad only in swimming briefs. These revealed him to be of rather large, athletic stature and evidently fit, which also accounted—along with his aquatics experience—for his ability to fight off two hired assailants in open water. The next series showed him in conversation with a young woman underneath columns on the seaside promenade, clad this time in silk shirt and linen slacks. The girl was caught both frontally and in profile. She looked younger than Thorsson and was almost as tall as he was. Attractive, in a healthy, voluptuous way, underscored by her short-sleeved blouse and tight-fitting skirt. Roundish face, with full lips and cheekbones framed by medium-length, light-brown hair. Slavic through and through. The attached text was minimal: "Yulia Petrenko, receptionist at Alushta RadissonBlu: *profile pending.*" Mikhailov made a mental note to learn more about her. He then moved on to the next summary:

Heather Robinson
Born 25 February 1976, age 37
Birthplace: Baltimore, Maryland
Citizenship: US
Ethnicity: unknown, presumed Anglo-Saxon
Family background: father, attorney; mother, teacher
Education: Chevy Chase, Maryland public schools 1981–1989; Sidwell Friends School (private preparatory), Washington, DC, 1989–1994; Princeton University 1994–1998, BA in history 1998; Middlebury College Summer Language Program (Russian) 1993; Nitze School of Advanced International Studies (SAIS), Johns Hopkins University, MA in international affairs 2003.
Employment: Intern, Ford Foundation, New York, NY, 1998–2000; commodities analyst, Black Oak Investments, New York, NY 2003–2007; US Department of State, Foreign Service, consular track, 2008–present, postings in Amsterdam 2008–2009, Kiev 2012–present.
Current residence: Kiev, Ukraine
Marital status: unmarried
Children: no known children
Religion: Episcopalian (Anglican)
Profile: little is known about Robinson's initial Foreign Service assignment in Amsterdam, though our residency in the Netherlands reported that she exhibited no signs of intelligence activity. Her duties in Kiev also appeared limited to consular work. Additional note: an article in the *New York Times* in May 2005 announced her engagement to Andrew Rutledge, a partner in a prominent Wall Street hedge fund. Apparently the engagement did not progress to marriage.

Two photographs of Robinson were attached, consisting of another head-and-shoulders passport portrait and a full-length shot taken on the sidewalk outside the US Embassy. Clean complexioned and slender; well coiffed and groomed; attractive though a little austere. Adroit in diverse milieu. Everything by careful measure. The US Foreign Service, in his experience, deployed such women in abundance.

He concluded with the dossier's internal analysis from the service's team of Ukraine specialists. The bottom line was clear: Moscow already considered it too vital for Kiev station to handle. Dexterous intervention was required. Exactly the kind of crisis that had become Mikhailov's stock in trade.

At the precise appointed time Rykov strolled up. He was now minus his shirt, his thick torso bearing traces of early-vacation redness. Mikhailov got up again to greet him, also noting several late-middle-aged women within hearing range. At Rykov's suggestion, they departed on a short walk into the grounds. Thirty meters in, they veered onto a segregated walkway, lined on one side sides by cypress and overhung on the other by a canopy of magnolia trees. Mulberry scents wafted down the hillside. Children's shouts from the beach became more muted. Rykov drew his hands behind his back. His first point of discussion was the conference.

"I reviewed the list of participants," Mikhailov said. "I noted that some of our own oligarchs were there. Burmistrov, Stepanov, a few others."

"I wish that was the extent of it. But you read what's ensued since then. The attempted hit on Thorsson. Krylov, the reporter, nearly beaten to death. Yesterday Thorsson's arrest for homicide. And it's only getting more chaotic. About an hour ago Thorsson's surviving assailant—known by his alias as Igor Moroz—was just released by police on his own recognizance. The charges against him have been downgraded from attempted murder to simple assault."

Mikhailov recalled Moroz's biographical data and mugshot from the dossier. Bull neck, shaved head, lengthy arrest record: classic thug-for-hire.

"You can imagine the levers that were pulled, both here and in Kiev," Rykov continued. "They all run back to Zherdev. Perhaps he's acted in coalition with others...perhaps accorded a wink and a nod from our friends in the SBU. But that's now beside the point."

Mikhailov could already trace the line of reasoning. Rykov continued, gazing forward. "As usual, the Ukrainians have blundered into a fiasco. Zherdev too...and in principle, he's our guy. Now it's deteriorated into a lurid circus. And the media has been on hand to chronicle it every step of the way."

"Not least because a foreigner is involved," Mikhailov observed.

"Precisely. And an American besides. Our main worry, of course, is that the Americans and Europeans will exploit this event for their broader political purposes," Rykov continued. "Use it, as they are wont to do, to promote their brand of democracy here. Which is exactly what we've been taking such great pains to avoid since 2004. Until now you've been involved in other countries in our near-abroad. But you know the score."

"Yes."

"You're also fluent in English."

To this Mikhailov only nodded.

"This case is already big, and it's getting bigger. We can't allow it to deteriorate further. The Ukrainians, as usual, are in need of some outside intervention."

The attitude was common back at headquarters. Mikhailov had heard it many times before and thought the bias rather misplaced. Again, though, he said nothing.

"I suggest you pay a visit this afternoon, Oleg Konstantinovich. Talk to the magistrate. Make contact with Robinson, if possible. Assess the situation, and make your own determinations. I'll wish to be kept in the loop, of course. But you'll have broad discretion on this matter. Our residency in Kiev and our local resources here in Crimea will also be at your disposal."

"Understood."

"Good. I'll arrange for a launch to pick you up at the dock at three o'clock."

"That won't be necessary," Mikhailov answered. "For my initial foray I prefer to take the ferry. Make a low-key entry. Catch them by surprise."

CHAPTER 39

From Chernigovskaya metro station, Yulia covered the last kilometer and a half on foot, towing her suitcase between an outdoor bazaar and clamorous traffic on Bratislavskaya Street. Her tensions were only aggravated by the illegally parked cars on the sidewalk. When she reached the National Emergency and Trauma Hospital, she showed her passport at the main desk and filled out a visitor's form. Five minutes later, after an elevator ride the seventh floor and another trek down a long corridor, she found Pavel's room. She knocked on the closed door and was bidden at once to enter by a voice that sounded like Alexander Brisiuck's.

Inside, Brisiuck stood alongside Pavel's stainless-steel hospital bed, where Pavel was lying down, his torso propped up at an angle. She'd girded herself but was still shocked by the mangling and bandages. Two thirds of his body, as well as his much of head, were wrapped in first-aid dressing. One side of his face was swollen out almost the point of disfigurement. She deposited her suitcase and laptop by the door and rushed over to his side, half crouching at her knees. "Oh my God, Pavel," she said, half choking and placing her hand on one his forearms, which was in a cast. He neither moved nor answered her; his only reaction issued through his eyes. "He's pretty much immobilized,

Yulia," Brisiuck explained from her side. "They broke both his legs, one of his arms, and smashed all the fingers on both hands...the worst kind of injury for a journalist. They also broke his jaw. It's now wired shut."

Yulia glanced at Brisiuck, then back at Pavel, then at Brisiuck again. She didn't know whom to address.

"I can talk," Pavel said with clenched syllables.

She looked back down to see his lips, underneath his plastered nose, now splayed back across his teeth.

"Just can't...carry on...normally."

She said she'd come straight from the station after an overnight train ride.

"Thanks, Yulia," he enunciated. His eyes flicked up to Brisiuck.

His struggle to speak triggered another wave of emotion, which she stifled. "I never should have started this whole thing," she said, struggling to get words out herself.

"No, Yulia...forget it...no regrets."

"Even after this?" She turned a palm upward and swept it down to his feet and back up again.

"Yes."

Belatedly Brisiuck put a hand on her shoulder to save Pavel the effort. "He's right Yulia. Pavel and I are both grateful you got this story started. So is everyone else on our team. We all knew you have a sound nose for this."

Yulia thought the praise was overdone, as usual. Nonetheless some of her distress subsided. Anger soon rushed up in its place. At the train station in Simferopol she'd read the latest reports on her smartphone. Three assailants in Pavel's case, rather than two. Followed or tracked after his dinner. Intercepted between the Lukyanivska metro station and his apartment building. Chloroformed and hustled into a waiting SUV, driven by a fourth man. Beaten violently in the backseat. Hauled out of the car in a remote wooded area. Knocked into unconsciousness and left for dead.

"Any idea yet of the perpetrators?" she asked.

From under his bandages Pavel flashed some rage of his own. "I have…a pretty…good idea."

"Multiple indicators point to Zherdev," Brisiuck interjected. "But it could have been any number of parties. We'll probably never know for sure."

"What about the police?"

"They were here yesterday afternoon taking down information. As if that matters. Pavel took precautions that night—varied his routes and so on—but they located him anyway in a secondary courtyard near his building. Most likely through cell phone tracking. Which in turn points toward complicity from the SBU or Interior Ministry. That shouldn't surprise us, either. The security services have become handmaidens of the oligarchs since the 2010 election."

Yulia had surmised as much.

"There was another element that makes this appear calculated and coordinated," Brisiuck resumed. "The forested area where Pavel was dumped is less than one kilometer where Georgiy Gongadze's decapitated corpse was found back in 2000. This was intended to send the same message…to reporters especially. That is, don't interfere with money and power."

The comment sent a chill down Yulia's spine.

Brisiuck checked his watch and said he had to return to the newsroom. When he'd gone, Pavel shifted his eyes and fixed his gaze on her again. "Really, Yulia…this is beyond…the call of duty."

She told him about the unexpected support from Nosko and her leave of absence from the hotel. The solidarity seemed to gratify him. When he asked where she was staying, she told him she hadn't thought the question through.

"Why don't you…stay at my place…it's empty now."

His fifth-floor apartment, which Yulia knew well, was situated in a leafy neighborhood of prewar buildings around *Lukyanivska* station. It also offered quick cross-town access to the hospital. Pavel suggested, again with effort, that she might also tend to Octavia, his cat.

"What about your girlfriend…Evgenia? I'd assumed she'd do that."

"That's finished…mid-June."

"I'm sorry."

"No need….please, Yulia…keep…a low profile," he said struggling on. "Plus you…won't be alone. My mother is…coming tomorrow."

Yulia had not yet informed her own mother of her transfer to Kiev but already suspected she would come too. From there it would only be a matter of time before her mother learned the full picture—which was bound to happen anyway, sooner or later.

Pavel told her where to find the keys, which were deposited in a side cabinet. "Please, Yulia…be careful," he said. "This is…far from over." He thanked her again, as best he could. As she turned back toward the door, he moved his eyes sideways and took in her laptop case, still lashed to the pull-handle of her suitcase—as if he had the same thought as Brisiuck. His eyes slid closed before she reached the door.

CHAPTER 40

Mikhailov was sitting on the left afterdeck, wearing sunglasses under the bright sunshine. Every stop on the coastal shuttle—Utos, Chaika, Lazurne—brought back summers from his childhood, and each docking and embarkation offered the same close-up views of beaches and bathers that he remembered. New hotels and apartment complexes had materialized here and there on the lush hillsides. But the itinerary and essential panorama remained the same. When Professorski Ugolok—Professors' Corner—emerged around a bend, he spotted the Alushta sanatorium, owned and operated by Moscow State. His parents had taken him and Ksenia there every summer but one. On all of them, they'd brought an ample supply of books. Now he'd set about writing one. It struck him as the fulfillment of a long arc.

Upon catching sight of Alushta proper, the last station, he forced himself back on task. At the quay he disembarked with the other passengers and made his way across town on foot to police headquarters. There was an assemblage of reporters milling about the entrance.

Inside, the duty officer observed his short-sleeved shirt and linen slacks and gave him an unhelpful look, until he examined Mikhailov's FSB identification and stiffened noticeably. Mikhailov informed him of his purpose, and added that his visit was unscheduled. The officer placed a call at once and Yosip Yezhov appeared from a side door two minutes later, wearing a suit jacket and tie. Yezhov invited him straight back to his office and dispatched his secretary for tea. The magistrate was aware of current balances, post-Soviet or not.

"I understand you're here about the American, Axel Thorsson," he said in the politest of tones. "How might I be of assistance?"

"First, our interest extends beyond just Thorsson," Mikhailov answered. "We've determined there is a backdrop here of wider importance. Starting, for example, with the Harcourt conference, in which some citizens of Russia participated. And leading, at present, to the current media firestorm. I saw evidence of it just now as I walked into your building."

In a further play at commonality, Yezhov placed one hand over the other on the edge of his desk. "Yes…most unfortunate," he agreed. "Particularly the attention from the Western media." The magistrate was more politically astute than Mikhailov had supposed. A little tense as well.

"Moreover Thorsson's arrest has only intensified the coverage," Mikhailov continued. "Same goes for the release of Igor Moroz. From our perspective the situation has become untenable."

By now Yezhov had gone immobile. "New information came to light in our investigation," he offered, blandly. "We've redefined this as an altercation rather than an assault—"

"Please spare me the rhetoric, Yosip Abramovich. We're aware of Moroz's record. And that of his dead associate, Maxim Grozny, as well. I expect different information than the trumped-up lines you've been feeding the media."

"I think you know the way these things work, Oleg Konstantinovich," Yezhov said.

"Which means what?"

"It means that this decision issued from higher up. Regional authorities in Simferopol. Ultimately, from Kiev."

Mikhailov had presumed as much. He asked about the plan going forward. The magistrate hesitated before answering. "My current instruction is to prosecute Thorsson all the way through to full conviction."

"Who are the ultimate stakeholders here...the ones pulling the levers?"

"I can make some educated guesses. But it's really not my place to speculate on those matters, is it?"

Yezhov was right. Based on the case file, Mikhailov could make some educated guesses of his own. For now, he decided there was no utility in pressing any further. "That, in fact, is what we already suspected," he said. "Let me be clear. The Russian state's main objective in this case is to minimize the news coverage and negative attention. In our view it is counterproductive."

"I agree," Yezhov answered, relaxing a little for the first time in their exchange.

"Good. Is there any other information you might be able to provide while I'm here, short of your investigative files? For example, videos of your interviews and interrogations of Thorsson? I'd also appreciate the chance to observe him live, through closed circuit."

"I'd be glad to accommodate the first," the magistrate answered, relaxing several degrees further. "As for the second, I can do even better." He checked his watch. "In about ninety minutes he'll be conducted to the interview room, which has one-way glass from the observation compartment. There he will meet the chief consul from the US Embassy in Kiev, a woman named Heather Robinson."

On the boat ride Mikhailov had already mapped out his plan. Based on what Yezhov had told him, he was now ready to put it into effect. "That's good timing," he said simply.

*   *   *

Through his many years of field work, Mikhailov had learned that biographic data and still images provided only cursory introduction.

Deeper insights came only by hearing and seeing an individual speak: his or her tone of voice, manner of expression, and other cues. If live contact was infeasible, the combination of video and audio comprised a sturdy substitute. Axel Thorsson was no exception. Mikhailov sat in front of a screen console in the station's technical room and studied the six video segments that had been compiled on him thus far, all taken without Thorsson's knowledge. Several features stood out.

One was that Thorsson reacted evenly to stress. Throughout his ordeal, he'd remained remarkably composed. Some slight signs of weariness around the eyes, perhaps. But neither his face nor his voice belied desperation or loss of self-control. The second was his precise verbal expression, in both Russian and English. Thorsson framed his thoughts logically and conveyed them with a clear, steady voice, devoid of either deference or aggression. The third was his emotional detachment, despite his relative youth. He was able to view his own situation in the abstract.

Among all the case subjects Mikhailov had encountered throughout his career, including numerous dealings with Americans, he'd never run across anyone quite like Thorsson. He turned to Yezhov, who'd remained seated next to him for the duration of the viewing. "I've reviewed our file on him," he said. "Well educated, early business success, which you also know by now. Apart from that, though, he's not standard issue."

"No, he's not."

"Any other observations you can make about him at this point?"

"In person, he's physically impressive. Very fit, by the looks of him. With an aquatics background, as I've learned. Probably explains his strength in the water."

"Can I now see him live?"

"Right this way."

Yezhov conducted him out of the technical room, down a short corridor, and into the viewing chamber, meant to accommodate four to five people. The adjoining interview room, colored eggshell white and brightly lit, was much larger. Mikhailov remained standing at the one-way glass as Yezhov closed the door behind them. Less than twenty seconds later, the sound of an opening door issued from the compartment's audio system, indicating Thorsson's arrival.

Mikhailov watched him enter the room, accompanied by a policeman. His height, in the flesh, was a good seven or eight centimeters taller than Mikhailov's own, which fell in more middle range. The policeman led him over to the interview table and instructed him to sit down in the nearest chair. Mikhailov also noted that the American had grown significant facial stubble. "The beard his choice?" he asked Yezhov, without taking his eyes off him.

"We didn't get around to giving him a razor until this morning. Apparently he hasn't used it yet."

"How long until he meets Robinson?"

"We still have a few minutes."

When the policeman stepped back to a position along the far wall, Thorsson was left alone in the center. He sat straight upright, his palms placed lightly on his upper thighs. He did however seem aware that he was being observed. After thirty or forty seconds he turned his gaze over to their one-directional window and held it there for ten long seconds, giving Mikhailov the chance to look him straight into the eyes.

In them he detected the same qualities he'd noticed in the videos. This fate hadn't befallen Thorsson by random. One way or another, the American was going to matter.

Mikhailov's main hope, just now, was that he would not bear on this book.

CHAPTER 41

Thorsson had not seen Vladimir Nosko since his arrest, despite the hotel manager's attempts. Access had been denied, according to Heather Robinson. That left Robinson as his only lifeline to the outside world. Thorsson had determined he could do a lot worse. He considered her for a moment as he waited for her to arrive.

At the various US embassies he'd visited during his sales career, women of her mien and age bracket were common, particularly in the consular sections. Most of them unmarried. Perhaps impersonal at times, hewing hard to boundaries. But also conscientious and competent.

Robinson was sleek and well-tended, with immaculately cut, mid-length hair. Thus far she'd been focused, professional, and on message.

He stood from his chair as she entered the room, wearing the same skirt-and-jacket ensemble as in the morning. When they sat down she extracted a legal pad and two folders from her briefcase and a pen from the breast pocket of her blazer. She then positioned pen over paper and examined his face and arms. Always aware, as Thorsson was, that they were being recorded and observed though the one-way glass.

"Any physical mistreatment since our last meeting?"

"No. They also gave me another decent lunch. All major food groups. Adequate portions."

"Good. What about contact with other prisoners and detainees?"

"None. I still have the cell to myself. I was even able to do some calisthenics this morning."

This fact yielded no reaction. She took in his face again. "What about shaving materials? I asked for those specifically."

"They did give me a razor and a tube of cream, soon after you left. But cheap, basic stuff. Plus I've already developed significant growth. I decided against hacking my face up."

She made a note. "I'll see what else I can do." She swept a glance toward the one-directional window, which by now had become a third party to these discussions. "What about your interactions with Yosip Yezhov? Any additional sessions for questioning?"

"Not since the one early yesterday evening."

She made another note. "Also good. The fewer of these the better, until you enlist a lawyer." She reached down and pulled out another sheet of paper from her briefcase. "On that note, I'm sorry to say, the three attorneys in Kiev whom you selected from my list yesterday have still not responded to my e-mails and phone messages. The problem, as I suggested this morning, is that this is early August. Many people are away on vacation. I've therefore compiled an additional list of five attorneys here in Alushta. However I should underline that the embassy has no previous experience with any of them." She slid the sheet across.

Thorsson examined the list. Three males and two females, with characteristic US evenhandedness. For him they could be individuals off the street. He drew a slow inhalation and told her he'd wait a little longer for the attorneys from Kiev.

"As you wish," she said, glancing back down at her pad. "In keeping with your request, I also e-mailed Ralph Waingrove, the president of your company. His response was almost immediate. He's very concerned, as you supposed. I told him I'd keep him abreast of further developments. Here's a copy of our exchange." She slid a sheet across.

"Thank you."

She glanced back down at her list. "What about your family members back in the States—your parents and brother? Shall I continue to update them?"

"Please do. Otherwise their only sources of information will be the news reports." He nodded toward the door through which she had just entered. "Speaking of news coverage, what's happening at present? Are the reporters still outside?"

"Seven or eight of them." Her expression remained level. "Here's another collection of articles." She reached under her first folder to extract the second, which she also slid across the table. Flipping open the cover, Thorsson beheld the latest collection of online printouts.

The article on top was from the *Wall Street Journal*, just three paragraphs long. The headline read, "Manager for Allegheny Energy, American, Arrested for Murder in Ukraine." In it he was identified by name, though otherwise just basic details were provided. Flipping through the twelve or thirteen remaining pages, he saw similar articles from the *Guardian, Le Figaro, Le Monde, Financial Times, La Repubblica, Die Zeit, Washington Post, New York Times*, most, apparently, picked up over wire services. Next were half a dozen Ukrainian and Russian-language publications, including *Ukrainskaya Pravda* and *Ukraina Sevodnya*, all much longer than their Western equivalents.

There was another series, also in numerous languages but less sensational, on Yulia's cousin Pavel. Thorsson was relieved to read that he was continuing to recover in the hospital.

Toward the back of the stack, a page in tabloid format from *Vecherny Vesti* grabbed his attention. The story carried bigger photographs than the others, in color. It featured him and Yulia Petrenko on the promenade in different poses and positions, set off by a bold, oversized headline: "Mystery Woman in Murder Case of American Businessman?" The most prominent, shot under the colonnade at the end, showed them standing at close range. The caption read, "The evening before his arrest, Thorsson in intimate dialogue with an unnamed woman who has been identified as an employee of the hotel." Robinson's eyes also flicked down to the page, then back up to his face.

Again she exhibited no reaction.

He checked the wall clock. By his count they had nine minutes remaining. "Do you mind if I take a little while to peruse these before we finish for today?"

"As you wish. My main purpose here, as I've said, is to assist and inform."

Thorsson had not told her yet about Yulia, given that they were being monitored. And thus far Robinson had not inquired. Yulia was in any case not a US citizen and therefore not within her purview.

Robinson was holding to boundaries. He could count on her for that.

*   *   *

"Her time's about up," Yezhov said to Mikhailov. "You're welcome to talk to Thorsson as well, before I send him back to his cell."

"That won't be necessary, at present." When the prosecutor reached over to the wall phone Mikhailov held up his hand. "But I would ask that you let Robinson remain a couple of minutes longer," he added, "and that you take your time processing her out of the station. I'd like to leave before she does."

Yezhov stopped in motion and looked at him, curious. "She's staying at the Radisson, if you'd like to make contact."

"That's not my objective at this stage. I simply want to know whether she engages any of the reporters outside."

The prosecutor reacted with a slight smile. "Of course."

Mikhailov shook Yezhov's hand and bid him farewell, casting one more glance through the glass at Thorsson and Robinson as he exited. On the station's front terrace, he donned his sunglasses and appraised the loose milling of reporters and photographers before descending the steps to the sidewalk. He then strode across the central plaza to one crosswalk, then another, and traversed to the opposite side of the square, blending among other pedestrians. Near the entrance to the outdoor market he pulled out his phone, contrived to check the screen, and drew up alongside a news kiosk, in the shade of a tree. Once in position he verified his sight lines back to the police station.

From Robinson's file he knew that she had never, in her diplomatic career to date, been approached by the FSB. That was about to change.

CHAPTER 42

At closing distance Mikhailov observed that Robinson was of statuesque proportions, particularly in her heels. Also that she threw off a slightly chill aura—the kind that forewarned all comers. Seconds later she passed within five meters of his location under the tree and turned down Khromuka Street. He took care to keep his face away as she passed, then after a brief pause, fell in fifteen meters behind her. Two Orthodox churches came into view on the stretch just ahead, bracketing Alushta's sole minaret. Mikhailov accelerated his pace, bearing down off her right flank. When he was two meters from her side, at last he spoke, in a timbre that was at once nonthreatening and businesslike—his best American-accented English.

"Pardon me. Heather Robinson?"

She startled only slightly, whirled ninety degrees, and stopped to look at him with a well-armored gaze. He removed his sunglasses to give her full-face view.

"Do I know you?"

"No you don't. My name's Oleg Mikhailov, and I work for the Russian government. Please excuse the sudden approach." He allowed her a long, hard look. She kept her own sunglasses on. "I'd like to talk to you about Axel Thorsson. I think I can be of help."

She processed this as well. Her response, when it came, was deliberate. "Can I see some identification?"

"Of course." Mikhailov handed over his diplomatic passport, which she flipped open and examined, looking up once to compare his face with the photograph. A flicker of recognition followed, which raised her guard even higher.

"FSB," she said. "Am I correct?"

"Yes."

"Have you just followed me from the police station?"

"I acknowledge that I have and apologize. However I wished to make contact without involvement from the police or prosecutor, and determined it was the best option."

Her armor stayed up. "My responsibilities do not include interactions with foreign intelligence services. In fact they're proscribed. Shouldn't this kind of contact be handled through diplomatic channels in Kiev?"

"Normally, yes. But I think you would agree that Thorsson presents an unusual and challenging situation. I really can be of assistance."

She handed his passport back and said nothing. A woman wearing a sundress passed them with shopping bags, her curiosity piqued by their use of English.

"I should also underline that this is no way an attempt to recruit you," he said when she had passed. "Can we talk for a few minutes? There's a small park just beyond the churchyard. We'll have more privacy there."

Robinson looked in the direction of his outstretched hand. "Okay, I'll give you a hearing. But this had better get right to the point."

"Agreed."

They walked in silence for ten seconds and turned right into the gate opening to the park, which was sunken and surrounded by a stone-masonry wall. Flowers and blossoming bushes colored the perimeter, as well as several raised planted areas in the center. The enclosure was empty except for a young mother with a stroller in the far corner, sitting on a bench and talking on her cell phone. Mikhailov gestured toward two other benches, both vacant, on the other side.

"We can sit over there, if you like."

"I'd prefer to remain standing."

She moved several steps toward the perimeter, keeping a high wall at her back and establishing a view of all the park's entry points. Mikhailov followed her. He also respected her training, particularly for a non-operative.

"Go ahead," she said when they were stationary again. "I'm listening."

Mikhailov obliged. "Okay, I'll cut straight to the core. We both know that Thorsson was an innocent bystander, according to all credible accounts. He got caught up in this affair by accident and was attacked without provocation. It was essentially a hit operation. We've determined it was ordered by powerful Ukrainian financial interests. His arrest is a sham, along with the evidence. The Russian government sees Ukraine as its sphere of interest, as I'm sure you know. Therefore we don't like the publicity that this affair has generated. We wish to put a stop to it."

Robinson gauged every word. Her face soured for an instant at his "sphere of interest" allusion. Nevertheless she said nothing, keeping her gaze fastened onto him through her dark glasses.

"I'll also be open," he continued. "Yezhov just showed me the video of your recent interactions with Thorsson, as well as audio of your first contact by telephone. I also watched the entire meeting you just conducted with him from behind the one-way glass. Therefore I'm fully aware of where you stand."

The consul didn't flinch. Mikhailov observed her. "And on that basis I've devised a solution."

Robinson remained rooted in place, which Mikhailov took as a good sign.

"I'm still listening," she said.

"I'm fairly certain I can exert appropriate influences over the next twenty-four hours or so—pull strings, as you say—in Simferopol and

Kiev, to at least get Thorsson released from jail. Also to delay the presentation of formal charges for several weeks. During this period, with a bit more scope for maneuver, I'm also confident that I can engineer complete dismissal of the charges so that Thorsson will be free for good." He paused for a downbeat. "To carry this plan out, however, I would also have to make certain requests of him, which at this point are best communicated through you."

"Go on."

"Once he's released, Thorsson should remain out of the media spotlight. Lay low until this is resolved. He won't be able to leave the country while the charges are pending, so that's not an option. At minimum I would suggest that he depart Crimea. Kiev comes to mind. There, he could lose himself in the anonymity of the big city, while remaining close to you at the embassy. He could also more easily enlist a lawyer, if he wishes. Meanwhile"—Mikhailov gestured back toward police headquarters—"some of this frenzy might subside."

"Which is the main objective of the Russian government, is it not?"

"Yes. I've been up front about that."

"What about Thorsson's assailant...the surviving one? Is he just going to walk free?"

"On that I can make no promises. But I'll consider all options."

For the first time Robinson unlatched her gaze from his and turned her head slightly toward the perimeter wall. Mikhailov sensed that she was visiting all angles.

"This exceeds my defined function," she said upon turning back. "Therefore, I'll need to run this by my superior at the embassy. The ambassador is on vacation. So just now that means the charge d'affaires."

Mikhailov nodded.

"Beyond that, even if I receive the green light, I can't make any promises on Thorsson's behalf. I'm going to have to consult him."

"Of course."

"You said twenty-four to forty-eight hours?"

"That's my aim."

CHAPTER 43

The alarm clock roused Yulia from deep slumber. She swung her legs out of bed and rubbed her eyes, while Octavia, Pavel's cat, also roused herself and jumped to the floor. First she made a brief foray to the kitchen to replenish the feline's food bowl, then returned to throw on jeans, a tee-shirt, and sandals over her sheer underwear. Minutes later she hastened out the door and downstairs toward the Lukianovska metro station. At the Zolotoi Vorota-Teatralna nexus she made swift transfer from green line to red and reached Vohkzalna with just a few minutes to spare. She strode into the main terminus and checked the arrivals board. The overnight train from Nikolaev was due in at 6:40 a.m., right on schedule. Her mother would be on the train with her aunt Ludmila. The two sisters were journeying north to take charge.

She drew a deep breath, aware of what was coming. She also told herself that their presence would be probably for the better.

En route to the escalator she passed a newsstand with a fresh rack of Russian- and Ukrainian-language dailies. Several of the latest headlines jumped out at once, and she stopped:

"Police Indicate No Leads in Beating of Reporter"

"Questions Mount on Arrest of American Businessman in Alushta"

"Zherdev Refuses Comment on Harcourt Conference and Pending Land-Reform Legislation"

There were others, all addressing the same threads. She pulled a couple off the rack and scanned their articles. She welcomed the growing coverage…as long as the primary focus stayed on the Harcourt conference and agricultural reform.

Thus far, to her relief, the images in *Vecherny Vesti*—published just the afternoon before—seemed to have made limited impact. None of the mainstream publications had yet seized upon them. She put the papers back on the rack, intending to digest all the articles online, when a photo cover caught her eye. The cover image, blown up and in full color, was from the *Vecherny Vesti* spread, proclaiming her and Thorsson in one of their more intimate-looking moments. The banner-line, in big capital letters, read, "MYSTERY BOMBSHELL IN ALUSHTA IDENTIFIED."

The magazine was *Ukrainski Insaider, Vecherny Vesti's* sister weekly. Suddenly wired, Yulia grabbed it off the shelf and flipped it open. The accompanying article encompassed multiple pages and a bigger collection of photos than the previous day's tabloid. Most of them seemed to emphasize her body curves. She snared the captions and other fragments: "Revealed as Yulia Petrenko, receptionist at the RadissonBlu Hotel…exact relationship with Thorsson still unclear…unexplained leave of absence…hotel refuses comment…"

She reexamined the images. In them she appeared to be veritably bursting out of her tight skirt and summer blouse, like a full-fleshed sexpot—a fecund farm girl, all dressed up and straight from the village.

An announcement came over the public address system: "Six forty train from Nikolaev arriving in two minutes on track five."

She cursed under her breath, rushed over to the cashier's counter, and pulled out a ten-griven banknote. The vendor, a woman in her forties, glanced at the cover and gave her a second look as she handed the money across. Yulia evaded eye contact as she took away the item and strode toward the escalator. On the way up, she rolled up the magazine in her hand and tried not to glance around. Countless eyes gravitated toward her all the same as she strode through the waiting foyer and down onto the platform, just as the train was pulling into the station. She took up position, on lookout for wagon ten.

Her mother, ten centimeters shorter than Yulia and a little on the plump side, looked alert and full of energy when she emerged from the door. Her aunt Luda, one year older, was showing more strain. Yulia rushed over to assist with their luggage, and at the center of the platform, following embraces and kisses, their expressions became more concentrated. In their usual forthright fashion, they examined her face.

Yulia knew at once they were on to her.

Her mother reached down into her satchel and pulled out the previous day's edition of *Vecherny Vesti*. "The attack on Pavel has been upsetting enough, Yuliochka," she said, holding the paper out. "Then we bought this at the station last night, which shows you with an American murder suspect in Alushta! What's going on here?"

Yulia glanced around nervously at the other people of the platform. At the same time her mother's eyes settled on the rolled-up magazine under her arm. It was now clear that any further concealment would be pointless.

"Mama. Please put that back in your bag. I'll explain to both of you. Just not here."

Her mother complied, though hardly satisfied. Both sisters bent immediately to take hold of their bags, disinclined to waste time. Again Yulia moved to help.

"Where to?" her mother asked. "The metro?"

Retracement through the main departure hall now struck Yulia as too risky. Same held for a metro ride.

"Better we take a taxi," she said. "We'll drop your bags off at Pavel's apartment and go straight to the hospital." Yulia headed toward the stairs, carrying two bags, her mother and aunt trailing behind. She decided their arrival carried an upside and a downside. The upside was that she now had some backup. The downside was that she would now have to tell them everything.

*   *   *

Thorsson's first inkling came when his cell door opened. He was expecting breakfast. Instead the guard carried a fresh change of clothes, retrieved from his hotel room and neatly folded.

"You're being released on bail," the guard said with a flat expression.

"Immediately?" Thorsson asked, standing from his cot and taking the items.

"As soon as you're dressed."

The guard retreated back to the corridor and stood with his back shoulder in the doorframe while Thorsson changed into the items and speculated on the fly. He'd started to resign himself to remaining in jail for multiple weeks, if not months, while awaiting trial. Upon their exit from the cell, the guard conducted him down the corridor past the ten other holding chambers, several of them containing new arrivals, detained overnight for drunkenness and hooliganism. In the outer station another policeman, through a window portal, handed over his wristwatch, belt, and smartphone. As he donned the first, he checked it against the clock on the wall; the time was 6:15 a.m. The guard stood next to him impassively.

"I'm ready," Thorsson said when he was done.

He expected to be let out the door into the station lobby. Instead the guard walked over to a smaller steel door on the far wall and proceeded to unlock it. "I've been instructed to release you through the back," he said, opening it.

It was Thorsson's first emergence into open air since his arrest. Heather Robinson stood right outside on a small rear porch. She wore her business-like expression. He held her gaze as he emerged, still puzzled.

"What's going on?" he asked her.

"Better if I tell you in the car."

She gestured toward the parking lot, past two patrol cars and a van. Along the far edge, about thirty meters away, Thorsson spotted one of the hotel cars, parked under a canopy of branches. Next to it stood Nosko, clad as usual in suit and tie, along with another man Thorsson took to be the driver. Upon making eye contact Nosko responded with a slight smile. Thorsson walked in tandem with Robinson across the asphalt, still wordless. When he reached Nosko they shook hands.

"I worried this day would never come," the hotel manager said in English.

"So did I," Thorsson said.

"Ms. Robinson pulled it off. I'm sure she'll explain."

Thorsson reexamined the vehicle, a long, dark-blue crossover vehicle emblazoned on the side with the RadissonBlu logo. It was similar to the one that had taken him in from the airport, almost two weeks earlier, except for the darker tint of its windows. Nosko seemed to note his reaction. "We usually employ this one for celebrity guests," he said. "With some help from staff I've packed up all your things. Your suitcase and laptop are already in the back. Slava here will drive you to the airport, along with Ms. Robinson. I can assure you he is discreet."

"Thank you."

This was the first indication to Thorsson that he was flying somewhere. Nosko discerned the only other missing piece.

"One more thing," he said. "I'm sure Yulia would have been here today, if she could have done. But she's on leave of absence from the hotel, for very good reason. She flew to Kiev the day after your arrest to attend to her cousin Pavel. You have her number if I'm not mistaken. Correct?"

"Yes I do."

"Good. I'll call her shortly to alert her to your release. But I also suggest you contact her when time allows."

"Thank you again. I will."

Nosko bid him farewell, and Robinson as well, while Slava opened the rear doors. Thorsson climbed in and settled into his seat, and the consul did likewise. Yulia apart, he still didn't know where they were going.

CHAPTER 44

The two sisters were in the back. Yulia sat in front with the taxi driver, twisting sideways and craning her neck to carry on the conversation. Her mother was now holding open the copy of *Ukrainski Insaider* with both hands, flipping insistently through the spread.

"So how did this photographer know about your connection to Pavel?"

"He didn't Mama. This American had just been the target of a murder attempt. But he ended up killing one of the assailants instead. He was just defending himself. Reporters were already there, thanks to Pavel's story."

The puzzlement on her mother's face only intensified. "This American, the target of a murder attempt?" She reread a portion of the text and looked up again, boring her gaze at Yulia between the two headrests. "It says here that he's the one who's been arrested for homicide!"

"He has been. But the charges are false. I can tell you that for sure."

"False? How can you know that?" When Yulia offered no immediate answer, her mother studied the images again, swaying in her seat as the taxi changed lanes. Next to her, Aunt Luda hung on every word.

"And that still doesn't explain what you were doing walking on the promenade with him. He was a guest, wasn't he?"

Yulia noticed the driver's eyes flick to the rearview mirror, then over to her. Already she'd divulged far too much for third-party consumption. "Please, Mama. This isn't the best time to talk about all this. I'll tell you more back at the apartment."

Another sedan cut abruptly in front of their taxi, prompting the driver to jam on his brakes and press down hard on his horn. At almost the same instant the melody sounded on Yulia's smartphone. The caller was Vladimir Nosko. Caught a little off guard, she collected herself and answered.

"Vladimir?"

"Yes, Yulia. Hello. Pardon the early hour." His speech was clipped and confident and carried incongruous up-notes, in view of recent events. He seemed to register the ambient noise from traffic. "Are you able to talk? I wouldn't be calling if it wasn't important."

Her heart fluttered for inchoate reasons. She looked at her mother and aunt in the backseat. Her next syllables twanged unevenly. "I'm in a taxi with some family members. But of course...go ahead."

"Good. I'll get right to the point. Axel Thorsson was released from jail here in Alushta this morning."

"So soon? Great...how?"

"It caught me by surprise, too. Heather Robinson, the American consul, apparently orchestrated some deal. But the main point is he's out, released on bail. In fact he's headed to Simferopol Airport now, together with Robinson."

As the news registered Yulia experienced a sudden unburdening sensation. Her heart fluttered a few beats. "The airport? Is he flying back to the States?"

"No. He's just out on bail. That means he can't leave the country. I'm not apprised of his exact plans. But I do know his first stop is Kiev."

"Kiev? You mean he's flying here?"

"That's right. He'll arrive at Boryspil Airport by 10:30. I informed him you're also there now, looking after Pavel. He said he'd call you as soon as possible."

Yulia glanced back at her mother and aunt again. Little to her surprise, they were more intent than ever. This would push them into overdrive. The street outside the windows blurred for a moment as wider frames came into view. Her heart fluttered again before she thanked Nosko and signed off.

And this time unburdening had nothing to do with it.

* * *

Heather Robinson had foisted nothing upon him, in keeping with her role. She'd behaved as neither executive nor enforcer but as the instrument of a free system, which Thorsson understood implicitly. In any case he agreed with her plan. All its components made sense.

The first and most immediate, which she'd noted as soon as the car doors had closed, was their destination. The capital, she'd suggested, offered escape from the media frenzy in Alushta and the relative anonymity of the big city. There were the additional pragmatic advantages of proximity to the embassy and to qualified legal representation. And it in no way precluded alternative destinations later, should he choose.

Moreover Yulia was already there, and she was just as entangled in this as he was.

Robinson's second suggestion was that he keep low profile once he reached Kiev, steering clear of the media in particular. This, she explained, would abet the political and diplomatic dynamic that had just yielded his release. He'd found no objection in this either. It had however prompted the question which had intrigued him most of all since he'd walked out of jail—namelyyy, how had he gained release in the first place?

He held the thought until they reached the airport, checked in their baggage, and passed through security. At last they reached their gate. Now he wanted some answers.

He purchased two cups of coffee, gave her one, and guided her over to a secluded corner with windows overlooking the tarmac. When they were stationary he also set down his laptop case. Each of them took their initial sips, as if by preface. "Okay, we're on our own here, Heather," he said. "Can you be a bit more specific about how all this transpired?"

"In fact, this has been developing for the past day and a half. It started on Tuesday evening, after I left my meeting with you at police headquarters. I was contacted by an FSB agent. He followed me into town, approached me covertly, and introduced himself. I was wary, of course, but I determined he was legitimate. We subsequently engaged in a short meeting in a nearby park."

"Just like that?"

"Just like that. His name is Oleg Mikhailov. I later learned from our own intelligence that he's a lieutenant colonel in the FSB. Just recently promoted, in fact, and one of the youngest in their service."

"An FSB colonel? And he's in Crimea solely for this reason?"

"That I don't know."

Thorsson mulled this for some seconds while drawing on his coffee.

Robinson did likewise. "Excuse me for not informing you earlier," she added. "But our conversations at police headquarters were monitored. Mikhailov's actions were behind the scenes. He didn't want to telegraph them."

"I understand. And he alone was able to pull all the necessary levers to bring this about?" he asked. "I wasn't aware the FSB held that kind of sway in Ukraine these days."

"Oh, they do. That part doesn't surprise me. And don't forget Mikhailov's high rank. One can assume that he's able to apply influence at high levels."

Robinson's phone beeped in her suit jacket, and she pulled it out and looked at the screen for several downbeats. "On more practical note, we've already found you an apartment on Kreschatik. A short-term rental, fully furnished."

"In Kiev I usually stay at the Hyatt. But I agree an apartment probably makes more sense just now. Kreschatik is also central. Thanks."

For security reasons she handed over her own phone rather than transmitting the information to his. While Thorsson was looking at the photographs—a luxury one-bedroom unit, on a high floor of the tallest building on the boulevard—Robinson's phone beeped again, and he handed the device back. This time she frowned as she examined the message contents. "This news isn't so benign. There's another big photo spread of you today in *Ukrainski Insaider*...this is public, so I'll send it to you."

An instant later the associated link popped onto Thorsson's message list. He clicked it open and scrolled through an array of photographs even more numerous and sensational than the first, with headlines to match. He also realized Yulia's profile was fast becoming just as prominent as his own. He drained the rest of his coffee.

"Incredible," he said after looking up. "Why such fascination with her?"

Robinson looked thoughtful as she took a sip of her own. "They're the same media instincts that prevail everywhere," she answered, casting a worried glance around the terminal. She examined his face for a moment.

"I was just reassessing your beard. Under the circumstances, it might even be an advantage."

Thorsson had half forgotten about it. He felt the growth with his free hand, including his burgeoning and spiky mustache, which now smelled of coffee. Coverage was already full and thick, obscuring most of the skin underneath. "You could be right. Who knows? I may even keep it." He also discerned that Robinson was mulling another subject. This one she didn't verbalize, in her usual delineated manner.

Namely Yulia Petrenko.

Thorsson extracted his phone, excused himself, and retreated five meters away along a wall. Without further ado he tapped Yulia's Skype moniker.

Robinson was still hewing to boundaries. That was the way he preferred it.

CHAPTER 45

The squeeze was tight for three people with baggage, forcing Yulia to wedge herself in near the control panel, where she managed to raise her arm and punch the button. Copious supplies from Nikolaev constrained her along both flanks. In one hand, looped below her rolled-up issue of *Ukrainski Insaider*, she clutched her mother's large plastic carrier, containing mostly fresh produce from her dacha, and in the other, a similar consignment from Aunt Luda.

Her smartphone stuck taut in the back pocket of her jeans with the vibrate function on.

The elevator whirred and clanked upward to the fifth floor, where she held the sliding doors open, then led her mother and aunt toward the apartment. Just as they reached the entrance and she extracted her keys, her smartphone sent a quivering pulsation through her right buttock, forcing her to extract the device and answer. The call was over Skype.

"Yulia? This is Axel. I'm calling from Simferopol."

He was speaking Russian. Her mother and Aunt Luda turned full around to look at her, standing up their wheeled suitcases.

"Can you talk?"

"Of course." Her voice cracked slightly and reverberated off the concrete walls of the landing. She registered the two other apartment doors nearby and glanced again at her mother and aunt. "The thing is, my mother and aunt have just arrived...but I have heard the good news from Vladimir. Can I call you back in a few minutes?"

"Sure. My flight boards in twenty minutes, but I'll be standing by."

She jammed the phone in her back pocket and tugged out her keys again, inserting them into the bolt lock. In her peripheral vision, she glimpsed her mother checking her watch. "It's not even seven-fifteen yet, Yuliochka, and you've already received two phone calls," she said. "Pavel's condition is already troubling enough. Is everything under control?"

Yulia swung the door open, relieved to gain some sanctuary. "For the most part, Mama...that second call was from Axel Thorsson."

"The American? The one now in jail?"

"Yes. The good news he was just released."

She stepped back to allow the two sisters to enter first, then bent down and took hold again of the two food bags. Inside Octavia was there to greet them. Her mother and aunt remained standing in the outer hallway. Unpacking seemed the last thing on their minds. "Let's put the food away and get you settled first," she said. "Then I've got to call Axel Thorsson right back. From there my plan there was to go straight to the hospital."

Yulia could tell that Pavel was her aunt's first priority. With her mother she wasn't so sure.

"But you will tell us everything, won't you, Yuliochka?" her mother said. "We really should know."

By now Yulia had resigned herself to it.

"Of course, Mama. That goes without saying."

*   *   *

For perhaps the first time since Thorsson had checked into the hotel some two weeks earlier, Yulia regretted that he spoke fluent Russian. Or at least that they'd never acquired the habit of speaking English.

Just now she would have preferred a language that was incomprehensible to her mother and aunt. Presently the circumstance drove her out to the balcony overlooking the street, where she shut the glass door behind her. Thorsson answered on the second ring.

"Please excuse the delay," she said. Twangs of anxiousness came through that she couldn't stifle. "It's been a busy morning."

"I gathered that. You said your mother and aunt just arrived?"

"Yes…mainly to look after Pavel."

Through the glass of the door, she observed the two sisters crossing to the bedroom, which she'd vacated in favor of the pull-out couch. They were accompanied down the hall by Octavia, in businesslike mode. The trio appeared eager to proceed on all fronts.

"Does that mean you're going to cut your visit short?" Thorsson asked from his end, realigning her focus.

"To be honest I haven't thought that far ahead."

"Good, because I may be there awhile. In fact, the US Embassy has already booked a rental apartment on my behalf."

She wasn't sure it was her place to ask where, but she did anyway.

"It's right on Kreschatik. You know the tallest building, right in the center, built in the Stalinist classical style?"

Yulia knew the building all too well. She also realized, simultaneously, that she was fortunate to be situated on the balcony. Pavel had warned her that his apartment might have been bugged. There was a public-address announcement on Thorsson's end. "I'm afraid I'll have to sign off. Of course I'll contact you again after I arrive, as soon as I can."

She managed to compose herself enough to wish him a safe journey, then opened the balcony door into the living room, just as her mother and Aunt Luda paced back in from the hallway, accompanied by the cat. All three looked determined to get answers, including the feline. "I'll call another taxi," she told them. "While we're waiting outside, I'll do my best to fill you in on more details."

Yulia tapped one of the taxi services on her speed dial as they headed toward the door. For now she didn't tell them about Pavel's warning about eavesdropping. She figured it would be too much for one morning.

CHAPTER 46

Mikhailov spotted the girl first, diligent and in motion. She wore a sunbonnet over her blond curls, a light cotton dress that bared her knees to vicissitudes and spills, and already appeared—at the precocious age of five—as if she was ready to take on the world. Her attentions were centered on the scooter, the pavement just ahead, and the constant adjustments to impetus and balance that the conveyance required.

In the fresh morning sunlight she presented a gentle, idyllic figure, resplendent with promise.

The girl was Rykov's granddaughter, and she'd accompanied him to a bright and open stretch of concrete walkway fronting the dolphinarium and skirting the multichrome fountain and its sculpture of Prometheus. She glanced over at her grandfather once to affirm his consent but he did not intervene, preferring instead to remain seated on an adjacent park bench.

Mikhailov did not have a daughter, which he attributed to fate. But as he drew closer he recognized what the girl represented. Women had always formed the true heart and soul of Russia, and probably always would. Even in this tender and still-emergent state this girl embodied the future, the next generation. Rykov, for all his power and authority and position in the state, saw himself as mere caretaker.

Only as Mikhailov bent around Prometheus did Rykov's wife come into view, standing apart and also keeping watch on the girl. He guessed they were giving their daughter and son-in-law some time to themselves. The older man glanced over at him when he was about fifteen meters away. Taking notice, the girl also looked his way with wide blue eyes, at once innocent and perceptive. Her grandmother did likewise, though she appeared to expect him. At the bench Mikhailov shook his superior's hand and turned to nod over at his wife. She nodded back with a slight smile and stepped forward to guide the child further up the walkway. Rykov invited him to sit down.

"Please excuse the intrusion, Anatoli Sergeiivich. I didn't mean to cut into time with your granddaughter."

Rykov, as usual, was aligned to the task at hand. "When duty calls, Oleg Konstantinovich, we have to answer it. Do we not?"

Mikhailov nodded. To this point he'd kept any generalized misgivings to himself. His agreement on such matters remained implied.

"I have an update," he continued. "Heather Robinson, the US consul, proved pragmatic and cooperative. Over these past two days I've also been able to pull appropriate strings in Kiev and Simferopol, thanks in part to our personnel in those locations. The result is that Thorsson was released on probation this morning and should arrive in Kiev shortly, accompanied by Robinson. To my knowledge he intends to stay there under low profile until further notice."

"Encouraging start. What are our next steps?"

"Our most pressing problem is still the media coverage. If anything, the frenzy has only intensified since we spoke last, particularly in the tabloids. Thorsson's departure from Alushta should help. But now a new actor—or actress, I should say—has now come on the scene—one who didn't even enter into our last discussion."

"You mean Yulia Petrenko, the receptionist at the hotel?"

As usual Rykov was keeping abreast of the case through other channels.

"Correct. She's proven more vital than we might have imagined. Through research into state and local birth and educational records, as well as passport data, we've discovered that she's the cousin of Pavel Krylov, the reporter at *Ukraina Sevodnya* who broke the original story on the Harcourt conference. Seems they grew up together in Nikolaev. In addition, Petrenko—despite her current line of work—is a recent graduate of the journalism faculty at Shevchenko University, the same institution from which Krylov graduated several years earlier. From that one might assume she carries certain journalistic inclinations."

"Insightful, though not entirely surprising," Rykov observed. "Do you suspect she was the initial leak of the confidential documents?"

"I'm now fairly certain that she was. Before Thorsson was released, I obtained copies of the digital video archives taken at the RadissonBlu during the period in question, which Yezhov, the prosecutor, had impounded from hotel management. Yezhov had already identified several key segments in which Thorsson discovers a flash memory stick in the elevator. He subsequently turns it into Petrenko at the front desk, on his way to the beach. Two of Zherdev's underlings later appear to collect the device.

"I sent these to our experts in Moscow for further analysis. Late yesterday they informed me that a minute-and-forty-five-second-long segment appear to have been excised. Precisely when the stick is in Petrenko's sole possession at the desk."

"In other words, Petrenko copied the files, and hotel management engineered some sort of cover-up on her behalf."

"It certainly appears that way. We're still seeking corroboration through other means. But those efforts may be superfluous, given what's happened in the interim. Three days ago Petrenko was granted a leave of absence from her job and is now in Kiev, where's she's made numerous visits to Krylov in the hospital. She is also now residing in his apartment. Meanwhile my efforts to obtain an appointment with Vladimir Nosko, the hotel manager, have thus far been rebuffed.

Based on impressions over the phone I sense that he retains certain anti-Yanukovich and anti-Russian sympathies."

"Where does that leave Thorsson? An inadvertent bystander, as we presumed?"

"Most likely. Though that doesn't quite explain all his interactions with Petrenko. And now they've intersected again in Kiev. Naturally we'll observe and assess their further contacts."

Rykov took a moment to mull the developments. For an instant Mikhailov's thoughts flashed to his novel. His early-morning writing sessions now looked more and more like a chimera.

"There's one key variable we haven't yet addressed," Rykov resumed. "That's Zherdev. We're already fairly certain he ordered both the botched operation against Thorsson and the attack on Krylov. And he continues to come under a barrage of media scrutiny, which must infuriate him. Once he also puts all these pieces together, he's bound to undertake further reprisals, including ones against Petrenko. Then we'll never be able contain this fiasco."

"Agreed, Anatoli Sergeiivich. And as luck would have it, Zherdev is still currently in residence at his villa near Feodosia. I would say some sort of tête-à-tête is in order."

"I would concur, Oleg Konstantinovich. As usual you've already envisaged next moves."

They rose from the bench and shook hands. Over Rykov's shoulder Mikhailov glimpsed the girl again, further up the walkway. She noticed them standing and glanced back. The thought occurred to him that she would need more, in the years ahead, than the material security and system of protections for which her grandfather labored. State power could only take Russia so far. She would also need fiction and literature—the redeeming kind, the sort that illumined the modern world and Russia's proper place in it.

Now more than ever, the second requirement looked more critical than the first.

CHAPTER 47

The proprietor offered a quick tour. It was a spacious one bedroom and living room/kitchen, recently remodeled and possessed of all amenities, including washing machine, coffee maker, HD television, and ultrafast Wi-Fi. Bed linens, towels, pans, and utensils in ample stock. Located on the tenth floor of Kreschatik 25, with a spacious balcony and encompassing view of the boulevard. Notably, he did not ask to see Thorsson's passport. Thorsson paid in US dollars, cash, for two weeks, with the option of a third. He did not request a receipt. After handing over the keys, the man departed with little fanfare.

"He's discreet," Robinson said when he'd gone. "We've organized rentals from him numerous times before, for visitors in special circumstances."

Thorsson refrained from asking what those circumstances were. "I've noticed this building during previous trips here," he said. "But I've never been inside. Impressive structure, like most of the others on Kreschatik. Built in the early to mid fifties, was it not?"

"To my knowledge, yes."

"I've long liked the Stalinist-classical aesthetic. Maybe it's an acquired taste."

Robinson volunteered no opinion and stuck to agenda. "I suggest you get settled," she said. "I realize you have to buy groceries and so on, but once again I implore you to keep a low profile. Particularly here in the center."

"Nobody on the plane or at either airport seemed to recognize me. I hope that bodes well."

"I hope so too." Robinson beheld his face again. "As I said, your beard helps. You might also consider sunglasses."

"Good idea. I wear them often anyway this time of year." Half by reflex, Thorsson reached up again to stroke his chin. Five days on, his facial growth still felt like a novelty. Trimming might soon be in order, but he'd decided on the plane to keep it until this ordeal was over.

"Will you revisit the list of lawyers I've given you?" Robinson continued. "Perhaps even make some telephone calls this afternoon?"

"It's my first priority."

"Good. Then as soon as possible, with whomever you select, I suggest we arrange a joint consultation with him or her at the embassy. For obvious reasons, I'd like to stay in the loop."

"That goes without saying."

Next Robinson paused, seemingly out of decorum rather than hesitation. Thorsson divined why. "I almost forgot," he said. "The cost of my airline ticket and taxi service." He reopened the zippered money pouch from which he'd just paid the apartment owner, to which Nosko had attended during his stint in jail. There were multiple envelopes inside, each containing a different currency. He made a spot inventory. "Will US dollars also be sufficient for the air ticket, converted at the current rate?"

"That would be fine."

Several minutes later she'd also departed. With his time now his own, Thorsson stepped onto the balcony again to behold Kreschatik. The boulevard was gleaming and rife with greenery in the late-morning sun, and the sky was expansive and blue. From below there was a hum of weekday traffic. Across the adjoining intersection, past the TSUM department store and up Khmelnitskovo Street, he could make out the corner of the Opera and Ballet Theater. After Alushta, the scale and anonymity of the big city carried sudden sensations of liberation.

His thoughts nonetheless remained on Robinson for a moment. In fact he hadn't been entirely forthcoming with her. He did intend to buy groceries before lunch. But after that his most immediate priority wasn't to contact lawyers. It was to call Yulia.

*   *   *

There were strict limitations on importation of foodstuffs to the hospital, particularly for patient consumption. The rules were precise, meticulously outlined, and posted in the lobby, elevators, and most waiting areas. Violators were subject to confiscation of prohibited items and expulsion from the premises by hospital personnel.

In their usual fashion, Yulia's mother and Aunt Ludmila completely ignored the regulations. Even the doctors knew better than try to stop them.

Today they'd brought food of soft variety, given that Pavel's jaw was wired shut. Moreover their insistences hardly ended there. Near the nurses' desk, Aunt Luda was now interrogating Pavel's main attending physician on her son's recuperation. "Should he still have so many bruises?" she asked him. "At this point I would think those would be healing."

"With respect, Mrs. Krylova, your son suffered a vicious beating just four days ago. Medically, he's lucky to be alive. His condition has now stabilized. But his recovery will take some weeks, particularly for the bones to reset."

"There's no risk of clots?"

"No patient who's been through such a violent trauma as Pavel is free of risks, but that particular one, I can assure, is under control. At present, all indicators are positive."

When the discussion concluded Yulia's aunt remained dissatisfied. Yulia and her mother joined her on the way back to Pavel's room. Cautiously, Yulia ventured a praising note. "I really do think the doctors and nurses are doing their best, Aunt Luda," she said. "Just since I got here, I can see that Pavel is improving."

"Do you remember how the doctors treated your grandfather and the result?"

"Yes."

The chapter remained a painful one in family chronicles, eleven years after the fact. Yulia believed Ukrainian medicine had advanced since then but decided to leave the theme alone. "Let's not forget about your status either, Yuliochka," her mother said. "Did you notice that woman just now in the waiting room? She was reading a copy of *Ukrainski Insaider*, with you right on the cover."

"I did notice, Mama. Fortunately she didn't seem to recognize me."

"You were just lucky."

When they reached Pavel's room, they refocused on him. That morning he'd already been attended by an orthopedist, a neurologist, and nurses administering salves and medications, and appeared on the verge of dozing off. He became alert again when his mother strode to his bedside, tears welling in her eyes. These were soon supplanted by a barrage of queries, which Pavel did his best to answer through his clenched jaw.

"Really, Mama," he said. "I'm making progress. The worst…is over. And I'm glad…you came…really."

His mother looked unconvinced. The two sisters walked over to the food bags they'd deposited earlier by the window and finally proceeded to unpack the contents. From beneath his bandages Pavel's eyes observed them with traces of fatalism. His mother turned back toward him.

"For lunch we prepared some apple sauce and pudding," she said. "I hope you're hungry."

"Please, Mama…I just ate…maybe…a little later?"

The two sisters reluctantly sat down on two chairs flanking the table, while the supervising nurse entered the room, carrying a clipboard. The woman walked to the end of the bed and consulted Pavel's medication table, checking off items on her chart. She also caught sight of the food items. For an instant she seemed inclined to object. Instead her gaze gravitated to Yulia and she did a double-take.

"Aren't you the girl in the magazine?" she said. "The one in Crimea…photographed with the American?"

Yulia stiffened and glanced over at her mother, who went immediately on guard.

"I'd rather not say," she answered, unconvincingly.

A fascinated smile spread over the nurse's face, as if she'd encountered a celebrity. "I read the issue this morning," she added. "I'm pretty sure it's you."

Yulia tried to ignore the woman's stares. She could hardly wait until she'd performed her function and left.

"I told you, Yuliochka," her mother said, still seated. "That nurse will run out immediately and tell all her colleagues. Word will spread all over the hospital. You won't be able to slip in here quietly to visit any more. I knew it couldn't last."

Yulia stared back at her mother and said nothing. She felt that she was being indicted for something that was not her fault.

"Does anyone here know you're Pavel's cousin?" her mother asked, pressing further.

"I guess I did mention it to a few people…maybe one of the doctors and a couple of the nurses."

Her mother took a deep breath. "Don't you see what this means?"

Yulia did but resisted the implications. She felt she had just escaped the fishbowl of Alushta.

"It means you'll now be even more exposed," her mother continued. She gestured over to Pavel on his bed. "The same people who did this to Pavel and tried to kill the American will put two and two together and realize you were involved in his original story. They'll set their sights on you next."

The room hung heavy and silent for a moment, troubled again by the specter of violence. It was Pavel who spoke next. "Your mother's... right, Yulia. Better to...lay low for now...stay away."

"And hide in your apartment?" Yulia asked. "You were abducted right outside."

"At least you're not...alone now...our mothers...are there."

As usual Pavel was the voice of reason. Another living arrangement would probably carry even more risks.

Yulia's mother concurred. "We'll be able to look out for you there, Yuliochka," she said. "It makes sense." She paused as another thought occurred to her. "On that note, do you intend to meet Thorsson, the American, now that he's here? I know you pulled him into this whole business and feel a responsibility. But wouldn't it be safer to stay away from him too?"

Before Yulia could answer her phone rang, now in the front pocket of her jeans, taut to her abdomen. With difficulty she managed to pull it out and check the screen, finding another call from Thorsson over Skype. Her first inclination was to move out and take the call in the corridor. But her discovery by the nurse made her think twice. Instead she turned her back and retreated to a far corner. To her slight chagrin, once again, he spoke Russian.

"Hello, Yulia. I've already settled here in Kiev. Are you able to talk?"

Yulia sensed the eyes and ears of her three family members on her from behind, especially her mother's. "Well, I'm in Pavel's hospital room right now, along with my mother and aunt..." She caught herself, wary of sounding standoffish. On his end, heavy traffic sounded in the background. "That's good news, though. Where are you now?"

"I'm on Kreschatik in an outdoor café..." He paused, as if to check the name of the place. "Coffee Time, just down from Maidan. I just ordered an iced latte to cool down and to celebrate my release."

Yulia was familiar with the café from her student days. What she remembered most were its broad sun canopy, central location, and proximity to pedestrians. Also that it was a favored venue of foreign men, keen on scoping out the unceasing flow of provocatively dressed young women in the warmer months.

"Coffee Time? Isn't that kind of public?"

"Well, let's put it this way. If you were walking by right now, you wouldn't necessarily recognize me."

"Why…what have you done to yourself?"

"Nothing extreme. But I'll leave the rest to surprise. Listen, I realize you're busy at the moment, but can we meet for lunch or coffee sometime soon, maybe tomorrow? I want to fill you in on the latest."

"Of course."

"Great. I'll call you back later to work out the details."

When Yulia signed off and turned around, Pavel was polite enough to retract his gaze from beneath his bandages. Her mother and Aunt Ludmila weren't quite so inhibited. She resigned herself to yet another update and justification.

CHAPTER 48

Mikhailov preferred to travel without trappings or entourage, which he knew set him apart from most others in the Service, particularly his contemporaries. Sometimes however, such as this morning, he had to adapt to necessity. The driver of his launch pulled up to the float, while another crew member threw out a line. Two of Zherdev's henchmen, muscled-up and wearing black tee-shirts, were already waiting. One secured the hull as he stepped out. "Oleg Konstantinovich Mikhailov?" said the second, from behind opaque wraparound glasses, hands crossed in front of his waist in a military-type pose.

"Yes."

The man offered neither smile nor welcome. Mikhailov had seen his type countless times before. If his intent was to impress or to intimidate, the effect was lost. Same held for Zherdev's ostentatious superyacht, moored about two hundred meters off shore.

"Right this way," the man said.

Mikhailov mounted the short ladder and followed him down the dock. Zherdev's villa loomed up on the bluff: an oversized amalgam of marble, polished granite, and incongruous motifs. On a scale befitting a czar, but without the taste. It had come into view amid the trees about a kilometer up the coast, just past Cape Aya. A portal emerged at the end, embedded in the rocks. The man opened a reinforced door and turned over his shoulder. "This is an elevator up to the main house," he said, pressing a button and beckoning Mikhailov to enter. The compartment was remarkably spacious. The hydraulics whooshed and whirred as they faced forward and started their ascent.

"No stairway?" Mikhailov asked. The man didn't turn his head.

"No," he answered.

Mikhailov decided he would reserve further questions for Zherdev. They had plenty to talk about.

Another muscled-up security goon met them at the top, together with one of Zherdev's young female assistants, leggy and well turned out. She carried more polish than the security muscle and smiled as she extended her hand.

"Mr. Zherdev has been expecting you," she said. "Right this way."

With elegant gait she led him through a palatial two-story foyer, encompassing a split-landing staircase and tall windows facing the sea, then through an extravagant living room, dense with gold-leaf furniture and brocaded pillows. Over a large stone hearth, Mikhailov's attention fell on an outsized oil-based portrait of Zherdev, his wife, and their dog.

The canine struck Mikhailov as the most virtuous member of the family.

The assistant gestured left with an open palm through open double doors, and they veered left onto a sun-splashed terrace, where he spotted the oligarch, sitting alone at cast-iron patio table near the balustrade. Mikhailov took in the 240-degree view over the sea as he walked across. Zherdev stood to greet him as he drew up, arch but respectful. Half the plundered assets of Donetsk were still no match for the reach and influence of the FSB. "Welcome, Oleg Konstantinovich," he said, shaking his hand with an effort at geniality. "I'd heard about you in Moscow. But I've never had the pleasure of crossing paths with you here, in my part of the world."

"My assignments have taken me elsewhere," Mikhailov answered. His new rank and status, he knew, required no advertising.

"I've understood you're on vacation."

"I was until a few days ago."

The no-nonsense tone of his pronouncement made Zherdev's smile vanish. The oligarch knew why he'd come. When they sat down a middle-aged maid appeared unbidden with a silver-tray coffee service. After asking Mikhailov for his preferences she poured out a cup and did likewise for Zherdev. Mikhailov took his time stirring in his cream and took in the view again for a moment. Zherdev opted to speak first, showing his unease.

"Compliments on the release of Axel Thorsson, Oleg Konstantinovich," he said. "I admit I didn't see it coming."

"You should have. This whole matter has spun out of control." Mikhailov paused to take a sip of coffee. As he did he heard the engine of another motor launch down near the dock. "Even worse, it's become a spectacle."

The word made Zherdev flinch. The oligarch knew that FSB's attitude toward adverse publicity in the West. Especially when it originated in Ukraine.

"I know that now," he said.

"You're just coming to this realization?"

"Yesterday, in fact. I finally saw the video from the hotel."

The only surprise, to Mikhailov, was that Yezhov had taken this long to provide it to the oligarch. He also surmised that Zherdev was now aware of Yulia Petrenko's role, quite apart from the magazine coverage. The oligarch's proxies in the Interior Ministry and the SBU had probably seen to that.

"How could this have happened?"

"Mistakes by my people," Zherdev answered. The oligarch struggled to give credence to his defense by reaching for his coffee cup and bringing it to his lips. "They thought Thorsson was responsible for releasing those files."

"And this was enough to order a hit? On a foreign citizen?"

Zherdev drew another deep breath. "Again, due to mistakes by my people."

"Your people? You're not giving yourself enough credit, Leonid Igorevich. I'd call it a blunder of your very own." The oligarch bris-tled, which was precisely Mikhailov's intention. Mikhailov paused for a sip of his own, only compounding the pressure. "How, then, did you progress from that blunder to yet another one? Namely, getting Thorsson arrested and thrown in jail?"

"By that point one of my men had died. The other one was in jail. I couldn't just let it stand."

Through his nostrils Mikhailov drew a deep inhalation, doing little to disguise his impatience. "What about the beating of Krylov? By that point the story was already all over the international media. The proverbial cat was out of the bag. You were instructed by Popov, our man in Kiev, to lighten up on the heavy stuff after the last episode. Didn't you listen?"

Zherdev saw an opening and decided to show some bluster. He pulled back his shoulders slightly with a smug look. Mikhailov could sense what was coming.

"I didn't realize the Russians favored soft treatment of journalists," he said.

The remark hit home, even from a glorified gangster like Zherdev. Mainly because Mikhailov knew it was true. However he sat up straighter himself and hit right back. "Listen, Leonid Igorevich," he said, returning his cup temporarily to its saucer. "You're missing the point here. This isn't about settling scores or getting your people off the hook. It's about keeping this whole business out of the headlines. Do I make myself clear?"

Zherdev had no other retorts in his quiver. He sat and stewed in silence.

"Listen further. We've helped you countless times over the years. And you've done favors for us in return. It's been advantageous for both sides. Now, if you had some sense, you would see that this is in your interest too." To punctuate the remark Mikhailov reached again for his cup and drew some coffee. Chastened, Zherdev did likewise.

"What do you want me to do?" the oligarch asked.

"First, lay off Thorsson. Krylov, too. No more attacks. No more harassment."

"You mean at Thorsson's current location in Kiev?"

Mikhailov exhaled hard again through his nostrils. Despite everything else the oligarch remained intent on showing off his access. Mikhailov wondered, hardly for the first time, how someone of such narrow bore became one of the richest men in Ukraine.

"Wherever he happens to be," he answered. "Hands off. Am I understood?"

"What if he starts talking to the media? As it is, I see his name and photograph these days every time I pick up a newspaper or magazine."

"I already have a plan in mind. The Russian government has some dealings with Allegheny Energy, Thorsson's company. Moreover Harcourt Bank is managing their initial public offering. And they do sizeable business with us as well. Let's just say I'll bring some influence to bear."

"I see," Zherdev answered. "But that still leaves the criminal case. If my man Moroz gets rearrested, the case will stay in the headlines."

"I'll address that separately. The first step is to get the charges dismissed against Thorsson. Naturally I expect you to stand back and not interfere."

"How can you be certain that all this will play out as you predict?"

Zherdev still had too much of the bilker in him to fall in line, Mikhailov could see. "That's not your place to ask," he answered, holding his hard edge. "And there's one more thing. You're not to interfere with Yulia Petrenko, either."

At the mention of Petrenko a wily, wolfish look flashed through the oligarch's eyes. "Ah yes, Yulia Petrenko," he said. "First, she's all over the tabloids with Thorsson. Next, I learn she's Krylov's cousin.

Then, yesterday…those videos top it up. Turns out she's been at the center of this business all along. She's become the bane of my existence."

Yulia Petrenko had obviously gotten under the oligarch's skin, perhaps for more reasons than one. Mikhailov would have none of it. "Whether she is or not it doesn't matter," he said. "Again, the rule is the same for her as for Thorsson and Krylov. Hands off."

"And how are you going to keep her quiet? Do you have a plan for that too?"

"Yes, I do."

"Might be wishful thinking. She's been nothing but trouble."

"I mean it, Leonid. That's not a request. It's an instruction. Am I clear?"

Zherdev fumed for a few long seconds. Mikhailov didn't like the hesitation.

"Clear," he said at last.

"Good." Mikhailov drained the last of his coffee and replaced the cup on the saucer. "I think we've concluded our business."

They rose to shake hands. Over the stone balustrade Mikhailov glimpsed a second launch near the end of the dock, tied up near his own. Closer to shore, some thirty meters below, he also spotted Zherdev's wife, walking out toward it. Trailing close behind her, with obvious enthusiasm, was the small, manicured poodle he had seen in the portrait over the fireplace.

"I was wondering where your dog was," he said.

"My wife is taking our yacht to Yalta to meet some friends for lunch," Zherdev answered. "After that they plan an afternoon cruise further down the coast. The dog enjoys it, so she brings him along."

"He doesn't prefer to stay here with you?

"Not really. The fact is, he's more my wife's dog. He doesn't seem to care for me so much."

Mikhailov was not the least bit surprised.

CHAPTER 49

On her way down Gorodetskovo Street from the metro Yulia couldn't resist several glances over her shoulder. By now she knew better than to linger at the newsstand near the crosswalk. Upon reaching the square she stopped and surveyed the outdoor seating area at Café Warsteiner, staying under tree shade. The tables of the café were shielded from the sun by an overhead canopy and filled with a standard lunchtime clientele, mostly businesspeople and tourists. She didn't take long to single out Thorsson.

She also did a double-take. Now she knew what he'd alluded to on the phone.

To her slight alarm he was seated right in the center, overlooking the fountain and in full view of the other lunch-goers. It was another choice which struck her as a little reckless. She adjusted her sunglasses as she entered and made her way to his table. Soon Thorsson spotted her as well. So did numerous male gazes, to her extra discomfort. When she reached him he rose to greet her, wearing a teal shirt and linen trousers that she remembered from Alushta. She also noticed his e-reader on the table, along with a half-finished beer. She settled in and exhaled.

"Is that your surprise?" she said. "The beard?"

"Yes." He smiled and reached up with one hand to stroke his cheeks. "Do you like it?"

She didn't know what to say. She was already nervous. She became conscious of the fountain bubbling next to them. "My first reaction is that you look like a Viking." She meant it. He really did.

"Well, I am of Scandinavian extraction."

"I thought you might be. Your name sounds like it."

"Half-Swedish and half-Norwegian, to be exact."

Their waitress came over and handed her a menu, after which Yulia ventured another discreet scan around other tables. Some of the reactions had abated, but people remained aware of them. She and Thorsson had claimed ongoing interest. She could feel it. She hoped they weren't summoning incidental news reports on their smartphones. Her face flushed a little when she found Thorsson examining her as well.

"Are those dark glasses your method of staying incognito?" he asked her.

"I'm doing my best." She made a vague gesture around the café and out toward the square, compact, half-shaded by trees and shaped like a wedge, on which several other outdoor restaurants and cafés were also located. "I know you're confident, thanks to your beard. And this isn't quite as out front as Kreschatik. But I still have doubts about being in the open like this."

"We should be fine. I don't see any reporters or photographers here."

"It's not just the media I'm worried about. It's Zherdev's goons." She met his gaze more directly through the barrier of her lenses. "With respect, I would think you would be too. After all, you were the one they tried to kill."

Her last sentence came out a little too loudly, also causing Thorsson's smile to fade. Luckily the fountain hushed her pronunciation. They paused to study their menus. Two minutes later the waitress came over to take their orders—a chicken salad and green tea for her and veal and fries for Thorsson. While they waited Thorsson recounted the details of his arrest, confinement, and ultimate release, as well as the decisive role of the Russian FSB, which struck her like a bolt from the blue. She in turn summarized Nosko's intervention, the arrival of her mother and aunt, and her visits to Pavel, including the episode with the nurse the previous day.

"How's Pavel doing, by the way?" he asked after taking a sip of beer.

This time she was careful to lower her volume. "They almost killed him. But now he seems out of danger. He'll probably need at least another three to four weeks to recover. But as long as all his broken bones heal okay, he should be fine, long term…apart from a few broken teeth and some scars."

"You've been thoughtful to look after him."

"I don't think so. After all I started this whole business" She could see Thorsson was about to reassure her but stopped him. "And now I can't even go back to the hospital. Thank God for my mother and aunt. I admit I had mixed feelings about them coming. But they've saved the situation."

He nodded before she continued.

"What about you? While you're waiting for all this to play out… for this FSB guy Mikhailov to intervene and so on…what's your plan?"

"This morning I had a meeting with my new lawyer at the US Embassy. Heather Robinson, the US consul whom I mentioned, was present. Certain processes are in motion. But the bottom line is that I'm simply laying low and staying out of view for the time being. In other words, I've got some time on my hands."

"Are you able to see some of Kiev, then? I mean on the sly, of course."

"I've been here eleven or twelve times before on business. So I actually know the city pretty well."

They paused again when the waitress appeared with their food. When the girl placed Thorsson's food on the table, Yulia saw her giving him an extended look, wearing a slight smile. As if she might have recognized him from her Facebook news feed…or more probably, because of the rugged effect from his beard. Either way he wasn't exactly out of view. When the girl was gone again, Yulia ventured her next query.

"I'd understood in Alushta you were some sort of businessman," she said. "How will this situation affect your work...and if you don't mind my asking, what kind of business do you do?"

He was already reaching for his knife and fork. Yulia remembered he'd just endured multiple days of jailhouse food. "No, I don't mind telling you," he said, looking down at his plate. "It is relevant. But I suggest we start eating first."

Yulia reached for her own utensils and followed his suggestion.

*   *   *

The cuisine was just as Thorsson recollected from previous visits to the café: rather appetizing for casual fare. He devoured his cutlet and his fries in parallel. Halfway through, he ordered another beer, which he'd also missed in his confinement. He then consumed another portion, leaned back, and blotted his mouth with his napkin, also wiping his mustache and beard, which he'd now recognized as an ongoing requirement.

"How much do you know about the energy industry?" he asked Yulia.

"Just the basics, I guess. Why?"

"What about hydraulic fracturing, sometimes called 'fracking' in English?"

"Isn't that where pressurized water is pumped underground to force up gas and oil?"

"Correct. That's the industry in which I work. My company is called Allegheny Energy, headquartered in Pennsylvania. We've developed a technology that covers a very specific piece of the process; namely, the drilling of small exploratory wells into shale deposits, at low cost, for purposes of sampling and analysis. We have proprietary software that goes along with the engineering. Our customers and clients employ us to determine the size of gas and oil deposits before they proceed with wider extraction projects and contracts. I'm the regional director for the countries of the former Soviet Union."

"Wow. That sound like a pretty responsible job."

"In some ways, I suppose. Most of it is sales work. Because most of the energy extraction rights in this part of the world are controlled by state-owned companies, my interactions are with national energy ministries...usually with deputy ministers, but sometimes even with the energy ministers themselves. I do some business in Russia, Azerbaijan, and Kazakhstan, but most of the demand is from countries without traditional energy reserves—for example, Ukraine and Armenia. Once we conclude a contract, we deploy a small team of engineers and analysts out into the field for evaluations. The ministries then take the data we provide them and determine whether their state-owned energy concerns are capable of proceeding on their own or need to involve one of the larger Western conglomerates."

"Does that mean you go out to remote areas?"

"From time to time. Mainly I just do the deals and see them through to fruition at the commercial level. That means I spend most of my time in the capital cities or other regional hubs, jetting from one to the other and essentially living in hotels. I also have to travel back to headquarters in Pennsylvania once per quarter to meet with the company president and other managers. Allegheny is a small, independent company, with about two hundred and fifty employees. Most of them are engineers and programmers. We're essentially still in startup phase. That means I have to cover a lot of bases."

Thorsson sensed that Yulia was impressed. He hoped for the right reasons. Moreover there was a less comely side to his activity. "It's not as glamorous as it sounds," he added. "The result is I spend more than seventy-five percent of my time on the road. I maintain a home base in Geneva, but I'm lucky if I get back there for a couple of times a month for three or four days."

This produced yet another reaction in her which he couldn't quite classify. He felt another surge of appetite and glanced down at his plate.

"But I suggest we finish our food before it gets cold," he said. "Then I'll tell you how my work relates to our current predicament."

CHAPTER 50

Thorsson's arrival and registration at the hotel now seemed to Yulia to have occurred ages ago. But her recollection remained vivid. Particularly that his original booking had been for two. She found herself reflecting upon this as he consumed the remainder of his cutlet and fries, and she addressed her salad. When he was finished he placed his utensils at a diagonal and took a swig of beer.

"All that doesn't sound too well suited to family life," she said, approaching the question obliquely.

"I don't have a family," he responded. "I've never been married. And I'll be the first to admit it. My private life has been rather disjointed, even decadent. My work has been a factor, I reckon. But not the only one."

"No kids?"

"No."

She felt a pang of sympathy for him, despite his jet-setting lifestyle. Thorsson sidelined her reaction by getting back on subject.

"My work relates to our current predicament on a number of fronts," he said. "The first and most obvious is that I've had extensive dealings with the Ukrainian government, especially over the past year or two. That explains all my trips to Kiev. In fact most of my meetings have taken place at the Energy Ministry at the other end of Kreschatik or the headquarters of Naftogaz across on Khmelnitskovo…both of them quite close to my current rental apartment."

Yulia nodded and suppressed, yet again, her association with Thorsson's building.

"That's given me an inside view into energy rights in Ukraine," he continued. "Namely who owns them and who ultimately benefits. Are you acquainted with Ukrainian law in this area?"

"Not the details. But as far as I know that the government has monopoly rights on both oil and gas."

"Also correct. Specifically through Naftogaz, which controls distribution and extraction on all national territory, including the waters off the Black Sea coast. Naftogaz and its affiliates have always been corrupt and opaque in their operations, going right back to Ukrainian independence in 1991. But up until four or five years ago, that corruption related primarily to distribution of Russian gas over Ukrainian pipelines. Now, with fracking technology, the venality has extended to energy extraction as well. It's become particularly acute since Yanukovich's election in 2010, when the president and his so-called family took overall control of the assets. Naturally I've always been kept a step or two away from the self-enrichment at the top. But I can tell you that the degree and magnitude of the corruption are mind boggling, particularly by Yanukovich and his inner circle."

Yulia's was hardly surprised. She'd long sensed the outlines. "In Ukraine it's unavoidable," she lamented.

"Yes, I'm afraid so—at least for now. Call it the seamier side of my work."

Yulia respected him for being open. She also wondered what he was driving at.

"But I offer that mostly as background," he continued. "What's relevant about my job—and about energy extraction in Ukraine—is that it relates very much to the question of agricultural reform. And by extension Pavel's story. Allow me to elaborate.

"Many of the shale formations in Ukraine where natural gas has been discovered lie under private farmland. This should be of little surprise. The vast majority of parcels handed over to private owners under the 1994 land distribution—most of them former workers on Soviet-era collective farms—were assigned these rights when fracking technology was practically nonexistent. Now many of these small farmers find themselves sitting on top of vast energy wealth, still mostly untapped. Unfortunately for them, however—given the circumscribed nature of their ownership—they are in no position to benefit.

"This is where land reform enters the equation. Even in other Western countries where the state has a full or partial energy monopoly on extraction—for example, Norway and to some extent in the United Kingdom—private property owners can at least benefit through royalties or lease income. In Ukraine, by contrast, they get nothing. However if the pending reform of agricultural land actually enlarges the property rights of farmers, that could change. That's one reason for the delays and obscurity of the surrounding political debate until now."

"In other words," Yulia observed, "Land reform doesn't just concern agriculture. It also concerns energy."

"Precisely. Yanukovich and his cronies like Zherdev want to keep that income stream to themselves. Moreover they're not alone. They get plenty of hidden support in perpetuating this scheme from one all-important quarter. Namely, the Kremlin. The Russians prefer the status quo as well, for different reasons."

"The Russians? I know Yanukovich has always been a tool of Moscow. But what's their angle?"

"As long the Yanukovich regime retains a choke hold on energy production—especially natural gas—the domestic energy industry in Ukraine will remain relatively underdeveloped. Or at least less developed than it would be with a more transparent and competitive market, driven from the bottom up by private landowners. That not only perpetuates the racket I've just described...it also prolongs Ukraine's longstanding energy dependence on Russia. Keeping Ukraine, in economic terms, a near-vassal state."

Hearing this, Yulia sat and fumed for a moment. However it was the sad reality. "Is that why this FSB operative Oleg Mikhailov has gotten involved?" she asked.

"That's a good guess. Russia probably prefers to tamp down this affair and make it go away. Hence Mikhailov's intervention in my case."

This didn't sit well with her either, even though Thorsson was benefitting in a roundabout way. The only positive part was that his view seemed to match her own.

"Here's the way I would summarize it," he said. "This reform doesn't just concern agricultural wealth and energy production. It concerns Ukrainian independence. The geopolitical stakes are huge."

Yulia took a deep breath. The bubble of the fountain steadied her a little. Finally she got her emotions under control. "Incredible. I hadn't grasped the full picture. No wonder Pavel's story caused such a violent reaction."

"No wonder is right. Though I'm sure Pavel is aware of these dynamics. He just hasn't had a chance, until now, to talk them through with you."

"No he hasn't. That's the kind of country he and I live in, unfortunately."

"Maybe that will change."

Yulia paused before responding. She knew foreigners tended to be more upbeat about the country's future than Ukrainians themselves. She tried to place herself in the optimistic camp as well. But it was difficult—perhaps now more than ever. "I hope so," she said. "Change is overdue."

With these words she noticed that Thorsson had thus far neglected his second beer. She'd continued to do likewise with her salad. The two of them had been too busy talking. She slipped in a few quick bites before they resumed.

* * *

Thorsson, she was realizing, had a loquacious streak and a capacity for verbal structure which she hadn't recognized in Alushta. She thought he would be well suited for academia or politics.

"Call those the macro influences," he said. "But there is also a very important micro factor which bears on our situation. Specifically: my energy company, Allegheny, is now preparing for an IPO, as it's called in English."

Yulia had trouble deciphering the acronym straightaway, which he detected.

"That stands for initial public offering. It's the financial mechanism that occurs when a private company offers sale of its stock to the public. Shares from such offerings are then traded on the stock exchange—in our case, the Nasdaq in the United States."

"I'm sorry...yes. Please go on."

"Well, take a guess as to which Wall Street institution is organizing the offering and serving as lead underwriter."

"Harcourt Bank?"

"You got it."

Yulia struggled to get her mind around the significance of this. At first pass, she did not succeed.

"My president back in Pennsylvania, named Ralph Waingrove, has been informed of everything over the past week," Thorsson resumed, "mainly through Heather Robinson. I also managed to reach him yesterday afternoon by phone and hear about the US end. Harcourt is already receiving a lot of unwelcome publicity thanks to Pavel's articles and the ensuing international news coverage. Now, if my case proceeds to trial, Harcourt's position will be complicated even further. But even more importantly, so will my company's IPO, which Harcourt is also managing, insofar as I'm one of their key managers."

"Oh no," Yulia responded. "The last thing Pavel and I wanted was to cause complications like that...for your company, I mean."

"You had no way of knowing. In your shoes I would have acted likewise."

She had heard this sentiment from him once before, on the promenade in Alushta. But that was before his jail time. Hearing it again bolstered her morale. She also relaxed a little inside and finally finished her salad. Seconds later their waitress appeared to clear away their plates.

"Would you like anything else?" the waitress asked them.

"Not for me, thanks," Thorsson said.

Yulia could see that Thorsson's beer was still more than half-full. In colder months she might have ordered tea. But this was midsummer.

"Do you have ice cream?" she asked the girl.

"Yes. Here are the choices."

The waitress handed her a dessert card. Yulia quickly perused the options and ordered a chocolate-covered sundae. She figured she'd earned the indulgence with her salad. She also waited to hear what Thorsson would say next. Whatever it was, she had the feeling it had been building in him for a while.

CHAPTER 51

There were numerous popular misconceptions about the sales profession, Thorsson had long believed. Among them that sales personnel spent most of their days schmoozing clients, talked more than they listened, and thought of little more than closing their next deal, thereby racking up their next commission or bonus. That money making was the begin-all and end-all, customer be damned.

However for the majority of its practitioners, in his experience, sales involved something more. Namely the elucidation and realization of mutual benefit. Integrity was just as necessary as the rest. How his customers distributed the benefits was almost an issue apart.

Another fallacy held sway. That was that salespeople had little time for intellectual pursuits. That they tended to be pragmatists rather than abstract thinkers. In reality he spent much of his working time alone: waiting in airport lounges, sitting on planes, eating solo in restaurants. Even with his smartphone at hand, he had plenty of time to himself. All of which left ample time for thinking…reading, too.

Prior to the Stoics he'd been on one track in particular. He put his beer mug on the table and refixed on Yulia, who'd already started her sundae.

"I should preface my next remarks with a disclaimer," he said. "Let me assure you that I am hardly antibusiness. On the contrary, I work in business and count myself a capitalist. Moreover I've had the unusual good fortune, at rather young age, of joining a start-up company in a fast-growing industry. I've therefore seen a business built from the inside out and come to respect the creative effort that is required—particularly from founders. In my company, these men have been true pioneers.

"I admit that fracking raises some environmental issues, which I'll address separately. But in the near term the technologies that Allegheny and its like have introduced have yielded enormous benefits to the US economy. Moreover, since the 2008–2009 financial crisis, they've provided a vital lifeline…at least until we can develop alternatives. Ukraine and other Western countries also stand to benefit—in particular, to reduce their energy dependence on Russia. That is, if they can get their own houses in order."

Thorsson paused to discern if Yulia was either bored or uncomprehending. She appeared to be neither, so he pressed on. "All of which leads me back to Harcourt Bank. By happenstance I started work at Allegheny in the thick of the crisis, and since then I've done considerable reading on it. Through it I quickly realized that Harcourt, along with three or four of the other largest institutions on Wall Street, played a major role in perpetrating the collapse. Even worse, they've reaped additional outsized gains in the aftermath, as national governments and central banks have intervened clean up the wreckage."

He stopped again, waiting for Yulia to consume another spoonful of ice cream. This time she interjected. "I've gathered banks helped cause the housing boom, which came crashing down," she said. "But that's about all I know."

"The role of Wall Street was much more insidious than that. Prior to the collapse, Harcourt and others created new-style debt instruments called mortgage-backed securities—essentially bundles of mortgages that yielded long-term, predefined interest, at least in theory. In reality many of these mortgages were unsound from the beginning. To Harcourt and others that didn't matter. They peddled them to investors as aggressively as they could. Ratings agencies legitimized the scam by assigning these securities high-grade ratings, which lulled everyone into complacency."

"Didn't anyone see the risks?"

"Very few, unfortunately. In part because Harcourt and other large banks further masked the downside through another new-style instrument called credit-default swaps. Most of these were sold by AIG, historically an insurance company but increasingly, in the mid-2000s, little more than a boiler-room operation. These contracts were supposed to protect against adverse price movements in the underlying securities. Through employment of this ruse, banks and hedge funds were able to dress up their books, perhaps Harcourt most of all."

"So what happened?"

"Unsurprisingly, the whole edifice did indeed come crashing down. All these new instruments proved to be bogus...often little more than worthless paper. The mortgage crisis exploded into something much larger, destabilizing the entire world financial system. If the Federal Reserve hadn't intervened, along with other national banks and governments in Europe and elsewhere, we would have plunged into an economic death spiral—the worst since the 1930s."

Next Thorsson paused for his own benefit, partly to contain his disgust.

"Didn't the banks suffer too?" Yulia asked. Her sundae was now more than half-gone.

"That's the thing. Hardly at all, in the end. Only one major bank was allowed to fail. Once the crisis hit, the rest were bailed out by the Fed. So was AIG. How? In effect, the Fed stepped in and liquidated most of these bogus instruments at face value, squaring the books of all the major players, including the big hedge funds that trafficked in this rubbish. Most of the financial big wheels who reaped obscene profits on the way up also got bailed out on the way down, losing scarcely a penny. And the sad fact is that the Fed had little choice. The financial sector now accounts for about eight percent of US GDP, an all-time high. As a result the whole economy is now rigged in their favor."

Thorsson paused and suppressed another swell of distaste. The bubble of the fountain made the effort a little easier. He examined Yulia again to see if he'd held her interest. He was also realizing she had more intellectual depth than he'd first supposed.

"What about the Harcourt guys at the conference?" she asked, pausing again between spoonfuls. "Were they connected with what happened?"

"Essentially, yes. Same crowd, same profit machine. Or better yet, same global racket. Now they're just trying to insinuate themselves elsewhere…even agricultural reform in Ukraine."

She displayed some distaste of her own.

"Their ravenousness knows no bounds. Marx was right about them."

"Marx?"

"Yes. Lately I've revisited him for the first time since university. Read almost everything he wrote. Engels and Lenin, too. Marx obviously got a lot of things wrong…you know that firsthand, having been born in the former USSR. But he also got a lot of things right. One was that in a capitalist economy the financial sector, if inadequately controlled, grows so large it hollows out the system from the inside—eventually, if the process is allowed to play out, engendering its very destruction."

Yulia stared back at him, her green-gray irises as intense as ever.

"How does that relate to the IPO Harcourt is organizing for your company? It seems you're mixed up with them as well."

"Good question. You're quite right; we are involved with them. And in our case, they are providing a real benefit—namely raising capital from private investors, which we need to grow our business. The problem is their role in the broader picture."

"Isn't there anything that can be done?"

"I'd like to think so. There have been some correctives during the Obama Administration, since 2009. But further action is clearly required."

At this Thorsson paused for a sip of beer. Despite Yulia's absorption he worried he had gone on too long. He was also ready to set the subject aside for now. He took another pull before speaking again. "Shall we call for the bill?" he said.

"All right. I've finished my sundae. In the meanwhile, if you don't mind, I'll excuse myself to the ladies' room."

Thorsson signaled to the waitress, then watched from behind as Yulia rose from her chair, exited the patio, and walked inside. Numerous other gazes swung onto her at the same time, for good reason.

Perhaps that explained why he'd underestimated her somewhat in Alushta. He'd been distracted by the obvious.

*   *   *

Yulia's head was swirling with Thorsson's pronouncements as she made her way to the restroom. She was impressed by his opinions and also a little startled. An American businessman singing praises to Marx? In the twenty-first century? Moreover he'd addressed all these obtuse subjects in Russian.

There was something else she'd noticed. In Alushta he'd always struck her as detached. Almost void of emotion, at least compared to her. On some of these bigger questions, however, he spoke with real conviction. He'd now activated her on many layers at once. On the way out she paused by the mirror to take in her image and adjust her hair, noticing also that her cheeks were flushed.

The aura didn't last. At the newspaper rack by the front door she stopped in her tracks. Sitting right on top rung, in full view, was the latest issue of *Vecherny Vesti*. With her photograph and Thorsson's blown up on the cover, under another garish headline.

The tabloid jolted her back to the present. She also realized she'd left her new sunglasses back on the table, leaving her face completely uncovered. She made her way back as discreetly as possible, avoiding the looks of the waiting staff and customers. The first thing she did when she sat down was to reach for the glasses and put them on.

"Have you gotten the bill?" she asked him.

"Already paid," he said, reaching for his e-reader. "Shall we go?"

"All right. And thank you for the lunch."

"Don't mention it. I'll walk with you to the metro station."

Yulia made an on-the-spot decision as they exited. For their next meeting, it would be better to choose a less public location. Someplace where they'd be more one on one.

CHAPTER 52

Vera's eyes were indistinct through her dark lenses. Mikhailov himself was wearing sunglasses besides. He was fairly sure though that she didn't bat her lids. It was the reaction he expected.

"You say you'll be gone just four days?" she asked him.

"Five at the most. A day and a half of engagements in Kiev, then two days' worth in London, if all goes well."

"That's not so long, I suppose. Dima and I can manage. And that still leaves a week after you get back. Right?"

"That's the plan."

For Vera, he figured, the trip actually held advantages. Any manner of FSB work was preferable to his writing. If all went well he might even forget about his book and abandon it altogether.

They were clad in bathing suits and reclining on two lounge chairs. Dima's towel covered the empty chair next to them. His paperback lay on top, while he swam toward the rounded hump of Medvedshonok Rock in the midmorning calm. As usual Vera refrained from delving. She knew only that Kiev and London related to his recent seaborne excursions and conferences with Rykov. On other scores, however, she'd grown somewhat concerned.

"You know I'll never stand in the way of your work, Oleg. What's worried me a little lately is your attitude. Not toward me or Dima. I mean some of your general comments."

"My comments on what subjects?"

"For example your remark this morning about Ukraine, as we headed down to breakfast. And a similar one just after your trip to Cape Aya. In both cases I believe you were referring to the Russian role here. This morning you used the phrase 'dubious rationale.' I can't help but notice."

"My job prevents me from being forthcoming with you, Vera. But I try nonetheless to remain truthful, to the extent that I can. I always have done."

"I know. Still…can I ask you if this relates to this assignment?" Her expression became slightly skeptical and defensive. "Or to something else, like this novel of yours?"

Through his intelligence work Mikhailov had come to appreciate the efficacy of questions. It was an approach he employed with his wife only when needed. The exigency now applied, provided he proceeded by careful increments. "I'll try to explain my standpoint as best I can," he said. "Let me ask you this, Vera. Have you ever felt unwelcome here in Ukraine over the years?"

"No, not really. The people are friendly. They all speak Russian fluently, even if Ukrainian happens to be their primary language at home. And my mother's from Kharkov, after all, even though she's lived in Moscow most of her life."

"Her example is relevant. What about here in Crimea? Anything to complain about?"

"Why would I complain?" She opened her palms outward and gestured toward the beach and then backward toward the resort complex with an encompassing motion. "It's like a slice of paradise here. This sanatorium is one of the best on the Black Sea. And we're given privileged access besides. Moreover the food is delicious…" She pulled off her sunglasses and squinted at him under the brightness with a perplexed and slightly wary look. "What exactly are you driving at, Oleg?"

"Please bear with me," he answered, before inserting several downbeats. He left his own sunglasses on. Seeing this, and apparently weary of squinting, Vera donned hers again as well as he continued.

"Can you offer any comments on the moral character of the Ukrainian people?"

By now her intellectual guard was definitively up. "Well, they are known for being corrupt," she answered, cautiously. "Bribery and graft are serious problems. You've said so yourself."

"Yes, I have. And it's most unfortunate...obviously we've been struggling with the same shortcomings ourselves."

This last sentence provoked a discernible reaction. Highly placed FSB officers did not ordinarily venture such remarks about Russia proper, even to their wives.

"What about their politics?" he asked.

"Chaotic, as far as I can tell...too many factions by our Russian standards...all struggling over the same small pie." Vera now leveled an even more appraising gaze. He could now see her eyes better through her lenses. "But you understand these political matters as much as anyone. Why are you asking me these questions?"

"I'm just seeking to establish context, that's all. So that I can address your original query."

"My original query? I asked you about the *Russian* role here."

Mikhailov smiled. His main intention was to coax out the essence. But he was not against a little amusement in the process. "Indeed you did," he said. "So now let me ask you this also. Do you think Russia is helping or hurting Ukraine at present, generally speaking?"

On this point Vera required little time for consideration. "Why helping, of course. They need us. First of all for our natural gas, which they can't get anywhere else at good prices. Also for our money. Let's face it: we're a rich country and they're not. Who else is going to invest here?"

As bright as Vera was, she was misinformed on the gas issue, like many Russians. Mikhailov blamed state-run media. But he ignored that variable for the moment. "What about their politics? Are we helping or hurting?"

On this point Vera was even more emphatic. "Helping, for sure," she said. "If it wasn't for us, they probably never would have freed themselves from the Turks. And we already talked about their corruption and chaos. Everyone knows they can't really manage on their own. That's been obvious since the breakup of the Soviet Union. They need us to create order and also to defend them."

"Are you asserting, then, that we've been excluded over these past twenty-plus years?"

Vera's guard rose higher still. Her next syllables were more cautious. "No not really…" She gestured again with one hand back toward the resort complex. "I mean the fact that we're here, at a place like this, says something. Russians still visit in large numbers. We're still involved in their economy…in their politics, too…we support certain politicians and so on…you know all that."

"Yes, I do. Therefore if we take that as a premise, is it fair to say that what's transpired here since their independence is partly our doing…indeed, perhaps our doing as much as their own? Or even before that…all the way back through the Soviet period to the Czars?"

Here Vera sensed she was being trapped. She also saw no path of escape. She nonetheless chose to stand her ground.

"Well, yes," she intoned, more aggressively. "I guess I would."

"Nonetheless our policies remain necessary and appropriate, in your view."

"Of course! Why wouldn't they be?"

Mikhailov paused, long enough for his progression to take hold. "The question I'm positing is this," he said. "Is it reasonable to indict Ukraine for all these national defects you've just defined, when we've never actually stepped back and let them decide for themselves in the first place?"

The circularity and feebleness of Vera's logic now lay bare and irra-
diated under the bright Crimean sun. She pulled off her dark glasses
again, this time more forcefully. She wasn't quite enraged, but her face
was simmering with redness.

She had clearly reached her limit.

"That's exactly what I was talking about! To me that notion seems
rather…unorthodox, to say the least. Especially from someone who
works for the Russian state. For God's sake, it's almost heretical!"

"My education and training taught me to take the macro view,
Vera."

"What exactly are you saying? That Ukraine doesn't need us? That
we should simply get up and leave? It's inconceivable! Any Russian will
tell you that."

In response Mikhailov finally removed his own sunglasses as well,
revealing the calmness in his own gaze. When he spoke again he also
modulated his tones and tempo, easing up on her. "Not at all," he said.
"We're too intertwined by the past for that. Kievan Rus gave us our
religion and written language, after all. Since then I would agree we've
done plenty for them in return. We suffered many ravages of history
together. And Russians and Ukrainians have intermarried for generations. You yourself are a direct result."

This family reference did little to sway her. "You make it sound like
it's been a sorry fate for both sides," she said, still defensive. "Nothing
but mutual grief."

"Hardly. At their best, our relations have been about common
advancement. Especially in the cultural sphere." He pivoted toward
Dima's empty chair and picked up his son's paperback from the beach
towel, page marked by an inserted postcard. The book was *Master and
Margarita*. He turned the cover toward Vera. "Take Bulgakov for instance," he said. "Born and raised in Kiev, but he wrote in Russian.
Gogol before him. Shevchenko and Les Ukrainka in the Ukrainian
language. There are a host of others."

"What about Pushkin, Tolstoy, Dostoevsky, Turgenev and so on?" Vera countered. "Your heroes, aren't they? We've given them more writers than they've given us."

"Maybe so. But the point is that the flow has run in both directions."

At this Vera's frustration reheated. "Once again you're evading my question," she said. "We were supposed to be talking about Russian policies toward Ukraine, not culture."

Here Mikhailov did not hesitate. "I'm evading nothing. What I'm contending is that our approach to Ukraine should be based on mutual reinforcement, not subordination of one side by the other. That if Ukraine is going to be drawn to us, it should be for the right reasons. In the political sphere and everywhere else. Isn't that a reasonable goal?"

He was still holding Dima's copy of Bulgakov in one hand. At last Vera gleaned both his argument and its implications. Only then did he replace the text on the empty chair. While she was still struggling to respond, he spotted Dima walking toward them up the beach, still glistening with water from his swim. "Here comes Dima," he added. "Once he dries off, I should probably tell him about my trip to Kiev and London. Wouldn't you agree?"

"Yes," Vera answered, still simmering but out of retorts. "That's probably a good idea."

As Dima approached them she continued to eye the paperback on the lounge chair. Her concerns, Mikhailov could tell, had re-centered on his writing.

And he had addressed her query exactly as he'd intended.

CHAPTER 53

From her seated position Yulia watched Thorsson from behind as he consolidated the items onto a tray. His summer-weight shirt hung loosely but outlined an idealized V: powerful shoulders tapering down to a cut waist. The effect was just as noticeable for his lower portions, clad now in trousers of light-gray cotton; his buttocks and thighs were dense-packed with muscle. She remembered his exercise regime in Alushta. Their subject matter the previous day had been so complex that she'd half forgotten.

He was actually quite a large, well-built guy.

This time they'd chosen a concession kiosk in the verdant confines of Mariinsky Park, on the back side of the palace and Parliament. Once again their table was situated near a fountain, though this one was about twenty-five meters away and of cast iron, pre-revolutionary vintage, with bigger streams and a more powerful flow than the one at Warsteiner. The park also offered more open space and fewer people, which she'd wanted. As he turned and brought their tray over he smiled at her through his facial growth, exuding a savage, Norse-style virility—more palpable than the day before.

She also remembered that he'd taken on two attackers in open water. And that he'd unleashed fatal blows on one of them. The

fact lingered in her thoughts as he unloaded the paper plates, nap-
kins, and plastic utensils from the tray, along with sausage rolls and
french fries, garnished with healthy portions of mustard; mineral
water for her; and a bottle of Chernigovskoe Beloe unfiltered beer
for him. "Not the healthiest meal," he said after sitting down. "But
we should indulge our appetites for animal fat from time to time,
right?"

"I guess so," she answered. "The main thing is it's quieter here and
less public."

"You're right about that. Sensible idea."

She looked around again to make sure they were unnoticed.
Traffic was audible from Grushevskovo Street, and the massive granite
and columns of the Cabinet of Ministers building were visible through
the tree limbs. But the rush of the fountain, together with the thick
foliage, provided a kind of muffled seclusion, separate from the city.
Most of the pedestrians in the vicinity were young mothers with children, pushing strollers and paying the two of them little attention. For
now they were the only patrons at the kiosk.

Thorsson wasted little time before reaching for his sausage roll.
Yulia waited for him to take several bites and gulps before posing her
next questions. She wanted to make sure she framed them right. "We
got so caught up yesterday in work and politics we neglected other
things..." she ventured. "Do you mind if I ask you some personal
questions?"

He glanced at her over his sausage roll through his sunglasses.
"Not at all."

She paused again, careful. "I was just remembering that you actually...killed a man. How did you do it? It was two on one, after all."

"I didn't tell you this earlier, but I swam competitively and played
water polo at high school and university. My water-polo experience
gave me a lot of training in evasive moves in the water. Let's just say I
know how to defend myself. I think my two assailants weren't counting
on that. In addition, though both of them were pretty muscled-up,

they seemed a little deficient in cardiovascular fitness. As the fight wore on, that began to show."

"I see...of course I remember you working out every morning at the hotel." At this point Yulia paused again, with a question that interested her even more. "What about the fact that one of the men died?" she asked. "I know you were acting in self-defense. But have you had any trouble adjusting to that? I mean morally?"

Thorsson finished chewing his mouthful of sausage and dough and added a couple of french fries for good measure. He also seemed intent on proper framing. "The whole episode still seems surreal," he finally answered. "And I have thought about it a lot, especially when I was in jail. A man's life was extinguished, which has been challenging to integrate. But the bottom line is that the attack was unprovoked. Would I have done anything differently? No. I had little choice. It was either them or me."

"Of course I agree," she said. "Still, I don't know how I would have reacted, afterward. Prayed for absolution, maybe."

Thorsson took a swig from his bottle of unfiltered beer, still appearing just as careful as she was. "That's a perfectly suitable response," he said after swallowing. "But in this instance I found philosophy more helpful. That's been true for me on a lot of fronts lately."

"Philosophy? What kind?"

"Stoicism in particular. In fact during my vacation I'd just completed some rather concentrated reading of its most formative thinkers: Epictetus, Seneca, and Marcus Aurelius, among others."

"I know little about them, I admit."

"I can try to summarize, as best I can. In general, the Stoics frame human existence as a fraught proposition...that the natural world is unpredictable, chaotic, and often dangerous to life and limb. That other human beings are malevolent just as often as they're well meaning, and in any case their behaviors are mostly beyond the control of the individual. But that's not a prescription for despair. It calls, rather, for pragmatism, objectivity, and detachment. As well as awareness that life can bring both setbacks and breakthroughs, often for random reasons. The key is to adopt the right attitude."

"I like that approach."

"I found it helped me form a context for the attack and for that man's death, intellectually and morally. I've also reminded myself in recent days that life can bring adversity and joys in close succession, though of course I'm not counting on the latter at the moment."

Yulia remembered how collected he'd been in Alushta, despite all the forces arrayed against him. The same seemed to holding here in Kiev. Now she better understood how he'd done it and figured she should apply some of the same concepts. She'd also taken note of Thorsson's remark about prayer. "Are you a believing person?" she asked him.

"I was baptized as a baby and raised as a Lutheran. Now I would probably call myself an ecumenist. However lately I've come to rely more on my own reason than spiritual doctrine. What about you?"

"Russian Orthodox."

"Practicing?"

"I try. But I admit I often fall short."

"Don't we all?" At this Thorsson took another swig of beer and smiled. Yulia smiled back. They'd gotten some sensitive subjects out of the way. It also seemed liked a good time to finish their lunch.

*　　*　　*

Where they went next remained unscripted. Which in turn had prompted her choice of clothing for the outing: light cotton blouse, shorts, and sandals. Thorsson suggested they stroll toward the Dnieper, and she agreed. To be safe both of them kept on their sunglasses. They rounded a bed of flowers, passed a statue of Lesya Ukrainka and proceeded down the walkway, shaded by a canopy of leaves. "You told me about your job yesterday," she said. "What you didn't say is how you got it. It seems to me like a pretty responsible position for someone as young as you."

To Yulia's surprise, Thorsson laughed. "First of all, I'm not all that young anymore," he said, smiling through his beard. "I've already been at this for almost five years. But yes, I admit I've been lucky. The beneficiary of random good fortune, as the Stoics might say. This was my first job after graduate school."

"Did you study petroleum engineering or something like that?"

"Hardly. I majored in Russian language. Back then I had the vague intention of entering the State Department or perhaps becoming a foreign media correspondent. But after graduation both of those notions proved unrealistic."

Yulia was struck by the parallel with her own situation. She'd found her solution. She was curious to hear how he'd found his.

"About the only sectors of the American economy that were booming at the time were banking and real estate," he continued. "But those didn't really interest me, so I widened my scope. To my disappointment that didn't yield any opportunities either. The result was that I resorted to a series of part-time jobs, including lifeguarding and some part-time swim coaching at the local YMCA, just to put some money in my pocket. With my fancy degree I was back to living with my parents, with few resources of my own and a negligible social life. It was a frustrating period. Graduate school seemed about the only way out. So that's what I did after two years."

To this point Yulia had become so engrossed she'd lost track of where they were. Looking around, she realized they were nearing the wood-themed amphitheater and the plaza overlooking the Dnieper. The latter was bathed with hot early-afternoon sunlight. "Shall we sit in the shade for a moment?" she said. "I want to hear the rest of this."

"Sure." They did as she'd suggested, settling on a bench just short of the intersecting alley. "Anyway...I decided to gain a business credential as well. So I entered the MBA program at Northwestern, in Chicago."

"And that led you toward the energy business?"

"Not right away. This time round, the overall economy was teetering, for reasons I broached yesterday. Almost no sectors were hiring. With one exception: the domestic gas and oil industries. Moreover, as luck would have it, one of the nation's primary new regions for natural gas extraction was Western Pennsylvania, which is where I'm from. Many of the companies there were also interested in expanding overseas. When I realized this I retraced to my parents' again and began circulating resumes. Within three weeks I had a job. Five years later, here I am."

"Great story," Yulia observed. "Your perseverance paid off."

Thorsson laughed again. "You might say that. But I'm also a realist. From the Stoical perspective I was probably just the beneficiary of random fortune."

Yulia wished she had been so lucky. Or that Ukraine could produce the same kinds of random fortune as the United States. "You're thirty-three, aren't you?" she said. "I recall it from your guest profile."

"Yes, that's correct."

"Same age as Jesus Christ…In his decisive year, I mean."

The remark came out spontaneously. It prompted him to smile again. "You're the second person in Ukraine who's mentioned that lately," he said. "The other happened to be the prosecutor in Alushta. But believe me, Yulia, I'm no moral exemplar. Quite the opposite, if you knew the sordid details. Or a Christ figure, either. I'm just trying to get through this in one piece."

Yulia wasn't sure how to react to the humor. But he smiled again, so she did the same.

"But enough about me," he continued. "What about you? I've gathered you went to university here in Kiev. After graduating, how did you end up working at the hotel?"

She recounted her own tale of uncertainty and tribulation and her gravitation to the hotel business. It lacked Thorsson's idealized ending but had actually played out reasonably well until a few weeks earlier. He listened with a sympathetic expression.

"At least you got numerous articles published," he observed. "That's more than I achieved. Did you write in Russian or Ukrainian?"

"Both. There were only fourteen or fifteen in total."

"Online or print?"

"Most appeared in both."

"Could you send me a few of the links?"

"Sure." Yulia was a little surprised by his curiosity. Apart from Pavel and her parents, and perhaps Alexander Brisiuck, he was the only person who'd showed interest in her journalistic skills for months. She also had to admit it felt gratifying.

"Now I have even more insight into your actions with the flash," he continued. "Shall we continue toward the river?"

Yulia did not object. Despite the hot sunlight she was infused with sudden energy. This talk with Thorsson, even more than the first, had bolstered her spirits.

*   *   *

Five or six young children played on the empty stage of the amphitheater, under the watchful eyes of their mothers in the gallery. On the plaza she and Thorsson steered around several teenage boys on skateboards and two girls on bicycles but attracted meager attention. When they reached the railing on the other side, they stopped and looked down the steep wooded incline toward the Dnieper. The river, more than one hundred meters lower, was wide, forceful, and iridescent. Through the leaves Thorsson spotted several crew shells out on the water and pointed them out to her.

"We've alluded to Vikings several times now," he said, "mainly in jest. But in all seriousness, I've long been fascinated by the role the Varangians played in the foundation of Kievan Rus. Maybe it's because of my Scandinavian heritage."

"So you're familiar with our history?"

"I've done a little reading on it. My understanding is that the foundation occurred in the 860s and 870s, when Rurik sent Varangian emissaries down the river in longboats from points north, seeking routes to the Black Sea and Constantinople. They identified these hilltops as strategic and made them their main base of settlement. They then integrated with the indigenous Slavic population—initially under Prince Oleg, then under a succession of Varangian leaders and their descendants. Then Kievan Rus was Christianized about a century later in 987, when Prince Volodomir converted. Is that more or less accurate?"

"Very much so. My compliments. Do you know that Askold, one of those emissaries from Rurik, is buried on this hillside, about a kilometer from here?" With an outstretched hand and extended fingers she gestured south down the bank.

"No, I didn't know that."

She racked her brain for additional facts. "Some accounts even say that Askold converted to Christianity very early on and was baptized in the 870s. If so, that made him the first Christian leader in Kiev. That was, until he was murdered by Prince Oleg, when Oleg traveled down the river from Novgorod and took over the city in 882."

"Rather brutal side chapter. I hope he wasn't nailed to a cross."

Yulia was suddenly sorry she'd mentioned it, after her earlier comment. Thorsson observed her reaction. "I was joking," he said, smiling again." To reassure her further, he placed his palm on her back, transmitting a precipitous, virile sensation through her thin blouse. "It's a shame our view of the river is partially obscured by the branches here...are you taking the metro back home from Arsenalna?"

"Yes."

"As I recall, the observation deck on the main plaza has an unobstructed view. Shall we stop there on our way?"

"There are often a lot of people about there. It may not be a good idea."

"If so, we'll just veer around it."

"Okay."

When they turned away from the railing and began walking again, he removed his hand—a politeness she almost regretted. They swung onto the broad connecting alley, with its canopy of chestnut trees and cooler shade. A slight breeze stirred in off the river, arousing fertile scents. She became aware again of his height and physique, which had made such an impression before lunch.

She also remembered that he'd paid for the meal, already for the second time. The fare had hardly been elegant. And Thorsson was a different sort of foreigner than Massimo. Less suaveness, perhaps, and more physicality. With philosophy and history thrown in besides, she now knew. But he was starting to provoke a similar unbidden attraction. She wasn't as detached as Thorsson. She realized she had to be careful. Given everything else that was going on, this was no time to repeat past mistakes. Or to surrender to her emotional side either.

CHAPTER 54

Pedestrians became thicker on the walkway as they progressed past Mariinsky Palace, which Thorsson attributed to the lunch hour. He also noted that he and Yulia were now attracting generalized attention, much as they had on the promenade in Alushta. At the endpoint, little to his surprise, they found fifteen to twenty people congregated on the observation deck, gazing out at the Dnieper or posing for photographs.

"You were right, Yulia," he said. "Too many people. The last thing we want is to get caught in someone's backdrop."

"That's for sure," she answered. "Let's get out of here."

They angled across the plaza and bent onto another canopied alley, into the south quadrant of the park, where Yulia seemed to relax somewhat. A little further along, Thorsson felt his phone vibrate in his back pocket. He pulled it out and checked the screen, finding a text message from Heather Robinson: *Axel—there is a new development regarding your case I should inform you about. Please call me this afternoon. Heather.*

"That was a text from Heather Robinson, the American consul," he said, slipping back the device back. "Apparently there's some new development in my case."

"Aren't you going to call her?"

He made a quick scan of passersby. "Not here. I'll wait until I get back to my apartment, with more privacy." He looked ahead and gestured forward with his outstretched hand. "Shall we bear right up here, toward the fountain? There are fewer people."

Yulia agreed, and as they adjusted course, she appeared to grow more thoughtful. "I've been meaning to ask you about the legal side," she said. "You now have a lawyer. A consul is also looking out for your interests. I have neither—just my mother and aunt, really. I hope you don't mind me asking…but are they thinking at all of my position in this?"

"That question has already occurred to me, Yulia. I'll raise it when I call Heather Robinson back this afternoon."

"Thanks. I appreciate it."

Thorsson observed her expression in profile. "I won't just look out for my welfare in the coming days," he added. "I'll look out for yours, too. I mean it."

Tears moistened her eyes, which caught him a little unprepared. In the next instant, she slanted closer and brushed his side, long enough to transmit dampness and flesh-warmth through the fabric of his shirt.

Both of them now fell silent.

They were now approaching the cast-iron fountain at the crest of the mound, almost identical to the one in the lower park. It was ringed by two concentric walkways, with flowers planted between them in swaths of vibrant colors. Thorsson drew in a bouquet of fertile scents through his nostrils and watched as Yulia squatted down and leaned over a cluster of irises, swelling out her hind-flanks and indulging their fragrance as well. Her shorts and light blouse had grabbed his attention before lunch. Now he couldn't keep his eyes away. His impressions from Alushta were only affirmed. Meanwhile she kept her gaze on the flowers.

When he reached her she stood again and looked him in the eyes. "We can't escape our challenges," she said. "Talking helps. But we also need to enjoy nature, right?"

"I agree."

"After all, what's more basic than nature?"

"Nothing. Moreover this whole thing originated from agriculture."

To his pleasure she released an uninhibited laugh, which he joined—another attractive side of her he was seeing for the first time.

The main gate to the park lay about 150 meters down the incline. A group of teenagers was approaching from the side—the very sort, Thorsson guessed, that made ample use of their camera phones. "Shall we continue on to the station then?" he said.

"Sure."

She seemed in no hurry to complete the journey. As they finished rounding the fountain, she walked alongside with him without touching but still near enough to permeate his senses.

Thorsson counted himself fortunate, again, to have just studied the Stoics. And that she found merit in them also. They did need to celebrate nature. But they also needed to stay aware of current dangers.

*   *   *

On Mazepi Street Thorsson resolved to reestablish an exercise regime of some kind for as long as he stayed in Kiev. For conditioning but also for general equilibrium. Without the Black Sea close at hand he would have to be creative. Yulia was silent until they were halfway down to Arsenalna Square. "Your joke about agriculture got me thinking," she said. "Have you ever visited the Ukrainian countryside? I mean the real interior?"

"Three or four times, for half-day visits…exploration sites."

"Ever been to a Ukrainian farming village?"

"Passed by them. Can't say I've ever stopped in one."

"Smelling those flowers reminded me of them. Any interest in an excursion? I have a female relative we might visit. Her village might give you some insight into rural life here, and why I did what I did in the first place."

"I like the idea. Just give me two or three days to make sure my court case is on track."

"Okay. Meanwhile I'll see what I might organize."

Arsenalna Square was bordered by vending kiosks and crisscrossing with pedestrians, which kept them on guard as they entered the station, passed through the turnstiles, and stepped on the first escalator. On their descent a steady flow of passengers swept past them on ascending direction, two tracks over, many making lingering scrutiny between the advertising tablets. Thorsson followed Yulia's example, keeping on his sunglasses on and turning sideways toward the wall to obscure his face. "Do you know Arsenalna is the deepest subway station in the world?" she said to him about halfway down, keeping her volume low to avoid attention.

"I know many stations here are deep," he answered. "But I didn't know that."

"The platform is one hundred and five meters below ground."

He glanced down. It was indeed a long ride.

At the intermediate level, they crossed left under the rotunda and stepped onto the second down escalator. This time the track next to theirs was activated, bringing the upward traffic even nearer. "If you look again," Yulia added, "you'll see this second escalator is even longer than the first." Thorsson cautiously rotated his head for another look. Almost at once, amid the line of ascending faces, he spotted a man about fifteen meters down: mid-twenties, with a trimmed beard similar to his own, making intent eye contact. His first intuition was that the man's interest stemmed from their shared facial growth…until he also noticed the high-end camera around the man's neck and a compartmented case slung at his hip. The man was a photographer—judging from his gear, a professional.

Instants later he was almost upon them. His gaze shot past Thorsson's shoulder toward Yulia, provoking another flash of recognition. Before the man could wield his lens, Thorsson swung his face back toward the wall and encircled Yulia's waist with his arm, holding her in place. He didn't hear any telltale clicks as the man intersected them and passed.

"Photographer," he said in a low voice, bringing his mouth to her ear.

"I saw. Just our luck."

"Let's keep our faces away as he moves higher."

Thorsson waited ten seconds. "Don't look yet," he added. "I'm going to check what he does next." He glanced cautiously around the edge of her hair and looked up. The photographer was now scrambling up past standers toward the intermediate level, clearly intending to reverse direction. This time Thorsson didn't pause.

"He's coming after us. Let's go!"

Hewing left and overtaking six or seven other riders, he bolted down the grilled metal steps as fast he could, while Yulia's sandals clapped close behind him. He made just one glance back. Twenty meters from the bottom he heard a train approaching through one of the tunnels and turned back over his shoulder.

"Come on!"

At bottom he reached back for her hand, which she grasped with some force of her own. They dodged half a dozen discharging passengers as they shot onto the platform, straight toward the first car. The train's automated public-address system sounded again in Ukrainian when they were three meters away: *The doors are closing. Stand back.*

Thorsson bounded over the threshold and pulled Yulia in behind him, a second before the doors shut. The engine's electric motor engaged and the train started forward again just as the photographer hurtled out onto the platform, out of breath. This time he made no attempt to raise his camera. Thorsson and Yulia watched him through the windows as he receded and disappeared down the tunnel.

They held hands for some live, extending instants. Thorsson then shifted his open palm up to her lower back, just as he'd done in the park. Like the photographer she was breathing heavily but more from excitement, as far as he could tell, than exertion. He felt her moisture and warmth again through her tee-shirt as he brought his mouth to her ear.

"Close call," he said.

"More like lucky timing."

"And you were pretty fast on your feet. Compliments."

From his side position he saw her cheek flush. Kreschatik station was only a minute away, but they were still standing close. She made no effort to separate. They remained in place until he got off at the next stop.

CHAPTER 55

Russian Embassies the world over flourished on routine, Mikhailov knew: precise opening hours, meticulous protocols, strict hierarchies. American embassies were little different. There were rules and frameworks for just about everything. Which helped explain the timing of his meeting with Heather Robinson at six o'clock on a Wednesday evening, when the US Embassy in Kiev was officially closed for business. For this meeting special arrangements were in order.

He arrived alone by taxi and presented himself by intercom at the east gate, where he was buzzed in immediately. Four solemn-faced security personnel put him through a thorough security check; he was then escorted by two of them through the receiving area and into the main building, left into the consular section, through a small open-office area where all the desks were deserted, and down a corridor where all doors were closed. And, it was safe to presume, locked as well.

The US State Department had businesslike, albeit well-circumscribed, contacts with FSB officials in some other parts of the world. Not here in Ukraine. Here an FSB officer was subject to extreme control.

Halfway down, he was ushered into a medium-sized conference room. Robinson was already there waiting, her notepad placed on the opposite side of a long table of polished wood. She rose to greet him, with the same watchful manner as in the first encounter. At her suggestion he took the seat across from her, near the head of the table. Somewhat to his surprise she was the only interlocutor present. Over her shoulder, though, he spotted a small, unobtrusive video sphere mounted on the ceiling in the corner. He figured there were others as well. This exchange was being monitored live, probably by two to three in-house CIA personnel. Robinson, as smart as she was, had been given a well-defined agenda. There would be no scope for mistakes.

"First Mr. Mikhailov, I should thank you again for your intervention with the Alushta prosecutor's office. You did just as you promised. Since then, we've also done everything possible to fulfill our end of the understanding."

"I'm aware of that. And we also appreciate your cooperation. It makes my task easier."

"You requested this meeting. So perhaps I'll let you start."

"Thank you. First I'll update you on my further actions to date. Two days ago I visited the individual who we believe ordered the attack on Thorsson. He is a Ukrainian citizen named Leonid Zherdev, who was also a participant in the Harcourt conference. I assume you and the embassy are familiar with him and his activities?"

"Of course."

"In that meeting Zherdev did not explicitly acknowledge his role. But he saw little purpose in denying it. I explained the position of the Russian Federation. That is, that we expect no similar occurrences in the coming days and weeks while this matter is being resolved. I have little doubt that he will comply."

Zherdev's back-channel associations and sympathies were well known in diplomatic and intelligence circles. Therefore Robinson did not inquire about the means of suasion. "For the US government, Thorsson's physical safety remains of primary concern," she said. "Therefore the question bears asking. What is your degree of confidence in this assurance?"

"In situations like this, there is always an element of human unpredictability. But short of placing Thorsson in a secure environment, such as the one here at your embassy, I can affirm my highest possible level of confidence. Thorsson will remain free from harm, not just from Zherdev but from other interested parties as well, including the Ukrainian SBU. I have also taken preliminary steps toward the dismissal of all criminal charges against him, which will require some additional time. Toward this end, however, I have also had to make certain assurances in return."

Mikhailov paused. The CIA observers in adjoining spaces were now listening, no doubt, with extra attention.

"The first is that Thorsson also agrees to drop any pursuit of criminal and civil charges against his surviving attacker, known as Igor Moroz, or against Zherdev, either here in Ukraine or in justice systems in Europe and the United States."

Robinson showed no outward reaction. "I met with Thorsson and his lawyer yesterday," she answered. "We discussed the abandonment of criminal charges against his attacker. Both he and his lawyer expressed their amenability to this. They will, of course, need to review the sequencing and details. On Zherdev I will have to consult them further."

"Naturally. The second is that if the charges are dismissed against Thorsson, the US government will drop all further referral to this matter, publicly and otherwise."

This was a request that Robinson appeared to expect. "That decision will require several days for formal approval," she said. "But that also strikes us as reasonable."

"Finally, I have also had to assure all interested parties that Thorsson will permanently refrain from discussing this matter with the media, both here in Ukraine and abroad, when the charges are withdrawn."

This time Robinson beheld him across the table. As unflappable as she was, her dismay was unmistakable. "Mr. Mikhailov, surely you must know that in the United States, rights of free expression are constitutionally protected, unlike those in Russia. The US government has no way of making such a guarantee and, frankly, would not even seek it from Thorsson in the first place."

"Of course not."

"Then how can you possibly issue such assurance?"

"This situation requires incentives and inducements, shall we say, rather than coercions. Thorsson is a Western businessman accustomed to the profit motive. The same is true of other Western parties to this equation. I've devised a corresponding plan."

Robinson held an unswerving gaze across the table as he elaborated.

"What does it entail? Harcourt Bank has played a central role in this matter, through their sponsorship of the conference and their relationship with Zherdev. By coincidence, Harcourt also is the lead underwriter of the upcoming IPO of Allegheny Exploration, Thorsson's employer. It also so happens they have extensive relations with the Russian Ministry of Finance. That gives me certain tools of leverage. I now intend to use them."

With each layer of overlap he'd mentioned—and each reference to Harcourt—Robinson's eyelids narrowed. He remembered her broken engagement to a Wall Street banker.

"I'm listening," she said.

"I'm flying to London tomorrow," he said. "There I have meetings scheduled with several top Harcourt executives, including one from the United States. If all goes as planned, the president of Allegheny Exploration will be present as well. I aim to find a solution that all sides will support, and that ultimately, Thorsson will accept as well."

"What form will this agreement take?"

"The form of a contract: the best kind of guarantee available in this situation. One that covers all the points we just discussed."

"Will Thorsson be informed of this directly?"

"Not of the details. Those will be communicated through you and his lawyer. Naturally I'll hope for your endorsement, when the time comes."

"I can make no assurances at this stage. But I'll be waiting."

"That's all I can ask. Is there anything else you'd like to discuss before we conclude?"

Robinson glanced down at her legal pad. A different kind of disapproval flitted over her features. "There is one more item," she said. "Normally I wouldn't raise this issue, in view of my responsibilities as consular officer. However Thorsson has made a specific request that I do so. It concerns Yulia Petrenko. From our perspective her role in this affair remains somewhat vague. But she's nonetheless assumed considerable prominence in the media, as I'm sure you're aware." She paused for affirmation as Mikhailov nodded. "For this reason Thorsson has grown concerned about her safety. He asked that you consider her welfare as well, as you move your plan forward."

"You can tell Thorsson that I already have," Mikhailov responded. "Those details will also be addressed in the contract, along with the rest."

"Good. Thank you."

Robinson made a mark on her legal pad. As if Yulia Petrenko was now crossed off her list.

CHAPTER 56

Thorsson boarded the eastbound metro at Kreschatik at 5:47 a.m., finding nine or ten other passengers already seated in his train car. Several glances flitted his way, taking his brightly colored training gear, but this time none lingered. Several minutes later he disembarked at Arsenalna station, filed through the base concourse, and mounted the escalator. Today the parallel descending track was almost empty. The same held for Arsenalna Square on ground level. From its northwest corner he began his jog down Mazepi Street, similarly void of people, including random photographers.

His smartphone was in his zippered side pocket, but this morning he'd turned it off before leaving his apartment, to avoid tracking. This morning he was headed out with a special purpose.

Halfway down the avenue, he crossed over and cut right through the intersection, circumventing the underground passage. The gray-granite obelisk of the Glory Monument came up on his left, one of its surfaces refracted with early sunlight. Thirty paces further, nearing the gold domes and crosses of Pecherskaya Lavra, he crossed again to the left and revisited his phone conversation with Heather Robinson the previous evening.

"Mikhailov told me he was meeting with several top executives from Harcourt," she'd told him. "He said he hoped that Ralph Waingrove, your CEO, would also be there. He planned to present them with a proposal along the lines he described to me."

"A proposal? Does that mean there's no predefined agenda?"

"I don't think Mikhailov needs one."

"How is that possible? I understand Waingrove's attitude, but Harcourt is an institution with worldwide size and reach."

Robinson had her response with a sour edge. "Let's just say that when the Russian government calls, international bankers usually heed the summons."

Her implication was that the FSB was dictating the terms. The imbalance had made Thorsson a little uneasy. All the more when his subsequent call to headquarters confirmed that Waingrove was already en route.

By time he reached the monastery, with its high perimeter walls and enclosed spaces, he became aware again of his vulnerability. And Yulia's, too. At the complex's main gate several small groups of women in head scarves were coalescing, bound for morning prayers. They presented a benign tableau but scant reassurance.

Today he had another solution in mind. One which related to Yulia as well.

To break clear of the area he ratcheted his pace higher until the Motherland statue came into view straight ahead. A short distance later he trotted down the interspersed steps to the fore plaza and accelerated again at bottom, shooting through a tunnel lined with heroic bas-reliefs from the Great Patriotic War. Finally, near the base, he drew to a stop and checked his watch.

The time was now 6:05. As he'd expected the plaza was deserted.

Before beginning he drew a long inhalation, taking in the scents of grass and trees on the surrounding hillsides. He also confronted reality. Discussions in London were beyond his control. The most appropriate response, therefore, was Stoical. To concentrate on more immediate factors, ones he could influence.

Like exercise.

Without further preliminary he chose an even quadrant of cobblestones and launched into an adapted version of his routine from Alushta: ten sets of thirty squat-leaps, alternated with equivalent sets of push-ups. By sets three, his pulse and breathing rose near his anaerobic maximum, and by sets five, his arms, pectorals, and quadriceps were burning with oxygen deficiency—exactly the sensations he wanted.

During his seventh set of squat-leaps an unwelcome noise intruded—a single car approaching the plaza up the opposite hillside.

He tracked the sound, and in his right-peripheral vision, saw the vehicle pull into the small parking area forty meters away. Its engine turned off at once. When he completed his repetitions he turned to take a look. The car was a black BMW Five-Series with dark-tinted windows. No one moved to get out: tabloid photographers or anyone else.

Zherdev's goons, back on his trail? Ukrainian or Russian security organs, alert to his new location? The license plate, from such distance, provided no clue. Their means of finding him was also puzzling, given that his phone was off.

Either way there was little sense in fleeing. Even less in showing fear. He made a quick decision. Rather than retreat he dropped to the pavement again and pumped out thirty push-ups, keeping his senses alert. When he rose to his feet, he glanced over again, and finding the vehicle inert and its occupants still inside, continued his workout, glancing over for verification at the parking lot during each changeover.

Upon completion of ten sets, he walked over to a bench along the periphery wall, positioned himself with a clear view of the parking area, and placed a foot on the wooden slats. He elongated one hamstring, then the other, and proceeded to address his Achilles tendons, calves, knees, and lower back. When he was done, he paused again for a long look at the sedan.

Its doors remained closed. At last he began to walk back across the plaza, the Motherland statue looming over him and the car at his back. He realized he presented an easy shot target, if the car's occupants wanted to do away with him.

The shot never came. He reached the hero-tunnel again, and as the passage bent left, calculated he had moved out of the sedan's direct line of sight.

It had not been his fate to die in the waters off Alushta. And it would not be his fate to die here this morning on this deserted plaza in Kiev either. Whoever occupied the car, he reckoned, their presence here seemed to be more signal than aggression. If they could find him here, they could find him anywhere.

Though for now Oleg Mikhailov's pledge was holding. Moreover, Thorsson hadn't even compromised his workout, which gave him some additional satisfaction. All the same he resolved to call Yulia soon after breakfast to warn her. Just in case she encountered similar trouble.

CHAPTER 57

The noise disturbed Yulia's dream in fragments and persisted until the vision and story line—such as they were—dissolved into a void. Seconds later Octavia stirred along her legs, and the feline's paws hit the floor. At last Yulia also engaged her senses and identified the source. The sounds came from the kitchen but penetrated the double door of Pavel's living room: metal utensils against plates, a knife against a cutting board, the opening and closing of the refrigerator.

Once again her mother and Aunt Luda were up fixing breakfast.

She groped down her body for shielding, but apart from her thin tank top and panties, found only bare, warm skin. The sheet lay off to one side. She rolled onto her back, opened her eyes and stared at the ceiling. Chirping birds became audible through the open window. With a slight groan she then reached for her smartphone, perched on the upholstered armrest, and focused on the on-screen digital readout. The time was 7:05, which meant the two sisters were bound shortly for the hospital. With a blend of exasperation and guilt she swung her legs out and sat up to collect her senses.

When she stood, she caught her image in the mirror of Pavel's bookcase. Her hair was a tangle and her eyes looked bleary and still half-asleep, but she took in the whole. Her lips swelled out as usual, too provocative looking. Lower down, though she'd never considered her-self big busted, her breasts this morning appeared to be bursting out from her top, nipples and all. Her waist remained narrow enough, but an expanse of exposed flesh swelled out just below, rendering her hips so lush and expansive that her panties—stringed and translucent in the first place—concealed practically nothing at all. Her thighs only exaggerated the effect—even more than the photo spread. Her moth-er and aunt were already feeding her too well. Once again she looked like an oversexed barn vixen, a milkmaid who'd indulged too much of her own sweet cream and honey butter. It was no wonder Thorsson's gaze had wandered down over her body the previous day at the park.

Same drawbacks as always. The bane that came with the blessing.

Octavia meowed from the doorway and redirected her attention, showing more important priorities. Yulia walked over and let her into hallway, where she made straight for the kitchen. Before following her Yulia replaced her tank top with a tee-shirt and pulled on some jeans. By time she reached the kitchen her aunt was already crouching near the door and feeding the feline.

"I would have done that, Aunt Luda," she said.

"She looked hungry. Why wait?"

"I feel like I'm doing nothing around here."

"No need, Yuliochka. Pavel is grateful you're here. And as his mother, so am I."

Her aunt and mother were one and the same. Once they were ac-tivated there was no stopping them. Her mother, indeed, had already laid out her breakfast, consisting of brown bread, cheese, sausage, yo-gurt, and apricots.

"Go ahead and sit down, Yuliochka," she said. "Coffee will be ready in a minute."

With a sense of inevitability Yulia did as she was told. The quanti-ties the sisters had prepared, as usual, were far more than she wished to consume at that hour of the day. "In fact, I'm glad you're up," her mother said from the stove, as she placed the copper pot on a burner and lit the gas. "We were just talking about you."

Yulia girded herself and took a bite of bread and cheese. She could already guess the gist. And she'd hardly cleared her head.

"It seems like you and this Axel Thorsson are spending a lot of time together since he arrived," her mother continued. "Several hours each time you meet, as far as we've counted."

Aunt Ludmila refocused her attention away from the cat onto Yulia, picking up her mug of coffee.

Yulia noted her gaze. "That included transport, Mama. And they were just lunches..." She took a deep breath. "Besides, I've already explained why. I got him into this mess. Therefore I feel responsible for him."

The water boiled up in the Turkish hand pot, and her mother turned off the flame. "I understand that, Yuliochka...here, your coffee is ready."

While her mother poured out the mug Yulia added a sliver of sausage to the bread and cheese and took another bite. The two sisters seemed to have already finished their own breakfasts. "Are you meeting him again today?" her mother asked.

Yulia had to swallow first. "I don't know yet. We haven't made any plans...perhaps not until tomorrow."

Both sisters were now arrayed around her, she realized, still standing and holding their coffee mugs. At last she lost her composure.

"Could the two of you please sit down for a moment? I feel like I'm under assault here!"

The two of them glanced at each other with forbearing expressions that Yulia found somewhat irksome. Finally they joined her at the table. "He's assumed a sudden importance in your life," her mother said. "Naturally we're curious."

"There's no romance between us, if that's what you're implying."

"We didn't say there was. We'd just like to meet him, that's all."

"Well, we certainly can't invite him here to the apartment. I'm sure Pavel would agree with me."

"That goes without saying."

"Good...let's leave the idea aside, then." In an attempt to head off further discussion Yulia took another bite, followed by a gulp of coffee. She'd already abandoned any notion this morning of reducing her calorie intake. Her added flesh wasn't going away anytime soon.

"Our idea is different," her mother resumed after a more modest sip. "It so happens we plan to go into the center tomorrow. Provided there are no seasonal thunderstorms, of course. Might we at least meet him somewhere for tea?"

"The problem is the media, Mama. You know we have to be careful in public. And I'm not even sure when I'm meeting him next."

"Will you talk to him this morning on the phone?"

"I expect to, yes."

"Then please mention the idea. There must be a quiet café somewhere. I'm sure you can remember one or two from your student years."

"I'll think about it."

"Good. Let us know."

Yulia was relieved when her mother at last abandoned the subject and reached for a piece of notepaper on the side of the table. She examined the sheet for a moment and slid it across within reading distance. "This is a grocery list we've put together," she said. "We plan to stop at that small supermarket on the way home from the hospital. Anything you'd like to add?"

Yulia scanned down the designated items. "I have a better idea," she said. "While you're gone, I'll do the shopping. Save you the trouble. It's the least I can do."

"What about getting noticed in the store?"

"The supermarket's only one block away. Plus I have those big sunglasses."

"All right...just be careful, Yuliochka."

Yulia said she would be. While her mother and aunt finished their coffees, she resumed her breakfast. She also restudied the grocery list. Anything to divert their interest from Thorsson.

*   *   *

Yulia could hardly remember the last time she'd used a grocery cart rather than a handbasket. Perhaps during a trip home to Nikolaev during the Christmas holidays. She also thought the quantities on the list were much more than they needed or that she wanted to eat. But through long experience she'd learned the futility of stymieing her mother and Aunt Luda—especially on matters related to the kitchen.

The same held true of their idea over Thorsson. By now she'd resigned herself to it.

She reached the last items of the list, to which she'd objected—in vain, as usual. Her mother and Aunt Ludmila planned to make sweet *syrniki* pancakes. She'd already placed the necessary eggs in the cart, together with the other cooking ingredients. Finally, near the cash register, she added four bars of dark Roshen chocolate, her mother's favorite. And one she was likely to indulge as well. She loaded the items onto a checkout belt.

She'd now resigned herself to big curves, for as long as this lasted.

To be safe she kept on her sunglasses in front of the cashier girl and paid with the cash her mother had insisted on giving her, along with a collapsible pull cart. She was now glad to have it. More often than not, she had to admit, her mother's advice was sound. She encountered only a handful of people on the way out, most of them elderly. Once she was clear of the store she congratulated herself on her stealth.

The sentiment vanished when she saw the car parked in front of the store on Tartarska Lane, right along the sidewalk. A midsize BMW with black-tinted windows. The car hadn't been there when she'd entered.

Her foot was already off the curb by time she considered alternative routes. To steady herself she took a deep breath when she pulled the cart to the opposite side, then turned right toward the perpendicular pedestrian stripes. She then ventured a glance back over her shoulder. The windows remained dark and closed. Her heart slammed hard again when she heard the car's engine start as she crossed again.

She quickened her pace down the sidewalk and tried to stay even. She only had to reach Pavel's short side street and then his courtyard. Within minutes she could be back in the safety of the apartment. For now the BMW was keeping its distance. Ten meters from Pavel's access it stopped alongside her, just one meter from the curb. This time her reaction was less controlled.

She turned toward the vehicle and froze. For five long seconds... then five more...she stared straight at its blacked-out windows, wondering if she should reverse direction and flee. The back passenger door opened before she had the chance, and a man stood up on the other side. Stocky and muscular. Tight black tee-shirt. Shaved head and sunglasses. She'd only seen him once before, from a distance, but she recognized him at once.

Igor Moroz.

He rested one forearm on the roof of the car and gave her a sneering smile, his manner and expression sending a shudder to her bones. "Need any help carrying up your groceries?" he asked. "We'd be happy to assist."

Yulia noted the first-person plural. For all she knew there were four or five men in the car. She managed to get two words out. "No thanks."

"Are you sure Yulia Borisovna? We could bring them all the way up to your cousin's apartment."

The use of her patronymic made her shudder again. She felt her voice crack as she responded. "I said no thanks."

Yulia watched him. To hold herself together she thought of her mother. In this situation her mother would maintain her ground. Yulia endeavored to do the same, as best she could.

"Okay. Just thought I'd ask," Moroz answered. He laughed as he lowered himself back into the car. Yulia thought she heard more sniggers inside before he closed the door. Her knees still weak, she stood and watched the vehicle back out again and continued down the street, the cart still in tow.

Upstairs at the apartment Octavia examined her face as she crossed the threshold, sensing at once that something was amiss. Yulia closed and locked the door, picked up the feline, and held her in her arms for a moment before putting away the groceries. She required another ten minutes of recovery in the living room, the cat on her lap, to fully collect herself. She decided Thorsson's Stoicism could take them only so far. Time had come, for both her sake and his, to appeal for divine assistance.

Thorsson rang her on Skype before she'd picked up her phone.

CHAPTER 58

The lobby of the Savoy on a Friday morning offered an inside view of twenty-first-century capitalism, live and up-close. If not its actual workings, Mikhailov reckoned, then the concentrations it yielded. These were the higher reaches. And his fellow Russians, after a seven-decade absence, were back out front.

From his silk-upholstered armchair beside a carved hearth, he observed and listened as he waited. There were as many hotel staff and personal attendants in evidence as guests, and their carefulness and hushed tones served to regulate the through-flows and ambient noise, notwithstanding the marble floor and vaulted ceilings. Very little of the world's jostle and harshness breached this sanctum. Apart from occasional muffled phone chirps from the concierge station and an intermittent cell phone, the most predominant sounds were the clinks of chinaware from the lounge, where liveried waiters poured coffee from silver serving pots.

He'd nonetheless heard his native tongue from all corners. Russian seemed to be the most utilized language after English.

In any case he could spot his compatriots from a distance.

By way of example, a middle-aged mother and her daughter approached from the restaurant. The daughter, a strawberry-blonde with pale skin and blue eyes, looked about sixteen years old, the same age as Dima. She was already as tall as her mother and wore elegant designer clothes. Their accents were Muscovite. He heard references to Harrods and residential properties before they angled toward the concierge station.

An English estate agent was already there waiting.

This was Friday. And that meant, even in midsummer, that there was other business to be conducted as well. At this stratum, he'd noted, the conductors were almost all male. He'd spotted several tête-à-têtes on his way past the lounge. The majority of the guests, either seated on the scattered divans and armchairs or in circulation around the lobby, were men wearing business suits, just as he was. Every few minutes a bellhop, chauffeur, or female assistant would materialize and escort one or two of them to a car, waiting outside. Their presence explained why the Russian Embassy had booked him here, and the FSB was willing to foot the bill. The Russians around him were the class of people he was serving. He had to operate in their chosen milieu.

The incongruity did not escape him.

For seventy-plus years, his organization had been the sworn enemy of global capitalism. Now, under different name, the FSB had flipped sides.

Mikhailov made no pretense of Marxism. But for him broader moralities had somehow gone missing along the way, here and back home. The deaths of his parents presented an example.

And so did Ukraine, the more he got involved.

He checked his watch. Stanislav Volodin, senior economic counsel from the embassy, was due to arrive any minute. As if on cue, Volodin appeared on approach seconds later, wearing the same category of elegant suit and silk tie as the business guests. Volodin was five years younger than Mikhailov and acted as the main local liaison of the Russian government with the City of London. Mikhailov rose from his armchair.

"Have you found the hotel to your satisfaction?" Volodin asked him, shaking his hand.

"More luxury than I need, really. But yes. It's quite comfortable, thank you."

Volodin smiled. High finance imposed its own protocols. "We try our best," he said. "Meanwhile I've reviewed the communiqué you sent yesterday, and your purposes are clear. I also understood that you wish to lead the meeting. Is that correct?"

"Yes, that's my intention."

"Of course I have no objection," Volodin responded. "However I would like to review some details beforehand. Shall we do that on the way?"

"Sounds suitable."

"Good. I have an embassy car and driver waiting outside. Harcourt's headquarters are on Black Friars Lane. The drive there is less than two kilometers, but with traffic that should give us ample time."

A liveried doorman reached out and propelled the revolving door forward for them as they exited the lobby. Their vehicle, a large black Mercedes with diplomatic plates, was waiting in the hotel's interior roundabout. Upon seeing them their driver started the engine, while another uniformed doorman stepped forward at once to open the car's rear door. As Mikhailov extended his briefcase and climbed in first, he saw Volodin slip the man a folded five-pound note. Their car edged out of the courtyard as they settled in and Volodin extracted a folder from his portfolio. Out on the Strand, as they merged into traffic, the river came into full view. Mikhailov gave the hotel one last thought before they addressed business.

His room had a large desk and an expansive view of the Thames. He'd already envisioned three or four hours of writing that afternoon.

He could live without five-star accommodation. But it did offer some advantages.

*　　*　　*

One of the lobby-level receptionists at the Harcourt building conducted them up by elevator to the sixth floor, where a secretary was waiting. After a precise, courteous greeting she led them out along a vast, horizontal trading floor, dense with computer screens and hundreds of youngish, well-groomed faces, taut with concentration. At the space's far corner she then turned through double glass doors and down a wide corridor of polished wood, modernistic artwork, and sleek fittings. The hum behind them receded. If the route and trimmings were intended to impress or to underscore Harcourt's heft, Volodin appeared unaffected and in his element.

"That was their trading floor for corporate debt," he noted to Mikhailov from the side, at discreet volume and in Russian. "Including our own, of course."

At last the secretary opened the door to a conference room and ushered them inside, compelling Mikhailov to realign his brain to English. He caught a postcard-worthy view through the large plate-glass windows, encompassing the dome of Saint Paul's Cathedral. Six people, all standing, were already arrayed along the near side of the conference table. A tallish man with styled hair and a charcoal-gray pinstriped suit, in his late forties, stepped forward. Mikhailov already knew him to be chief of Harcourt's European investment banking operations and a Briton.

"Pleased to meet you Mr. Mikhailov," he said, extending his hand. "I'm Niles Fletcher." He then turned to Volodin. "Hello Stanislav," he said. "Good to see you." He gestured down the table, along the side closest to the door. "Allow me to introduce everyone else here."

Fletcher presented each in turn, all men, as Mikhailov and Volodin moved down the table to shake their hands: Alexander MacPherson, head of Harcourt's Ukraine desk; Hugh Curtis, head of fixed-income trading for Harcourt in London; Ralph Waingrove, the president and CEO of Allegheny Exploration; Michael Bequette, Harcourt's lead underwriting manager for Allegheny's initial public offering; Gennadi

Kuzmenko, ambassador of Ukraine to the United Kingdom; and David Lancaster, Harcourt's lead counsel in London. Volodin was already acquainted with half of them.

Fletcher invited Mikhailov and Volodin to take seats along the other side, facing the view of Saint Paul's. Mikhailov had not spelled out his exact position in the Russian government. But all six were well aware of the organ he represented.

As they sat down, he could see he had their full attention. Fletcher opened the discussion. "The political and legal developments in Ukraine which we're here to address are naturally of great concern, Mr. Mikhailov," he said. "We've also all read the preliminary memorandum you sent two days ago. Given that this was your initiative, we'll let you begin."

Mikhailov took one token glance down at his notes. He then looked back up across the table, directing particular attention at Waingrove, something of an odd man out among the finance wheels. The energy entrepreneur was a solidly built, ruddy man in his early fifties, with sand-red hair and blazing blue eyes, a little more on edge than the others.

"I've summarized the events of the past twelve days in my memorandum," he said. "So they require no elaboration here. Allow me to start, then, by noting what I perceive to be the overlapping interests of everyone at this table. None of us have welcomed these events. They've produced a wave of negative international media coverage, an unprovoked assassination attempt on a foreign citizen, and an ongoing criminal case with potential ramifications for Ukraine's political and economic stability. Though the Russian Federation has not been a direct party to these events, we also view them with serious concern. Mr. Volodin and I are here to help find a way out."

He paused to gauge the reactions of everyone across the table. They remained locked on.

"I am not here to assign blame," he continued. "Nonetheless, I think the first step should be to define the parties responsible and also the parties aggrieved."

Fletcher maintained a poker face. Ambassador Kuzmenko became more sober.

"First, the parties responsible...let us be forthright. Harcourt Bank organized the conference in Alushta, in cooperation with the Ukrainian government. Many of the Ukrainian business figures in attendance are clients of Harcourt. Various Ukrainian government officials were also in attendance. The leak that resulted in the initial wave of media coverage occurred from the conference. That's where this trouble began.

"What happened next—when the American Axel Thorsson was attacked—transformed it into an international sensation, a growing diplomatic issue involving the United States, and a potential political crisis in Ukraine. Leonid Zherdev, a figure with close ties to the current presidential administration, was the perpetrator of the attack. He is not represented here, but in addition to his political ties he is a de facto constituent of Harcourt Bank. Several representatives of the bank, for example, hold board seats on Zherdev's companies. Responsibility therefore lies with Harcourt Bank and the Ukrainian government."

Mikhailov paused. Fletcher's stare became more acute, the Ambassador Kuzmenko's more fatalistic. Both could guess what would soon follow.

"Now to those aggrieved," he continued. "Axel Thorsson had neither connection to the conference nor direct links to any of its participants. He came under attack due to an inane mistake on the part of Zherdev and those who work for him. He was subsequently arrested for homicide on false pretenses and jailed, and has since come under an intense media barrage. His employer, Allegheny Exploration, represented here by Mr. Waingrove"—he nodded at the CEO—"has seen its business in the region jeopardized. The company has also experienced adverse media coverage that—as I understand—has been detrimental to its upcoming initial public offering in the United States. Am I correct?"

Bequette seemed to consider a comment. But Waingrove spoke first. "That's an understatement," he said in a graveled voice. "But our primary concern now is Thorsson's welfare. I want to make that clear."

"Rightly noted," Mikhailov responded. "The first requirement, in our view, is therefore for Thorsson to be cleared of all charges. He should also remain unharmed afterward, in Ukraine or elsewhere. Leonid Zherdev will be obliged to stand down. Secondly, safety guarantees should likewise be provided for Yulia Petrenko, a receptionist at the hotel who has also been inadvertently caught up in this controversy." Mikhailov waited for comments or interjections. There were none. "Thirdly—and just as importantly—Thorsson must stay out of the media spotlight going forward. Call this, if you will, the price of our intervention. How you achieve this, and how you persuade him to cooperate in this, is a matter I'll leave up to you."

Fletcher and the two Americans seemed to discern at once what Mikhailov had in mind. They raised no objections. Kuzmenko was less sanguine. "With all due respect, Oleg Konstantinovich," he said, "enlisting the cooperation of Thorsson and Petrenko is one thing. And I understand you've already spoken to Zherdev. But our judicial system and security structures can be...how shall I put this...slow to act. The dismissal of charges may take time."

Mikhailov expected such protests from the ambassador and gave them no oxygen. "There is no extra time in this case, Gennadi Dimitrivich. Certain processes are already underway in Kiev. We expect you to urge them along. Am I understood?"

Kuzmenko blinked. The reaction was tantamount to a flinch. "Yes."

Mikhailov kept the press on. "However as I said, the Russian government also assigns responsibility for this affair to Harcourt Bank," he said. "Accordingly, I will now cede to some brief remarks from Counsellor Volodin."

Volodin was adept at his role, despite his youth. He performed on cue, directing his primary attention at Fletcher. "I am here to underscore the support of the Ministry of Finance on this matter," he said, looking at the banker evenly. "Four Russian companies, all told, are planning forty-five billion dollars in corporate bond offerings in October and November, Niles, as you're well aware. One of them is Gazprom. All are controlled by the state. Harcourt is currently slated to be one of the lead underwriters on all four. However final announcements are not due for three weeks. In the meantime, we would appreciate your full cooperation on this matter."

Fletcher was just as adept at these exchanges, with considerably more experience. He held a practiced, unwavering gaze on the younger Russian, then swept his eyes back to Mikhailov. "Your expectations are clear, gentlemen," he said. "However, they're also very general. To fulfill them on our side, we'll have to consider the specific means toward those ends."

"Quite so," Mikhailov answered. "I'll therefore leave the details up to you." He looked around the table, reserving a particular gaze for Waingrove. "My time in London is limited. Counsellor Volodin and I will return at this same hour tomorrow morning. I'll expect commitments then."

There were no objections from Fletcher or anyone else. Everyone, even Waingrove, understood the bottom line. On matters such as this, the FSB did not negotiate.

CHAPTER 59

Tabloid photographers now struck Yulia as benign, relative to other hazards. All the same she donned her sunglasses on the up escalator. Outside, however, on the busy plaza fronting Lev Tolstovo station, skies were clouding, signaling a summer downpour. She found her mother and Aunt Ludmila already waiting. Both carried umbrellas, despite leaving the apartment much earlier. Each also carried a small shopping bag. She asked them how their excursion went.

"We ended up buying items for Pavel," her mother answered.

Yulia expected as much.

To her exasperation she found herself growing nervous as they crossed Antonovicha Street. On the opposite sidewalk she tightened her clasp on her handbag, looked down at her muslin sundress, and smoothed the lightweight fabric along her thighs. Her appearance was hardly her only concern. In these situations her mother had a way of embarrassing her.

"You said you know this café, Yuliochka?" her mother asked when they reached the corner.

"I used to come here from time to time. It's sort of a student place. Now that it's summer, I hope it will be fairly quiet. It's also air conditioned." The sign for Café Bravo came up ahead on their left, across from Shevchenko Park. "Thorsson is punctual and often early," she added, "So he may be there when we walk in. Before we do I should warn you that he has a beard. Therefore don't be shocked."

"A beard?" her mother responded. "I thought he was a businessman."

"He is. He started growing it in jail. Now he's kept it to stay incognito."

Her mother considered this as they went inside, where Yulia spotted Thorsson seated at a table along the wall with a clear view toward the entrance. He rose to greet them at once, smiling and polite in a way that softened his stature. He also employed the precise grammar that by now she took for granted. During introductions she observed her mother's reaction. Her mother had already seen him in the photographs. But now she appeared to like what she saw, beard or not. Same for her Aunt Luda.

She tried to stay composed as she took the chair next to him, with the two sisters opposite, and a student-age waitress approached with menus. To her relief just one additional table was occupied, by a man in his sixties, taking tea with a newspaper. Along with the waitress, there was only a bartender. She hoped that would make this exercise a little easier.

Once they'd ordered, Thorsson framed the meeting as a pleasure, circumstances aside. Her mother seconded the notion but was also contrite. "Of course we regret that you were dragged into this," she said.

"By now that hardly matters," he answered. "I should also say straightaway that I don't blame Yulia in the least. Your daughter did the right thing."

Her mother's estimation only appeared to trend higher. Yulia felt her face reddening and cast a glance at her aunt, who was looking Thorsson over with equal interest. When he asked her about Pavel, she recounted their visit to the hospital that morning and summarized his condition, which continued to improve.

Thorsson held the upbeat tone. "I'd like to say that I believe Pavel's stories on agricultural reform were courageous and necessary," he said to her, "just like Yulia's initiative. He suffered consequences much more severe than my own. I consider journalists like him to be critical to Ukraine's future, in order for the country to overcome this corruption problem and realize its potential."

Her aunt thanked him. It was clear that Thorsson had now won them both over.

The waitress came with the tea, supplying a brief respite. But Thorsson's comments had given her mother an opening. "Do you know Yulia studied journalism at university?" she said when the waitress had gone. "In fact she had quite a number of stories published."

"I do know that, and I'm very glad you mentioned it..." Thorsson grasped his teacup with his fingertips and looked at Yulia from the side. "I clicked through the six or seven links you transmitted and read your articles, Yulia. I'm not a native speaker, of course, but as far as I can judge, they're excellent."

"That what I say!" her mother responded. "Her father and I have always thought she's talented!"

Yulia hurried a swallow of hot tea, causing some discomfort in her throat. "Mama, please. You've always exaggerated about that."

"I don't think so, Yuliochka. And your father and I aren't the only ones with this opinion. I've said so many times."

Thorsson replaced his teacup on the saucer and transferred his open palm to Yulia's lower back, just as he'd done in the park. Once again the contact prompted a spontaneous quiver along her spine. "You do have talent, Yulia. It's evident from your articles."

Her mother observed his gesture before he withdrew his hand again. Now she was even more emboldened. "I know your job at the hotel pays well, Yuliochka. But I still feel your talent is going to waste."

Yulia felt her face going even redder. "Could we please just drop the subject, Mama? We have enough other things to deal with." She checked her watch. "Just a reminder...I plan to take Axel to a high service at Saint Volodomir's right after this. The service starts at five o'clock, and the church is about a ten-minute walk from here. So we don't have a whole lot of time." She turned to him. "That is…if it's still okay with you."

"Of course it is, Yulia. I'm looking forward to it."

Her mother then shifted in her chair and looked out the window. "Looks like rain," she said. "You're welcome to take one of our umbrellas, Yuliochka."

"I wouldn't want to do that, Mama." Yulia also looked out toward the skies. "With luck, the rain will hold off until we get there."

She still felt a tingling sensation under her muslin where Thorsson had touched her back. There were still fifteen minutes to withstand. But she really needed to get to church, for more reasons than one.

*   *   *

At the nearest intersection they crossed over to the corner of Shevchenko Park. Thorsson waited until they entered before commenting. "I really like your mother," he told her. "Your aunt Ludmila, too. They're both very nice."

Yulia was doubtful. "They asked you a lot of questions. My mother also got on the subject of my career—one of her favorite themes. You're sure you didn't mind?"

"Not at all. I enjoyed it."

"Truly?"

"Truly, Yulia."

His remark sounded sincere. He really *did* seem to like them. Almost to the point where he seemed reluctant to part ways when they left the café. Yulia realized her apprehensions had been overblown.

She and Thorsson turned onto the shaded, winding walkway that fronted the university. Precipitously, her emotions took full hold… she'd resisted them for as long as she could. Thorsson was much more than someone with whom she'd been thrown together in crisis. And who *happened*, by coincidence, to be attractive. He was also someone who could help her leave the romantic pains and disappointments of her university years behind, once and for all. Who could even herald, if she dared...

The thought, just now, was almost too much to handle.

Her emotions began spinning off in yet another direction, tangled up with all the others.

To her relief he addressed practical matters, which had gotten side-lined the day before due to her brush with Igor Moroz—which she'd already recounted to Thorsson over Skype. "Before we get to church I want to give you an update," he said. "I spoke to Heather Robinson earlier this afternoon. Oleg Mikhailov called her from London. He told her that a solution is in the offing. Also that we should expect some kind of definitive answer tomorrow."

"Did Mikhailov tell her what this solution might be?"

"No. But he did say that it will include both of us."

Yulia welcomed the report. Just now, though, she had more imme-diate concerns. She looked up at the skies, removing her sunglasses. Clouds were darkening fast. A clap of thunder boomed from the direc-tion of the Dnieper.

"Oh no," she said, quickening her pace.

"Your mother was right," he said, following suit.

She glanced ahead. They were approaching the towering monu-ment figure of Shevchenko on their right. The red façade of the main university corpus stood across the street on their left, just fifty or sixty meters away. Its portico offered a refuge. He saw the direction of her gaze and gestured toward it.

"Should take shelter there, under the columns?"

Yulia slowed for several steps and considered the idea. She also looked ahead up the walkway. If they paused, she worried, they risked missing the service. And at the moment she needed church more than ever.

"I don't know," she answered. "Saint Volodomir's is just minutes from here."

"Shall we try to make it, then?"

"I'm in favor."

They made it halfway from the monument to the park's far corner before first drops splattered on the sidewalk. An instant later a furious peal of thunder rumbled over the trees, followed by a crack of lightning that rattled the hollow in her chest. Branches began to sway violently. Just five or six steps further, as if by preordainment, the skies unleashed a downpour. Yulia raised her handbag over her head. It was a futile gesture. Drops pelted her face and ran down her hair. She struggled to pronounce her next words through the din. "Oh no!"

"Let's run!" he implored her in return.

She took off with him at once along the walkway, a half step behind. She did her best to keep up, but her mid-heeled sandals offered meager balance and traction on the wet pavers. At the next curve one of her feet slipped sideways, sending her skidding. He slowed and reached one arm back, looking at her through the veil of water streaming off his forehead.

"Take my hand!" he urged, even louder.

She looked back at him through the deluge. They were both without protection.

She didn't hesitate.

CHAPTER 60

Thorsson soon realized the rain would soak them whether they ran or walked. He opted to keep running.

Along Shevchenko Boulevard water coursed over windshields and bodies alike, stalling all four lanes of traffic and rendering the pedestrian signals almost superfluous. Under another crack of lightning he bounded a torrent at the far curb, leading Yulia over, and swerved left toward the churchyard entrance. Just behind him her foot slapped a deep puddle on the sidewalk, flinging out indiscriminate splashes and prompting a shriek that sounded half disbelief and half elation.

The onslaught was propelling dozens in the same direction. They dashed across the church's fore plaza to its front steps and arched doorway, where he finally released her hand and wiped the water from his eyes. One of Saint Volodomir's massive outer doors was open to accommodate the inflow, while about fifteen others huddled near the threshold, deciding what to do. In the half shelter, Yulia seemed to lose whatever giddiness she'd exhibited during their sprint.

"Hold on," she said, "I've got to put on my scarf."

She reached into her handbag, pulled out the item, and folded it into form. The patterned silk fabric seemed to have remained at least partly dry, in contrast to her other coverings. As she tied the wrap around her head she looked down at her dress with a horrified expression.

"Oh Lord. I'm hardly decent."

She was right, Thorsson saw at once. The thin muslin was drenched through to her skin and undergarments. The effect was provocative. So much so that she had obvious second thoughts.

"Maybe we shouldn't go?"

Another sheet of rain blew in and struck them in the doorway. Thorsson could feel his hair plastered against his skull and drops running off his beard. They'd made their bid to evade nature, he reckoned. Now that they'd arrived he was inclined to cede to it.

"Let's at least go inside the vestibule. We can decide there."

"All right," Yulia answered, still doubtful.

They rejoined the inward movement, at last escaping the rain, and edged to the periphery of the antechamber. An elderly woman selling prayer candles took in Yulia's drenched clothing and appeared about to object. Then noted him too and for some reason refrained. Water continued dripping off their clothes as they collected themselves. The interior light was refracted and subdued by the stained-glass windows. Thorsson faced her from the front and made a shoulders-to-feet appraisal.

All the features and allocations that had first summoned his attention in Alushta were now on vivid, flagrant display, from Yulia's full lips and round cheekbones on down. Her bra was just as soaked and translucent as its overlay, while lower, the gossamer material outlined the sensuous indent of her waist and swelling counterpoise of her hips and thighs, exclaimed by sheer panties at the center—the very part of her that had mesmerized him two days earlier at the flowerbed. She now held him more rapt than ever, forcing him to redact his stare.

Even the babushka selling the prayer candles glanced over for another concerned look.

"What do you think?" Yulia asked him, still unsure.

He drew a deep breath through his nostrils, but instead of clearing his thoughts inhaled a heavy dose of incense from the sanctuary. "We're here. I'd say we should just go ahead."

"You're sure no one will be offended?"

"People will understand. Don't forget. They're here to worship, not to ogle other congregants. Perhaps your dress will dry off during the service."

"Okay, let's hope so…you've been to an Eastern Orthodox service before, right?"

"Just two or three times. I admit I'm not really acquainted with the details."

"If you have any questions, feel free to ask me."

"Will do. You lead the way."

Yulia adjusted her headscarf and checked the tie under her chin before they advanced inside. Eight or nine steps into the sanctuary she stopped to genuflect, facing the altar. Thorsson considered doing likewise but instead stood a respectful distance behind her, one hand clasped over his wrist.

Preliminaries were already underway. Straight ahead, inside the railed-off enclosure of the intermediate sanctum, two junior priests were setting the stage, one swinging a wand of burning incense on the periphery and the other arranging an ancient-looking Bible. Meanwhile the church was filling up at a rate that Thorsson wouldn't quite have expected, given the weather.

"The service should start in a few minutes," Yulia whispered to him over her shoulder. "Shall we get a little closer?"

"Sounds good."

They wove through the thickening assembly toward the railing, stopping three lines back, Thorsson still standing slightly behind. Their repositioning proved well-timed; less than two minutes later a curtain drew open behind the altar and a door opened to the inner sanctum, followed in short order by a bell chime signaling commencement. Right on cue, some fifteen prelates issued out single file, led by one priest swinging a smoking urn and another hoisting a bejeweled crucifix on a golden staff. Toward the end of the procession, the patriarch of Kiev made grand entrance, denoted by his towering, jewel-encrusted miter, white ecclesiastical vestments with gold embroidery, and distinctive, ornamented crosier, topped by two snakes and a cross rising between them—a symbol, Thorsson had once read somewhere, that represented the Christian triumph over sin.

The patriarch reached the front railing and initiated the liturgy in the Ukrainian language. Thorsson understood enough Ukrainian to grasp the essence but was familiar with the schema in any case.

Yulia genuflected again along with the other worshippers. From behind Thorsson saw that she was fully absorbed and also, now that she was out of the rain and bathed in the gauzy refractions of the sanctuary, that she'd acquired a radiant glow. As she closed her eyes in prayer he let his gaze wander down her back. Her muslin dress was beginning to dry in spots but in most places remained plastered against her skin, accentuating her youth and fecundity more acutely than ever. On her lower, most hallowed portions, he indulged another up-close view from behind, which, in his current state, seemed to hearken full deliverance.

On reflex more than reason, he closed his eyes and rendered a prayer of his own.

When he reopened them and redirected his gaze to the service, he tried to regain a measure of Stoic detachment. To concentrate on a historical lineage that stretched back through Kievan Rus and more than a millennium of Byzantine civilization, across centuries of practice under the soaring chambers of Hagia Sophia, all the way to the emperors Justinian and Constantine.

The aspiration was fruitless. The incense and sensuality were going to his head.

*   *   *

Finally the rearmost priest disappeared behind the curtain into the inner sanctum, concluding the service. Thorsson remained spellbound, his senses brimming. Yulia looked back at him over her shoulder.

"Well, what did you think?" she asked.

"Impressive. Made me appreciate the effect these rituals have had on the Slavic world over the centuries."

"Did you understand, even in Ukrainian?"

"Enough to follow it."

Others around them were already stirring back toward the main entrance. Thorsson looked back and saw both sides of the double door splayed open. Sunbeams were visible through the aperture. "Looks like the rain has stopped," he said. "Shall we head outside?"

"Sure."

Amid the slow outward migration Thorsson felt his male appendage, still stiff, prod the flesh of Yulia's behind. The contact provoked glimmer of recognition in her, discernible in profile. Several steps further on, nearer the vestibule, she turned back toward the altar and performed another genuflection.

As she did he checked his watch. The next couple of hours, until dinnertime, were unscripted. Same held for the days to come.

The sunlight dazzled him for a moment on the front steps, prompting him to don his sunglasses. At the bottom, Yulia turned back toward the door, crossed herself one last time, and removed her scarf. She was folding the item to return it to her purse when Thorsson caught sight of a wedding party, just twenty meters away on the fore plaza. The group included a photographer, who'd just completed one round of photographs and was preparing for another. The man lowered his lens and glanced over at them, a glimmer of recognition crossing his face. The bride and groom soon did likewise.

Thorsson reached around Yulia's waist to guide her in contrary direction. For a moment the photographer looked tempted to follow. Fortunately he was otherwise engaged.

CHAPTER 61

Mikhailov and Volodin took the same two seats they had occupied the day before. So did the other parties. Fletcher got straight to the point, his gloss of civility notwithstanding.

"We have endeavored to fulfill all the conditions you outlined, Mr. Mikhailov. Indeed, our legal team was up much of the night, working with their counterparts in New York on the specifics. We recognize that we just transmitted the draft document a little more than three hours ago. Nevertheless have you and Mr. Volodin had adequate time to review it?"

"We have," Mikhailov answered. "Our legal secretary and private counsel have also rendered their opinions."

"And does it meet with your approval?"

"It does. No amendments are necessary."

"That's excellent to hear. We will transmit digital copies to Heather Robinson and Thorsson's lawyer at once. For your convenience we've produced paper versions as well."

Fletcher reached toward a console, pressed a button and communicated a clipped request by intercom. Seconds later a secretary entered, bearing a stack of document copies. She distributed them first to Mikhailov and Volodin, then to everyone else around the table.

While she did Mikhailov scanned across all faces opposite, according particular attention again to Ralph Waingrove. At last he addressed them as a group. "I realize these agreements contain numerous moving parts and required accommodations from many of you here. On behalf of the Russian government I wish to say that we appreciate this. I also hope that the outcome will prove, in the end, to be the best one available." He paused and scanned the faces once again. "Before we conclude, does anyone have anything to add?"

"I do."

Mikhailov looked down the table. Little to his surprise the speaker was Waingrove.

"I'll be blunt, Mr. Mikhailov," he said, his bass voice edged with the hardness of the drilling rig. "I haven't signed onto this agreement with any enthusiasm. And certainly with no gratitude. Thorsson has been one of our most valuable employees over the past five years. The way I see it, what's happened had nothing to do with him or with my company. It's the result of the corruption that pervades your part of the world."

Mikhailov understood it was meant as indictment. Nonetheless he returned the American's stare impassively.

However Waingrove's broadside didn't end there; he pivoted his gaze toward Fletcher. "This outcome may solve problems for Harcourt," he continued. "But for Allegheny it arises from necessity… nothing more. I'll be straight, Niles. If not for our client relationship and our upcoming IPO, I would have pursued other options."

Fletcher looked back at Waingrove with similar impassiveness. The Briton knew the rebuke was symbolic, as did everyone else present.

Finally the oil man then swung his gaze back across the table. "The only reason I've agreed to it is to ensure Thorsson's freedom and safety," he declared. "Therefore I expect you to uphold your end of the bargain, Mr. Mikhailov. Full freight. Nothing less."

"I also will accept no shortfalls, Mr. Waingrove. About that, you have my utmost assurances."

Mikhailov pronounced these words with the authority instilled in him by his service. He wished, inside, that his conviction equaled his tone.

CHAPTER 62

Many categories of intelligence work, in Mikhailov's experience, hinged on preparation. Setting stages. Creating conditions. Arranging pieces before the fact. After that there were never any guarantees. But at least an operation stood a chance. The logic applied to Thorsson and Yulia. To personal domains as well.

Even if timing was still to be determined.

He pulled a last drag, exhaled a plume of smoke out toward the Thames, and flicked his cigarette over the balustrade. The ember arced out and extinguished upon contact with the water. It would be his last until after dinner.

He'd also reached a decision.

When he turned back toward the Savoy a clutch of Japanese tourists was descending the stone steps by Cleopatra's Needle, scanning the river view with cameras in hand. He ceded his position in the frame and ascended in the opposite direction, between the obelisk and one of its companion bronze sphinxes. Up on street level he traversed the crosswalk to the leafy belt of the Victoria Embankment, turned right toward the hotel, and found an empty bench next to a flowerbed. When he was seated he checked his wristwatch. Since Sasha's death his sister's schedule had become more regularized. At four thirty Moscow time, he could guess where he would find her. He hit her speed dial on his phone screen. His call reached her at once.

"Oleg?"

"None other, Ksusha. Hello from London."

"So I heard from Vera yesterday. She said you were there." His sister sounded surprised. He seldom called her while on assignment, especially impromptu.

"Short-term matter. Already complete on this end. Flying back to Ukraine tomorrow. Can you talk?"

"Sure…in fact I'm sitting on our balcony having tea. Your beloved Rufus is lying alongside me, looking out toward the ponds…almost as if he's waiting for you."

Mikhailov visualized the scene with a stir of affection. His presumption of tea had also been correct. He asked her how she was doing.

"There have been more bright patches this week, thanks as always to church. Rufus has also helped…by coincidence he just sat up and looked at me. He seemed to hear your voice."

"He couldn't be in more caring hands, Ksusha…" He took a pause of his own, albeit more deliberate. "I'm actually calling about a different matter, which I've been pondering over. Something we may as well resolve sooner rather than later…namely the disposition of Mom and Dad's property."

His sister fell silent, waiting to hear what he had in mind.

"You know how fond I am of the dacha. And now that your girls will be at Moscow State, you have more interest in the apartment than I do. I still have to run this by Vera, but would you be opposed if I take the dacha and you the apartment?"

Ksenia took this in for several seconds. To this point they'd set this question aside. "Are you sure Oleg?" she responded. "We've both figured the apartment is worth about one-third more."

"I know. But we're both well off. So why split hairs?"

"What if Vera disapproves?"

"I think she'll come around."

"And Dima? He's approaching university age himself."

"He's an independent sort. Even if he attends Moscow State, he'd probably be happier in a dormitory. Anyway you and the girls would be close by."

His sister was quick to endorse the idea, contingent on Vera's approval. Before they signed off, she asked him about the London weather.

"Splendid and sunny this afternoon, actually," he answered. "I'm sitting out of doors just now, along the Thames. My flight for Kiev won't leave until morning."

"Doing some sightseeing, now that you've completed your business?"

"More constructive activity, you might say."

Ksenia was too discreet to inquire further. Thus far she remained uninformed about his novel. Vera had not mentioned it to her, in the hope that the aberration would fade away.

Upon rising from the bench he strode at brisk pace back toward the Savoy and spotted his room window. Several minutes later he was seated on the other side of the glass, laptop open and fingers poised over his keyboard, with a more encompassing panorama of the Thames than he'd held down below.

His book was not going away. Quite the opposite.

CHAPTER 63

As usual Heather Robinson displayed no outward markers. She was too professional for that. But Thorsson knew her well enough by now to perceive her more subtle cues.

What he couldn't grade was the part she detested most: Harcourt Bank, or the influence of the Russian state over the City of London.

The hour was approaching seven and most of the embassy complex was empty. Their conference room on the second floor was an exception. Robinson commanded the head of the table, while Thorsson was positioned halfway down one side, next to his lawyer. Seated opposite them, and now speaking, was David Lancaster, a mid-forties attorney with bespoke tailoring and an Oxbridge accent who served as Harcourt's lead counsel in London. He'd participated in the meetings with Mikhailov in London and had just arrived at Boryspil Airport on private jet.

This evening Thorsson felt as though he had reentered his old milieu. For the first time since the start of his vacation he was wearing a suit and tie.

"You've now had about five hours to review the contract," Lancaster said. "On our side we wish to resolve this matter with all possible dispatch. Therefore I'll start by summarizing what we have proposed."

With clipped syllables he enumerated the seven main elements of the contract, starting with the dismissal of criminal charges, proceeding to the financial disbursements and employment terms, and finishing with the nondisclosure requirements. Thorsson was still startled by the amounts involved.

"Do you have any questions?" he said upon conclusion. "Or objections to the document as now formulated?"

In keeping with prior arrangement Robinson ceded to Andrei Krilenko, Thorsson's attorney. "The financial and professional stipulations are all clear," he said. "My client has also had an opportunity to discuss them with Ralph Waingrove, his company's president. The timeline and conditions surrounding the dismissal of criminal charges against my client are also explicit and give rise to no questions." Krilenko paused before proceeding to his next item. "However I should underline that my client is unable, of his own volition, to avoid spontaneous media coverage, with or without the other conditions in the document."

"We're aware of that, as are the other parties. For that reason we have included no specific obligations of that kind."

"Good…however, the security guarantees, as formulated, do present more serious concerns. In this domain I'll defer to Ms. Robinson."

When Lancaster rotated his face down the table, Robinson locked her eyes onto his, unintimidated. "Because Axel Thorsson is a US citizen, the US government has two main priorities in this matter," she said. "The first is dismissal of all criminal charges against him. The second, as Mr. Krilenko noted, is his ongoing physical safety in Ukraine and elsewhere in the region. I'll address each in turn."

Lancaster readied a pen over his legal pad.

"First, on the criminal matter, we believe the charges against Mr. Thorsson have no basis in evidence. On the contrary, the facts indicate he was the victim of a premeditated attack in an apparent case of mistaken identity. Therefore we view the dismissal of criminal charges against him not as a concession, either on the part of the Ukrainian and Russian governments or on the part of Harcourt Bank. But rather as a proper administration of justice."

"Duly noted," Lancaster responded.

"In the same vein, we believe that justice should be rendered for Thorsson's attacker..." She glanced down at her own notepad. "A Ukrainian citizen known as Igor Moroz. You did not mention him in your summary. Will he be charged and prosecuted for the crime?"

"He will not. That was part of the overall arrangement offered by Oleg Mikhailov of the Russian government. Will that form an obstacle?" Lancaster directed his gaze at Krilenko and Thorsson. Robinson did likewise.

"It will not," Krilenko answered.

Lancaster scribbled a line on his pad. Robinson, already aware of Thorsson's decision, was ready with her retort. "Nevertheless the US government will lodge a formal protest with the Ukrainian government."

"Also duly noted," Lancaster answered.

"Second is the matter of Thorsson's physical safety," Robinson continued. "In your draft contract you've offered various general assurances but assigned all responsibility for them to the Russian government. There are also no financial or legal commitments associated with these assurances. What guarantees will Mr. Thorsson have that these assurances will be fulfilled?"

"This is a legitimate question and you are correct in raising it," Lancaster answered. "I will therefore be forthright. Harcourt Bank has been given these assurances by Oleg Mikhailov, an emissary of the Russian state. For us they have the status of government guarantee. Accordingly, we have no practical means of enforcing them."

"How, then, can you be confident that the Russian government and Oleg Mikhailov will make good on these promises?"

"I would only offer this. Since the fall of the Soviet Union—and particularly since the 1998 financial crisis—the Russian government has been true to its word in their dealings with the City of London and the financial world generally. That includes Harcourt Bank. Based on self-interest alone, in our estimation, they have every incentive to uphold their reputation. The same would therefore seem to hold true, I would think, for Russia's government-to-government relations with the United States."

At this point Thorsson interjected himself into the dialogue for the first time. "Yulia Petrenko is mentioned once in this regard," he said. "Still, I wish to verify her status. Do these assurances by the Russian state apply to her also?"

"They do," Lancaster answered.

It was the confirmation Thorsson wanted. Robinson mulled Lancaster's response a moment longer. But she had already reached a conclusion. "Speaking on behalf of the US government," she said, "I should note that we find these assurances vague and unsatisfactory. Therefore we will refrain from formal endorsement of this proposal. However we have also determined that it is probably the best Mr. Thorsson can achieve under the circumstances."

Lancaster turned his gaze toward Thorsson and Krilenko. "Ms. Robinson's reservations aside, have you made your determination?" he asked.

Krilenko glanced toward Thorsson for verification. Thorsson nodded in return.

"We have," Krilenko answered. "My client has decided to agree to the proposal as now presented."

"Is Mr. Thorsson ready to sign, then?"

"He is."

CHAPTER 64

Their driver held the rear door as Yulia stepped out and up onto her heels, smoothing the salmon-colored silk dress that she'd chosen for the evening. Thorsson placed one palm on her lower back, in a gesture that was already becoming a habit. With his other he gestured toward the entrance. A liveried doorman was already there waiting.

"Shall we?" Thorsson said.

"Yes."

Yulia was too overwhelmed to say much more. This restaurant, Leo, had a reputation. Besides, they were expected. The doorman welcomed them as they crossed the threshold and accompanied them to the maître d' station, where another welcoming party awaited, consisting of the maître d' and two young female attendants, all bearing receptive smiles. Yulia was further startled when the maître d', speaking Russian, greeted Thorsson by name and appeared to notice his beard, as did the two attendants. Still smiling, the latter pair conducted them through the lobby and an interior dining room, inveigled by cool-age jazz from a pianist in the corner. In the foreground she glimpsed a scattering of elegant patrons, whom she made an effort not to look at directly.

All she really knew thus far was that the criminal charges against Thorsson would soon be dropped: "Likely a matter of two or three days," he'd said over the phone. Otherwise the evening had unfolded with a whirl. The first indicator had been his request that she dress "as elegantly as possible on such short notice." Second was that he'd abandoned their previous discretion and collected her in a hired limousine outside Pavel's building, while her mother and Aunt Luda looked down from the living room windows. The third was their destination. Even Massimo had never taken her to this place.

Yulia was further stunned when the two girls escorted them to a table on the outermost arch of the terrace, bracketed by greenery, with a privileged view of the Dnieper. On a summer evening such as this, it was the best table in the house. Two male waiters in vests and black bowties stepped out of nowhere, pulled out their chairs, and proffered opened menus once they were seated.

At last she dared to glance around. Many other diners, whatever their status, were unable to resist a look in their direction. She and Thorsson, as usual, had claimed attention. "I associate this place with celebrities and oligarchs," she said over the top of her menu. "How on earth did you get a reservation here on a Saturday evening?"

Thorsson smiled. "It's the vacation season. That probably helped."

"The staff also seems to know you. Is that true?"

"I've taken Ukrainian business contacts here on numerous occasions...government officials and executives at Naftogaz for the most part, for lunch as well as dinner. My most recent visit was in mid-May." He paused to consider his next remark, as if he was embarrassed by it. "I've also made a point of tipping decently."

She allowed herself another look around. Thorsson seemed to guess, correctly, that she was scanning the clientele for famous faces, and smiled at her again.

"I don't know any celebrities or oligarchs, though," he added.

"Maybe it's for the better. Think of Zherdev."

They shared a laugh before directing attention to their menus. Yulia also tried to keep hold of herself. Thorsson had mentioned on the phone that they had cause for celebration. And the dismissal of criminal charges against him presented reason to rejoice. But he hadn't provided any details in the limousine. Moreover he himself didn't appear thrilled. Upbeat and relieved, maybe. But hardly ecstatic. She wanted to hear more. It was too soon to get dazzled.

She ventured another glance at him over her menu. It was the first time she'd seen him in a suit and tie since his arrival in Alushta at the hotel. Different color this time—light gray—but just as fashionable. European cut, just like the previous one. His shirt was an immaculate white, and his tie was patterned silk. The only major difference was his beard, which was now trimmed, together with somewhat longer hair. Just now: a Viking in a suit. But she had to concede that the label didn't do him justice.

"There are so many choices," she commented. "Do you have any suggestions?"

"The head chef specializes in seafood, so they're mostly oriented that way."

"Seafood is fine with me."

"Perfect. I was thinking the same." He consulted the menu. "For the main course, I'm considering the Atlantic turbot with keps mushroom sauce. I've had good experience with it before."

"Sounds great."

He glanced down again. "For appetizers, I'm also considering caviar and oysters. Are you game?"

"Caviar? Won't that be expensive?"

"As I said, we have reason to celebrate."

"All right, then. You can order for me."

Thorsson picked up the wine list for a moment. When he closed it their waiter arrived at once to take their orders, including a bottle of 2010 white burgundy, the price of which she could only guess. And there really was no denying that he looked fabulous in his suit.

"That waiter also seems to know you," she observed after the latter had withdrawn.

"He's waited on me once or twice before," Thorsson answered. "Though don't place much stock in it. People are often impressed by the wrong things…anyway, those days are over."

"Over? What do you mean?"

"I'm leaving Allegheny Exploration."

The announcement hit Yulia like a bolt out of the sky. She thought this was a celebration. It was the last news she expected.

"What?"

"Along with dismissal of the criminal case, that's one of the outcomes this agreement. Not right away…that wouldn't be feasible. But in six months or so I'll be completely free and clear."

"Do you mean to say that you're quitting?"

"Not exactly. I basically enjoyed my job and expected to stay another three or four years. This has been foisted on me through the agreement. Though it's actually been developing ever since Oleg Mikhailov met Heather Robinson here in Kiev several days ago. Since then I've had numerous phone conversations on this issue with my boss, the CEO, who's currently in London. My lawyer and I also spent most of afternoon today reviewing the documents…"

He was interrupted when the waiter made another discreet appearance at their table, bearing fresh bread in a silver basket, along with the white burgundy, which Thorsson sniffed and tasted before the waiter poured out both glasses. Afterward he continued. "Oleg Mikhailov didn't exactly impose this condition. But let's just say he prodded all parties in that direction. Harcourt and the others simply concluded that my wind-up would be consistent with their main objective, which is the waning of media interest in this matter. But make no mistake. My exit is mostly Harcourt's doing. My CEO, Ralph Waingrove, was essentially forced to go along."

"Harcourt? That hardly seems fair. They're largely responsible for this mess in the first place."

"True. But by now it's probably sensible. I haven't seen any of my business contacts since all this began. If they haven't heard about my arrest and detention by now, they soon will. I've no doubt acquired certain notoriety, for better or worse. Let's not forget that I killed a man."

"In self-defense!"

"That hardly matters now, does it? My ability to do business here has been compromised. My CEO eventually reached the same conclusion, albeit with reluctance. If this is the price Oleg Mikhailov demanded for my freedom and one that Harcourt is prepared to underwrite, then it's a reasonable transaction. I should also note that written guarantees of your safety are included as well, along with Pavel. I'll get to those in a moment."

Yulia was glad to hear him mention her status and Pavel's. But she remained a little confused. She didn't really understand Harcourt's "underwriting" role. She refocused instead on what to her was still the main question.

"Are you really going to be cleared, then?" she asked.

"That's what this contract stipulates—the one I signed this evening. In just two or three days."

The confirmation gave her an additional dose of relief. Also of balance, which she needed. The evening really was unfolding in a swirl.

Their waiter made another understated appearance. This time he bore their platters of oysters and caviar, which he laid out on the table alongside their bread basket, still untouched. To this point they'd gotten so absorbed in conversation they'd also neglected their wine. Once he'd departed Thorsson at last raised a toast.

"To my freedom and your safety," he said, "And to breaking clear of this once and for all."

Yulia raised her glass in return. "Yes…salvation at last."

She put her lips to the crystal and gained her first taste. She couldn't have told whether it was burgundy or sauvignon blanc but knew it was excellent. They then sampled the caviar, which was served in small pockets of hand-folded blini, as well as the raw oysters. Both were delectable. She also remembered, vaguely, that the latter was supposed to be an aphrodisiac. But she forced *that* notion out of her head for the moment. There was too much swirling going on there already. She still wanted to hear more about the agreement he had just signed—not just about the part related to her but also about his employment situation, which still worried her. Before she had the chance to ask about it, however, he resumed where he had left off.

"The second major concession I had to make, in order to get the charges dropped, was to agree to a 'gag rule,' as it's called in English. Do you know what that is?"

"Isn't that when someone agrees not to discuss something publicly for a certain period of time?"

"Exactly. Mine covers eighteen months. During that time I'm forbidden from making any public statements about the criminal case or the attack episode, or even the Harcourt conference at the hotel. I'm also prohibited from making any defamatory statements against Harcourt and from bringing lawsuits against them, either in the United States, the United Kingdom, or any other legal jurisdiction. I'm also forbidden from returning to Crimea for the remainder of 2013."

Yulia was disappointed to hear the last part. She said it sounded like a straitjacket.

"It is, I suppose. But to the Russian government and to Harcourt Bank, my silence and departure from the scene are critical. Their main priority is our removal from public attention…which in turn leads me to the part covering you and Pavel, which I perhaps most want to tell you about." He paused and looked down at the platters again. "But first, let's not forget about our caviar and oysters."

Yulia plucked another serving of blini and caviar from the platter while Thorsson transferred two more oysters to her serving plate. The caviar dissolved on her tongue, and she washed down the blini with a sip of wine. Already she felt the alcohol going to her head and told herself to slow down. The agreement sounded pretty complex. She wanted to understand all the details. Especially what Thorsson was going to next, now that he would soon be out of a job.

"Specifically," he resumed, "Zherdev will be prevented from visiting further harm upon either you or your cousin. If he does, the gag order is obviated."

"What will restrain him, after everything he's done? Let's not forget those stunts here in Kiev just a few days ago."

"Harcourt's counsel assured me that both Harcourt and the Russian FSB have means of keeping him in line. Moreover they've written the commitment into the contract. Not ironclad, I know. But it was the best I could do."

"Thanks, Axel. I appreciate it. I know Pavel will, too."

"No need for gratitude, Yulia. It's done...oh yes...there is one other major concession I had to make. I had to agree to abandon all criminal complaints against Igor Moroz, the guy who attacked me in the water...the same one who trailed you back from the supermarket."

"A shame. That guy is a nasty piece of work."

"That's the way it goes...more caviar and oysters? The main course should be here soon."

She agreed and contemplated these additional threads while Thorsson transferred two more oysters to her serving plate. When he was done she plucked off another blini pocket with her thumb and index finger. The caviar oozed around her tongue again before she swallowed and reached for her wine glass. This time she was careful to take a more moderate sip. She tried not to get caught up in the moment. She needed to keep her head for at least a while longer. "I know you gained your freedom," she said. "But haven't you also given up a lot? It seems to me that your life has been turned upside down. I mean...what are you going to do for work?"

"That's no longer such a pressing issue."

As if he was embarrassed by this topic, Thorsson consumed another caviar and blini. He followed by grasping his shellfish fork and addressing his second oyster. Out of politeness Yulia joined him. She hesitated before speaking again. She wasn't sure it was her place to delve.

"Does that mean you have some money saved?" she asked, a little cautiously.

"I do. But that won't form my main base of support. That will come from the financial settlement from Harcourt, to which I have now agreed."

"Financial settlement?"

"That's correct. Harcourt is underwriting the cost. Call it Harcourt's means of ensuring my cooperation."

"And it's enough to live off?"

"More than enough. Indefinitely, you might say."

At this Thorsson directed his eyes down at his serving plate and addressed his sixth and final oyster. He still looked reluctant to discuss it further. While she followed suit her thoughts ran wild. Finally she couldn't help herself.

"Millions?" she asked.

He looked back at her with a slight smile and hints of discomfort. "To be honest, I'd hoped to avoid those details, at least up front..." He then caught sight of their waiter, approaching from the side. "Here comes our main course," he said. "I suggest we enjoy our turbot and burgundy and revisit that piece later."

He'd allayed her concerns somewhat. She couldn't say, though, that her head was spinning any less.

CHAPTER 65

Yulia tried not to flounder in comparisons, when it came to men. She was more likely to lump all of them into the same self-centered, deceitful whole. Especially the foreign ones. They seemed worst of the lot.

However Thorsson, it was now clear, was different. At first she'd resisted the notion, wary of guilt-traps. But he'd steadily overcome her doubts.

Halfway through her Atlantic turbot with keps mushroom sauce she determined for sure that there was no likeness. Thorsson *was* superior to Massimo. To Vitali as well…and to all the other males of the species who had insinuated themselves into her misbegotten romantic life thus far.

Thorsson inhabited a category all his own. It was okay to be dazzled.

When she finished she angled her utensils across her plate, reached for her wine, and examined him over the top of her glass. For someone about to receive more money than he'd expected—significantly more, as she'd understood—he looked less than overjoyed. Content, maybe. Inclined to celebrate: that also. But short of euphoric. She wondered why. Before she had a chance to ask him, their waiter came to clear away their plates. Meanwhile Thorsson turned his gaze toward the Dnieper.

"Superb view of the river from here," he said.

She followed suit and agreed. The vista *was* fabulous.

"I was just thinking again about the Varangians."

She recalled their conversation in the park, just up the slope.

"When they reached this location, they didn't opt for a quiet, agrarian life. They built a flourishing city and a base for trading to the Black Sea and Constantinople. Along the way, they Christianized and tried to overcome their barbarity. Then, for their time, they created the most advanced culture in Europe. In short they always wanted better."

With that, Thorsson fell silent, leaving her to wonder why such a thought had occurred to him just now, in light of the day's other events. "Are you thinking about that because of your settlement?" she asked him. "I mean...do you feel you deserved more?"

"No, not at all. Not in terms of the amount I'm receiving." He paused again, thoughtful. "No," he continued. "My dissatisfaction stems from the way in which I've acquired this windfall. And even more, from the way in which this whole affair has played out."

"I hope you don't blame yourself for it. Or your company, either."

"I don't."

"Blame Ukraine. We're a corrupt country, unfortunately."

"Sadly I would have to agree. We took conditions here as we found them and responded to all this as best we could...no...my misgivings are more delineated. Remember my remarks on Marx and the financial sector?"

Yulia nodded. She still found them peculiar, coming from someone she saw as such an emblem of free enterprise.

"And the causes for the crash five years ago?"

Yulia still didn't grasp all the specifics but nodded again.

"Capitalism is in a bad state. The rot isn't limited to Ukraine...it spans the globe. And I say that as a capitalist myself."

At this Thorsson seemed to worry he had gone on too long. He glanced out over the Dnieper again and took a sip of wine, as if descending from the abstract. "Please excuse my monologue, Yulia," he said.

Yulia shook her head to show the apology was unneeded.

"Anyway...why do I discourse again on all these subjects...the Varangians, corruption, Marx, the influence of global finance, and so on...on an occasion like this?"

Yulia waited. Now he had her attention more than ever.

"Harcourt, as I said, is funding my big payoff. In short, I've benefitted from the very corruption and preponderance of finance that I've just bemoaned."

"I also mention them because they will shape, in part, what I will do from this point forward."

CHAPTER 66

One of their waiters appeared to clear away their plates, bringing her back to the here and now. Another presented dessert menus and refilled their glasses, finishing off their bottle. She'd already drunk too much burgundy, even if Thorsson had consumed more.

"Inclined to indulge?" he asked her.

"I don't know. I've been trying to watch my calories lately—especially sweets."

"This is a special occasion. I suggest we make an exception."

When Yulia opened her menu and saw the selections on offer, she required little persuasion. Upon the waiter's return, Thorsson chose the chocolate mousse with truffles, while she went even richer and more indulgent, ordering the chocolate torte with raspberries and cream. Only then did she recall that he'd been leading up to something and that that something was his future. His allusion to it caused her a little trepidation, now that their other troubles seemed out of the way.

"So what *arerere* you going to do next?" she asked him.
"All these resolutions have just fallen into place. So I've had little time to reflect. But I do know things need improving," he added. "On a macro level, let's say."

Yulia reached for her wine again, though she couldn't tell whether her next sip helped her clarity or further compromised it. "Wow," she said after swallowing and repositioning the glass on the table. "That's a tall order. If I were in your place, as an American, I can't imagine where I'd start…"

Before she could pose a follow-up question, Thorsson asked one of his own. "On that note Yulia, what are *your* plans, now that all this seems to be winding down?"

"Good question," she answered. "This agreement has happened rather fast…probably stay in Kiev another week or two to help my mother and aunt look after Pavel. Then Vladimir Nosko has already promised to keep my job for me back in Alushta…so I suppose I'll go back to the hotel. I've got job security there. I don't want to give that up."

"Understandable. What about Pavel?"

"Unlike me, he's still as determined as ever to improve things. Once his recovery is complete, he plans to get right back to work. The problem is that *Ukraina Sevodnya* is barely surviving. They've gotten a new lease on life thanks to his articles. But from what I understand, they need at least a half a million dollars just to stay afloat. They'll be lucky to last another six or twelve months."

"Maybe now they'll be able to turn it around."

"I wish I could be so optimistic."

Both of them fell silent and addressed their desserts. To Yulia's delight the cake was exquisite. She was also glad for the break. Thorsson's plans were now what interested her most. She still wanted to sate her curiosity, on two counts. She began with the first.

"Back to your future, Axel…even if you haven't made any decisions yet, can't you give me any hints?"

He inserted a spoonful of mousse and took his time before responding, cautious. "I guess politics and government are one option," he said when he'd swallowed. "Some role where I could make a difference."

"Politics? Wow…"

Thorsson laughed, as if amused by his own grand schemes. "I know it's a long shot. Anyway there are some intermediate phases. For the next year or so, I'll be anchored in Europe, thanks to this agreement…it's still early."

Yulia realized he was right. Her curiosity was a little out of place.

"I do know what will guide me at the baseline, though," he added. "Remember our discussion a few days ago on the Stoics?"

She nodded.

"There was one tenet I didn't mention. That is, their indifference to riches."

"Indifference? You mean riches didn't matter to them, one way or the other?"

"That's right. For them money was secondary. I now intend the same."

This was another comment that surprised Yulia, coming from such a self-described capitalist. Ever since graduation she'd been struggling for a toehold. Material security was top of the list. This was one element of Stoicism, and to Thorsson too, to which she had trouble relating. How on earth could he be indifferent to money, when he'd just received a big payout? And he was American besides.

What she still had *not* heard were details of his financial settlement. She knew Westerners were private about their finances and hesitated. Finally she decided to sate her curiosity on count two, which she'd wanted to do ever since the appetizers. "Do you really have so much now that you can afford to be indifferent?" she asked.

"I prefer not to frame it that way."

Again she had trouble relating. "You don't have to tell me if you don't want to, Axel…But if you don't mind my asking, how much money is Harcourt giving you? I can hardly make a guess."

Thorsson, his elbows on the table, interlocked his fingers in a fresh bout of discomfort. He then wrapped one hand around the other. "I guess I don't mind," he said. "I was planning on showing you the written document tomorrow anyway, since it concerns you. The structure is rather complicated, so I won't elaborate upon it in detail. In short, it covers existing stock warrants with a revised vesting schedule, some new warrants granted immediately, and some additional stock options related to the IPO. I'll be obliged to cash out and liquidate all my holdings in Allegheny during the next twelve months, prior to August 2014. That's earlier than I would have preferred. But thanks to these circumstances and the conditions to which I've now agreed, I'm now receiving about triple what I projected, and three to four years ahead of schedule."

When Thorsson told her the total, she pulled a sharp, involuntary inhalation through her nostrils. It comprised an extra digit and six or seven multiples beyond what she would have guessed.

Her bloodstream was already coursing with wine, sugar, and concentrated chocolate. And now her head was spinning more than ever.

CHAPTER 67

Thorsson knew this about himself. When he veered into the abstract he acquired more self-mastery. Of the Stoic variety, one might say.

But he also knew something else. Newfound material wealth could compromise his judgment—most of all with women. Make him feel advantaged and invulnerable. Propel him toward rash, impetuous advances, of the kind he invariably regretted later.

It was the very tendency he'd resolved to overcome in Alushta.

Tonight he was in the moment. And the two forces were entering open battle.

He and Yulia were descending the stone staircase from Leo to the pedestrian walkway that traced the upper hillside, enveloped by verdant foliage and lush scents. Through an aperture in the branches, he glimpsed the pedestrian bridge below, stretching across to Hydropark. And around the next bend was the towering, cast-iron figure of Saint Volodomir, wielding his cross and staring skyward over the water.

His gaze then revisited Yulia's luxuriant, swelling backside and upper thighs, swathed in the salmon-colored silk of her evening dress. He'd gone rapt again in the limousine, under the influence of her perfume. His discourses at the restaurant had provided a respite, but the dinner and wine were now taking full hold.

He next caught sight of the Friendship Arch beyond the next downslope.

"Are you sure you don't mind walking in your heels, Yulia?" he asked her. "I can summon the limousine again when we reach the arch."

"No, I like this."

"I do too. If you're up for it, maybe we can even continue all the way up Kreschatik."

She cast a slightly timid smile at him and edged closer, transmitting another dose of her perfume. Tonight her heels were higher than ever, bringing her almost eye to eye. His next move had been conditioned over previous days and now seemed almost foreordained. With an unhurried twist of his shoulder he circled his arm across her lower back and rested his hand around her hip. He also told himself that he would stop there, at least for tonight. To think and act like a Stoic. To be indifferent to luxury and riches. Establish a direction and plan before plunging ahead. Decide first and mate later.

The proposition already felt tenuous. It didn't help that she was flashing no stop signals.

The walkway zigzagged down the embankment. To make sure Yulia didn't put a foot wrong in the dimming light, Thorsson fixed his eyes on the pavement and, at the fifth bend, caught sight of the titanium facets of the huge, fifty-meter-high arch. An instant later its illumination came on.

"Great timing," he said.

"Yes. It's beautiful."

"Never seen it from this angle."

"Me neither."

Thorsson glanced sideways at her profile, glimpsing her lips and cheekbones. He wasn't the only one who was thoughtful. This culmination had been building all week. On the broad stone stairway to the plaza, she pressed her hand closer to his and gave him another timid smile before releasing it again. The gesture was intimate—beyond what she'd ever shown before…and it revealed some tension as well. For the first time, he sensed that she was engaged in an internal struggle of her own.

The recognition touched him in a way that only fed their combustions. Everything between them, with each additional step, suddenly felt more pending and unbound.

Their onward movement carried them through European Square onto the lower portion of Kreschatik, followed by Maidan, with its blurred kaleidoscope of bright lights and gushing fountains. At the square's southern edge the heart of the boulevard stretched out before them: eight lanes of open pavement through the city center, closed to traffic from now through the weekend. Their further path was unobstructed. Yulia pressed even closer, supplying a fuller helping of perfume and body warmth.

Neither helped his clarity. "I like this practice," he said. "I mean closing the boulevard to traffic on weekends. I've always thought the center is best appreciated on foot. Wouldn't you agree?"

"Yes."

Her monosyllable seemed about the most she could pronounce at that instant. Thorsson looked up the thoroughfare.

"Given the hour, I can now suggest two options," he said. "Prorezna Street is coming up on our right. On weekends there are usually several taxis waiting there. We can grab one and I can take you home to Pavel's apartment. I can then retrace back down here to my own place. Alternatively, we can extend our walk a little longer. There's a taxi stand around Bessarabski Rinok. We can find one there and do likewise."

"What do you want to do?"

"And you?"

"Frankly, I'd prefer the latter."

He glanced down. "How are you holding up in your heels, by the way?"

"Okay."

She pressed his hand to her hip again and nudged her breast to his side, then held the pose as they fell silent, skirting the center line. His apartment building, the tallest in downtown, emerged into fuller view on their left. The fountain in its lower fore plaza—this one much bigger than all the others—was now illuminated and shooting jets of water up toward the night sky. Its rushes and emissions quickly pervaded his senses. This was the first time they'd passed the complex in tandem. When Yulia glimpsed it he felt her back grow tauter against his forearm, as if she was as stirred up as he was.

"My home away from home," he said, nodding up at the façade.

In the ensuing seconds Thorsson wasn't sure whether he was the first to slow or she was. All he did know, for certain—in the early morning hours right afterward, when he replayed the moment again and again in his head—was that they slowed together and that seconds later they were standing face to face in the blank middle of the intersection, with no center lines to guide them. Also that he grasped her other hip with his free hand and pulled her closer.

Her reaction this time was nonverbal and immediate. She reached up, encircled her arms behind his neck, and pressed her midsection hard against his, so that all her contours were tactile through her dress fabric. Her lips were moist and already open.

Whatever shreds of clarity he'd retained from his earlier flights to abstraction, over dinner, now evacuated him. All his endeavors toward philosophical improvement, all his reading of the Stoics, he realized, had come down to this.

Another capitulation to lust.

When he finally drew his mouth back, even that realization was gone. "Would you like to come up to my apartment?" he said, half in a trance.

Yulia continued holding tight for drawn-out seconds. At the same time she looked over his shoulder, toward his building. Her tension seemed to flow back just as quickly. She shuddered, and a tear rolled down one cheek. "I can't," she said in a trembling voice.

At the same instant the fountain behind them paused, bringing the jets back to their basin and a sudden hush to the area. Thorsson's own desire receded just as abruptly. They retracted their bodies and separated.

"I'm sorry, Yulia. I didn't intend that…it's far too soon."

She wiped the tear away and pulled several abbreviated breaths. "It's not you, Axel…I just want to go home. I'll take the metro by myself."

"The metro? Can't we at least find a taxi?"

"No. I'll just go on my own," she half turned and looked across the intersection. "Teatralna station is right over there." She took a pained, tentative step toward it.

"Can't I at least walk you over?"

"All right."

Thorsson drew alongside her, now keeping less intimate distance. He felt the reflex to replace his hand around her waist but thought the better of it.

He also wondered if he'd lost her for good.

CHAPTER 68

Yulia wasn't sure when and where the switch occurred. There was no exact moment or location, no sudden flip. Afterward, she decided that it had probably been a fitful shift. That it had started around the Friendship Arch and unfolded all the way down Kreschatik.

Maybe the precipitant was Thorsson's fancy suit. Maybe it was his knack for well-turned phrases. Or maybe his aura of money, which now dazzled her more than ever. To top that, he'd wowed her in Russian. In *her* native tongue, not his own...she had to admit he was smart. Meanwhile the number he'd mentioned at dinner continued to ring in her head. What did that kind of money even mean for a guy who was only thirty-three years old?

All she did know for sure, as they strolled up the boulevard with his arm around her waist and her desires growing, was that Thorsson gradually stopped cancelling out Massimo and began bringing him back. That all the pain resurfaced, one gnawing installment after another. And that the location in front of Thorsson's building where they'd come to a halt—practically the same spot where she'd stood with Massimo in front of *his* building on that reckless and ill-fated night sixteen months earlier—set the stage. Thorsson's move was just the final trigger. By then the changeover became complete.

She'd been bought once. She wouldn't let it happen again.

Her shakeout became inevitable.

Still, as they started up Khmelnitskovo, past the scaffolding and shell of TZUM...she started to feel embarrassed and ashamed. Yes, her response was explainable...but there was a complicating factor. She knew—deep down—that Thorsson was superior in all ways to his predecessor. He didn't deserve this. Her emotions were over the top. They were now approaching the entrance to Teatralna. Another tear rolled down her cheek. She hesitated before wiping it away.

"Can I at least accompany you home by metro, Yulia?" he said with another bout of concern. "It's the least I can do."

"No, I'd rather go by myself."

"I'd prefer not to conclude this way."

She was so disconcerted she simply resumed walking, while he fell back in step alongside. Wordless again, they descended the steps into the outer station and crossed to the entrance doors, where they separated to face one another. Looking at him, she could see that he was suffering turmoil of his own. As if he was disappointed with himself as well.

"What about our trip to the country tomorrow?" he asked in a flatter tone. "Are we still on?"

His reminder tipped her further off balance. During her shakeout she'd forgotten all about it. "You don't mind driving?"

"Not at all. I've already arranged a rental car."

"I'm not sure...let me think."

Yulia thought of Sofiya Yaroslavovna, her relative. The woman lived alone in the village, was sixty-seven, and almost certainly in bed at this hour. Moreover she had been planning on their visit for days. It was too late to cancel now.

"I guess we should," she answered in a wobbly voice.

"Good. Nine o'clock then, outside your apartment, as we agreed?"

"Okay."

The most she could manage was a feeble "good night" before turning into the station entrance. After their fancy dinner and celebration, it seemed like degrading, unworthy ending. When she reached the turnstile and deposited her token, she realized that she'd even forgotten to thank him.

He deserved at least that, after all she'd put him through.

Her shame flamed higher on the down escalator. Only then did she remember that she remained dolled up in a sexy dress, makeup, and four-inch heels. Another round of attention awaited her in the connecting tunnel to Zolotoi Vorota.

Tonight she couldn't wait to get home.

To her relief she found an open seat on her subway car and did her best to endure the four-minute ride to Pavel's stop, where she steeled her eyes against tears and exited as quickly as she could. On the sidewalk she accelerated her stride along the tree-lined street and saw the apartment windows dark, indicating her mother and aunt were already asleep. All she wanted now was to crawl under her sheets and sob into her pillow, consoled, if she was lucky, by the feline succor of Octavia.

She paid little attention, at first, to the dark sedan parked just up ahead along the curb. When she drew closer she realized she recognized it. An instant later its doors flew open and three men jumped out, wearing black jeans and tee-shirts. Before she could run two of them grabbed her by the arms from both sides.

Her next reflex was to scream. Her cry for help lasted just one or two seconds. A third man grabbed her behind and closed his hand over her mouth.

CHAPTER 69

Yulia was almost the same size as her assailants and fought back with as much force and fury as she could, lashing out with her heels and elbows. She succeeded in gashing one man hard on the shin, provoking a grunt of pain and a curse. But there were three of them and one of her. A driver was also waiting, who turned on the motor. In less than ten seconds the trio corralled her into the backseat and closed the doors, with two men pinioning her arms from the sides and the third scrambling in the front passenger seat. She attempted one last cry for help before the latter closed his door and the car sped off. At the first intersection they took a sharp turn and accelerated from the scene.

The entire operation had been so coordinated and swift she doubted there were any witnesses. She next expected to have a gag shoved into her mouth and a hood yanked over her head.

When neither one happened she recovered enough to glance around the vehicle. It was a BMW, as she'd surmised, with black-leather upholstery—the same one that had menaced her three days earlier. The man in the front passenger seat bore a shaved head and was bending forward, tending to his shin. He sat up and turned to look at her with a sneering smile. She recognized him at once.

Igor Moroz.

"We knew you were a big, strong girl, Yulia Borisovna," he said, using her patronymic as a slur, "so we came prepared. Still, you cut me pretty good. If we weren't under orders I'd give you what you deserved." Yulia tensed her arms but saw little sense in struggling anew. They were now zooming down Melnykova Street in light traffic, already several blocks from Pavel's apartment. She caught a smirk from the driver in the rearview mirror. She looked down and noticed her bare knees. In the scuffle her hem had hiked up to a revealing level. She did her best to steady her voice.

"Whose orders?" she asked.

Moroz only smirked again, along with the driver and the other two.

"Okay, then. At least let me fix my dress."

Moroz considered her request and nodded back to the goons at her sides, who relinquished their hold long enough for her to raise her hips off the seat and pull down her fabric partway over her thighs. All four pairs of eyes tracked the maneuver to completion. Their stares aroused another swell of fury.

"You work for Zherdev, don't you?" she snapped.

Moroz flashed another smirk and glanced forward through the windshield. As he did Yulia examined the other two more at length. Their hair was so close cropped as to be practically shaved as well. One had a bull neck and a busted-up nose. The other had deep scar down his cheek and half his earlobe missing. Both thugs of the crudest order. They reestablished their grip on her upper arms.

"What do you want from me?"

There was no response. She came at them a second time.

"Okay...what does *he* want from me?"

Moroz took his time turning around. He cast snide, complicit glances at the two goons on either side of her before responding in the same derisive tone. "Let's just say Mr. Zherdev wants to keep it a surprise," he said.

Yulia shuddered again, more deeply. Her shakeout with Thorsson was now well past. Her brain had cleared and her senses were now on full alert. She looked out the side window, then forward through the windshield. Streetlights ticked by, infusing the city with a surreal glow. They were speeding back toward the center from which she'd just come by metro.

She was lucid enough to draw two conclusions. One was that Thorsson had been too much confident in the commitments of Harcourt Bank. The other was that they'd both placed too much trust in the guarantees of Oleg Mikhailov.

*   *   *

Sidewalks became more populated nearer to downtown, mostly by the same young crowd she'd just seen in the metro. Yulia could see their faces, uncomprehending through the tinted glass. When the BMW stopped at a traffic light at the end of Sophiaskaya Square, a gaggle of students loitered around the Bogdan Khmelnitsky statue just thirty meters away, vivid in their closeness. Just beyond them she also spotted two policemen. She considered a lunge toward the window or a blow against it with her heel and a shout for help.

Then she recalled that the driver had activated the window lock. The glass also looked reinforced and bulletproof. She stayed in place.

It turned out to be her last chance. The car zipped uninterrupted down Volodomirskaya Street, past the Golden Gate and the floodlit façade of the opera, then turned into the entrance to an underground garage, attended by a suited security man. She recognized the office building above, located just up from the main university campus. She'd gathered it was the swankiest business address in Kiev.

The door to the garage lowered behind them, giving her an ominous sense of enclosure. On the mostly empty first level, another suited security man stood near the elevator as the BMW pulled into an empty spot alongside. Before they got out Moroz twisted back to look at her again. At the same time she felt the goons on either side of her reestablish their grips on her arms.

"You'll be a good girl, won't you Yulia?" he said. "No stunts."

She looked straight back at him but said nothing. To insure that she complied, he exited first and stood by as she climbed out. As she did she noticed a tear in his trousers and a sizeable stain of wet blood where her heel had made contact. He sneered at her again and brought his mouth close to her ear so that she could feel his breath on her skin.

"You got away with it once," he said. "You won't again." He sounded like he meant it.

Her trio of escorts ushered her into the elevator, turned a key in the console, and pressed the button for the eighteenth floor. Seconds later they ascended into a glass shaft in the atrium lobby, bathed in the soft light of off hours. She looked down and out as they rose higher, past a hanging sculpture and some potted ferns on the periphery. Otherwise the space was empty on Saturday night, except for another suited security man patrolling the floor. At the uppermost level the doors slid open to reveal an outer-office reception area, decked out with gray carpeting and red-brown hardwood. Moroz got out first. Behind him the curved reception desk was empty. She glimpsed a raised emblem for *Donbass Holdings*.

"Right this way Yulia Borisovna," he said, contriving a polite tone and gesturing to his right.

They turned down a corridor of empty offices, their footfalls muffled by the carpet…as if she was marching toward some sort of private doom. Near the end, they turned right into an outer office, where another man waited alongside a vacant secretary's desk: about thirty years old, wearing a suit and open collar, muscled-up like the others but with a bit more polish. Glancing down and past her, he took note of the bloodstain on Moroz's pant leg. "I'll take over from here," he told him. "Go get that cleaned up."

Moroz sneered at her one last time as he withdrew. The man in the suit took light hold of her upper arm and knocked on the inner door, while her two original escorts took position outside.

When it opened she caught sight of Zherdev about twelve meters away. His office and desk were huge—larger than she'd ever seen. He reclined imperiously against the high backrest of his leather chair as she entered, wearing the same entitled expression she remembered from their first encounter. Tonight he wore a blazer, along with a striped shirt with an open collar that emphasized the stoutness around his neck. The man in the suit conducted her about halfway across before halting her there in space and pulling back against the wall. Otherwise the office was empty. She became conscious of plusher carpeting underfoot.

"Please excuse the way in which you brought here, Yulia," Zherdev said, with the same false solicitousness with which he'd opened at the hotel. "Regrettably I had no choice. I'd ask you to sit down, but it's probably best if you remain standing for now…at least until you hear me out." He next looked her up and down. "Before we continue, are you hurt?"

It was not a question Yulia expected. She still felt some soreness where the men had gripped her arms. But despite their violence, they'd done no serious damage. "No."

"Good. I say that because I asked you here with a purpose. Note that I chose my office." He swept his hand across the room with traces of vanity. "This isn't a hotel lobby. This is where I do real business."

CHAPTER 70

Yulia performed a quick survey of the room. It was done up with more ostentation and paneling than the outer area, with gold inlays in the moldings and a fancy furniture ensemble in the corner. Four or five large oil paintings adorned the walls. Behind the oligarch, though big plate-glass windows, she glimpsed a sweeping nighttime view over downtown. Thorsson's apartment building, with numerous windows alight, was visible down Khmelnitskovo.

Her emotional shakeout on the boulevard, and Thorsson too, now seemed like a world away.

Running her gaze back to Zherdev, she could see that he expected her to be impressed. She refused to give him the pleasure. She stood at fuller height on her heels and glowered back. "I don't call this doing business," she said. "I call it kidnapping. I also call it a crime."

He reacted with a look of bemusement then appraised her more at length, from head to toe and back up again. Once again she regretted her sexy presentation. Her silk dress had been for Thorsson only.

"Ah yes...crime. Not a word we hear that often, here in Ukraine. But that's the sort of country we live in, is it not?"

Yulia didn't like the description. Least of all from someone like Zherdev. "Thanks in no small part to you," she answered.

This elicited the same reaction from the oligarch. "Bravo, Yulia. I admire your attitude. You've reminded me that you're a girl with spirit. I'll be frank. Along with your looks that was one of the things about you that impressed me most in Alushta, during our first and altogether-too-brief encounter..." He paused and smiled again, as if relishing his recollection from the reception desk.

"What do exactly you want now?" she said. "I thought this was over."

"Over? Not quite. All I ask first is that you hear me out."

"For what? Haven't you done enough harm already?"

At this Zherdev's smile vanished. In its place he hardened his gaze and snorted through his nostrils. He still didn't like being refused. "Harm, you tell me? I guessed you'd react that way. Therefore I've prepared a little presentation...to put you in the proper frame of mind, shall we say." He reached for a handheld remote and pointed it toward a bookshelf. Two panels slid open to reveal a super-large flat-screen television, almost big enough for cinema. Next he dimmed the lights and pointed the device again. Yulia stayed in place but turned for better view. The top-down image that materialized—silent with no audio, black-and-white with a digital time clock in the corner—was of a lone young man emerging from his hotel room, wearing shorts, sandals, and a tee-shirt. He slung a beach bag over his shoulder and traversed a short distance down a corridor to an elevator, where he pressed a button and the door opened.

She recognized both man and setting at once. The man was Thorsson, minus his beard. The corridor was on the second floor of the RadissonBlu.

The next image came from the elevator, also top-down. As the car started down, Thorsson spied a small, dark item, barely visible on the carpet, and bent down to pick it up. He then raised it to eye level for further examination. He paused, as if considering what to do. The item was unmistakable, even in black and white.

The flash-memory stick. Yulia took a deep breath, aware of what followed.

In the next instant the video cut abruptly to another camera angle, a downward view covering the lower stairwell and most of the lobby. In it she was sitting alone at the reception desk. Thorsson exited the elevator, strode across the space in front and smiled. He addressed her briefly and held up the memory stick between his thumb and index finger. After another brief conversation, which she could recall word for word, he handed it over. Seconds later he continued into the lounge, toward the beach. She was then shown sitting alone at the desk, holding the item in her fingers and staring at it with a concentrated expression. Before any further action, Zherdev pointed his remote and froze the image in place.

"This is where it gets interesting, Yulia," he said. "Please note the digital time clock in the corner."

The digits read 08:15:47. By now about two minutes had elapsed since Thorsson had picked up the flash in the elevator. In the image, she remained sitting in the same position for almost ninety additional seconds, alternately staring at the flash stick and into space—critical, decisive seconds that she also could recall as if they'd happened yesterday. The image then jerked suddenly. She was still sitting alone at the counter but no longer holding the flash stick. Upon closer inspection it was visible, instead, on the counter next to her computer. Several seconds later Zherdev refroze the video.

"Now," he said, "please note the time once again."

Yulia looked at the bottom corner for verification. The digits now read 08:19:04. Zherdev remained calm and cold but pronounced his next words with relish.

"Rather odd, isn't it Yulia? Seems almost two minutes are missing…any comments?"

She looked back at him and said nothing. Her first worry was Vladimir Nosko.

"As I expected," he said. "Well, you obviously enlisted one or more accomplices in the hotel, whom I plan to identify. And your admission is redundant anyway. From here on, there are only a couple of sections that really matter."

He then fast-forwarded through much of the ensuing eighteen or nineteen minutes, including Anna's arrival at the reception desk and her interactions, along with Yulia's own, with several guest parties. He slowed the video to normal speed again only when his grim-faced lieutenants appeared to recollect the device. After Yulia spoke with the men and handed the device over, and they'd departed, he froze the recording and raised the lights.

"Nice little acting job, Yulia, if I may say so," he observed. "If you hadn't performed your little subterfuge and been honest in the first place, I wouldn't have blamed Thorsson. He'd still be on vacation, enjoying himself." The comment hit home but she tried hard not to let it show. He fixed another hard stare on her and continued. "Unfortunately I didn't get hold of this video until about a week after the fact. And by then, of course, events were already in motion. Does Thorsson now know what you did, in the name of your own little agenda?"

This remark struck target even harder. She reached up to the corner of her eye to suppress a tear, barely managing to fight it back.

"But let's leave Thorsson aside for the moment," the oligarch continued. "I'll return to him later. Your cousin Pavel, on the other hand, falls in a different category. Unlike Thorsson he was a willing and active participant in your scheme. Worst of all, he chose to single me out for his most pointed attacks, for reasons I can't fathom. Allow me to read you some lines from his original article." With that he reached toward a side table and grabbed a copy of *Ukraina Sevodnya*, recognizable by its masthead, which he brandished toward her. He then grasped it in both hands and furrowed his brow as he focused on the front page. "For example, it says here, 'Most prominent among them was Leonid Zherdev, one of the richest men in Ukraine, who reportedly stayed offshore on his private yacht for the duration of the conference, commuting daily to the hotel by motor launch...'" He scanned down the page. "And then this: 'Materials obtained by *Ukraina Sevodnya*, which include presentation outlines and detailed written proposals from Harcourt Bank to individual participants, indicate that Harcourt convened these prominent figures and their associates with one main overarching objective: to conceive means of influencing the agricultural reform legislation now under consideration in the Ukrainian Parliament and to formulate plans for a wholesale takeover of the Ukrainian agricultural sector by a limited coterie of wealthy industrialists and well-connected political insiders. Judging from these documents, Zherdev intended to play a leading role...'"

Zherdev put the newspaper down on his desk and refocused a hard gaze. "At that point, of course, I didn't know Pavel was your cousin. That also came to me later. But it didn't change the fact. He attacked me, so I responded in kind. I had little choice in the world I inhabit. Your cousin deserved what he got."

The oligarch punctuated his remark with a look of vindication. In it, Yulia saw what she should have recognized more explicitly all along. The man not only lacked conscience. He was a sociopath. She shuddered, just as she had in the car. She could also see that he wasn't done and braced herself for more.

"I wished it could have ended there," he resumed. "But to my regret it did not." With that he reached over to his side table again and picked up two additional publications: a color tabloid and a glossy magazine. He held up one in each hand and also brandished them in her direction. She had no trouble recognizing either one, even from across the room. One was the *Vecherny Vesti*; the other was its sister weekly *Ukrainski Insaider*. Zherdev made a show of opening the latter, flipping through to the relevant pages and photographs and furrowing his brow as he focused on its contents.

"Let me see here," he continued. "I'll read a few segments straight from the text. It says, 'We can now identify this mystery bombshell, who was first photographed last week by our sister publication *Vecherny Vesti* in a discreet rendezvous with accused murderer Axel Thorsson.

She is Yulia Petrenko, aged twenty-three and a receptionist at the RadissonBlu Hotel…since Thorsson's arrest, further reporting has revealed that he was a guest at the hotel during a mysterious and secretive business conference that took place there just a week earlier… Thorsson is now awaiting trial, though his proceedings have not yet been scheduled. In the meantime the hotel has placed Petrenko on extended leave of absence. The hotel refuses comment.'"

Zherdev raised his eyes from the magazine and reapplied his hard gaze. "Harm, you say? The first articles were bad enough. And now the tabloids are really dragging me through the muck. Thousands of people are vilifying me on social media, too. The way I see it, I've been harmed plenty myself."

This remark was just further confirmation to Yulia. He'd detached from reality; in his own mind he was culpable of nothing. "That wasn't my doing," she said. "I didn't seek that attention from the tabloids or on Facebook. Neither did Thorsson."

In response the oligarch gave her a sharper, cunning look. He put the publications aside. "Really? As far as I've gathered, you've picked up in Kiev right where you left off."

Yulia already suspected Zherdev was apprised of her recent meetings with Thorsson but recoiled anyway. "What difference does it make?" she retorted. "We were never photographed by the media again."

"You're lucky you weren't. The two of you have been flaunting your relationship all over town, often in public places. Allow me to show you some examples." He picked up the remote control again, pointed it toward the television, then re-dimmed the lights. An image appeared, still and in color, of her and Thorsson during their first rendezvous in the capital, sitting in conversation at their outdoor table at Warsteiner Café. This was followed by another from somewhat different angle. A third showed them walking to the metro stop afterward.

"Why perform a running commentary?" Zherdev added. "I'll just let the rest of this little slideshow speak for itself."

The succession of frames that followed, each projected for about five seconds, covered each of their ensuing meetings: from Mariinsky Park to Arsenalna station, to lunch with her mother and aunt, to their dash through the rain to Saint Volodomir's Church, to their exit from Leo, to their nighttime stroll under the arch and up Kreschatik. Most distressing to Yulia were the final two images: one of her and Thorsson in passionate embrace in the middle of the boulevard and another, taken just after her shakeout, with the two of them holding glum distance as they walked to Teatralna station. They'd been taken less than an hour earlier.

The oligarch observed her reaction with shrewd eyes through the semidarkness and raised the lights. She tried to contain her anger. She also felt suddenly restive, until she remembered Zherdev's muscled-up henchman, still standing against the wall. "What's the point of this show?" she asked him. "Isn't this supposed to be settled?"

"You mean by Oleg Mikhailov?"

"Yes. And by Harcourt Bank also."

"Maybe. But I have just one more piece I'd like to conclude, if you'll permit me. Let me start with Thorsson. He may have been an unwitting participant in your scheme at first. But he certainly doesn't look like one now. Did you tell him all the facts? I mean about your original subterfuge?"

"That's none of your business."

"In any case he now seems interested in you in more ways than one."

His insinuating, proprietary tone smacked of their original encounter at the hotel. She felt another rise of anger. She was therefore caught a little off guard by his follow-on.

"My compliments, Yulia."

"Compliments? For what?"

"For co-opting him. For getting him to do your bidding. The same goes for Pavel, too, for that matter."

The characterization was so far off the mark that she didn't know to respond—all the more when the oligarch reassumed his original pose.

"I will admit. I underestimated you at the beginning. Please forgive me. Shall we put all this behind us now, Yulia, and get off on different footing?"

"I just want this to be over."

"Good. I do too. In this spirit I have a proposal for you." He paused for effect, keeping his eyes on her but softening his gaze. "In short, I'd like to offer you a job."

After all the violence and harm he'd inflicted, Yulia was appalled. He really was delusional. A megalomaniac of the first order.

The oligarch sensed her reaction. To preclude it he held up his hand. "I can guess what you're thinking," he said. "But before you make any hasty responses, allow me to fill out some details. I don't want to hire you as receptionist...nothing of the kind. I've learned more about you over these past weeks, including your education, your previous work as a journalist, your English, and so on. And I now know, through firsthand experience, that you're capable of much more than what you've been doing at the hotel." He paused again for build-up. "In short, I'd like to offer you a position as my spokesperson to the press, in charge of all media communications for me personally and for my group of companies at large."

First she'd been appalled. Now she was astonished. He continued.

"The job will be centered here in Kiev. You will be given a large office of your own, just down the hall. However the position will require extensive travel, some within Ukraine but much of it international. In additional to my business interests in the Donetsk region and my villa in Crimea, I also maintain residences abroad in Zug, London, Courchevel, and New York. When I travel to them, naturally, you will accompany me on my private jet—just one of three or four employees accorded this status. At times my wife will accompany us. And like everyone who travels with me, you will be accommodated in premium, five-star hotels. And given a generous personal budget besides. Not to mention six weeks of paid vacation per year."

Yulia remembered the magazine spread she'd seen on Zherdev and his wife, together with their dog. She also wondered just how often his wife and dog would come along on these trips. Somehow she guessed their presence would be the exception rather than the rule.

The oligarch paused to observe her reaction. He seemed to misperceive it. "Oh yes," he added. "I shouldn't leave out the rather important matter of your salary. I've learned what you've been making at the hotel. And if I may say so it's rather modest for a girl of your talents. Therefore I'd now like to multiply it by ten. And that's just a starting point."

Yulia performed a quick calculation, momentarily stunned by the number. That kind of pay in Ukraine, especially at her age, was almost beyond belief.

The oligarch paused to observe her again. "So now you see why I've brought you here tonight. My means were regrettable. But I had a good reason…well, what do you say?"

Yulia's head was spinning again, for different reasons now than over dinner.

Zherdev smiled, as confident as ever. "Take a minute or two, if you wish," he added. "It's obviously a big decision."

She took a deep breath to collect herself. The thought occurred to her, despite all her loathing, that this was a dream job. Zherdev had apparently thought this through. It drew upon everything. Her writing talent. Her journalism degree. Her practical experience as a reporter. Even her languages. And she'd live the high life besides. First-class travel to Switzerland, London, and New York. All at age twenty-three.

By irrepressible increments, though, facts reclaimed her. She remembered his debased proposition at the hotel and his leering appraisal when she'd first walked into his office. In between those two bookends, he'd dispensed hideous violence—against Thorsson and

Pavel most of all. She now knew his real nature, close up and firsthand. He'd done deep, corrupting damage to Ukraine and now wanted to do the same to her. Her anger rose higher and her defiance along with it. All her emotions, all her ups and downs of the previous three weeks, crystallized into a single response.

Her mother had not raised her to curse like a shoemaker. But in this case, Yulia reckoned, her mother would make an allowance. She straightened her back, stood at her full height on her heels and stared Zherdev squarely in the eyes.

"You can take that offer and shove it up where it belongs."

Her words almost seemed to reverberate off the paneling, unreal in their audaciousness. When they subsided a hushed silence fell over the office, amplified by the plush carpet. She also realized that she'd been reckless beyond imagination. That she'd hurtled herself, in all probability, straight toward her own doom.

Zherdev appeared startled at first. She'd refused him once, and now, to his disbelief, she'd done it again. During the next edged seconds, while she watched with a sense of encroaching doom, his eyes blazed with wrath. In her peripheral vision she also saw his henchman step forward to intervene. She fully expected to be grabbed anew, hustled back down to the car, and taken outside the city to the forest, there to suffer the same fate as Pavel—or worse.

Instead the oligarch's eyes turned cold again, and he held up his hand. "No more of that," he said. "She's had her chance. Just take her home."

CHAPTER 71

The realization had come to Thorsson as he'd lain in bed, staring at the ceiling in a state of moral disquiet and profound disappointment with himself. Soon thereafter he'd obtained a restful night's sleep. When he awoke, the idea seemed to him more valid than ever. Over breakfast he'd only affirmed it.

Yulia had done both of them a favor. In the heat of the moment—just when philosophy had deserted him and he'd succumbed to his usual impulses, when all his struggles for improvement seemed to have come to naught—she'd exercised prudence and moderation. Her instincts had been true.

Yes, his interest in her was genuine. But neither one of them had committed. The timing was way too fast.

Now he appreciated her more than ever. And they probably stood a better chance going forward.

There was almost no traffic at this hour on Sunday, and his car came with a GPS system besides, easing his passage. When he reached Tatarska Lane he turned left and found the number to Pavel's building. Skies were bright but for now temperatures were comfortable. Nevertheless he parked under the shade of a chestnut tree, partly so that the car would not be visible from above. He wanted to surprise her.

Thus far he'd kept the top closed. A white Mercedes SLK coupe: stylish and top of the line, which now suited his frame of mind. He'd dressed for the countryside in shorts and a sports shirt. His bathing suit and towel were in a bag in the trunk.

He got out and stood on the sidewalk as the minutes ticked past nine. Finally Yulia emerged from the building, clothed in tight denim shorts, a summer blouse, and sandals, carrying a canvas bag with gift items for her relative. Her eyes showed little enthusiasm when she saw the car. Her gloom made him even more intent to rectify his error. When she drew closer he opened the passenger door.

"Is this a convertible?" she asked in a lifeless tone.

"We're headed into the country. I figured why not?"

She didn't respond. He endeavored to stay upbeat. "Well, do you like it?"

"I don't know. I've never been in one."

She offered no further reaction as she climbed into her seat, avoiding eye contact, as he hastened around and climbed into the driver's seat. His first impulse was to place his hand on her knee. Instead he kept his hand on the shift, placed his elbow on the wheel, and twisted toward her.

"Look, Yulia. I know I pushed too far, too fast last night. It was way too early. You were right to respond the way you did."

Instead of looking back at him she kept her eyes forward. A tear streaked down her cheek.

"You still want to go, I hope."

She wiped it away. "To be honest, I wasn't sure last night. However, when I got up this morning my mother convinced me stick to the plan." While Thorsson mulled this remark, she at last turned her face toward him. "It isn't because of what you did. It's because something that happened after we parted ways."

"Why? What happened?"

"I was abducted. By Zherdev's men. They took me to see him."

"Zherdev? I thought he was finished with us."

"Turns out he wasn't…at least not with me."

His first worry was that she'd been beaten, like Pavel. He hadn't noticed anything awry and reexamined her face, arms, and legs for signs of injury. To his relief, there were none. "Tell me exactly what happened, Yulia," he said. "Don't leave anything out." He kept his elbow on the steering wheel and the car in place as she related the episode from start to finish, spilling out each detail with emotions that seemed to have been building up for weeks. Almost ten minutes later, when she was done, she directed her face toward him again. Now there were streaks down both cheeks. All her accruals of anger, grievance, and determination had now come full surface. "Well?" she asked him.

"I understand how disturbing it was. But in the end you returned unharmed. That's the main thing. Let's not forget Zherdev is now operating under the dictates of the FSB and Harcourt Bank. Sounds to me like this was the last installment."

She heaved a deep breath through her nostrils and wiped away her tears, first one and then the other. She still looked uncertain.

"The best we can now is to reclaim some normalcy. We can't live the rest of our lives in fear, can we? Let's also not forget your original rationale…that is, to expose me to village life. To show me why you and Pavel though agricultural reform is so important in the first place."

"I admit I'd almost forgotten."

"This might even help provide closure."

"So you think we should go ahead?"

"Yes, I do."

By now her tears had dried. Her deliberation didn't last long. "I agree," she said. "My relative has been planning on us. And the weather's nice too. Let's do it."

Thorsson faced forward, strapped on his seatbelt, and donned his sunglasses. Yulia did likewise. Without further pause he activated the ignition, and the 3.2-liter V6 engine sprang to life under the hood. He was now glad he'd rented the car after all.

Before he shifted into gear and pulled away from the curb, he glanced at her profile. Despite her decision, she still looked tentative.

*   *   *

Mikhailov returned to the position he'd chosen by the plate-glass window, placed his cup and saucer on the side table, and settled into his upholstered lounge chair. He took several sips of coffee, enjoying the view over the runways, then checked his watch. Given the three-hour time-zone difference, he figured the timing was about right. With his free hand he extracted his phone from his computer case and tapped Vera's number. She answered at once, with more enthusiasm than he expected.

"Are you and Dima already on the beach?" he asked her.

"Yes. We just got set up. Dima's out swimming."

On standard schedule, just as he'd assumed. He inquired about the weather. She said it was idyllic. In Crimea, at this time of year, the question was almost redundant.

"Are you already at Heathrow?" she asked him.

Mikhailov glanced out over the runways again. He watched a Delta Airlines 747 jumbo come in for landing, its tires kicking up smoke when their rubber hit the pavement. "Checked in and ready to go," he answered. "I'm now in the British Airways business-class lounge in terminal five. My flight boards in less than an hour."

"What about breakfast? Have you had time?"

"I left my hotel at five o'clock this morning, so not yet. I may have a little something here in the lounge, but I'm sure I'll get a big breakfast on the plane. The flight will be more than three hours long."

He spotted another jumbo jet out the window, descending toward the runway. Further across, on a parallel strip, three other jets had queued for takeoff. He raised his cup and drew another sip of coffee. His plan included an additional activity on board, which he opted not to mention.

"Do you still have some obligations in Kiev when you touch down?" Vera inquired further.

"I'm afraid so…just some final pieces of business. To wrap up this assignment, you might say. However I'm still booked on the one-thirty flight to Simferopol tomorrow. By four in the afternoon, I should be back on the beach with you and Dima."

"We're looking forward to it."

"So am I, Vera."

"Have a pleasant flight."

"I will. I'll call you this evening from Kiev."

When they'd concluded Mikhailov gazed out again over the runways and drained the rest of his cup. Vera had refrained from asking him about details. In fact both of his appointments—one with Heather Robinson and the other with the Ukrainian Security Service—were not until the next morning. That left his flight free for separate pursuits and his entire Sunday afternoon as well.

He'd been honest with her, in the main. He was looking forward to seeing her again. Dima, too. What he hadn't told her, though, was what he was looking forward to most.

His assignment was nearly complete. His writing could now reclaim first priority.

CHAPTER 72

One consequence of Yulia's late-night ordeal, it seemed to Thorsson, was that his proposition on Kreschatik—just ten hours or so earlier—had now been displaced. On the other hand she was still not quite herself, for understandable reasons.

On their way out of the city he tried therefore to reassure her. To cast the episode for what it seemed to be. One final convulsion. The last of a succession.

His words had the effect he intended. By time they attained the MO3 highway toward Poltava, her mood had stabilized. The surrounding countryside only accentuated the trend. Sensing that she preferred to stay silent, he also kept the top secured and the radio off. Their SLK, with its air conditioning, heavy glass and leather, muted the sounds from passing cars—as much moving cosset as convertible.

Expanses of farmland swept by on either side: fields of wheat, corn, and potatoes, broken up by patches of lush forest. The Stoics, he remembered, cherished rural spaces and agrarian life, finding them conducive to detachment. The same appeared to hold for Yulia, who soon gazed out her side window, deep in thought. He then looked forward again over the steering wheel and engaged some reflection of his own. On both her situation and his, over the coming months. He also thought about Ukraine.

All three beckoned for answers, on different levels. They also intersected in a way he hadn't previously registered. Over the next eighty or ninety kilometers, as they moved deeper into the countryside, he fleshed out an idea. By time they turned off the highway, it was fully formed.

*   *   *

The village where Yulia's relative lived was situated about one kilometer off the paved secondary road and consisted of about fifteen wood-and-concrete houses, spaced out down a narrow dirt lane, four meters across and cleaved by ruts. With the low-slung SLK, Thorsson had to navigate with care, weaving across the mounded-up surface points. All the same he scraped bottom more than once.

"I admit I didn't think of this when I chose the sports car," he commented.

"Are we going to make it?"

"We should be okay. I'll just take it slow."

About halfway in two middle-aged men made way, appraised their car, and scrutinized them through the windows—frank, though not unfriendly. Visitors from the big city, Thorsson sensed, were a rather rare occurrence. At last they rounded a slight bend and Yulia gestured ahead.

"It's been quite a while since I was here," she said. "But that's it."

Thorsson took in the dwelling she'd indicated. It was modest in size, with stucco walls, a slate roof and several smaller outer structures. The surrounding yard was enclosed by a slatted fence, which contained some well-tended vines and a patch of grass. Several apple trees lent some shade to a simple courtyard. Large plots of vegetables were visible in the background, behind the house.

"You said this woman is your second cousin, right?"

"That's right. But her relation is actually closer than that. My mother also did her university studies in Kiev…back in Soviet times in the eighties. The rest of her family was abroad in Hungary, where her father was stationed as an army officer. So she often traveled out here to the village on holidays and vacations. At the time, this woman and her husband had three kids, all teenagers. This woman almost became a surrogate parent. I suppose I could call her my aunt. But I've always called her by her patronymic, Sofiya Yaroslavovna."

"And her husband is now deceased?"

"Yes, already more than five years ago. That was just before I came to Kiev to study. My parents and I came to visit her when they drove up to get me settled. After that Sofiya Yaroslavovna gave me an open invitation. But it was the last time I was here, I regret to say."

"What about her kids? Do they still live around here?"

"No, they all moved away when they became adults. One's in Kiev, and the other two are in Poltava."

"And Sofiya Yaroslavovna is able to cope out here all by herself?"

"She has until now."

"Even in winter?"

"The villagers here look out for one another. They help with certain work, when needed. Her kids also visit her from time to time. But her pension is very small. That means she mostly manages on her own. She's a strong woman."

They were now almost to the house. Thorsson glanced at the yard again, where he also noticed several walnut trees and a chicken coop, with an outer wall near the road. He didn't doubt it.

"Before we arrive I should also tell you about the meal," Yulia added. "We visited here several times when I was a kid, when Sofiya Yaroslavovna and her husband always organized big *shashliki*. Unfortunately she can't really barbecue now by herself anymore. Today's lunch will be a little simpler."

"I'm sure it will be splendid."

"Oh...there's one more thing. Here in the village people speak Ukrainian for the most part, not Russian. Sofiya Yaroslavovna speaks Russian too, but it's not her primary language. You might bear that in mind as you talk to her."

"I will. Thanks for alerting me."

Sofiya Yaroslavovna was waiting when they reached her property and opened her gate so that they could drive in and park. She hardly glanced at the Mercedes. Instead her eyes went straight to Yulia when they got out and then to Thorsson, garnished by smiles for both of them. For someone in her late sixties, she was a robust, vibrant woman, not as tall as Yulia but just as full bodied. She wore a cotton dress and apron that Thorsson associated with Ukrainian peasant motifs. Despite Yulia's long absence she gave her an embrace and kisses before Yulia introduced him.

Sofiya Yaroslavovna only warmed further. She also seemed a little intrigued by his beard.

Yulia gathered the chocolates and cookies she'd brought from the city. On their way toward the house, just past the chicken coop, Thorsson glimpsed a wooden table in the courtyard, already adorned by a patterned tablecloth, utensils and glasses, a carafe of cranberry juice, and a tray of dried walnuts. Scents of cooking wafted out from the nearby kitchen. Lunch would be ready in about an hour and a half, Yulia told him. First, though, she would show him around and take him down to the river.

Once they were out in open air, Thorsson felt the sun on his face. Skies were even brighter now, no longer obscured by clouds. He also became aware of a symphony of birdsongs, animal calls, and chirping insects from fields and forest alike. He sensed, already, that the setting would be unlike any that he and Yulia had experienced in Kiev. Same held for the meal.

This promised to be a day he would remember.

*   *   *

Thorsson came up from his dive after touching bottom and found Yulia looking out at him when he surfaced. He shook the water from his hair and beard, unable to repress a smile.

"Lately I've been partial to saltwater," he said. "But perhaps I should reconsider. This water is amazingly clean. It feels so pure."

She reciprocated with a more modest smile of her own and squatted lower onto her thighs. The small dock from which she was watching, she'd told him, had been built by Sofiya Yaroslavovna's husband, many years earlier. Above all she seemed relieved that he was enjoying himself.

"You said this is a tributary that feeds into the Dnieper?"

"That's right. The Poltavski region, just east of Kiev, is combed through with them. Moreover it's considered the most ecologically pristine region in Ukraine. Here, you can almost count on purity."

Thorsson took several strokes back toward the dock so he could talk at closer range. The channel traced the back of the property and was about forty meters across. Based on his dive, he guessed it to be five or six meters deep in the middle. He looked up at Yulia and asked her if his estimate was accurate.

"I'd say so," she answered.

"Rather ample. Plus you said there are many others like it in this region. That would seem to afford plenty of irrigation for crops."

"Exactly so…these tributaries run all through central Ukraine. It's one reason the farmland here is so fertile."

"The most fertile in the world, right?"

She grew more thoughtful again, as she'd been in the car. Thorsson had meant the comment to be upbeat.

"That's why I wanted to show it to you," she said after a pause.

"I know, Yulia. Thanks."

During his dive Thorsson had seen numerous fish. Now that his head was above water, wider sights and sounds engulfed him again. Tree branches overhung both riverbanks, thick with leaves and underscored by reeds and marsh grass. Two large birds alighted from one of them. Croaking frogs were audible from around the dock. Another more guttural sound issued from behind him, on the bank opposite. When he turned around to determine its source, he noticed a rustle in the grass and reeds and spotted a dark mound, just detectable above the surface and moving at steady speed.

"Is that a beaver?" he asked Yulia, twisting his face back.

"That's typical. The river is full of them."

Thorsson watched the creature for a moment longer. In his countless outdoor swims over the years, this was a first.

"Don't worry," she added. "They don't bother people. Except, of course, for the occasional unwanted dam."

He laughed, and she smiled back. She then raised herself to full height. "As I said, I wish I could join you. But I really should go help Sofiya Yaroslavovna in the kitchen. You're sure you don't mind if I leave you alone here for a while?"

"Not at all…you're sure I can't help too?"

"No need. You're a guest here."

Still treading water, Thorsson then watched her turn around, retrace down the dock, and climb the bank along Sofiya Yaroslavovna's farmland. Their shakeout on Kreschatik now seemed inconsequential, like a flutter on a trend line. He felt suddenly purified of the errors that had caused it.

They still had some uncertainties to confront. And he hadn't yet told her about the idea that had occurred to him in the car. But at the moment he felt nothing but harmony—with nature, with surrounding wildlife, and toward his future overall.

He blew a hard exhalation and launched into a crawl-stoke down the river, gaining power with each pull through the water. The swim, he realized, was his first since Alushta. He decided it would serve as absolution. Not just for himself but for Yulia too.

The worst was now behind them.

CHAPTER 73

S ofiya Yaroslavovna was too generous and polite to expect help from her guests. Yulia almost had to beg her for kitchen assignments. One, which she assumed with great relief, was to stir the soup: an aromatic mixture of chicken, baby potatoes, green onions, parsley, and *salo.* The chicken, she learned through some queries in Ukrainian, was one that Sofiya Yaroslavovna had purchased in a regional market about ten kilometers away. To reach it, she had walked to the end of the village road and taken the bus, the only one of the day. Her own chickens, those in the coop, were for egg laying only. Seven ovules from their morning output were now laid out on the counter, ready for frying.

Yulia had not visited for five years. And yet Sofiya Yaroslavovna was opening her home and table without restraint. Receiving her— and Thorsson too—with the same generosity she'd shown her mother some twenty-five years earlier. With slight shame Yulia remembered why she'd refrained for so long from coming—reasons she hadn't admitted to Thorsson. Truth was, she'd considered the village boring. The bright lights and excitement of the big city offered more fun. The men too, though she'd eventually learned their downsides.

Her mother had urged her to make the effort. Once again she should have listened.

There was a deeper angle. One she'd only grasped recently. The village was more than a settlement or place on the map. The village and villagers formed the heart and soul of Ukraine.

While she continued to stir the pot, she glanced again at Sofiya Yaroslavovna. Here was a woman who'd been born little more than a decade after the brutality and starvation of Stalin's Holodomor. Who'd spent much of her life toiling on the nearby collective farm. Who since independence had been exploited, neglected, and even disdained. Yet she bore no grudges. She simply rose every morning with the same cheerful approach and carried on.

There were many social dysfunctions in rural areas, Yulia knew. Drunkenness among the men. Out-of-wedlock births among the teenage girls. Frayed marriages.

But the baseline decency remained.

Like so many other reforms in Ukraine, therefore, agricultural reform had to be done in the open and done right. For the sake Sofiya Yaroslavovna, for the sake of countless villagers like her. For the sake of the country as a whole too.

She was now more convinced of it than ever.

And that, in turn, required journalists. Her mother had been right on that question as well. She'd been so all along. Yulia had made her decision in the car. And now, standing in the kitchen next to Sofiya Yaroslavovna, she was surer of it than ever.

*   *   *

Yulia's preemptive apology was unnecessary, just as Thorsson had suspected. The reality was evident as soon as Yulia and Sofiya emerged from the kitchen with the first batches of food to the shade of the picnic table. There was nothing modest about their lunch. It was a feast.

They debuted with fried eggs, sausages, and salo, garnished with cabbage salad and fresh cucumbers. Their second course, building on the first, consisted of green-onion borsch, augmented by brown bread larded with butter. Their penultimate and primary installment was a rich chicken-and-onion soup, of which he consumed several large bowls, supplemented with more baby potatoes. The only indulgence missing was alcohol, because he was driving. He compensated with multiple glasses of fresh goat's milk drawn from the udder that morning.

Through this procession he did more eating and drinking than talking, urged along by Yulia and Sofiya Yaroslavovna. Only when they progressed to the raspberries and desserts—small *vareniki* topped with sweet cream and complemented by hot tea, as well as the chocolates and cookies Yulia had brought from the city—did Yulia invoke the purpose of her visit. On that she was true to her declaration.

"In the kitchen I had a chance to chat with Sofiya Yaroslavovna about conditions out here in the village," she said to him. "They're even worse than I realized. In fact worse now than ever, since Yanukovich became president." She turned to her relative. "Am I right, Sofiya Yaroslavovna?"

"Well, yes…unfortunately."

It was the first time since they'd arrived that Thorsson detected a melancholic note in the woman's voice. He asked where the deteriorations had occurred.

"Pensions are lower than ever," she said. "And there's no maintenance. The asphalt road into town is falling apart. Bus service has been cut. In winter, it takes days before we see a snowplow."

"Meanwhile, the head administrators in town are driving hundred-thousand-dollar cars," Yulia interjected.

Thorsson was well aware of the phenomenon, which prompted another uncharacteristically rueful look from Sofiya Yaroslavovna over her teacup. "What about the younger farmers?" he asked her. "Are they still trying to make a go of it?"

"Some are hanging on. But they can't get bank loans. Then there are the problems of getting their products to the market in town... others just give up."

Before Thorsson could query her further, Sofiya Yaroslavovna suddenly cast off her baleful expression and her irrepressible smile returned. She excused herself to the kitchen to brew another pot of tea. When she was gone, Yulia lowered her voice a little. "She doesn't like to complain, especially with guests. But you get the picture."

"Pretty bleak, overall," Thorsson observed, draining the rest of his cup. "I'm amazed she stays so upbeat."

"Many villagers are like that. But most are essentially subsistence farmers. They're barely scraping by."

"Despite the fact that she lives in the breadbasket of Europe...or at least what should be, in terms of its potential."

"Exactly. And the villagers know this. All they really want is better infrastructure, decent laws, and a cleaner financial system. Then for the government to get out of their way. They'd do the rest on their own."

In the next instant, Sofiya Yaroslavovna rounded the corner from the kitchen again, with a fresh pot of tea. She was still smiling. "But let's stop talking politics for now," Yulia suggested, "and enjoy the rest of our desserts."

Thorsson agreed. All the same he sensed Yulia still had something to say. He also sensed, somehow, that it concerned redemption. Much like his own idea.

*   *   *

Some forty minutes later, after engaging lighter topics, they at last rose to clear away the dishes. Little to Yulia's surprise, Sofiya Yaroslavovna again declined Thorsson's offer of help. Yulia helped her with the transfer, but in the kitchen the older woman would hear nothing of additional assistance with the cleanup. She insisted instead that she rejoin Thorsson and keep him entertained. When Yulia returned to the table, she and

Thorsson exited the shade of the courtyard and set out for one last walk, down toward the river and back. Though the sun was still bright, temperatures remained mild and pleasant, thanks to a freshening breeze.

"You told me the lunch would be simple," Thorsson told her, placing both hands on his belly, "while in fact, it was one for the ages."

"You enjoyed it, then?"

"Immensely. If that were my last on the planet, I think I'd die happy."

Yulia beheld his stomach with a slight smile. It really was bulging a little. He had eaten a lot.

"Sofiya Yaroslavovna is an extraordinary woman," he added. "Thanks for bringing me here."

"It was my pleasure. And hers too."

"One question, though. She seemed rather curious about my beard, even if she never said anything about it…any particular reason?"

"I noticed that too. Then I remembered. Here in the village, the only men with beards are the priests."

"Ahh…now I get it," Thorsson answered, smiling.

Over the next ten or twelve steps Yulia fell silent and focused her thoughts. They were now skirting a tomato patch on a path of well-worn grass that led to the water. "I said I wanted to tell you something…" she began. When Thorsson turned his head again she got straight to the point. "I've decided to work as a journalist…" The words seemed to resonate in the sweet air, once they were out. She took a breath. "It's what my mother has been urging all along. Even you said the same thing. Now I realize she was right, as usual."

"Do you intend to start immediately?"

"I hope so…full time, if I can. I'm not going back to the hotel. That wasn't realistic anyway. Vladimir Nosko is a great guy. But too much has happened. Let's say Zherdev finally pushed me over the edge last night."

She took a deep breath before continuing. "Maybe it's futile. But it's still a job that needs to be done. Today, when I saw what Sofiya

Yaroslavovna is facing out here in the village because of people like Zherdev, I became even more convinced of it."

"Where? At *Ukraina Sevodnya*, Pavel's newspaper?"

"That's right. Alexander Brisiuck, the editor, has given me a standing offer, ever since graduation. He can't pay me much. And as I mentioned the paper may not last beyond six or twelve months. But I've decided to go ahead anyway." Yulia paused to await his reaction. When it was slow in coming, she turned to examine his face more closely. He looked pleased but also thoughtful. The expression was not quite the one she expected. "You approve?" she asked him.

"I more than approve," he answered. "I applaud. To be frank, I was even hoping that would be your announcement."

Yulia knew he held a high opinion of her writing. And that he wanted the best for Ukraine. All the same she was a little puzzled. Before she could probe, he spoke again.

"Do you know how much financing the paper needs?" he asked her.

"You should remember that *Ukraina Sevodnya* is one of the few truly independent news operations in Ukraine. In other words, they're not backed and controlled by an oligarch, with all that entails. I don't know details, but Pavel has mentioned something like half a million, just to keep going. They can't get bank loans any longer. The current owners are just trying to unload the paper. Sell it in full. They're seeking an even million dollars, as I understand."

Upon hearing this he fell into a focused state of his own. First he gazed forward into space, then down at the ground, and then forward again, while clasping his hands behind his waist. It was the first time Yulia had seen him in this pose, which she associated more with older men. They'd now attained a ripening patch of cantaloupe and watermelons. The slope down to the river was just fifty meters ahead.

"I should also tell you now that I've conceived an idea of my own," he said. "It occurred to me in the car and is one that I was going to tell you about even before you told me yours. I'll need to explore more details. But our visit here with Sofiya Yaroslavovna has only reinforced it."

He drew a deep breath through his nostrils and exhaled again. Yulia searched his profile again. At last he angled his face toward hers.

"I'd like to invest that million dollars and buy the paper," he said. "This new windfall of mine comes from Harcourt. That makes it of dubious provenance. And the Stoics counseled indifference to wealth anyway."

CHAPTER 74

At first Yulia was too stunned to respond. Thorsson seemed to be taking on a burden that wasn't his. He wasn't Ukrainian. He was American. She figured he'd suffered enough already. Her second worry was that he was acting out of some sense of obligation toward her. The way she saw it, she owed *him* a moral debt, not vice versa. She wondered if their blossoming but uncertain romance had clouded his thinking. That he was moving in haste.

She looked down at Sofiya Yaroslavovna's dock and at the gently flowing water around it. She remembered the near-lethal attack he'd suffered in the water in Alushta, everything he'd endured since, and tried to bring the reckonings full circle. Finally she collected her thoughts enough to ask him:

"Are you doing this for Ukraine, for me, or out of some kind of conscience?"

"All of the above," he answered.

The answer did little to quell her misgivings. When Thorsson observed this he elaborated. "I also admit I'm doing this for myself," he said. "I started my vacation in Alushta seeking redemption. This gives me an important means toward it."

Yulia was stunned by this as well. "Redemption? Here in Ukraine?"

"That's right."

"But can't get you get that in the United States? I mean...it's probably the freest, richest country on the planet."

"Maybe so. And I'm likely to head back at some point. But Ukraine is now a country in transition. Struggling against defects, largely of its own making, but aiming for something better. Much like I am. At this particular moment, it's a perfect match."

"But what if Ukraine continues to get worse?"

"That's a risk I'm prepared to take."

"Or if you lose the money?"

At this Thorsson smiled. "Here's another way of looking at it," he said. "One million is a fraction of the total. I've got plenty more to invest, if necessary. And lots in reserve after that."

Yulia drew a deep breath. He still seemed to be risking himself across too many fronts.

"Moreover," he continued, "under the terms of the agreement, I have to spend six to eight months in this part of the world anyway, to hand off my responsibilities to my replacement. Geneva has been a waystation to this point. Even if I keep my apartment there, I can easily make Kiev my home base."

There were obvious implications for their romance. She wondered if this might even be his main motive. Carefully, cautiously...measuring her words and trying to control her emotions, she asked him what he meant by "all of the above." He looked out at the river, while his expression grew reflective again.

Like her, he appeared to weigh his words carefully. "You mean, where do you fit?"

She nodded.

"This plan of mine will not only place us in the same city. It will unite us in common purpose. That only buttresses the arguments in favor."

Yulia pondered these last phrases. Before she could sort them out he suddenly closed his eyes and drew a deep breath. His serious look vanished, replaced by exultation. He tilted his head and turned it to one side, then the other, as if listening.

"Let's take a moment to exercise our senses," he said. "I mean to smell...listen...to engage with nature."

A little puzzled, she did as he suggested. The air, as usual this time of year in the village, was resplendent with the scents of lush grasses, wildflowers, and billowing trees, along with the crop fields. There was a plethora of cackles, birdsongs, and chirps, too numerous to identify. She'd been so caught up in the other priorities of the day she'd hardly noticed.

"There's another argument in favor," he said. "It occurred to me only here at Sofiya Yaroslavovna's. Maybe it's one of the main factors that drew the Varangians here in the first place."

Yulia looked back at him. She still didn't understand the sudden reference to nature.

"This is a land where life flourishes and thrives, in all its forms. Beavers and fish...birds and insects...trees, plants, crops...you name it. There's probably no more abundant place on the planet. Why shouldn't humans also thrive here to the fullest extent? Ukrainians as a whole and the two of us included?"

The phrase "common purpose" was still singing in her head. This only amplified it.

"Shall we head back to house, thank Sofiya Yaroslavovna for her wonderful hospitality, and be on our way to Kiev?" he added, looking up at the sky, now bright blue and cloudless. "On our return trip, if you're not opposed, we can also put the top down...to keep on enjoying nature."

Yulia seconded the plan. As they turned and retraced toward the house she realized he hadn't quite offered the precision she'd desired. He'd offered something larger. Her turmoil and trial of the night before now felt like a receding memory. New paths suddenly stretched out ahead, wide open and full of promise. She resisted the urge to reach out again to hold his hand. Instead she asked herself a question.

What was it about him that stood out the most? Was he her collaborator, deliverer, or the man of her future?

The answer seemed suddenly simple. All of the above.

*   *   *

The lead flight attendant came over the address system and announced the plane's descent, breaking Mikhailov out of his thrall. He held his concentration long enough to complete the sentence he was writing and to perform a quick review of the preceding paragraph. The passage struck him as adequate, at least for an early-stage draft. After an inhalation through his nostrils he stored his work, closed the cover and slipped the laptop into his case on the floor.

Only then did he recline against his backrest and expand his field of vision around the forward cabin. He also took stock. One benefit of air travel, he now recognized, was its disconnectedness from the wider world. Since breakfast he'd managed almost two hours of focused work. Moreover his brain was now primed for further creation after touchdown.

Two flight attendants strapped themselves in at the head of the business-class cabin, while the plane banked back to the east for a southerly approach into Boryspil. With the tilt of the fuselage he looked out his portside window and caught sight of the Dnieper and central Kiev, about two thousand meters below, and seconds after that, the golden domes of Pecherskaya Lavra. Skies were sparkling and clear, just as the pilot had indicated. Direct sunlight shone on his face, bringing a new flush of energy.

The rest of his afternoon also stood free and clear. He'd declined a car and driver from the embassy. His only obligation upon landing was to check in with the FSB duty officer by phone. From there he planned to catch a taxi directly to his hotel and get straight back to writing. He didn't plan to call Vera until evening. This would not be a Sunday of rest. He intended to put this particular Sabbath to use.

The landing was smooth, and at the gate he was the third passenger to disembark. On the gangway he turned on his phone. The device sounded before he'd even replaced it in his pocket. Mikhailov shed his abstraction and focused. Just inside the terminal, he detoured to a quiet corner and answered. The duty officer sounded relieved when he came on-line.

"Oleg Konstantinovich this is a code-red communication over an unsecured link. Please specify your location."

"Terminal D, Boryspil Airport. Just off the plane at the gate."

"Are you alone and able to communicate?"

"I am."

"This concerns the subjects Axel Thorsson and Yulia Petrenko. Two hours ago one of our sources in Zherdev's inner circle alerted us to a hit operation against them, now in progress. According to our information it is to occur somewhere in the Poltavski region, where the Thorsson and Petrenko have traveled by car."

Mikhailov's pulse accelerated. He centered himself on the here and now.

"What assets has Zherdev deployed?"

"Seven or eight men, to our knowledge. We have reason to suspect a roadside bomb."

"How far are Thorsson and Petrenko now from the airport?"

"Eighty-nine kilometers, according to phone tracking. At this point they remain stationary, in the village of Gurbintsy."

Mikhailov made a spot decision to rent a car. He also recalled the new covert teams in the east that Rykov had mentioned. "What about our own assets?" he asked. "Do we have any teams there who might be able to intercept them?"

"To this point I've been unable to obtain that information, Oleg Konstantinovich. Those are mostly GRU. This is Sunday. I'm still working on it."

"I don't care if they're GRU or not. Find one!"

Mikhailov broke off the call and took off running down the concourse. He was no longer thinking about his book.

CHAPTER 75

Yulia saw only one drawback with the convertible, now that the top was retracted. Her hair was whipping about in all directions. Her only protection came from her sunglasses. Otherwise she loved it. The car offered liberation and communion with nature, just as Thorsson had suggested. Daring confrontation with the wider world. It was the perfect vehicle for what had become a perfect day.

They'd just turned onto the wide-shouldered secondary route toward the highway. No cars were in view, ahead or behind, and Thorsson was picking up speed past fields and forests, vibrant with green. Yulia pulled part of her hair back with one hand and drew in their bombarding scents. Thanks to the fresh air and the hospitality of Sofiya Yaroslavovna, she felt renewed and unburdened, purified of all the vileness and distress that Zherdev had inflicted the night before and during preceding weeks before that.

Best of all…these sensations now extended forward. There would be challenges ahead, she knew. Hostility and persecution from the powers-that-be. But she now felt stronger, worthier, and less afraid. Ready to confront them head on.

Thorsson had played the leading role, though it wasn't one he'd sought. And he'd embraced her along the way, although she hadn't always made it easy. Now they could press forward together, wherever that led…

She looked over at him behind the wheel, as healthy and strong as always. He was also wearing sunglasses now, his own hair in turbulence. His beard, though, was matted smooth against his face. She affirmed her conclusion at the village. He really was all she wanted and required. He sensed her gaze and looked back.

"Well, how do you like the convertible?" he asked.

She pulled several locks back away from her mouth and smiled. "I love it," she answered, raising her voice a little, "Everything except my hair getting blown around."

He turned his head and considered her before flicking his eyes back onto the road. "What about your headscarf?" he asked. "The one you wore at church?"

Yulia had completely forgotten. She reached down for her purse and found the item still inside. She pulled it out, refolded it into proper form, and tied it around her head and under her chin. The covering did the trick. Her vision was unobstructed.

"Much better!" she said.

He smiled again and gestured toward the center console. "How about some music?" he said. "Don't forget we have a radio."

She'd been so absorbed in thought on the way out that that idea had not occurred to her. "Sure. Why not?"

He extended two fingers, pressed a button, and activated the system. It was already tuned to a music channel. One of her favorite songs came on, in the English language. It had just started playing.

His hand still lay on the center divider. Before he could return it to the steering wheel, she reached out and grasped it, which she'd been yearning to do ever since the village. He smiled at her again from behind his sunglasses, turned his palm over, and clasped hers back.

With that, the day now felt perfect. All their worst problems really did seem behind them.

*   *   *

Mikhailov spotted a gravel turnoff and spun a quick left, then a U-turn, kicking up a cloud of dust and pebbles. Once he was facing the road he grabbed his phone off the passenger seat. Since he'd left the airport he'd relied upon just one number, following operational protocol for emergency situations like this one: Kiev station.

"I've stopped moving east and am now stationary," he said. "You can see my location. How far away are Thorsson and Petrenko?"

"Less than two kilometers now, headed toward Kiev," the duty officer answered. "They should intersect any minute."

His adrenaline ratcheted higher. He pushed his sunglasses against the bridge of his nose, struggling to contain his impatience.

"What's the latest with the ops team?"

"One moment please Oleg Konstantinovich. I am awaiting information."

Mikhailov drew a deep breath and surveyed the area. The segment of road on which he'd stopped was straight and surrounded by open farm fields. The nearest patch of trees lay about a kilometer back toward the northwest. There were no other vehicles in sight. He looked next down the long stretch to his left. Within seconds he spotted Thorsson's car. It was a white Mercedes convertible, just as the duty officer had indicated. Yulia became visible through the windshield before he could make out Thorsson. She was wearing sunglasses and a headscarf. They were closing ground fast.

The sighting brought him to full alert. He glanced at his phone screen again, while gripping the steering wheel hard with his other hand. He seldom raised his voice in operational situations. For this one he did.

"*Hurry, for God's sake!*" he shouted.

The Mercedes was upon him less than ten seconds later. Thorsson and Yulia turned their faces toward him, in plain sight in their open car, seeing him but unaware who he was. Once they were past he put his rental sedan in gear spun onto the road straight after them, determined to maintain view contact. He was gathering speed when the duty officer came back over the link. Mikhailov cut in first.

"I'm right behind them now on Route 39. Where the hell is the team?"

"I regret to report a change, Oleg Konstantinovich. Moscow has overruled your request."

"Overruled...why on earth would they do that?"

"'Larger strategic considerations,' they said. That's all we were told."

Mikhailov glanced ahead at the Mercedes, about four hundred meters ahead. His speed was up, and he was maintaining separation. There seemed to be only one option remaining.

"Then at least send me their telephone numbers, dammit! There are two lives are at stake here. I'll handle this myself."

"I'm not authorized to do that, I'm afraid. Those are also Moscow's orders."

"Orders? Have they lost their minds?"

The duty officer did not respond and an instant later broke the connection. Mikhailov gripped the phone hard, resisting the urge to hurl it against the dashboard, and stuck it back in his shirt pocket. He'd just returned both hands to the wheel when he spotted three black SUVs in his rearview mirror, coming up hard from behind. Before he could react they moved into the adjacent lane and zoomed past.

Through the window of one he caught the flash of a cell phone screen. Another image came back from six months earlier. It was from the snow and ice outside Moscow.

All three vehicles were Range Rovers. And they were closing down fast on Thorsson and Yulia.

"*Please...NO!*" he shouted, only this time louder. He stamped his accelerator and gave chase.

CHAPTER 76

The speed was a giveaway. So was the formation. Mikhailov deduced what was about to happen.

He was also powerless to intervene.

The three Range Rovers, all with dark-tinted windows, continued to pull away from his underpowered rental sedan and bear down on the Mercedes, maintaining their tight grouping in the left lane. From his trailing position 150 meters back Mikhailov watched Thorsson take note of them in his rearview mirror, then his left-side one as well. He said something to Yulia, who rotated her head. He then increased his speed.

The acceleration came too late, even if the American was inclined toward evasive maneuvers. In the next instant the first SUV passed and veered in just ahead of him, while the third moved right in behind. An instant after that the second drew up outside his left-front fender. The coordinated maneuver took all of three seconds. By now all four vehicles were traveling at about 140 kilometers per hour. Thorsson and Yulia were now trapped in a vise, unable to speed up or slow down. The grove of low trees was approaching rapidly on the right.

The driver of the second Range Rover then executed a violent swipe from the outside, clipping the Mercedes hard on its corner fender, yielding a crunch and snap of metal. The effect was instantaneous.

But what followed, from Mikhailov's rear vantage, appeared to be disconnected from time.

The rear of the Mercedes vaulted up on a right diagonal and cartwheeled off the roadway, giving him an unobstructed view into its interior. Thorsson and Yulia were secured by their seatbelts, and their airbags deployed at once. Still, each bounce lashed them in several directions at once. Their car appeared to gain velocity as it left the roadway and careened down the embankment. Mikhailov counted two and a half full rotations before they hit level ground at the bottom.

For the first time the convertible now met hard, immobile earth, striking rear first. The impact emitted a blast of soil and wheat stalks together with a vicious thud, with Thorsson and Yulia facing skyward. Mikhailov saw their upper bodies hurl hard against their headrests and seatbacks, and bounce back again into the airbags as the car's trajectory bent off on a forty-five degree angle.

It now appeared to take flight, moving in higher arcs. What had been a cartwheel became a vaulting somersault, accompanied by additional eruptions of dirt and wheat and crunches of metal.

Mikhailov could also see they were headed straight toward the grove of low trees.

In a sole flash of providence, the car's undercarriage made contact first. Its mass and momentum obliterated a sapling on the periphery and cut through heavier branches behind, snapping them off. Violent cracks reverberated across the field, together with screeches of contorting metal. Through his open side window Mikhailov heard what sounded like a puncturing of the airbag and a hiss of air. Finally the car came to rest in a vertical position, suspended about a meter off the ground and tilted at slight side-angle. Thorsson and Yulia now faced skyward with their airbags half-deflated.

Neither one of them was moving. Mikhailov pulled over and jumped out of his sedan, also glancing up the road. The three Range Rovers had drawn together about one hundred meters further. One had parked across the center line. The two others were completing three-point turns, while he lacked even a pistol. He let loose the same reaction as before.

"NO!"

Before they started back, he clambered down the bank and took off sprinting through the wheat field, refixing on the Mercedes. Yulia had dropped to the ground and was now staggering around the vehicle to Thorsson's side, pushing through leaves and broken branches. Abrasions were evident on her arms and legs, but she appeared free of broken bones. Her sunglasses were gone but somehow her headscarf had remained in place.

Thorsson remained immobile. Blood was visible on his forehead and soaked through one side of his beard. A gash had also opened on his left forearm, which was dangling out of the car. Yulia looked up at him as she rounded to his side.

"Axel!" she screamed.

Still fighting his way through the wheat stalks, Mikhailov watched her balance on a downed tree limb, yank open the driver's-side door with a high-pitched grunt, and reach in to pull Thorsson's legs from under the airbag. They came out suddenly, sending her reeling backward and leaving his body twisted out at an awkward horizontal, the safety belts still strapped around his torso. Yulia screamed again, even more loudly, and struggled back up. She unclasped his seat buckle, setting his torso loose as well and tumbling his body into vertical position.

Thorsson remained tangled around the shoulders, suspended a meter and a half off the ground. His head was drooping forward, and his arms were splayed outward. Yulia stumbled off the limb back to the ground, clasping his legs and sobbing in desperation.

The scene resembled a latter-day crucifixion, with Yulia as Mary Magdalene. All that was missing was the cross.

*   *   *

Yulia had only vaguely registered the lone figure running through the field. She'd assumed he was a passing motorist who'd happened upon the crash scene—if she was capable of perceiving or assuming anything at all. Never in her life had she sustained such violent shocks to her head and body.

She was surprised she was still conscious.

To her desperation the same could not be said of Thorsson. He now hung suspended off the ground, limp and unresponsive. Half choking on sobs, she whirled around to appeal for help. But what she saw stopped her from screaming out again.

The man she'd noticed had stopped running. Instead he'd turned around to face the roadway. When she looked there herself she understood why.

Two of the three black SUVs that had just forced their Mercedes off the road pulled up and stopped. Six men got out, all of them bearing guns. Several looked like Kalashnikovs. She noticed Igor Moroz in the group, identifiable by his shaved head. He raised phone to his ear, as if awaiting an order. The man on the other end, she was almost sure, was Zherdev.

The oligarch had started the violence. Now he was finishing it.

In an instant of acute, crystalline recognition over the sunlit field, Yulia became certain that she and Thorsson were about to die. And probably the passing motorist too, if he didn't have the sense to flee, and flee quickly.

What the man did next, though, was quite different.

He did not turn and run. He did not dive low into the wheat. He continued to stand upright. Holding ground right where he was. Even more astonishing to her, he stared straight back at the group, including Igor Moroz.

From behind he presented a solitary figure. Exposed. Vulnerable. Possessed of obscure, futile motives known only to himself. Just as defenseless as she and Thorsson.

His audacity struck her as madness.

Moroz locked his gaze on the interloper through his wraparound sunglasses, his phone still held to his ear, his scowl even more malevolent. As if awaiting confirmation of their sentence. Ten seconds passed. Then twenty. And then thirty. Yulia heard the squawk of a bird and the croak of a cricket. She twisted back to take one last look up at Thorsson and then up at the blue sky. The accompaniment of nature seemed a fitting end.

Finally Moroz lowered his phone with an impassive expression and held it as his side for few seconds longer, while the other gunmen awaited their cues. She expected the command to come in short order and for the group to descend the bank with guns drawn, ready to turn the wheat field into a kill zone.

Instead Moroz stiffened, clenched his fists, and swore. When he uncontorted himself he cast one more malevolent glance at her, Thorsson, and lastly at the man in the field. He then issued the command. The other men lowered their weapons, slowly, reluctantly, and began piling back into the two SUVs.

Yulia couldn't believe her eyes. She then re-concentrated on Thorsson and screamed out to the solitary man in the field, just as he turned back toward her and resumed running.

"Please hurry! He needs help!"

The man drew up while she boosted herself onto the tree branch, fighting pain in her thigh. To her astonishment he appeared as wrenched by Thorsson's condition as she was.

"Here," he said in Russian, "Use my shoulder for balance."

The man then anchored himself to the ground around Thorsson's feet with a wide stance, enveloped his lower legs with his arm, and boosted him about ten centimeters higher. She freed one arm, then the other, then stabilized Thorsson's torso while the man lowered Thorsson's feet all the way to the ground.

Together they dragged him to a level patch of wheat several meters away and lowered his body to the ground, creating a bed of compressed green stalks underneath his body. A gold crucifix came free from the man's shirt, under a flash of light-blue eyes. The cross continued dangling downward while the man checked Thorsson's vital signs.

"He's still breathing," he said. "But he's in shock and is losing a lot of blood. Do you know CPR, if we need it?"

She choked back a sob. "Yes."

"Monitor his pulse. I'll call for help."

The man stood, extracted a phone from his shirt pocket, and placed the call. He then knelt opposite her, across Thorsson's inert figure. The three of them were now enveloped in green so that they could hardly see outward.

"My name's Oleg Mikhailov," he said. "I'll stay here with you until they arrive."

Yulia startled and looked back at him. His gaze, once again, looked just as overturned as hers. Suddenly nothing made sense.

She didn't try to understand now. Instead she looked back down at Thorsson, keeping her fingers on his pulse with one hand and wiping away tears with the other.

Her only hope was that Mikhailov's crucifix might confer some grace.

CHAPTER 77

Mikhailov and Rykov were seated at a diagonal with an open view toward the sea. The café tables around them were empty. Gentle swells lapped the pebbled waterline below. Few beachgoers had yet to arrive. Mikhailov did not know if Rykov had been in the loop on the culminating day. In all likelihood, he would never know.

He now wondered if the morning calm, together with the expanse of water, on Rykov's part, were meant to induce wider perspective.

"We were both aware that Moscow has new initiatives in Ukraine," the section chief said after sipping his demi-cup of espresso. "We were also both aware, without details, that these were most pronounced in the east."

Mikhailov absorbed this and said nothing, choosing instead to draw a sip of his own. He wondered again whether he'd been set up by his rivals, those in other departments.

"We also knew that Zherdev's primary economic interests are centered on Donetsk," Rykov continued, still gazing out toward the water. "The villa here in Crimea and the head office in Kiev? They're accessories. You're acquainted with his dossier."

Mikhailov had anticipated the explanation. Again he stayed wordless. Another light swell lapped the beach pebbles, while an elderly couple walked past the far end of the café, on their way to the lounge chairs below. When they'd passed, the section chief then turned his gaze to establish more direct contact. His expression was dispassionate, dutiful, and one Oleg had seen hundreds of times before. Too many times, in Rykov and those like him.

"In the end, for Moscow, these two realities collided with the operation."

The choice of words was more lamentable than Rykov realized. Finally Mikhailov responded. "And rendered Axel Thorsson and Yulia Petrenko expendable."

"Yes, for better or worse."

"What about Zherdev's misjudgments and the risks he poses?"

"Moscow determined that our objectives in Ukraine override those concerns," Rykov answered. "His continued loyalty was deemed a higher priority."

"Loyalty to what purpose, exactly? I'd thought our main priority here was something else."

The observation was sharper than Rykov was accustomed to receiving from a subordinate. Nonetheless he stayed even, forever consistent with the tenets of his profession. "That's not for us to decide, is it Oleg Konstantinovich? It never is, in the line of work we've chosen. Both of us knew that when we joined. Correct?"

Mikhailov had to admit the statement was true.

Now both of them fell silent. Rykov took another dose of espresso and evaluated Mikhailov over the rim of his demi-cup. Mikhailov could tell what he was thinking. He could also guess what he would say next.

"Look Oleg, I understand your discontent. And I suspect our superiors in the Kremlin do too, though they will never acknowledge it. Your assignment went awry for external reasons beyond your control. Moreover it transpired during your vacation. Therefore I've already obtained approval for a ten-day extension of your stay here at the sanatorium, right up until the start of the school year for Dima. The Service, of course, will cover all expenses."

"That won't be necessary."

At this Rykov lowered his demi-cup for a frank, unobstructed view across the table. In the Service, one didn't reject an offer like this without explanation.

"Personal obligations in Moscow..." Mikhailov elaborated. "Namely, my sister is taking care of our dog. And she's planning a vacation of her own."

It was the line of a good soldier. Rykov smiled. "Moscow appreciates your dedication, Oleg Konstantinovich. So do I. Believe me, I've been through assignments like yours in my own career. The sting will subside. One has to bear in mind the larger balance. Build toward the future."

The section chief was misguided on the larger questions but more on the mark than he realized. Mikhailov made no comment and drained the rest of his coffee. Something caught Rykov's attention behind him.

"Good timing," he said. "Looks like your Vera and Dimitri have just arrived for the beach."

Mikhailov swiveled to look. His wife and son were now hesitating, wondering if they should continue. Rykov waved to them and held out a palm, indicating they should wait. "Go join them," he said. "You and your family still have a week left here at the seaside. From this point on you can relax. You deserve it."

Mikhailov shook his hand and parted company. The section chief remained seated at the table while he crossed to the end of the café. As he drew closer, Vera searched his face for clues but refrained from speaking as they descended down the stone steps to the beach. When they reached their preferred lounge chairs she reached into her beach bag and handed him his folded towel.

"How did it go?" she asked him in an undertone, palpable with concern.

This time Dima paid closer attention than usual. He'd sensed a juncture of importance. He waited for his father's response, still holding his beach bag.

"Fine," Mikhailov said simply.

Rather than elaborate he shook out his towel and spread it on the lounge and then did likewise for Vera.

The gesture didn't distract her. It was clear from her expression that she wanted more. "No changes...nothing for the worse?"

Mikhailov couldn't resist an ironic smile and snorted through his nostrils. "They're satisfied, if that's what you're asking. I did my duty."

Vera released an exhalation. Dima, by contrast, examined him more closely.

"Thank God," she said. "I thought something bad had occurred at the end."

Mikhailov opted to leave this comment unaddressed. Instead he slipped out of his beach sandals and pulled off his tee-shirt. "There will be one small change to our outlook," he added. Vera looked at him through her sunglasses, stiffening a little.

"I'll be taking a little detour on the way home. Not a long one... we should reach the airport in Moscow about the same time. It's something that concerns my assignment. Call it a final element I have to wrap up."

Vera relaxed again. Anything that had to do with the Service was fine by her. "I understand," she said, resuming her preparations.

Over her shoulder Mikhailov glimpsed Rykov again up on the terrace, standing to leave. Mikhailov made final, polite eye contact. The section chief was not a malintended sort. Through his loyalty to the state, he thought he was accomplishing good. His efforts were just misapplied.

Rather like his own, Mikhailov now recognized, since the affair had started. He knew that he'd been spared in the wheat field not because of his courage or his integrity or his righteousness, but because—in the end—he was one them. Just as much as Zherdev, Igor Moroz and all the rest—part of the same noxious, oppressive power structure that emanated from Moscow and kept Ukraine forever stunted and under heel.

However he did have to thank Rykov for one thing. Mikhailov settled into his lounge chair and looked out again toward the sea. The view corresponded to the one he'd just held from the terrace.

And he now had all the perspective he needed.

*   *   *

The very first feature Yulia noticed, this time round, was his light-blue eyes. The second was that he was carrying flowers.

Oleg Mikhailov was not someone she expected to see in these environs, either.

Mikhailov held her gaze and continued walking, converging toward her along opposite path. She stopped in place and waited, as startled by the flowers as she was by his presence, until he acquired the same proximity she remembered from the accident scene. His expression was straightforward and somber but also penitent. The same held for his voice, when he finally addressed her.

"Excuse me for arriving unannounced, Yulia," he said. "I'm relieved to find you here. I'd hoped that you could accompany me."

Yulia was too off-balance to respond right away. Her whole world had been upended over the previous week, even more than before. Mikhailov seemed to understand. He looked up at a directional sign on the corner and some identifying numbers.

"He's this way, isn't he?" he said, gesturing to their side at perpendicular angle.

"Yes."

They turned and walked along in tandem. When Yulia composed herself she figured she should thank him, despite the way things had ended.

"Pavel and I are grateful for your help with our Schengen visas," she said, "Especially on such short notice."

"Don't thank me. Thank Heather Robinson. I just got the process going."

Yulia made a mental note to thank the American diplomat before she departed. They passed an orderly, pushing a cart.

"How's your cousin Pavel doing, by the way?" Mikhailov asked.

"Better, thank you. I just came from seeing him. He's due to check out in about a week."

They approached their endpoint. The Russian slowed before she did.

"This is it, isn't it?" he said.

"Yes."

"Why don't you go first? It would more appropriate."

The Russian stood back while Yulia applied a light knock. There was no answer. As quietly as she could, she cracked the door open and poked her head inside.

Her heart skipped a beat when she saw Thorsson's bed-dais empty.

She panted slightly while she cast her eyes about the room. A second or two later she spotted him, on the side opposite, wearing a bathrobe and siting in a hospital armchair. He was fixed on his e-reader, deep in concentration.

"Axel? Oleg Mikhailov is here to see you. Shall I let him in?"

He startled slightly and raised his head. "Mikhailov? Yes, of course."

Thorsson rose, still holding his e-reader, and walked across the room as she and Mikhailov proceeded inside. His limp was mostly gone, as were the bandages on his head. He looked less surprised than she did. Upon seeing the Russian he appeared neither hostile nor suspicious. When the Russian extended his hand he reciprocated with an even expression.

"I've come to make apologies," Mikhailov said. "Not on behalf of my Service. Of my own."

Thorsson looked back at him. Before he was able to respond the Russian spoke again. "I thought I was in a position to make guarantees. I wasn't."

"Thank you," the American said, still holding their handshake. "Though perhaps apologies are unnecessary now, given what's transpired during the past week."

Mikhailov offered no affirmation of the remark, instead maintaining his penitent expression. He extended the bouquet with his other hand. "I've gathered you're scheduled to check out in a day or two and then depart Kiev," he said. "I realize this is a rather unusual gesture from one man to another, before you go. But I've brought some flowers."

Thorsson's face flickered with irony. In the next instant he seemed unable to resist a slight smile, framed by his beard. "I haven't died, you know."

At last the Russian's exterior broke open, and he smiled as well. Yulia sensed this had been a long time coming.

"I know," he responded. "And you've saved me as a result, whether you realize it or not."

CHAPTER 78

The hillcrest was blanketed by October leaves now, rather than snow. And the air was milder, imbued with the sharp scents of autumn. The only constants were the topography, the trees, and the quiet. Still, Rufus circled and sniffed each time they passed. Mikhailov was sure the canine remembered the spot on the trail just as much as he did.

And when winter returned, he was just as sure, the reflex would still apply. And during the spring and summer after that.

The dog completed his remembrance and took off running again, ears flopping and kicking up leaves with his hind paws. Mikhailov paused a moment longer, concluded his own tribute, and followed, reacquiring his steady stride over the matted foliage.

He looked ahead along the downslope. There were several undulations over the remaining distance. But he and Rufus were on the return leg now, headed home. At this stage in his life, even before his commencement and renewal, he'd grown familiar with every dip and rise, which rendered it easier and reinforced him.

His father had traversed it countless times, in all seasons. But the images that he retained most were of him on skis, lean and athletic, gliding along at a pace that belied his age and cerebralism, with an aptitude that exceeded Mikhailov's own.

Winter would arrive in about a month. Soon thereafter he would be back on skis himself for the first time since his outing with Sasha. Three weeks had now elapsed since he'd committed himself. The urge to smoke had now left him completely. He could already feel himself getting fitter, thanks to his daily hikes with Rufus. This season, he would be ready... readier and more vital than he'd been since university. He now realized, as he broached forty, that he had to optimize his abilities while he still possessed them. Not just physical ones but his intellectual ones too.

At the top of the next rise, he crossed through a cluster of birch trees. Drier leaves crackled underfoot. Rufus continued racing ahead, intent on completion.

The canine had understood the change almost as soon as it happened. Mikhailov had supplied the cue. No more morning disappearances and evening returns. No more long absences. The apartment in the city remained, which the dog still visited on occasion.

But for both of them, this was now home.

Here in the forest, Rufus never went on the leash. Here he could always roam free. Make the most of his capacities. Just like his master.

Several bends and dips later, through a grove of pine trees, the dacha came into view. Mikhailov looked toward it and remembered his mother there over the years, in different scenes and seasons. Welcoming his arrival on Friday evening in autumn, along with Vera and Dima, for a weekend visit. Reading a book on the porch in summertime, a glass of watermelon *kompot* at hand. Busy in the kitchen around the New Year's holiday, with windows aglow.

He'd squared matters with Ksenia. With the Service too, to the extent that that was possible, overriding Vera's objections and anxiety in the process. She would come around, he knew. And Dima already had, in the ever-adaptable manner of youth. There were no material obstacles. No purposes in evasion.

Individual efforts mattered, in the sum of things. One had to make proper choices.

He traversed a bed of pine needles at the edge of the clearing. Rufus had already reached the back porch of the house and released a bark of excitement. The canine knew the next steps to the ritual. Mikhailov would climb the steps and enter, add another log to the main fireplace, and brew a pot of tea. Mug in hand, he would then repair to his desk in the study, where his laptop remained plugged in and opened. Finally, without further preliminaries, he would settle into his chair, bring his fingers to the keyboard and return to work, while Rufus settled into position on the rug beside him.

Over the previous three weeks, he'd revised his first chapter and written about eight thousand words more. Untold thousands remained still ahead, rife with challenges, toil and uncertainty, along with relentless editing after that. But he was now fully underway. Time had come for true courage. There was no going back.

From this point forward he would be receiving no further assignments from third parties. Not from the state or from anyone else. This was an assignment he had given himself.

He'd made his decision. Chosen his means.

He had some things to say. At last he was saying them.

CHAPTER 79

Yulia sat up on the edge of the bed and glanced at digital clock on the nightstand. She was sleeping a little later now as months progressed. The habit was now intentional. Her priorities had changed with the circumstances.

This was also a Saturday.

She remembered events in Kiev and zinged more awake. Without further hesitation she thrust her toes through her slippers, stood and reached for her short cotton wrap on the settee, then padded out of the bedroom toward the kitchen, tying the sash as she went. In the kitchen she poured a half liter of milk into a small saucepan and placed it on the stove at low heat. Next, by reflex, she extracted an oversize mug from the pantry, along with a packet of mix.

Morning hot chocolate was another of her new rituals this winter. She didn't chastise herself for that one either. She'd also developed the habit, while the milk was warming, of gazing out through the living room and its large-paned windows, over the crystalline surface of Lac Leman toward downtown Geneva and the snow-capped peaks beyond. It had become her way to greet the day. Also to remind herself, and sometimes marvel, that she was still in Switzerland at all and filing an occasional story besides.

This morning, instead, she grabbed her computer tablet off the serving counter, where she'd left it the night before. She reloaded the *Ukraina Sevodnya* main-page. The lead story, once again, was written by Pavel, who'd never used his visa after all. The headline zinged her even wider awake:

Yanukovych Flees to Kharkov; Parliament Declares Presidency Vacant

The milk bubbled up before she could read much further. She finished preparing the hot chocolate as quickly as she could and strode around to the living room and plunked down on the couch, where she took her first sip and then a second as she sped through the ensuing text and secondary headlines:

Riot Police Desert Ranks...Government Buildings Occupied by Protesters...Parliament Orders Release of Timoshenko...Activists Overrun Mezhyhirya, Yanukovych's Private Estate in Novi Petrivtsi...

Each new detail seemed more incredible than the last. Events of the previous several days had riveted her, along with millions of others in Europe and around the world. But she had hardly imagined the protest movement would come to this. Even less that it all would happen overnight. She glanced at the calendar by the refrigerator for confirmation:

22 February 2014

In the history of Ukraine, she imagined, the date would endure forever. And her dream had burst into reality.

She wondered if Thorsson had already gleaned the news, pre-dawn, when drinking his morning coffee. He was never from her consciousness these days, but she'd been so distracted by the cascade of reports from Kiev that she'd lost track of his workout plan. Her heart racing, still clutching her mug, she sprang up from the couch, cornered around to the dining room, and opened the door onto the balcony. The frosty air braced her face and pierced her thin wrap as she stepped outside. She drew her arms closer for warmth as she stood by the railing and looked down at the lakefront.

She spotted him almost at once on the frosty promenade, in his customary location. He was facing the water toward the empty boat docks, his back toward her, performing squat leaps, followed at once by a set of push-ups. His lacerations were long healed by now, and he was clad in winter fitness gear rather than summer, including a cap and gloves. She took another sip of chocolate to warm herself and was about to retreat back inside to the apartment when he finished, checked his sports watch, and walked over to a nearby bench to stretch. By coincidence he glanced up to the seventh floor and spotted her. She waved at him and he waved back, smiling. He also changed direction toward the building.

Toward *their* building. This apartment was hers now too. That was another new reality about which she had to remind herself.

She also figured she should get out of the cold, given her condition. Back in the dining room, with the door closed, she held out her left hand and beheld the two gold bands on her ring finger, which she was only now getting used to after four and a half months. One bore a sizable diamond, which she remained a little embarrassed about.

With her other hand she felt the growing swell of her belly.

She and Thorsson hadn't quite waited until their wedding, but they had waited until they'd gotten engaged, a timeline they'd both favored. Thorsson in particular had been intent on the point. After his miscue on Kreschatik he'd wanted, above all, to *decide*. And she'd become pregnant, she was sure, only after their wedding. Just days after, maybe. But she had no reason to be embarrassed about *that*.

She retraced to the living room and stood near the entryway, still sipping her hot chocolate, while Thorsson rode up by elevator. Upon entering, he appeared enlivened, as usual after his workout, his cheekbones ruddy with the cold. He encircled her waist with one hand and planted a kiss on her lips, almost before she'd had the chance to speak.

When she did she was hardly able to contain herself. "Did you read the news this morning?"

"I know…it's stunning. Have you turned on the television yet?"

"Not yet…just Internet."

She briefed him on Pavel's latest report while he bent over to unlace his sports shoes and deposit his other gear by the coat rack, before they proceeded together into the living room together and sat down on the couch. He then picked up the remote and turned on CNN International. The screen filled at once with cheering throngs on Maidan, throbbing with joy and near disbelief. For the first time in weeks there were no riot police to be seen. The female correspondent, in her delivery, seemed almost as thrilled as the protesters. They both watched in captivated silence for several minutes, flicking between additional channels in English and French. Similar images flashed everywhere.

With each new account Yulia's thoughts began running along one track. She sensed Thorsson's were too. Finally he diverted his gaze from the screen and turned toward her. "You realize what this means, don't you, Yulia?" he said. "Zherdev already hasn't been seen for weeks, and now he's probably fled, too. We can go back, just as we've talked about…you can even start doing some reporting on the scene, at least until the baby is born."

Everything was coming together so suddenly. Yulia was too overwhelmed to respond right away. It all seemed too good to be true. Or to last, either.

"Don't forget I'm the publisher now," he added, smiling. "I think we can choose whatever formula and proportions we like."

Her disbelief aside, Yulia couldn't restrain a smile of her own. "Will we have the baby in Kiev?" she asked him.

Thorsson paused and reached his opposite hand across, placing it on her belly. His touch brought a frisson of tenderness. "The due date is in late July. But who knows? We could even return to Crimea and have it there. That's where our story started, right?"

The question, for the moment, required no response.

"Either way, we can decide the specifics later."

Yulia stirred with another swell of emotion. Nowadays, in contrast with the past, they almost all tended positive. And this one was perhaps stronger than any other. She reached up and placed her fingertips on his cheek. His beard was gone now, but her associations from summer remained.

"It's what you wanted, right Yulia?"

"Yes, it's what I wanted."

ACKNOWLEDGMENTS

During the creation of this novel I benefitted from the assistance of a group of versatile and perspicacious first-line readers, all of whom valiantly delved into a rough, early-stage manuscript and offered feedback. Their incisive comments and criticism enabled vital improvements and refinements, now reflected in this published release. This exemplary and steadfast circle comprised: Anna Dmitrenko, Ann Johnson, Bill Mackintosh, Chris DiNapoli, Dave Johnson, Irina Guliaieva, Jim Haas, Marina Telen, and Thibaut Behaghel.

In separate category and earlier in the process, Milos Duletic volunteered essential insights into water-polo tactics.

I am forever grateful to each and every one.

That said, I hold none of them responsible for the outcome. I alone am answerable for that.

NOTES BY THE AUTHOR

I had the good fortune to make two summertime visits to Crimea before the illegitimate Russian takeover and annexation of the peninsula in March 2014, while it was still part of Ukraine. My renderings reflect this time frame, including the RadissonBlu Hotel in Alushta where Yulia Petrenko works and Axel Thorsson is a guest. (Since then the hotel has come under Russian ownership, changed names, and to my knowledge is now largely inaccessible to Western and other international travelers—in part because of visa restrictions.) Otherwise I can assume my physical depictions of Alushta and other coastal locations, including street names, remain more or less valid.

My portrayal of Kiev, by contrast, derives not just from the recent past but also the present. I resided in the capital during much of 2013, the year the story is set, witnessed the genesis of the Revolution that ultimately triumphed in February 2014, and have been on hand to observe its aftermath into 2015 early 2016. My experiences throughout this period have therefore defined more than places; they've also informed my story and characters. And—I hope—imbued them with extra retrospective context.

That the revolution occurred during my writing of this book was pure chance—one might even say creative providence, in that it made me more determined to get it right. Now more than ever, I share the aspirations of the Ukrainian people for national self-determination, the rule of law, and an end to Russian interference and oppression.

I hope readers will too.

Kiev, June 2016

ABOUT THE AUTHOR

Eric Almeida was born in Ithaca, New York in 1962 and raised in Rhode Island. He attended Tabor Academy and majored in History at Brown University, where he also competed on the rowing team. Upon graduation in 1984 he worked as a Sports Writer at *The Providence Journal* for one year, then resumed his education at The Nitze School of Advanced International Studies (SAIS) of Johns Hopkins University, receiving an M.A. in International Affairs in 1987.

From graduate school he detoured into business, working as international sales manager for an American high-technology company for five years, primarily in Europe. He proceeded to co-found a software-development venture based in Belarus, France and the Netherlands, for which he also served as President from 1996-2001.

Soon thereafter he returned to writing, his core interest. He currently divides his time between Ukraine and the New England coastline. For more information about Eric Almeida and his books please visit www.ericalmeida.com.

www.ingramcontent.com/pod-product-compliance
Lightning Source LLC
Chambersburg PA
CBHW070751280626
47162CB00016B/160